SURPRISE PACKAGE

In the container was the body of a young woman. She looked as if she were made of silver. Her skin, stretched over long, fine bones, was covered with a fine downy hair that had a luster which reflected back the blue light of stasis. Erect and awake, she would stand about two meters tall. Her head was topped with long, straight, black hair arranged about her shoulders. She was definitely humanoid—but she had wings.

THE
ALIEN
WITHIN

JOHANNA M. BOLTON

A DEL REY BOOK

BALLANTINE BOOKS • NEW YORK

THE
ALIEN
WITHIN

CHAPTER 1

Malvern, capital city, 2473 Terran Standard Calendar

The afternoon sky was heavy with clouds, and the city shone like a wet opal—or a garbage dump in the rain. From a distance the city and even the dump had a sort of aesthetic appeal. However, closer observation revealed their true state, the despair, the dirt, and patches that were more often than not an attempt to make something beyond repair useful again.

The streetlights were haloed with rainbows, their glow dissipating in the fog that crept beneath the covered street, billowing out of ventilator shafts and filling the alleyways. Water dripped down the fronts of buildings and ran along the pavement, turning it into a mirror that shattered with every footstep or passing vehicle. Fog smothered the city, changing color in the neon signs above the small shops that lined the streets, and swirling around the pedestrians.

Even in the rain traffic was heavy, and Shaw hunched his shoulders as he moved through the crowds, walking as swiftly as the press of people and vehicles would allow. A cab would have been quicker, but his credit chip was at zero and he did not have time to steal another. He had also decided that going on foot would be quicker. If anyone had discovered the real reason he was on Malvern, the authorities would have been looking for him, and the first thing they would do would be to put a monitor on all public transportation. They might watch the pedestrians, too, but there was less of a chance they would spot him in the confusion of the back streets.

A secondary entrance to the spaceport was just ahead, the gate topped by a small blue sign. There was a lot of traffic going in and out, past a couple of bored-looking guards. As Shaw moved toward them, he opened the front of his raincape and flipped the left side over his shoulder. Beneath the cape he wore a one-piece suit of gremlin silk dyed forest green. The color of the suit, as well as the embroidered badge attached to the breast pocket, identified him as a member of one of the major business guilds. The guilds were an important power on Malvern, and although the guards at the gate glanced at him as he went by, he was not stopped.

So far everything was going according to plan, and inwardly Shaw relaxed a little. The guards' disinterest and their mental boredom meant that the hunt was not on yet. While he realized that he would not be completely safe until he was off planet, the odds against him did not seem so great anymore.

Bad posture and loose-fitting clothing hid Shaw's slender height and long fine bones, both of which would have been distinctive among the stocky inhabitants of Malvern. His face was altered, too, the hollows beneath his high cheekbones filled out with a thick application of synthaskin, but he had left his long, straight, black hair alone. There was no way he could pass as a native on Malvern, but one of the main rules of disguise required that he at least blur his appearance to avoid seeming too remarkable on that planet of xenophobes.

Shaw was a spy and he was very good at his job. No one knew anything about him: where he came from, what he believed in, or even what he really looked like. He was as evasive with his employers as he was elusive to his victims, and that provided the basis for a lot of speculation. Few people could claim to have met him face to face, and if those few ever compared notes, each of them would describe a different man. The only thing anyone would have agreed on was Shaw's almost uncanny ability to tell falsehood from truth, one of the talents that enabled him to avoid many of the dangers inherent in his profession.

Shaw owed loyalty to no one but himself. He was not

bound to a government and he did not work for a cause, and that lack of what they considered commitment created problems for some of his employers. More than one attempt had been made to recruit him, but always without success. Because of that, as well as his access to sensitive materials, it was feared that he might one day prove an embarrassment. To alleviate the problem, some of his employers had hired assassins, but none of them had succeeded, and that, too, added to Shaw's reputation. His skills at retrieving information and secrets were vital for the players in the game of interplanetary politics, but Shaw, the mysterious man, was feared and hated by everyone who knew him.

When Shaw entered the port he moved immediately to the inner area where a number of ships were cradled in enormous elevator racks, waiting to be lifted to the surface. His goal was the *Nighthunter*, a slim racing sloop, her metal sides washed by rain that streamed down through the shaft above her, glistening in the light like a silver curtain. The base of the elevator was dark with moisture, and above the other noises in the port he could hear the rumble of distant thunder.

As Shaw continued to walk to his ship, he pressed a button on the tiny remote that he carried in his pocket, and an opening appeared in the ship's side. He hurried up the entry ramp, ducking his head just enough to clear the top of the hatchway.

His long fingers stabbed at the control panel inside the door. As soon as the ramp had withdrawn and the hatch sealed shut, he ran forward to the cockpit where Dree was in the midst of preflight checks. She gave him a quick nod, acknowledging his presence without taking her attention or her fingers from the panel in front of her.

Shaw left her to the task and lifted a piece of floor mat, feeling beneath it for a hidden latch. There was a click, and a small section of the floor opened. Swiftly he transferred a flat package from inside his suit to the hiding place. After setting a dial, he closed the floor again. Nothing showed to indicate the existence of a hidden locker, and if anyone tried to force the floor open, the materials inside would be destroyed.

"Countdown prepared. We're ready to lift," Dree announced in her deep voice.

Shaw strapped himself into the pilot's seat. "I will get the clearance," he said.

"Hurry up. I can't wait to get off this hell world."

"You are no more anxious than I." But Shaw took a moment to peel the synthaskin from his face and pop the contact lenses from his eyes. He sighed with relief.

"Hurt?" Dree asked sympathetically.

"Not really. But they do restrict my vision." He tossed the remains of his disguise in the disposal. Unprotected, his eyes were silver-gray, with very little white showing around the edges; they were unusually luminous in the shadows of his thick, black lashes.

Shaw turned to the instruments before him and activated the radio link to Malvern Port Control.

"This is *Nighthunter* preparing to lift. Please engage docking elevator for Port Seventeen B," he said into the mike.

There was a crackle of static and a woman's voice replied. "*Nighthunter*, this is Port Control. Have you filed your clearance?"

"Not necessary," Shaw replied. "We landed under a twelve-hour refueling permit."

There was a moment's silence on the other end of the link. "Am I speaking to the *Nighthunter*, registry is zero zero two, A, six niner five sixty-three, Savarada origin?" the woman asked finally.

"Affirmative."

"We have you listed for a sixty-hour pleasure permit. You cannot lift without customs inspection and clearance. You must also record your destination."

"Your records are in error. Please check again. My vessel landed here less than six hours ago."

Dree looked up at Shaw, a frown on her face and her eyes narrow with suspicion.

"*Nighthunter*, please unlock your entry. The inspectors are standing by. We will expedite your departure as much as possible, but I'm afraid you cannot lift until you comply with regulations."

Shaw snapped off the mike. "Blast regulations!" he muttered as he activated the external cameras. One after another, images of the area around the base of the ship appeared on the monitor before him. He pressed a key and froze the scanner when he saw what he was looking for.

The group of people standing in front of the hatch could not possibly be customs officials. They stood with military posture, and all of them held laser rifles. The insignia and color of their uniforms identified them as members of the Malvern Special Forces.

"What's happening?" Dree asked.

"I do not know, nor do I want to stay around to find out," Shaw replied. He adjusted the outside view and saw sky at the end of the tube above them. At least the port officials had not thought to close the lid on the landing pit. "We're lifting now."

Dree's face split in a wide grin, and her short fingers pushed the buttons that opened the engine's mixing chambers.

At Shaw's command the sloop began to move. The roar of the engines must have been deafening in the underground terminal; he saw the pseudo—customs officials clutching their heads as they scurried for cover.

The *Nighthunter*'s first movements were hard to see. She seemed to sit stationary on her launching pad as the fumes from her exhaust rose, obscuring her sides, then only seconds later she was a speck in the sky. Shaw did not even pause to consider the damage they had caused by lifting from the tube instead of ground level. One of his prime rules was to take care of himself first and worry about details later.

Within minutes the black of space surrounded the racer, and Dree sagged in her seat with relief.

"Whatever you stole this time certainly has them angry," she said. "Or did you violate some taboo while you were in the city?"

"That would not be difficult," Shaw commented. His eyes were busy watching the monitor, looking for Malvern ships. He was not sure that they would want him enough to chase him into space, but then he did not know the value of the materials he had stolen either. They might be worth the effort of pursuit.

So far there was nothing around the *Nighthunter* but the serene void of space. He shot a glance at Dree and found that she, too, was searching the emptiness before them.

Dree was a dwarf. Her bones, though they were of the normal diameter for a mature human female, had somehow stopped growing before they reached their full length, and as a result, she stood little over a meter tall.

When Shaw had first seen Dree, she had been in the middle of a shouting mob of children. At first it had seemed that she was one of them, and that they were all involved in a noisy game. He was about to pass by when he realized that the children were armed and violent. He felt for thoughts and heard Dree's desperation amid the frightened anger of the children's minds. Time was running out for Shaw, but her terror was so great that he stopped and went to her assistance.

Shaw could not imagine what Dree's life had been like before they met; he never asked, and she never volunteered the information. But whatever it had been, it had left her with a cynical outlook that almost matched his own.

Dree had been born during an age when medical science had eliminated the possibility of birth defects. Either her parents had not bothered to take advantage of prenatal care, or the treatments had not been effective. Because she was so very different, Dree would have been a source of shame to her parents and the object of either pity or derision from her fellow humans.

Shaw had outstayed his welcome on Dree's home world, and stopping to help her had delayed him dangerously. In his need for immediate departure, Shaw took Dree with him. He had intended to leave her on some other world where she would be safe and could possibly make a better life for herself, but Dree had ideas of her own. She also had a mind quick to learn and an almost instinctive feel for the controls of the *Nighthunter*. So Shaw had let her stay.

Like Shaw, Dree was a loner, not inclined to intrude into his mental space or personal life. She had already proved her worth in emergencies more than once. So Shaw had admitted her to a tentative partnership. As long as the relationship continued to their mutual advantage, Shaw was content to have her.

Dree's attention was claimed by something on the instruments in front of her. "We've got a blip."

Shaw saw the light on his screen at the same time. "There are three of them, coming up fast. What is their beacon?"

"They're not broadcasting, but they look like Proxima fighters."

"What in hell are they doing here?" Shaw's fingers flew over the controls. "Evasive, set. Prepare for—"

"Shaw," she whispered.

He looked up at the screen and froze. The three blips were escorts, each one not much larger than the *Nighthunter*, but the fourth ship that appeared behind them was a Proxima dreadnought. It was enormous, a behemoth passing the fighters and seeming to approach the tiny racer slowly, almost languorously. She knew that the representation on the screen was deceptive, for very few ships could challenge the dreadnought's speed or might.

"We're not going to make it," Dree stated softly.

"We cannot give up without trying. Not without a fight," Shaw said. Dree turned back to the nav computer, her face pale but her fingers sure on the controls.

The *Nighthunter* was only seconds away from a hyperspace jump. Once it made the transition from real space they would be safe, but they had to act quickly. If the mass of the other ship was too close, the nav computer would not allow the *Nighthunter* to make the jump. The dreadnought continued to approach.

The *Nighthunter* gave a lurch, and the sound of her engines rose to an agonized shriek, signaling approaching overload.

"Damn!" Shaw slammed his fist down on the edge of the console.

"*Nighthunter*," a voice boomed over the comlink. "We have you in a tractor. There is no escape. Cut your engines and prepare to be boarded. I repeat, cut your engines."

"We're going to overload," Dree said. Her voice was calm as she reached for the cutoff switch.

"No!" Shaw said, catching her wrist. Dree's eyes opened wide with surprise. "Let it overload," he told her. "They are going to kill us anyway. Let us at least take the dreadnought with us."

"You mean blow up the ship?"

"The explosion will ride back on their tractor beam. Even if we do not manage to destroy them, we will do a hell of a lot of damage."

"Are you certain that we can't escape?"

Shaw shook his head, his eyes locked with hers.

Dree looked again at the giant ship that held them. "Then let's get them."

"*Nighthunter*," the voice said again. "Your engines are overheating. Cut—"

Shaw hit the switch that deactivated the entire communications system.

"We do not have to listen to that," he muttered. He unhooked his seat harness and reached over to Dree, putting his hands gently on her shoulders. "I am sorry. We have been in some tight spots before, but . . ."

"Never mind," she told him. "I knew what I was in for when I asked to join you. My life was better these last months than it would have been if I'd stayed on Summerland." She did not like emotional scenes, and even though she was moved by it, Shaw's apology made her uncomfortable. In the time they had been together, he had always treated her with consideration, but he had never before shown her any sign of affection. One of her hands came up and quickly touched his. "Let's make a bad taste in their mouth," she said, pointing at the screen and the large open hatch through which the *Nighthunter* was being drawn.

Shaw nodded and went to the engine compartment in the rear of the ship. The racer had an automatic safety device designed to shut down the engines when they approached critical. He would have to disconnect those circuits before the engines would blow.

The *Nighthunter* was straining, and various resistances set up, causing vibrations that would soon become strong enough to tear metal from metal. The ship was in agony, and the sound was a scream waking a corresponding pain in Shaw. The air in the engine compartment was dense with blue smoke that made him cough. Sparks danced across the panels as the wiring protested abuse.

Shaw found the control box for the engines' failsafe, but the access panel was vibrating too wildly for the catches to release. He worked frantically, his eyes tearing from the smoke. He was beginning to sweat in the rising temperature, and his fingers were slippery. He wiped his hands on his pant legs and tried once more.

Suddenly the *Nighthunter* lurched again, slamming him against the engine casing. Hollow thumps echoed through the hull on both sides, and then the ship steadied. Magnetic grapples, Shaw thought, distracted for a moment. It seemed the Proxima were not going to risk losing the *Nighthunter*. He returned to his task, anger replacing earlier care. His slender fingers found the crack where the panel joined the wall, and with much more strength than was obvious in his lean frame, he pushed the two pieces of metal apart. With a jerk he ripped the panel from the casing.

"Cut your engines and prepare for boarding!" The words boomed out as the Proxima used the grapples to carry sound vibrations into the captive ship.

Hurry, hurry, his mind said. Shaw's eyes were still watering from the acrid smoke. He brushed tears and sweat from his face and tried to remember the sequence that would deactivate the failsafe, but it was hopeless. Not caring what damage he did, he began tearing blindly at the wires.

The engines went dead. The shrieking began a diminuendo, down through the octaves to a dull bass rumble that faded to silence. Shaw realized that he was too late. Some kind of external control had been used to deactivate the *Nighthunter*'s engines. There was an intermittent sputter and crackle as circuits continued to short, but no other sound until a loud blast as the entrance hatch was blown open. Armed troops crashed into the *Nighthunter*, their heavy boots resounding on the deck.

Shaw came to his feet, running from the engine compartment. He was just in time to see Dree rise from the nav console, a pistol in her hand. There was a whining burst as a laser fired, and Dree fell to the deck, a small, still shape, smoke curling up from her burned body.

Anger engulfed Shaw like flame, a blinding rage that erased the last of his earlier fear. A trooper entering the *Nighthunter* after his mates was the first one of the Proxima to notice Shaw. The man raised his rifle, but before he could fire, Shaw hit him with a mental blast that destroyed his mind.

The troopers began to fall as Shaw broadcast his fury. Their screams wove a confusion of sound for a second, and then they all died—except one. For some reason he was not affected. Shaw did not stop to wonder why, but launched himself toward the armored figure. The trooper turned, flicking his rifle's setting, then fired, engulfing Shaw in an intense light. The captain of the *Nighthunter* fell, and total silence settled over the ship.

CHAPTER 2

Space, 2473 TSC

The woman's arms moved like a flower unfolding, opening slowly as if underwater, all of their power disguised in grace. There was no water in the gym, but free-fall presented many of the same conditions, and the reaction sent her floating toward the wall. Her back arched as she swung feet over head to touch the padded surface with her toes, recoiling and turning in the air as she came back toward center to meet an invisible opponent, ready for the next strike, the movement beautiful and quite deadly.

Winter was tall and extremely fit, the definition of muscle visible under the tight-fitting shipsuit that she wore while she worked out. Not that she did not appear feminine: her structure displayed none of the bulging muscles of a male body or a weightlifter, but the sleek lines of a dancer. She wore her brown hair in a short cap, a style affected by most of the ship's crew, and her hazel eyes were slightly slanted by high, pronounced cheek bones. Her skin was dark, more golden than brown, and although she really fit few of the criteria by which society defined beauty, she was a very attractive woman. She was also a starcaptain, and her ship was the FSS *Venture*.

Dr. David Wilson was unaware that he still held a cup and that the coffee inside of it was getting cold. He stood in his office in front of the comscreen, watching his captain as she worked out in the free-fall gym. Since it was well into the ship's night cycle, Winter should have been asleep, but for the second night in a row David watched as she put herself through a strenuous series of exercises.

As the *Venture*'s chief medical officer, Wilson had certain powers and privileges. He was the only one who had any authority over the captain. If he felt it was in her best interest, or for the safety of the ship and its mission, he could even question her orders. But such an extreme action would have to be justified both to her and the other ship's officers, and to an inquiry board when the ship returned to base. The doctor's responsibility was the physical and mental well-being of the crew, and thus he had access to all of their activities, whether personal or professional. From the special comscreen on his desk, Wilson could eavesdrop on everything that happened in the ship.

When he first had been assigned as ship's physician, Wilson had considered the use of that device the most distasteful part of his work, but since his own inhibitions prevented him from abusing it, he soon recognized the monitor for the useful tool that it was. It had enabled him to intercede on a number of occasions, preventing situations from becoming serious incidents. At the moment, he was using the comscreen to follow his captain as she battled her unseen demons.

Apprehension furrowed Wilson's brow as he stood and watched Winter. He recognized the movements of a sunbas mote, a katalike exercise of the free-fall martial arts. On the previous night she had repeated that particular mote until she could barely move, and even then he knew that she had not been able to sleep.

David began to think it was time for him to interfere. He shifted his weight and felt the now cold coffee slosh in the cup he still held. He looked at the cup with distaste and then put it down, precariously balanced on a stack of papers and a couple of data cubes. His attention shifted back to the figure on the screen. While he was responsible for everyone on the ship, his feelings for Winter were special; during the four years he had served aboard the *Venture*, he and the captain had become friends.

Not many people could claim any kind of a personal relationship with Winter. In fact most people said she was aptly named after the coldest months of the year, but David had discovered the truly warm human that lay behind the chill, efficient exterior of the starcaptain. She did not display that side of her personality easily, and their dealings with each other were usually conducted with the formality required by their military service. Still, David was the one person on the ship who could approach Winter on a personal level, and he decided that it was time to do just that.

The stress of the past month had been severe, especially for the captain. At the crux of the matter was Princess Isaten, the granddaughter of the Matriarch of Malvern. Isaten had served as her planet's representative to a series of meetings that the Federation had held in an attempt—another vain attempt, David reminded himself—to reconcile the growing differences between the colonies and the government.

It was another case of too little and too late. For years the colonies had pleaded their cause to the Council of Ruling Houses without success. If his interpretation of the situation was correct, that most recent conference would probably be their last attempt at peaceful negotiation. As well as reports in the news, he had seen evidence during his travels that a large number of the colonies—more than a hundred planets—were already in revolt, fighting for autonomy. The conference had been a last-ditch effort by some of the more conservative worlds to make changes, but it appeared that most of them would join the rebels. The way things looked, there was nothing the Houses or the Federation could do to stop them. Although David sympathized with many of the colonists' complaints, he still could not condone their methods; as far as he was concerned, war was never a viable alternative.

Perhaps because she had not been successful at pleading her planet's case, the Princess Isaten had been a demanding and peevish passenger; nothing the ship's crew did had seemed to please her. She spent much of the voyage in her cabin, in the company of her attendants and personal guards —all women.

"Isaten," he said to himself. She was a glorious creature, her head held high on a slender neck, her shining blond hair arranged intricately and twined with gems, flowing down her back in soft waves. Every time he had seen her, she had been dressed in bright silk gowns and jewels that were no less brilliant than her blue eyes. He had been more than half in love with her at first.

David had been standing at attention with the rest of the *Venture*'s officers, an honor guard to greet the ambassador when she boarded the ship. He had to admit that he had stared in stunned admiration as she and her attendants swept regally past, disdainful of the ceremony. David remembered Winter starting after her, a slight elevation of her chin and her narrowed eyes the only sign of irritation at the ambassador's rudeness.

David sighed at the memory. The mission had not started at all well, and perhaps he might have anticipated the problems that someone like the ambassador could cause, but he had been so dazzled by her obvious beauty. Who could have imagined that such a woman possessed a soul as vicious and amoral as Isaten's had proved to be? She was the cause of the trouble they had experienced, but as usual, Winter was taking the blame on herself.

David's attention was called back to the present as he heard the communicator in the gym begin to chime. He saw Winter kick herself away from the wall to float over to the receiver by the door, and he turned up the audio on his comscreen so he could listen in.

The voice of the watch officer came from the speaker. "Captain Winter," he said, "You have a priority message from Alpha Base Seven. It's Command Headquarters."

"Relay it down here," Winter ordered. Hooking her leg around a padded holdtight by the door, she settled down to wait. There was a muffled crackle of static as the link was established.

"Captain Winter, are you there?" a male voice asked. David recognized the voice of Oliver Gerny, one of the chief advisers to Admiral Jammeson and head of Information Services at the base.

"This is Captain Winter."

"We have just received a transmission from the Malvern government. The Matriarch extends her gratitude for your swift return of her ambassador. She also requests an additional service before you leave the Malvern system."

There was no definable expression on Winter's face, but

the doctor could see her shoulders rise slightly, reflecting the increased tension in her body.

"Have you seen my report on the results of the last 'favor' we did for the Matriarch?" she asked, her voice very smooth and controlled. "The minor task of returning her ambassador cost me two members of my crew, one of them an officer."

The doctor perched on the edge of a chair, prepared to listen to the rest of the conversation.

"I have seen your report, Captain," Gerny replied. "The incident was regrettable, but the importance of the Malvern Matriarchy to the Federation is such that we must overlook certain misunderstandings. We have already informed the Matriarch that you will be happy to comply with her wishes."

Winter's eyes narrowed to angry slits, but her voice was carefully controlled. "And what is this favor, Official Gerny?"

"You are to deliver two containers to Gyler Laboratories. There will be no personnel this time, just cargo."

"Cargo," Winter echoed. "Gyler is at least two weeks from here, and it's in the opposite direction from Alpha Base."

David could tell that Winter was at the end of her patience. It was out of character for her to argue with her orders. He was torn between watching the rest of the transmission and leaving immediately for the gym. His hand hovered over the cutoff key.

There was a moment of silence, then the face of Admiral Jammeson replaced that of Gerny on the screen. David felt a prickle of apprehension. Apparently the favor was more than it seemed.

"Captain Winter, you are ordered to comply with the Matriarch's wishes. We are aware that this request is somewhat unusual, but it can be used to our advantage. You will take the Malvern containers to Gyler Labs. Once there you will request a tour of the facility. Afterward, you will make a comprehensive report on your observations. You are to include a description of the physical plant and any activity you may observe there. In a way the Matriarch's request is fortuitous; it enables us to appease the Malvern and at the same time gain entrance to the labs on a legitimate errand."

"Aye, sir," Winter responded, but her tension did not abate. "Were we informed of the contents of the containers? It would be useful to know if they require special handling."

"We were not, but whatever they are, I'm certain the *Venture* will be able to accommodate them. Your formal orders and additional information will be blipped to your ship's computer."

David saw Jammeson square his shoulders and tilt his head as if posing for an audience. On the wall behind the admiral was a large plaque, the bright enameled surface a reproduction of the emblem of the Federation of Ruling Houses.

"I don't think I have to remind you, Captain," the admiral continued, "that the Malvern system is important to us—to the Federation. Now that we are aware of the unique customs of the planet, you will be able to prevent another incident such as the one that killed your crew members on the previous mission. You might have prevented that in any event."

David switched off the monitor and left his office. He had never really liked Admiral Jammeson, although he knew that Winter respected him. Hearing the admiral imply that the captain was responsible for the death of her crew pissed him off.

David used a drop tube to get to the null-g hub of the ship. By the time he arrived at the gym, the transmission had ended and Winter had returned with renewed vigor to her exercises.

David clung to the bulkhead as he floated in the doorway watching her. He had always found the movements of the martial arts fascinating. He had studied hand-to-hand combat as part of his basic training, but he had not continued the discipline, and sometimes he was sorry. Winter on the other hand had earned a cinquodez zudan in Sunbas and a second-degree black belt in Karate. She knew the movements so well that they were second nature, and watching her work out was like watching a very skilled dancer or the movements of a healthy predator—both beautiful and frightening at the same time.

David shook himself from his reverie as he remembered why he was there.

"Captain," he called from the doorway.

"Go away," she replied as she spun slowly past him.

"I will not go away, Captain. Not until you talk to me."

"Leave me alone. That's an order!"

"Captain," David snapped. "I am responsible for your safety. Stop what you are doing immediately and come with me."

She flew in his direction, stopping her movement at the last minute by snagging a holdtight with her foot.

"What in hell are you talking about?" she demanded.

Such a display of her anger was rare, but David stood firm.

"You're off shift. You've been without sleep for more than forty-eight hours. Two nights now, you've been here working yourself into exhaustion, but it hasn't helped, has it?"

She was silent.

"You're like a bomb about to go off." He changed his tone. "Winter, what's wrong? Can't you talk about it?"

Winter wiped the sweat off of her face but did not answer. David noticed that she would not meet his eyes.

"It's Dow, isn't it?" he continued, but still she did not speak. The sound of her breathing was harsh in the silence. "Winter, I'm supposed to help you, but I can't do anything unless you let me."

She went past him out the door and used the grav tube to rise up into the ship's outer ring. David followed as best he could. He did not like null-g very much—he always felt so awkward.

"What do you want from me, Doctor?" she asked when they were standing in the corridor. "Of course it's Dow. And Mechlin, too. The complete, total uselessness of what happened."

"You couldn't have prevented their deaths. You weren't responsible." David kept his voice low and, he hoped, soothing, but his words had the opposite effect.

"No!" Winter almost shouted, whirling on him, her eyes blazing. "No, I couldn't have stopped what happened, and that's what's so hard to take. I thought we were supposed to be civilized. Don't we have laws? Isn't murder illegal?"

"Of course—" David began.

"So what makes *her* exempt? I was told that we must overlook such misunderstandings! Why should that spoiled ambassador and her lousy chauvinistic culture be allowed to practice their short-sighted, murderous customs—" Winter paused, appalled by her outburst. Her hands went to her face as she fought for control. David wanted to say something, to help, but he knew he had to be still.

"Dow was the best Exec I've ever worked with." Her voice had lost the hysterical edge. "We were together for over eight years. To kill him for no good reason . . . and Mechlin . . ." She leaned against the wall. "I've never felt so helpless," she whispered.

"Dow was your friend," David began, but she interrupted him again.

"We were lovers, too, a long time ago. But that isn't the

reason. Dow was a good officer. So was Mechlin. They didn't deserve to die for no reason." Her shoulders were slumped as if her anger had been all that held her up.

"Come on." David took her arm. "You need some rest. And your muscles will stiffen up if you stand here any longer."

Winter moved down the corridor with him. "I need a soma; that is, if you have one that will keep me from dreaming," she replied. "I'm almost afraid to close my eyes."

"I'll do better than give you a pill. I think about twelve hours in the tank will straighten you out."

"I hate that damned tank," she returned, but her voice lacked force.

"It serves a purpose."

"Sure. Taking people's bodies apart and prying into their minds."

"You've had reason to be grateful for the tank before."

Winter's steps slowed as they neared the door to sick bay. "All right, I'll get into your tank, but only for six hours. I have new orders. We have work to do."

"Twelve hours—and those are your doctor's orders. Right now they come first. You can get someone else to shuttle the Malvern containers up. Delegate authority. That's one of the captain's privileges."

Winter stiffened at his words. "You've been snooping!"

"If you mean, have I been watching you? Yes. I knew something was wrong, and since you didn't come to me for help, keeping an eye on you was my job."

"I don't like that." Winter muttered as they entered sick bay.

"Neither do I, but sometimes it's necessary."

She was silent, considering his earlier words. "The only other person I can send down is Lieutenant T'Gal, and she's about as ready to murder the Malvern as I am."

"I can go. What's so difficult about picking up two containers? I'll be diplomatic, even subservient if it's necessary. Stop worrying about petty details."

Winter sat at David's communicator and started punching buttons. A man's face appeared on the screen.

"Commander Thomas here."

"Commander, this is Captain Winter. Please record. I'm instructing Dr. Wilson to take the shuttle down to the Malvern capitol at oh nine hundred hours. He'll be accompanied by a work detail. Four people, no more, and all women, if possible. They will pick up two containers and bring them back to the ship. We'll leave orbit as soon as this is completed. Prepare a course for minimum distance from planetary mass and prepare for hyperspace jump at seventeen hundred hours. Inform all necessary personnel and log this message. Winter clear."

"Recorded and logged, sir. Bridge clear."

Winter leaned back in the doctor's chair and looked up at him. "All right, Doctor, you can hook me up. Just remember, you were the one who suggested I delegate authority. It's in your hands now."

"You worry too much, Captain."

"That's part of my job," she reminded him with grim humor.

"Okay, I've been warned. Take a shower while I set up the machine." He gestured to a doorway. "I'll be waiting for you in there."

Fifteen minutes later Winter climbed onto the slab projecting out of the huge diagnostic and therapeutic computer that took up an entire wall of sick bay.

"Remember, no more than twelve hours," she said as she lay down.

"Relax, Winter. You're in good hands."

"And don't get yourself killed down on Malvern," she continued, closing her eyes as she pressed a defuser against her thigh. The device hissed as the sedative entered her muscle.

He waited a moment until her breathing slowed, then pulled the lid down over her body. A clear, pink liquid began to fill the container as David sat down at the console to monitor her body chemistry and brain waves.

That was the biggest problem with people like Winter, he thought. Outwardly she was cool, direct, and extremely efficient, but her repressed emotions would eventually turn on her.

David frowned and tapped out a command to the machine. He watched one of the readings rise to normal.

No one of the crew was immune to the strain they had been under. He wished they could take a break, but the *Venture*'s next scheduled maintenance was months away, and R & R would have to wait until then.

The *Venture* was a ring ship, one of the twenty star cruisers commissioned with the new Dillinger drive. The ship carried a crew of one hundred and twenty-four men and women—twenty-two now, he reminded himself. Originally the *Venture* was to have been a science ship. They were on their way to the yards at Gallandry to be fitted with an additional ring containing labs and staff quarters when their orders were changed—all because of the damned rebellion. Since then the *Venture* had caried out a wide variety of missions ranging from diplomatic courier to exploration and survey, while the original crew served as both technical support and research personnel. Fortunately they were overstaffed for such missions. The loss of two crew members, while tragic, would not impair the efficient running of the ship.

The doctor tapped another adjustment into the machine and sat back, watching carefully. Satisfied at last, he set the controls to automatic and headed for his own bed.

CHAPTER 3

The discovery of thermonuclear power paved the way for space flight, although learning to harness such an awesome energy took decades. In contrast, designing a ship was much easier, for away from gravity there were fewer restrictions on form, and engineers had known the secrets of stress and structure for centuries.

The *Venture* and her sister ships were only one of the many designs that eventually evolved. What made her special was the massive Dillinger drive that propelled her through hyperspace, that maze of warped space which shortened the previously impossible distance between the stars. The power represented by the drive and the *Venture*'s other engines was tremendous. They lay in the ship's central shaft like restless dragons, their awesome fires under the control of the people who manned the bridge.

The *Venture*'s brain was the bridge, and it was a study in elegant logic, every inch of space carefully fitted with a complexity of controls, computers, monitors, and keyboards. It held the regulators that maintained the internal life-support systems, the sub and superspace radios, and links to the sensors which served as eyes in the void outside of the hull. No one appreciated the efficiency of the *Venture*'s bridge more than the crew. The design enabled them to fulfill their tasks quickly and with an ease that was lacking in many of the other ships.

David entered the bridge and stood watching while Winter finished working with the navigator as they prepared for the jump into hyperspace. The captain was dressed in a fresh uniform, and though her face was unsmiling as she concentrated on her task, the lines of fatigue were gone. Twelve hours in the tank had worked wonders as usual, he thought.

Winter looked up and gave David a nod, but turned to speak to the helmsman before joining the doctor at the door.

"Our cargo is on board, Captain," the doctor reported.

"Did you have any problems?"

"Of course. Did you think I wouldn't?" he replied with dry humor.

"I had hoped you would be able to carry out the transfer without creating another incident," she replied.

"Oh, there wasn't an incident," David told her. "I just had to contend with the normal officiousness and bureaucratic red tape. Then, after wading through all that, I had to convince them I had your authority before they would release the cargo into my care."

Winter made a small sound of irritation. "We jump in an hour. It'll take us that long to get the minimum distance from the planet." She turned to leave, but David stopped her.

"Aren't you curious about the cargo?" he asked.

"Not in the least," she said. "Tie it down, lock it up, post a guard if you think it's necessary, but whatever it is, it can take care of itself until we reach Gyler." She went back to her duties.

"Aye, aye, Captain," David said, and he left the bridge.

A shower and a nap helped David ease the mental distaste left from his jaunt to Malvern. Looking at his reflection in the mirror over the sink, he felt his jaw, wondering if it was time for another application of inhibitor and toying with the possibility of growing a beard. His hair was blond, lightened by a liberal sprinkling of silver, but the last time he had grown a beard it had been a shocking red color. No, he told himself, better keep a clean jaw. He sprayed the inhibitor into his hands and rubbed it across his cheeks, closely watching the process with his bright blue eyes. More and more, when he looked at himself he saw a reflection of his father staring back at him. David grinned at the face in the mirror.

As he dressed in a fresh uniform, he realized that the *Venture* must have made the jump to hyperspace while he was asleep. He was glad; it meant that he had slept through the dizzying wrench that always accompanied transition. Although he had been in space for many years he still disliked the jump. He felt it as a moment of such intense disorientation that he was afraid he would lose his lunch. David had been ashamed of his reaction and kept it to himself until he learned that a lot of other seasoned spacers felt the same.

When David was dressed he went into his office and called the galley, asking for a meal to be brought to him. He had decided to eat in since there were reports to be completed and some reading he wanted to do.

When the meal arrived, he absently thanked the steward, his attention distracted only for a moment as he tried to concentrate on the words parading across the viewer. They kept coming, but David was having trouble remembering what they said. He finally gave up, snapped the viewer off, and sat back in his chair, a troubled frown on his face. There was a plate on the tray beside him, and he realized that he had eaten half of the food without either identifying or tasting it.

David gave a gusty sigh. Winter might say she was disinterested, but he could not get the thought of the Malvern containers out of his mind. Their shape worried him more than anything—they looked like coffins.

He turned the viewer back on and requested the information about Gyler Laboratories.

GYLER: G-3 PLANET, NUMBER 198764-306G.
SUN: 61 CYGNI AB.
DISTANCE FROM EARTH: 3.43 PARSECS—11.187288 LIGHT-YEARS.
PLANETARY DIAMETER: 450 KM
ROTATION: 18.0 ER
INCLINATION: 3.8 DEGREES

David increased the scanning speed until he was past the astronomical data.

HISTORY: GYLER, A COMPLETELY BARREN WORLD, DEVOID OF ATMOSPHERE. CHARTERED FOR COLONIZATION ON 7/10/2153.
PURPOSE: TO PROVIDE A TOTALLY ISOLATED LOCA-

TION FOR THE FEDERATION R-3 LABORATORIES. THE
ORIGINAL SITE (A MODULE ATTACHED TO THE NOBEL
SCIENCE COMPLEX, EARTH ORBITAL STATION #74) WAS
ABANDONED BECAUSE OF THE NATURE OF THE RESEARCH
SCHEDULED THERE. IT WAS CONSIDERED TOO DANGER-
OUS TO BE CARRIED OUT EXCEPT IN A TOTALLY ISOLATED
AREA. R-3 RESEARCH = BIOLOGICAL AND ORGANIC CHEM-
ISTRY, [CROSS REF: FED INDEX CHEM VOL 233]. CUR-
RENT (PAST 20 YR TSC) = GENETIC MANIPULATION USING
BOTH VIRAL AND BACTERIOLOGICAL AGENTS, AS WELL
AS MECHANICAL MANIPULATION [CROSS REF: FED INDEX
GENE VOL 104]. THE ARTIFICIAL ATMOSPHERE REQUIRED
ON GYLER CAN BE MAINTAINED BOTH TO INSURE THE
INTEGRITY OF THE EXPERIMENTS AND TO AVOID CONTAM-
INATION OF PERSONNEL.

David's eyes raced through the rest of the history: he already knew most of it, and he had even helped make some of
it.

The Gyler Labs had had remarkable results, he reminded
himself, at least during the early years. He himself had been
grateful to use many of the techniques they had developed,
such as virally induced tissue regeneration and accelerated
bone knitting. Those discoveries not only had eased pain and
made his job easier, but also had healed people who would
once have remained crippled for life. But the labs had also
developed some of the most terrifying biological weapons in
man's history. Thank God the Federation had the sense to
realize that those weapons caused indiscriminate destruction,
and since they had no regard for political conviction, decided
they were not useful as weapons.

It was about that time that the labs had been reorganized
and directed toward another line of work: genetic manipulation. The object was to provide human colonists with the
means to survive on some of the less hospitable but still eco-
nomically desirable worlds. As a result there were human
types suited to live in a variety of conditions: in heavy gravity,
in low gravity, and even under water—again a plus mark for
Gyler.

Then there had been a public uproar about Gyler's work in
genetics. Certain special interest groups decided that such
drastic alteration of man's natural form was immoral. At first
those fanatics were ignored. Then a routine government in-

vestigation of the labs revealed that Gyler's work for the Pioneer Program had deteriorated into unusual and highly unethical experimentation. The labs' scientists insisted that what they were doing was a logical extension of genetic research. But what the investigators found could only be described as monsters.

David's thoughts of the labs were tinged with revulsion when he remembered the investigation. He had been one of the professionals assigned to accompany the government inspectors, and he would never be free of the memory of what he had seen there.

He got to his feet and paced to the wall where he stood staring at the duty roster for the coming week. He did not see the names listed there as the past came flooding back.

No one knew what to do with the surviving subjects of the research at Gyler. The subjects that were obviously nonsentient were mercifully destroyed, but there were others who were alive, thinking and feeling, even though their outer forms had been altered, sometimes beyond recognition. What to do with them was a problem that no one felt qualified to solve. There were too many issues, many of them conflicting, to take into account. Because the survivors were all so different from each other, there was no unity or group support among them. Each one had to be considered as an individual, and by law, they could not be kept as either prisoners or wards of the state.

By that time the public had become aware of the plight of what the media presented as pitiful victims of injustice. Various religious groups rose up demanding that they be released.

And so Gyler's creations were set free, cast adrift in the mainstream of life, to make of it and of themselves whatever they could. But few of them survived the outrage of humanity when the reality of the Gyler horrors was made manifest, and many of their attackers were the same people who had once clamored for their release.

David was haunted, and despite the years that had passed, he still felt ill when he thought of the events he had witnessed. Although the labs had been placed under strict Federation control, they were still run as a private institution and had their own board of directors. Because of the highly competitive business interests throughout Federated worlds, the work at Gyler was classified. No one could ever be certain what was being done there.

David's personal knowledge of Gyler was a spur to his curiosity about the Malvern containers. Each one, despite the machinery that was attached to it, was the right size and shape to hold an adult human. Unlike the stasis boxes that he was accustomed to, they were opaque, so whatever they contained was hidden from view. But, he mused, perhaps the cases were not immune to his medical instruments.

The lights in the storage room obligingly came on as they sensed David's presence in the doorway. Before him were the long flat containers, each one attached to a broad, cradlelike support by a heavy cable consisting of wires and tubes twisted together. He could not see any controls or monitoring devices. Only two small, amber lights showed that the machinery was operational.

David went to the nearest container and took a reading with his hand-held scanner. The contents were not complicated: basic liquid chemical stasis material surrounding inert organic material. The absence of any bioelectrical readings indicated that the contents had ceased to live, and the chemical composition of the liquid meant that it had died before it had been placed in the container.

He made an adjustment to the scanner, and the tiny screen produced an image of sorts. He could only see a small portion at one time because of the size limitations of the hand-held unit, but he pressed the record button, making an end-to-end scan of the figure. He could reproduce an entire picture later on the big screen of the medical computer in sick bay.

"Dr. Wilson, is that you?" a man's voice called from the doorway. "Is there something wrong with these machines?" It was Thomas, the *Venture*'s engineer.

"No. Nothing's wrong. I'm just satisfying my professional curiosity," David responded.

"I don't blame you. I've been curious about them, too." the engineer said, entering the compartment. "They look like stasis units, don't they?"

"I believe that's what they are."

"I wouldn't trust those Malvern witches not to have some poor unfortunate soul locked up in there. What have you found?"

"I've only scanned one of the containers so far. Whoever's in it was dead when they placed her inside."

"Her? You don't mean they're sending one of their own to Gyler?"

"I'm not sure. I can't tell very much from this tiny screen, but the size indicates that it's a child. She was dead before they placed her inside."

"A child? What did she die of?"

David adjusted a setting on the scanner. "Looks like burns."

He moved to the second container. Having found one corpse, he was surprised when the readings were positive on the second.

"Is this one dead, too?" Thomas prompted when David did not speak right away.

"Alive," he said, without looking up. "But maybe better off dead." He shook his head in bewilderment. "I don't understand what they've done here. Look at this. There's definite electrical potential in the muscles. Chemical stasis accounts for the lack of activity in the organs . . . but the brain wave readings are too low. This is either a severely retarded individual, or the brain waves have been suppressed in some way."

Thomas looked over his shoulder and made a small sound of disgust. "I could never understand that biology stuff," he grumbled. "Might as well be alien."

David was frowning over the readout. "Could the brain be dead?" he wondered out loud. He made another adjustment to the scanner. "No, there are faint responses, but they're abnormally low, and I can't imagine what would account for that." He turned his attention to the support mechanism that surrounded the containers. "I don't see any controls or monitors on this thing."

"They're probably behind a panel somewhere," Thomas said. He was an enormous Welshman with an almost instinctive way with anything mechanical. "I wouldn't go messin' with the controls on this thing," he continued, contradicting his words with his actions. "At least not until we've figured out what they do and how they work. Here you go . . ." As he spoke, a panel on the machine slid aside to reveal a small console.

"How did you do that?" David asked. He had not seen a button or even a seam to indicate that the panel was there.

Thomas grinned. "What I'd like to know is how they power these things. I may not like that crew of women back there, but they do have some good ideas when it comes to technology. This is a very elegant device."

David studied the console, trying to relate what he saw to equipment he was familiar with. He ticked items off in his mind, then straightened up and turned back to Thomas.

"As far as I can see, there is nothing in here that would account for brain-wave suppression."

"You've figured it out then?" the engineer asked. "What's this for?" He pointed to a switch that was set a little apart from the others.

"I don't know. Probably controls something in the case. It doesn't seem to be part of the medical equipment."

"Here, let me see that." Thomas shouldered in front of the doctor and bent his tall frame until his head was at the level of the opening. "You're right," he said after a moment. "It's a light switch."

"A light switch? On a stasis unit?"

"Well, sure. I suspect these containers are made of berdieum. It's as hard as steel. You can't break it, and it's noncorrosive. They use it for ports in ships, tanks, things like that. It's good for one-way windows, too."

"You mean . . ."

"If you put a light behind it, it's transparent, but with the light on the outside, you can't see in. Here, I'll show you." Before the doctor could protest, Thomas threw the switch. As he had predicted the inside of the container began to glow with light.

Inside was the nude body of a tall, slender male. He was floating in a dense silvery liquid with trails of tiny bubbles rising up around his sides.

"Ye Gods," Thomas breathed. "There's your brain wave suppression."

He was referring to the black metal helmet that completely covered the figure's face and head. There was a small box built into the top of the case and connected to the helmet by a dozen or so wires. Blinking red lights indicated the box's activity.

David stepped closer, his scanner forgotten. He could see thick lines of scar tissue running down the back of the arms that were bound across the figure's chest. Scars were almost unheard of in a time when tissue regeneration was so common.

"What are you going to do now?" Thomas asked, calling David's attention back.

"Huh? What do you mean?"

"You aren't going to leave him there, are you?"

"That's up to the captain. I'll have to report this, of course. I think she'll want to know that we're taking a live human to the labs."

"She won't like it."

"No, she won't, but it may not be in her power to do anything about it," David said grimly, remembering the last transmission from Command.

"Power or no, she's not the kind to let something like this happen," Thomas stated firmly.

"No, she isn't," David agreed, and hoped it was true.

"Get him out of there," Winter told David several hours later.

He was startled. When he had first told the captain of his discovery she had listened. She accompanied him down to the storage area and looked at the containers themselves. But in all that time, she never said a word.

David found he was almost arguing with her, so percussive was the manner in which he presented his findings. He described the conditions, gave voice to all of his suspicions, backing everything, almost frantically, with medical and historical fact, clutching against the wall of Winter's silence. The longer she said nothing, the more vocal he became. He realized he was almost begging her to allow him to release the captive. But it was impossible to read her, to know what she was thinking or feeling when she was in such a mood, and David became desperate at his lack of ability to get a response.

They were still standing in the storage area when David finally let his words stop. He knew he had done all he could, and knew he had failed.

He had closed his eyes and waited at the door while Winter walked slowly around the containers one more time, her tall body erect in her dark blue uniform. She did not take her eyes from the machinery and the man in the black helmet.

Finally she spoke. "Get him out of there."

"What?" His eyes flew open at her words.

"I mean exactly what I said. You can do it, can't you?"

"Yes. B-but—" David stammered. "But what about Command? And Gyler?"

"Don't worry about them. I'll make a report and give my reasons for this decision. My initial orders were based on incomplete knowledge. I'm not carrying a live human to the Gyler Labs, and the Federation won't expect me to do it. You of all people should understand that."

"But are you sure about him?" David pointed to the figure in stasis. "We have no way of knowing why he's in there. He could be a criminal. He could be insane, maybe even dangerous."

"Does it really matter? If he committed an offense, it was against Malvern. Nothing he could have done deserves being sentenced to Gyler."

"You don't think Admiral Jammeson will be angry?"

Winter gave a short laugh. "My orders were to deliver two containers to Gyler. Nothing was said about the contents. I want both of those cases opened and the bodies removed. Prepare a report on everything. Since Command suspects that something's going on at the labs, our delivery of more experimental material without investigation might prove to be a serious mistake."

"I'll get a medical team down here right away," David said. "It will take some time. Removing a living body from chemical stasis is tricky."

"But you can do it?"

"Of course," he promised.

"Good. I'll be on the bridge. Let me know how you progress."

CHAPTER 4

Karth, 2452 TSC.

Spring came to Karth in a haze of green as new growth pushed up through the last patches of snow. Slowly the winter constellation, Felis major, slipped beneath the night horizon as the northern hemisphere turned back toward the sun. Spring meant longer days, warm breezes blowing up from the south, and bright blue skys filled with birds flying back from winter havens. Most important of all, spring was the birthing time for the cassia. The fawns danced stilt-legged among the herds as they gained the strength and endurance that they would need for their annual migration. At first their coats were dark, almost black, but as they grew during the summer months the fleece would lighten to the rich browns, tans, and even whites of their parents. And that precious cassia fleece that was the wealth of the seminomadic herders of Karth.

As spring days began to lengthen into summer the cassia grew restless. Gradually they began grazing farther toward the northern end of their pasture. Memories teased them, memories of the plains, the vast expanse of new grass growing knee-high as far as the eye could see. The sweet grass lured them after a winter spent grazing on the hard salt-grass that grew along the southern beaches. Coastal mountains sheltered the beaches from the devastating winter storms that swept the plains, but in summer the storms abated, life returned to the plains, and the cassia remembered.

The herdsmen watched the animals very carefully, and when the scouts returned with word that the snow had melted from the lower levels of the mountains, the gates in the passes were opened. The cassia wandered out, grazing and moving slowly. In time, the clanspeople packed up their families and followed, keeping with a tradition that had been repeated every year since the colony's founding.

First came the herdsmen themselves, mounted on the strong ponies that were descended, like the people, from Earth stock. Later came the caravans, tents built on floater platforms that carried everything the clanspeople would need on the trek. Soon the big stone winter houses beyond the fishing villages stood empty, abandoned for eight months until fall when the clanspeople returned to the southern sea.

Life for the clanspeople was not easy. Their survival was linked to the cassia, and the life of the cassia was the annual migration across the vast plains. Every year they followed the same pattern: the spring restlessness and then the long slow movement away from the sea. In four months the herds would reach the Turning place, the northernmost point of the trek. There beneath towering mountains, all of the migratory paths met. Before humans had come to Karth, the cassia had rested there, the males looking over other herds for choice females and young studs trying for a herd of their own.

With the arrival of humans, Turning had evolved into a place where the seven clans met. It was a time to greet old friends and to exchange news and breeding stock. Merchants from the city came to the Turning, as they visited the Snow Festival in the middle of winter, bringing aircars full of manufactured goods to trade for cassia fleece, hides, or the woven goods for which the clans were famous. Turning was also the time when the council would meet, sitting with the clanspeople and ruling on local affairs as well as deciding government policies. As such, the Turning was one of the two major celebrations on Karth.

Sixteen-year-old Ilya rubbed down her tired pony and turned him loose in the pasture. He trotted away to join the other saddle stock, scattering a small herd of drifters that was in his way. Although the drifters were wild, they understood that safety from predators was to be found in the vicinity of humans, and there was usually a herd or two of the tiny goat-like animals following the caravan. The drifters ran in a wide arc, slowing as they returned to the place where they had originally been grazing. They moved swiftly for such small animals, but they were not so much frightened as they were reluctant to have anything to do with the pony.

Ilya watched them for a minute before turning away. She was sweaty and streaked with dust from a day of helping to chase strays into the holding pens at the Turning place. She took a long drink at the communal well and splashed her face with the cool water, rubbing off some of the grime. Ilya's hair was confined in a long braid that reached her waist, but ten-drils had escaped to straggle in a tangled mess around her face. She pushed her hair out of the way with the back of her hand and wished she had time for a swim, but it was late, and Hanna would have dinner ready soon. Ilya was not too tired to eat, but she also was not eager to face Hanna with a new rip in her pants. It was the third time she had ripped them in a six-day, and Hanna was sure to scold her.

Ilya wandered over to a thick stand of trees where Yoko, her dace, was resting in the shade, his eyes half closed in the glare of the setting sun. Not many of the clans still kept the big striped animals. Although the dace could be trained to work the herds, their predatory nature occasionally got the better of them, and cassia was their traditional food. Like the cassia and drifters, the dace were native to Karth. They looked like a cross between a Terran wolf and a large cat. Ilya was especially fond of Yoko; perhaps because of the close bond between them, he had never threatened her herd.

Ilya settled her back against Yoko's soft shoulder, reaching up with her hand to scratch behind one relaxed ear. Yoko rumbled his response, the sound coming from deep in his chest, but he declined to make the effort to give a more enthu-siastic greeting. The heat was intense, and though his thick fur gave him some protection, he was very tired from the day's hard work chasing the stubborn cassia.

Insects buzzed in the bushes around them; the hard sunlight was deflected by a thick roof of leaves while a fitful breeze brought some cool air to where they lay. Ilya let her eyes close and became aware of sounds beyond the thicket. Another clan had arrived sometime that afternoon and was busy setting up camp. That would be the Sanders, she realized. They were the closest eastern neighbor of the Winter clan to which she belonged. She listened, idly trying to pick out individual voices.

Despite the wide separation of the herds during most of the year, children of the clanspeople had ample opportunity to be with each other during the five-month school year. Many lifelong friends were made that way.

Eric was a Sanders; he was seventeen, a year older than Ilya, and they had been close friends for many years. Even when they reached adolescence, Ilya and Eric were still able to talk through the shyness of their new sexual awareness and, as a result, became even closer than before.

That was the best part of their relationship, Ilya decided. They could talk about almost anything—until lately, she remembered with a frown. Eric had been different at the previous two festivals. Though he had still appeared happy to see her, he had spent most of his time with his male friends.

Ilya's mother, Alisia, told her not to worry about Eric's sudden change. She pointed out that young men had to spend time with each other before they were ready to pair off. But Hanna had scolded, telling Ilya that she was too much like her mother—too bossy and too independent. If she didn't settle down, Hanna had said, she would never be accepted by a partner.

Ilya did not agree with Hanna's advice. Alisia was the clan leader, but she was also a working herder. If she had to be like anyone, Ilya hoped she would be just like her mother, rather than settling into the quiet life of a weaver or a clanmother like Hanna. Ilya loved the excitement of being out on horseback with the herds and even preferred the danger and discomforts to traveling with the tent floaters or sitting behind one of the big looms. Yes, if she stayed on Karth, she wanted to be a herder just like her mother.

But Ilya had a fantasy, a secret dream of one day going into space. She had never told anyone except Eric about it. She loved Karth and did not like to think about leaving her family and friends, and yet there was something so compelling about the stars. Now that Space Service had begun recruiting from the colony planets, she began to dream again, to think about the possibility of joining them. She had even started to take some of the prerequisite courses in advanced math and science.

Ilya slapped at an insect that was buzzing around her face. Yoko grunted his disapproval as her elbow dug into his ribs.

As she soothed him, she noticed that the sound of voices was growing louder. Someone was coming down the path. She heard the clanking of buckets and realized that the newcomers were going to the communal well.

"Why didn't Eric want to come?" she heard a young voice inquire.

"Probably didn't want to get mixed up with Ilya again," another voice sniggered. "She's the ugliest, bossiest girl at the whole Turning."

Ilya recognized Ralf, a Sanders boy she had beaten in the pony races last summer. She curled closer to Yoko, glad that she and the dace were hidden from the path.

"I don't think she's ugly at all," the first voice protested. "And that's not why Eric wouldn't come."

"Yes, it is. Did you see her today? Filthy dirty and her clothes all torn. No wonder Eric is taking Maris to the Festival. She's a weaver. They smell better than herders."

"You're just saying that 'cause you like Maris and you're going to be a weaver..."

The conversation blended into the other voices around the well, and Ilya could no longer hear what was being said, but what she had heard had been enough. So Eric thought she was ugly, did he? Smelly, dirty cassia herder? Well, she would show him! She wanted to punch him, but not until she had beaten that nasty Ralf to a pulp! Sneaky rotten weaver! She imagined the scene with little satisfaction, and when she thought of Eric, sudden moisture came into her eyes.

Ilya was very late for dinner, and when she finally arrived, everyone else had eaten and gone. Only Alisia was still seated under the big awning, lingering over a cup of tea. Hanna bustled in the background, clearing away the remains of the meal and setting her helpers to wash up the dishes. Ilya hesitated, loath to expose her wounded feelings to a double scolding, but Alisia saw her daughter and called her in.

"You missed dinner," her mother observed, patting the cushions on the bench beside her.

Ilya sat stiffly, hunched down as if making herself smaller would keep her from attracting Hanna's attention. "I wasn't hungry," she replied quietly.

"Unless you're coming down with something, you should be starving. I know I was, and you were riding with me most of the afternoon," Alisia said. "Do you feel ill?"

"No. I'm just not hungry."

Alisia looked closely at her daughter, noting the torn, dirty clothing, tangled hair, and dust-coated skin—and the girl's troubled eyes.

"The Sanders arrived this afternoon," she said matter-of-factly. "Did you see Eric?"

"No. I didn't look for him."

"I thought you were best friends."

"Not anymore. Eric has a new girl friend . . . a weaver. He thinks I'm just a stinking herder."

Alisia laughed, understanding her daughter's problem. "Just like your mother."

Ilya looked at the tall woman who lounged gracefully at her side. Alisia was dressed in a flowing violet-blue robe, rich with embroidery. The blue intensified the gold of her hair.

Ilya's face mirrored her thoughts. Alisia was a herder and had spent as hard a day as any penning the last of the clan's stock. Yet she sat there as clean, beautiful, and cool-looking as any of the weavers.

Alisia laughed again. "Once you've had a bath and changed, you'll feel differently."

"But not 'til she's been fed," Hanna interjected, as she put a brimming bowl of stew in front of her nursling. She carved thick slices of bread and put them in reach with a pot of butter. "The child has to eat," she added as she refilled Alisia's cup.

The smells were tantalizing. The stew was redolent with herbs and the tomato-like cahicha on which the broth was based. Ilya decided that it would be silly to continue to insist she was not hungry when her stomach was growling a contradiction.

"Guess I might be hungry," she muttered and set to eating. Yoko prowled just outside the awning, snorting in the smells and whining until Hanna finally put down a big pan of leftovers. She fended off the dace's grateful tongue with good-natured grumbles.

Evening closed in around the campground, turning the sky a clear deep blue that was echoed in Alisia's gown. A breeze stirred the smoke from the cooking fires, spreading the sharp warm smell of burning wood. Torchlight and lanterns made bright spots in the growing darkness, and voices called out as friends greeted each other. The day's work done, the festival mood was donned like bright clothing. People moved about, talking, while the children ran among the tents, hoping to prolong their play and escape the bedtime call.

Footsteps sounded outside the awning, and Eric's voice called to Hanna as she clattered about the kitchen. He had not seen Alisia or her daughter where they sat at the far table in the shadows.

Ilya recognized the voice and jumped up, leaving her mother's protests behind her as she fled into the night.

Karth was a beautiful blue-green world named for Bernard G. Karth, the well-known environmentalist and explorer. It was in the twenty-third century that he petitioned the Council of Ruling Houses for a charter to colonize a planet. His plan was to establish a colonial administration based on the principles of ecological management proposed by the Carsonites in the late twentieth century. His case was famous, for it was the first time that the Council had been asked to finance a colony because of a moral issue rather than economic interests. As might be imagined, the opposition was fierce, but in the end, Karth won.

He was an old man by then and although he set off on one of the first colony ships, he never reached the world he had fought for during those long years. His body was buried on Karth and the gravesite marked by a monument in the city that eventually rose around the first landing site.

The early colonists kept to Karth's original plan. Their planet had been selected by the Pioneer Program because it was a G-type world that would require no additional modification to make it habitable. It also was accessible since it lay within easy reach of several established commercial routes. But one of the main reasons it was chosen was because the initial research teams decided that it had little to offer other than its benign atmosphere and bucolic beauty. There was certainly a wealth of minerals, but there were other mining worlds productive enough that no one cared to develop Karth in that way. No, no one cared about the minerals on Karth until years later. In 2452 the population was more concerned with the everyday business of survival.

A majority of the people who came to Karth settled on Asterid, the largest of the planet's three land masses, and developed a seminomadic life-style following the annual migration of the cassia. While enjoying the lucrative interstellar market for the fleece, the clanspeople also became adept weavers, and the cloth they made on their big looms was prized throughout the Federated worlds.

A port city grew around the colonist's original landing site and was called Havensport. It contained a university, light industrial complexes, and anything else the city dwellers might need, for not everyone who came to Karth was willing to face the rigors of clan life.

Years after the first colonists arrived, the grasslands still stretched beyond Havensport, seemingly untouched by man. Bernard Karth and the original settlers would have been very pleased. Even many of the city dwellers were proud of the unspoiled beauty of their planet.

In the last hundred years a second interest group had grown up on Karth. Settlers in the mountains stumbled upon several surprisingly rich deposits of gold. Their discovery lured prospectors into the area, and the resulting boom had stirred up quite a controversy. A group of landowners contacted the Federation Mining Consortium and began negotiations to begin large-scale mining operations.

The residents of Karth were divided. There were those who anticipated great wealth and were prepared to begin mining immediately. They were stymied by others who argued that such an abuse of the planet was contrary to the original charter. Those objectors insisted that mining would mean the need for industry, smelters, and more people who would come to Karth, destroying the planet's balanced ecology.

The arguments lasted for years. There was even violence against some of the more adamant of the charter's defenders. Only when the government decided to hold a planet-wide election to determine the fate of the charter did an uneasy peace descend on the planet. In the meantime, the interest of the Federation became focused on the previously insignificant little world.

Early in the year 2452, Willa Bronsky came to live with the Winter clan. Willa was an anthropological pscyhologist from the I.G. University who was making a study of the nomadic clans.

"An obsessive romantic," was what Willa had called Ilya. The subject of that discussion, tucked snugly in a pile of furs, had been asleep. When she woke she heard the muted drone of voices from the adults gathered around the fireplace and wondered sleepily about Willa's name for her. By morning she had forgotten all about it.

Alisia did not take it seriously either. She had laughed. "I was very like her as a child. It's a troublesome time, but she'll outgrow it as I did."

"Have you ever wondered if all of your children are content with their life on Karth?" Willa persisted.

Ilya's mother had taken her eyes from the fire and leaned back into her furs. "There is a lot here to be content with. The life is good, the rhythms secure. Why would anyone want more?"

"I think there are certain personalities who do not do well if they settle into a life-style before they have had a taste of adventure. I think Ilya may be one of them. I think the time will come when she may have to choose between adventure and the life of the clans. It won't be an easy choice for her."

"We don't keep the children from making their own choices," Alisia said. "Next year when Ilya is seventeen she will go to the university in Havensport. If she finds something there that she wishes to pursue, she will be encouraged to do so. But she is always part of the clan and nothing that happens can change that. No matter where she goes or what she does, she will always be welcome here."

Willa chuckled. "An attitude like that will make her choice all the more difficult. Actually, after living for a year in the impersonal atmosphere of the university, I couldn't blame her if she came right back here, but I think she should consider something else first—something more than just the school."

"What would you suggest?"

"I'm not sure. There are a lot of options. You might suggest that Ilya contact me when she gets to Havensport. I might have something concrete for her then."

A year later Ilya did contact Willa and, through her, met the representatives of the Federation Space Service Academy. They were recruiting on Karth, as well as other planets, and because of her excellent scholarship and interest, Ilya was eventually accepted to the academy.

Thinking back, Winter never could be certain what kind of a life she would have led if circumstances had not interfered. From the beginning she was torn between the two: Karth and Eric, or Federation service. She always hoped to find a compromise, a way to have both. A part of her mind always insisted that it would have been possible.

Ilya Winter was born of Karth, and it was so much a part of her that she could never lose her feeling for the land and the life she knew there. Years later, in her cabin aboard the *Ven-*

ture, she would sometimes dream of riding her spotted pony after the cassia. In her dreams she relived the cold months, remembering the warmth of the enormous fireplaces that helped to heat the clan's big stone winterhouse. The roaring flames had been so impressive to her as a small child.

She dreamed of the nights when she would sneak out to join her friends on the beach. There they would race their ponies, the animals snorting streamers of smoky breath as their hooves pounded the hard sand. Later she and her friends would build a fire to cook something for a late supper.

Winter remembered looking up at the stars as she sat in the fire's warmth with Eric's arm around her and her head on his shoulder. Eric had laughed at her then, teasing her about her fascination with the night sky. Little did either of them know that those stars would one day be her only home.

But fate made decisions for Winter, fate in the form of war and the Federation's needs. Soon all she had left were memories and dreams. She tried to ignore the memories, but she could not control the dreams. When they came, she knew they were a sign of her desire to return home to the clan and the love and security she had once known. But Winter could never return. The war had made sure of that. And the Ilya who lived on Karth and the starcaptain she had become were two very different people. The world of a starcaptain had no place for love or security.

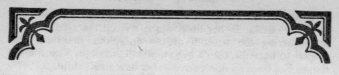

CHAPTER 5

Shaw could not remember ever wondering about death before. He had always accepted dying as inevitable, unavoidable, and when the time finally came, irrevocable. He did not believe in any kind of an afterlife, or even a new beginning in some other form. To him death was the long sleep through eternity's night, something that gave meaning to the word "forever."

Shaw faced his death at the moment he was shot down by the Proxima trooper. As far as he was concerned, his life ended when the blackness came, and he was therefore surprised when he realized he was regaining consciousness. The surprise lasted only an instant, for he quickly became aware of the messages being relayed to his brain by the outraged nerves in his body. He woke to pain, agony that filled him beyond endurance. His muscles contracted, trying to escape, but the pain had him, consuming him, and it was unavoidable.

David was monitoring the medical tank when Shaw woke. The sensors recorded the sudden return of nervous activity and the frantic reactions of the muscles. Almost immediately the medical computer compensated, stimulating an endorphin release from the brain, but it was not fast enough to keep Shaw's mind from reacting and sending one defensive burst before he sank back into unconsciousness.

David almost fell from his chair at the intensity of the mental blast. The medtech working beside him let out a cry and sank to his knees, his face contorted with shock and pain. David sat very still, willing his mind and body to be calm, the sound of his own breathing loud in his ears. He tried to understand what had happened and at first did not connect the mental shock with the figure in the tank.

"Bristol?" he called to the medtech.

"I'm all right, now," the man replied. "At least I think I am. What happened?" He staggered to his feet, holding onto the edge of the console.

"I don't know."

David checked the monitors and saw the recorded peak in brainwave activity from the body in the tank. He keyed for an increase in sedatives. Using drugs on a patient who was just coming out of stasis was risky, but until he understood more about the man, he thought it would be best to keep him unconscious.

The communicator chimed. David keyed it open at his end.

"Sick bay," he responded.

"We need a medtech on the bridge, fast," the captain told him. "Something strange is happening. I've got half my staff down with blinding headaches."

David nodded to the tech, who grabbed a kit and rushed from the room.

"You felt it, too?" the doctor asked.

"We all did. Do you have any idea what it was?"

"I think so. It was the man we took out of the Malvern container."

"What happened? What did he do?"

"He began to regain consciousness, but the transition was too fast. His body reacted—it probably hurt pretty bad. I don't know what he did, but from the result I'd guess he's a telepathic sender."

"Pretty strong sender if he could reach everyone on the ship. I hope you've got him under control," she said.

"For the moment, yes. He's sedated," David replied.

"Good."

"I think we'd better think of something to do about this when he finally wakes up," David told her. "I can't keep him sedated forever."

"What do you suggest?"

"I'm not sure. He was wearing some kind of a supressor when we found him. Maybe Thomas can help me . . . maybe he can come up with something like that."

"Talk to him about it immediately," the captain ordered. "Couldn't you have anticipated something like this happening?"

"I don't think so."

Winter let her breath out in a hiss. "See that he doesn't cause any more trouble," she said. "When can I talk to him?"

"I've slowed his wake-up time. Unless there's something physically wrong with him, the tank should bring him back gradually over the next six hours."

It was a little more than six hours before Shaw woke for the second time. He became aware more slowly, but he still anticipated the pain he had experienced before. He willed himself to physical and mental stillness as he searched for it, but mercifully, it was gone. In its place he felt as if he was insulated, tightly wrapped in something thick and soft that kept the sharpness of reality away. Even sounds were muffled. The sensation was comforting at first, but then it began to confuse him. He tried to understand what was happening and realized that he could not hear telepathically. His eyes opened in panic, and his hands moved up, reaching for his head.

"No. Don't do that," a calm voice told him. Hands caught his, drawing his arms back to his sides. Shaw did not resist. "You're wearing a wave shield," the voice said. "It won't hurt you, but you won't be able to use your telepathic abilities while you have it on."

Shaw looked up and saw a man with short, graying hair and light blue eyes that matched his smock. The voice was soothing, and Shaw vaguely remembered it speaking to him before, although he could not recall the words.

"Do you know where you are?" the man continued.

Shaw looked around at the light blue walls and masses of machinery that surrounded him.

"No," he managed to croak. "Who are you?"

"I'm Dr. David Wilson, medical officer aboard the FSS *Venture*. You're in my sick bay and you're safe here."

"Safe," Shaw echoed. He blinked, trying to become accustomed to perceiving with less than half his normal senses. "I am on a ship? Not on Proxima or Malvern?"

"No. You're not on Malvern and definitely not on Proxima."

"How did I get here? Am I a prisoner?"

"That depends on you. There's someone here who would like to talk to you. I think she's the best one to answer your questions."

The doctor went to the door and admitted a tall woman with short dark hair. If Shaw correctly understood the significance of the uniform she wore, he was in the hands of another military force.

"I'm Captain Winter," she said. "You're on board my ship, and we want you to know you are safe here."

"Thank you, I think," he replied.

"Who are you?"

Shaw could think of no reason to evade her questions. "I am called Shaw."

"How did you come to be in the Malvern system?"

"I was on a ship. I had business there." Shaw felt dull and lethargic. He wanted to sleep, but he also knew that he had to know more about his situation before he could rest. If answering questions might buy him information, he would try to answer.

"I am surprised to hear you say that. Malvern rarely conducts business with off-worlders."

"Nonetheless, I had business there." Shaw responded, but there was little strength in his voice. "How did I get on board your ship? Was I alone? Was there anyone else with me?" He wondered about Dree, but he also knew that he had seen her die.

Winter glanced at David, who was standing where he could watch the medical monitors as well as Shaw. His patient was tired, but he did not think it would harm him to hear the answers to his questions. He nodded to Winter to go on.

"There were two of you," Winter told him, "but your companion was dead. I'm sorry. Was she someone close to you?"

"Close? No, not really, but I rescued her once. Her name was Deirdre. She told me that the name means someone who wanders and grieves. It describes her life very well. I remember . . . she was dead before they captured me." Shaw took a deep breath. "She did not deserve that." He looked back at Winter. "What about me? Am I your prisoner?"

"Not unless you're a danger to my ship or my crew. We

know nothing about you except that you're a strong telepathic sender. Where do you come from?"

Shaw managed a whisper of a laugh. "I come from many places, from far away. I come from nowhere."

"That's not an answer." Winter's voice showed her irritation.

"It is all the answer I can give you."

"Why?"

"There are things I cannot explain."

"Can you tell me why you were a prisoner on Malvern?" the captain asked.

"Malvern? I was captured by a Proxima II ship. Are they allies of yours?"

"Hardly," she responded, stiffening at his words. "This is a Federation vessel, and the beliefs of the Proxima and the Federation aren't compatible."

"I see," Shaw said.

"Are you aware of what's happening in galactic politics?"

"Not unaware, just uninvolved. I had business on Malvern, but apparently they did not approve and sent their allies after me."

"Malvern and Proxima have formed an alliance?" she asked.

"You did not know that?"

Winter frowned. "If it's true, then this is the first I've heard of it." She looked at David again, then back to the bed. "You seem to be a source of useful information. Can I have your word that you're not a threat to this ship or to the Federation?"

"For the moment, yes. I'm not in a position to be a threat to anyone." He indicated the wave band with a weak movement of his hand. "I can barely move, and with this on, I have lost the better part of my senses."

"You're still heavily sedated. We thought it best after you almost knocked my crew out," Winter informed him.

Shaw stared at her. "I do not remember doing that."

"He wouldn't remember, Captain," David said, coming to the stranger's defense. He moved closer to the bed. "I told you I thought it was just a reflex. You were coming out of the stasis too fast," he told Shaw. "That stresses the nervous system, and it can be pretty painful."

"I remember hurting, but nothing else." Shaw looked from the doctor to the captain. He wished he could read the emotions behind her face. "I am sorry," he said simply. "It was not deliberate."

She relaxed. "No one was badly hurt," she told him. "We'll reduce your sedation, and when you've rested, I would like to talk to you again. I have to make a report to my superiors, and I'm certain they will be interested to learn of Malvern's dealings with Proxima."

With a nod to the doctor, Winter left sick bay.

Shaw's eyes followed her until the door closed. "She is not pleased," he said.

"Captain Winter? Why do you say that?"

"She seemed angry. I think my presence here disturbs her."

"No," David told him. "It's not you. She's just concerned with the news that Malvern is allied with Proxima. It was hoped that the Matriarchy would ally itself with the Federation, and the captain has been personally involved in the negotiations."

"The government there isn't exactly noted for their cooperative nature," Shaw pointed out.

"I know, but Malvern is a major outpost in this sector. We were so sure they would join us—until now." David shrugged.

"And these Federation matters concern your captain so deeply?"

David raised an eyebrow. "She's the captain of a Federation starship. She doesn't take her position lightly." He grinned at his patient. "She's also the one who gave the order to have you taken out of stasis. When she did, she interrupted your trip to a rather unpleasant destination."

"What destination?"

"Gyler Laboratories."

Shaw could hear the loathing in the doctor's voice through his own flash of fear. "The last thing I remember is being shot down by a Proxima trooper. Perhaps you could fill in the gaps in my knowledge?"

David checked the medical monitor. There were no undue indications of stress. "Sure. I'd be glad to, unless you're too tired?"

"Not tired. I feel lethargic, but I suppose that is the effect of the drugs."

"I've already reduced your sedation, but the effects will take a couple of hours to wear off. After a good night's sleep, I think you'll feel as fit as you ever did."

It did not take David long to tell Shaw how they had found him. When he finished speaking, the only time left unaccounted for were the days Shaw had been in the hands of the Proxima and down on Malvern. Shaw was silent, and David went into his office, leaving the stranger alone with his thoughts.

Shaw was finally coming to accept the fact that he was still alive. Throughout these years he had courted death; he had teased, cheated, and almost welcomed an end to his existence. It had been a game to see how close he could come, an exciting game pitting his skills against danger. He had even chosen his career because of the challenge it offered, and when he thought the end had finally come, he had been able to accept it.

The colonial war was making some people rich, including Shaw, but he was not interested in wealth except that it bought him the best tools, such as his ship, and certain other advantages in his work. No, his was a private battle. Part of him, the basic drive that seeks genetic continuity, wanted to live. Another part wanted just as badly to die, putting an end to a life in which he could find no meaning.

Shaw reached up and gently felt the light metal band that encircled his head. He had been told that it was a wave shield, and he had promised David he would wear it. He would honor his word for the time being. As he lowered his hands, his eyes went to the ridge of scar tissue running down his arms. The scars had been left there on purpose, a reminder of what he had been and could never be again. A feeling of loneliness and alienation washed over him, and he closed his eyes, trying to banish the memories. But they were there, as always.

Shaw sighed. Nothing had changed. He had only cheated death one more time. He drifted into sleep and dreamed of flying.

CHAPTER 6

Karth, 2452 TSC

"Gee up!" Ilya shouted, leaning over the lathered shoulder of her galloping pony.

There was one maverick cassia that seemed determined to go anywhere except back to the herd, and Ilya smacked its butt with the coiled whip she carried, trying to drive it that way. The cassia kicked out and caught Ilya's pony in the ribs with the hooves. The horse gave a grunt and swerved. Ilya pulled the pony back in order to go after the stubborn cassia again when Yoko dashed in, jaws snapping and low growls coming from his throat. The cassia gave one bleat of terror and fled back to the herd, trying to get as many other bodies between herself and the predator.

The objective achieved, Ilya pulled her pony around and cantered down the flank of the herd, looking for more strays. Yoko ran after her, his tongue hanging out as he panted in the heat. Alisia passed them, galloping the other way with two other herders, and gave her a thumbs up signal.

Dust rose in soft clouds around the riders as the animals' hooves churned up the dirt. The sun bore down on man and beast alike, the heat and dust making breathing difficult. The air was filled with sounds: the pounding of hooves, the whistles and shouts of the herders, and the bleating of the cassia.

Ilya's shirt felt as if it was glued to her back with sweat, and strands of hair were sticking to her wet, dusty face. She tried to wipe her eyes with the back of her hand, smearing more dust into the sweat. Nothing helped.

She turned her pony and rode easily back up the herd. The cassia were obediently heading toward the pens by the camp, where they would be sorted, some traded to other clans, some sold and shipped to the cities. The greater part of the herd would be released the next evening, to return to the wide plains and the rich pasture of summer grass.

When the last cassia was finally penned, Ilya trotted her pony to the horse pasture. Yoko dropped down beside the gate with a gusty sigh and panted mightily, his chest and sides heaving. He watched as his mistress unsaddled the pony and gave him a good rubdown before turning him out. The pony walked wearily through the gate, snorting at the ground until he found what he wanted. Dropping to his knees, he rolled over onto his right side in a sandy wallow, and grunting with pleasure, swung his body back and forth, scratching sand into his back and shoulders.

Ilya leaned against the gate for a moment, then picked up the saddle and bridle and headed back to camp. Yoko lurched to his feet and trailed after her.

Giant galoba trees were scattered over several acres where the clans pitched their tents every year. Interspersed with the huge tree trunks were thickets of shrubs and young trees that made a natural division between the campsites. The ground there was densely packed clay beneath a layer of fine sandy soil. Native grasses mingled with a few Terran species that had sprung up from seeds dropped from the horse feed that the colonists brought with them. Oats, bran, and wheat flourished in Karth's soil, as did an occasional alfalfa plant. On the eastern shore of Astride, near the cities, there were fields of Terran crops, but the clans were never in one place long enough to grow anything. Their summer was spent on the migration and, although there were greenhouses at the winter camp to supply the clan's need for vegetables, open fields on Karth had to be carefully watched, to protect the crops from drifters and wild cassia that had developed a taste for imported food.

The lower branches of the galoba trees had been stripped

by the wild herds, and the tops formed a sort of roof over the camp that diffused the occasional summer rainstorm and otherwise provided a cool, shady place for the tents. Each clan had its traditional area, as well as a fenced pasture and smaller corrals for their stock.

Birds flirted among the tree branches, filling the day with their chirp and chatter. They settled to sleep when the sun set and the lanterns and torches turned the campsite into a wonderful city of colored light and shadow.

The Winter clan had already been at Turning for two days when the last of the clans finally arrived. The stragglers were just in time for the official opening of the three-day fair that raised its tents and built its booths beyond the corrals. No one was immune to the excitement of the event and everyone who was not working either lent a hand or came to watch the fair go up. Children, dogs, and even a couple of tame dace ran through the confusion, getting in the way and escaping disaster by centimeters.

Ilya flinched as Alisia snagged the comb on a stubborn snarl. She was barefoot on a thick rug of unshorn cassia hide in the middle of her mother's tent. Just out of the bath, Ilya was dressed in her underwear, standing with her back to Alisia who was trying to work the tangles out of her hair.

Ilya wiggled her toes in the soft wool of the rug, trying to ignore the pain in her scalp as Alisia caught another bad knot with the comb.

"You shouldn't have washed your hair before it was combed out." her mother said. "I didn't realize it was such a mess. When did you comb it last?"

"She didn't," Hanna answered, pushing through the flap and into the cool interior of the tent. She dumped a pile of clean clothes on a chest and turned to survey Ilya. "I have to catch her before I can get her cleaned up and combed. She's worse than a wild cassia when it comes time for curryin'. You'd best shear her the same way you do them."

"No!" Ilya protested, turning abruptly toward Hanna, half believing the threat. The movement jerked her hair out of Alisia's hands, but her mother firmly pulled her back into position.

Hanna ignored Ilya and continued grumbling. "Most youngsters have given up all this nonsense by the time they're sixteen." She began to sort the clean clothes. "Ilya's just being stubborn—as usual."

Alisia smiled and attacked Ilya's waist-length hair again. "Your hair's much too pretty to cut. Why don't you take better care of it?" she asked her daughter.

Ilya shrugged. "There isn't always time."

"From now on, you should make the time. Hanna's right. You're getting to be too old to depend on her for everything. You'll be going to the university at Havensport next year. Who will look after you then?"

"Maybe I should cut it. Then it would be easier to take care of." Ilya suggested.

"We'll see," her mother told her. "Now," she said, standing back, "I have a surprise for you. Close your eyes."

"What is it?" Ilya demanded, curiosity and excitement mingled in her voice.

"Close your eyes," her mother insisted.

Ilya obeyed and heard the sound of a trunk opening followed by a rustle of material.

"Hands up over your head," Alisia instructed.

Something soft was fitted over her arms and head.

"Lift your foot."

Ilya caught hold of her mother's shoulder, struggling for balance and fighting the temptation to giggle. "Can't I look now?" she complained.

"Let her look," Hanna snapped, "before she falls over!"

Alisia was laughing when Ilya opened her eyes. "Here, look at yourself!" She turned her daughter to face the big mirror.

Ilya gasped with delight. She was dressed in trousers and a tunic of a rich golden green. The tunic was embroidered in bright colors and decorated with beads that caught the light and reflected every color of the rainbow. Alisia was holding out a new pair of boots, the soft hide dyed to match the rest of the new clothes.

"I have a very beautiful daughter," Alisia said with pride.

"Pity she didn't get your coloring," Hanna grumbled.

"She has her father's, and that's even better," Alisia replied.

"Festival clothes," Ilya breathed with delight. "Oh, Mother, they're wonderful! Thank you! Thank you!" She hugged Alisia.

"Just stay away from the ponies while you're wearin'

them," Hanna said. "You'll have them ripped in no time, anyway."

"No, I won't. I'll be very careful!" Ilya promised. She put the boots on and looked at herself again in the mirror. Her clean hair curled around her face in a dark cloud. Ilya crowed her delight.

"Go on, now. Find your friends," Alisia told her. "I have to get dressed, too, or I'll miss Festival."

Ilya hugged her mother again and even embraced the still grumbling Hanna before she danced off into the twilight.

"She'll be a mess in no time," Hanna predicted.

"I don't think so," Alisia said calmly. "I think Ilya is finally growing up."

"I hope you're right. It's about time."

Alisia smiled and started to dress in her own Festival clothes.

For a couple of minutes there was nothing but the hiss of the lamp and the rustle of clothes. Cautiously, Hanna broke the silence. "Are you going to see Knox tonight?"

"I'm supposed to meet him, yes." Alisia twined a strain of gold-colored beads in her long braid before wrapping it around her head. She watched her reflection in the mirror as she fastened the hair in place with hairpins.

Hanna's disapproval was patent in the way she kept her back turned and the sudden jerky movements of her hands as she put the clothes away. "You won't change him, you know," she said.

"I don't expect to," Alisia told her. She leaned into the glass as she applied eyeliner and shadow with deft strokes.

"Then why see him at all?"

Alisia turned around to look at her friend. "Because tomorrow is Lorin's name day. And Knox is his father, after all."

"Humph," Hanna snorted. "That was a mistake, is all I'll say."

"Lorin?" Alisia raised an eyebrow. "Let me assure you, even though he's only twelve, Lorin is nothing like his father."

"And that's no small blessing." Hanna finished stowing the clothing in the chest and sat on it, facing the blond woman. "I've heard Knox wants to take Lorin to live with him. In the city."

"I know." Alisia shrugged. "After tomorrow it will be Lorin's decision."

"And do you know what he'll choose?"

"No. I haven't spoken to him about it." Alisia fastened her gold earrings and leaned back to survey the result.

"What if he decides to go?" Hanna persisted. "Knox can be very persuasive when he wants to be—as you well know!"

Alisia's face was full of mischief when she turned to Hanna. "Do you really think so?"

"He evidently is, if fathering Lorin is any proof," Hanna said in a huff.

Alisia burst out in laughter. "Hanna!" she gasped. "Do you have such a low opinion of me!"

"Humph! I suppose you think you knew what you were doing with that slick-faced trader?"

"Yes, I did. And the year he spent with us proved to be an excellent opportunity to increase our economic standing. That was the first year the clan was completely out of debt."

"Yes, and I guess the two of you running around all starry-eyed had nothing to do with anything?"

"He is attractive, even you have to admit it."

"If you like the type." Hanna sniffed. "I saw him yesterday, though, and he's lookin' his age." She fingered a fold of her gown. "You're not going to let him take Lorin away are you? He'll fill the lad's mind with all kinds of nonsense about letting the miners in here. They'll turn Astride into a big nasty pit, good for nothing, much less the cassia."

"I don't think Lorin will want to go. He hasn't seen his father in almost seven years."

"Which is another blessing, I'd say." Hanna got to her feet and started toward the doorway. She paused and turned back. "Do you know what name Lorin will choose tomorrow?"

Alisia smiled and nodded. "Maxim, after my father."

"Aye, that's a right choice." Hanna beamed. "He was always the old man's favorite. Made his last years happier, too, them always being together."

> "No matter where we lay down to sleep,
> I know I have come home,
> Across light-years and through time,
> When my eyes awake to see you
> Softly sleeping here beside me,
> Your long-lashed lids,
> Like shutters closed and hiding,

But only for a moment
All the brightness that's inside you,
Then I know I have come home."

The minstrel accompanied himself on an old-style guitar as he sat singing to an audience in the refreshment tent. He was singing the love song from the Ballad of the Rim Wanderer, an old favorite. Ilya heard the last words as she ran to join her classmates.

"I have come home, I know it now.
In the misty dawn of morning
Watching you before you wake,
I am home."

Ilya and her friends went out into the night while behind them the song was saluted by loud applause from the rest of the audience. The air was rich with wonderful smells, and the sounds of excited voices blended with the music from a band at the far end of the grounds. Merchants called out to the pedestrians, announcing their wares, and customers argued and bargained as they tried to get the best deal on goods from the city or from off world. The fair was intoxicating: bright and shadow, color and sound, up, down, hard, soft—all mixed together and whirling like a kaleidoscope. It was all joy, and the joy was contagious.

Except to Ilya. She was walking with a group of other Winter teenagers between the brightly lit rows of stalls when they encountered Eric and his friends buying ice cream. She had carefully avoided him since the day the Sanders clan had arrived at Turning and she overheard the conversation revealing how he felt about her. Now, even in her new clothes, she was afraid to see him.

The two groups of young people mixed, exchanging loud greetings. Ilya turned to escape into the shadows, but a hand on her shoulder held her back. She turned her head and saw a handsome face topped with a smooth cap of fair hair from which one unruly lock escaped over the forehead. The face was smiling at her, the blue eyes merry.

"E-Eric?" she stammered.

"Where were you going?" he asked, looking down at her, his eyes crinkled with laughter. "I've been looking all over for you."

"You have?" Ilya cringed inside at the inanity of her words.

"I've been busy, you know. Rounding up strays," she explained, trying to give the appearance of some dignity.

"The cassia have been penned for days now," Eric said, sliding his arm around her shoulder.

She relaxed against the warm side of her old friend.

"Have you been avoiding me?" he probed.

"No. Not really."

He cocked a skeptical eyebrow at her, but the grin never faded. "I missed you," he whispered in her ear.

"I missed you, too," she admitted.

Their lips met in a swift kiss. In that instant all of the misunderstanding vanished, and they were laughing as they rejoined the rest of their friends.

For Ilya it was the most memorable opening night, perhaps because it was the last one she ever spent with Eric. The food had never tasted so good, and the sights and smells were more wonderful than she had ever experienced. Not even the memory of Ralf's words could dim her happiness as she moved through the fair with Eric's hand in hers.

The sky was growing light when the opening night of the Festival ended. Eric walked with Ilya away from their friends into the shadows by her tent. He held her in the circle of his arm while his free hand brushed her loose hair back from her cheek, his eyes smiling down at her.

"I was worried when I couldn't find you," he whispered. "Then I saw you tonight, all dressed up, so beautiful . . ." He held her close against him and kissed her, his lips very gentle.

"I was afraid," she said, breathless. "I thought you were seeing someone else."

His arms tightened around her. "How could I be seeing anyone else when we're promised to each other?" he asked.

"That was a long time ago. We were just kids. You could have changed your mind."

"I'll never change my mind. I love you, Ilya," he said softly.

"And I you," she responded.

Eric's lips met hers again in a kiss that spoke eloquently of his feelings. He drew a ragged breath as he pulled back from Ilya. "Never doubt me again," he said.

"And don't you doubt me," she told him.

"Next year at this time, I will be at the university, but I'll be waiting for you."

"I'll come," she said. "I promise."

"Will you sit with me at the Meeting tomorrow?"

"Yes."

He kissed her again, quickly, before he left her in the sunrise.

CHAPTER 7

The communications technician, Lieutenant Delieus, sat at Winter's right on the bridge of the *Venture*, separated from her by the helmsman's bank of controls. Delieus was almost finished coding a message to be sent to Alpha Base Seven. He was dressed in fatigues, a gray jumpsuit with his name emblazoned over the breast pocket and the bars of his rank on his shoulders beside the round insignia of the Space Service. The insignia was a small golden twin of the huge shield that hung behind Admiral Jammeson's desk.

Winter was in her command chair, working on a report. When she was finished she signed off and linked her console to the ship's main computer.

She typed: RETRIEVAL: NAME=SHAW. SCREEN ONLY— SOUND-OFF, and pressed the "run" button.

The screen flashed a WORKING message and she waited, drumming her fingers on the edge of the keyboard. She hoped that the vast stores of the computer library included the data she was looking for.

Winter stilled her fingers and checked the ship's functions on one of the smaller monitors beside her. The *Venture* was cruising at sublight, still heading toward Gyler. Their speed was less than it might be, but Winter was in no hurry to arrive before she was ready. She was eager to hear from Alpha Base, since she felt that her report about Shaw would be sure to affect her assignment.

The stars on the wide view screen above her console were fixed around the *Venture*, blue ahead and red behind, as the ship moved through space.

The computer signaled READY, and the information that Winter requested appeared on her screen.

NAME: SHAW, NO TITLE OR SURNAME USED.

SPECIES: HUMANOID / NO DETAILS AVAILABLE.

PLANET OF ORIGIN: NOT KNOWN

AGE: NOT KNOWN

PHYSICAL DESCRIPTION: HAIR, BLACK; EYES, VARIOUS RE-
  PORTED, TRUE COLOR NOT KNOWN; HEIGHT, 1.83
  METERS; WEIGHT 78.02 KG.

DISTINGUISHING FEATURES: MASSIVE SCARRING, DORSAL,
  ALL LIMBS; POSSIBLE ESPER ABILITIES, RATING NOT
  KNOWN.

VISUAL: NOT AVAILABLE.

ADDITIONAL INFORMATION AVAILABLE: SECURITY
  CLEARANCE ONLY

Winter typed her command code and the computer continued.

A-ADDITIONAL: SHAW

OCCUPATION: SMUGGLER SPY

AFFILIATION: NONE, NON-ASSOCIATION. HAS WORKED FOR
  A VARIETY OF CLIENTS WITH CONFLICTING IDEOLO-
  GIES.

ARRESTS: THREE: ALL NON-FEDERATION.

SENTENCED: THREE YEARS REHABILITATION, HAVERLOCK
  COLONY—ESCAPED.

SENTENCED: DEATH, MALTAN SEVERARD LEAGUE—
  ESCAPED.

ARRESTED & ESCAPED BEFORE SENTENCE: NEW HOME
  CAPITOL LAW ENFORCEMENT. CURRENT STATUS, APB,
  SUBJECT TO IMMEDIATE REARREST.

BOUNTY: TEN THOUSAND GALACTIC CREDITS ALIVE,
  SEVEN THOUSAND GALACTIC CREDITS DEAD, MALTAN
  SEVERARD LEAGUE—CONTACT GRAND MASTER, MAL-
  TAN SEVERARD LEAGUE.

B-ADDITIONAL: SHAW

SHIP: FIFTEEN-METRIC-TON INTERSTELLER RACING SLOOP
MANUFACTURED BY BLESSARD ASTRONAUTICS, INC. . . .

Winter skimmed the rest; she had already learned what she wanted to know. Shaw was a smuggler and a spy, someone who worked for the highest bidder. She turned off the computer and sat back, thinking, her fingers drumming on the arm of her chair.

"Captain," the radio officer's voice interrupted. "There's a ship approaching. Bearing zero zero nine, point three two. Speed, sublight point seven and accelerating."

"Identification?" Winter asked, raising her head to search the view screen.

"They're too far away for visual and their automatic beacon seems to be off. Should I hail them?"

"Yes. I want to know who they are. Alert the *Venture*; go on stand-by, status three."

The pace of activity on the bridge increased as the crew went into action. Winter switched on the proximity readout at her console and noted the other ship's distance: 82,603 kilometers. It was definitely close enough for radio contact.

"No response on any frequency, Captain," the comtech said. "They're not acknowledging our hail."

Winter keyed for magnification so that she could see the other ship on the *Venture*'s view screen. According to the information on the smaller screen in front of her, there were positive bio-readings and nothing unusual in the other ship's power expenditure, so it did not seem to be in any trouble. The ship continued to accelerate and was heading straight for the *Venture*, moving precisely along their line of flight.

"Activate the main deflector shields," she ordered. "Change to alert status one, ship wide. We must assume we're under attack." She watched the figures on her monitor: 47,251 kilometers, and closing.

The *Venture*'s interior lights blinked off for an instant and returned glowing red as battle conditions were assumed. The crew strapped themselves in and the bridge fairly hummed with energy and anticipation. Main power was routed to the deflectors and weapons. Winter adjusted her position so that she could reach all of her control console and then snapped the seat restraints tightly around her.

"Status report, all stations," she requested, her voice deliberately very calm.

"All stations report battle ready, Captain," came the immediate reply.

Winter watched the screen as the other ship continued to accelerate. Unless it deviated from course, it would collide with the *Venture*. Despite the evidence in front of her there was a part of Winter's mind that could not believe that anyone but a suicidal maniac would deliberately crash head on with another ship. Yet she knew that the safety of the *Venture* depended on her response. She could not make assumptions about the attacker; she had to act on the evidence.

"Helm, lay in evasive, preset maneuver D. Implement on my order."

"Aye, Captain."

"Captain," Lieutenant Delieus called. "I have an identification on the ship. It is a Proxima II short-range interceptor. There's still no response to our hail."

"Mr. Thomas, implement evasive now. Speed, point eight."

Despite inertial damping throughout the ship, the *Venture*'s abrupt change of direction could be felt by all aboard. Winter unconsciously braced herself with one hand on the edge of the console, her eyes busy watching to see how the Proxima ship would react.

Space is vast beyond human comprehension. Even those who had spent their lives among the stars found it hard to realize the incredible distances that stretched in every direction. They dealt with the problem in a rather Zen way, by concentrating on their immediate position, the here and now of wherever they were at any one particular moment.

In all the emptiness of space it was difficult for two ships to contact each other without the cooperation of both vessels. Even in populated systems where there was regular traffic, there was still enough room to keep ships at a distance from each other. In open space, the encounter of the *Venture* and the Proxima ship would have had to be carefully planned.

Winter frowned at the view screen. Unless the Proxima ship was experiencing simultaneous malfunction of navigation and radio, which she somehow doubted, its behavior could only be interpreted as an attack. The test was to see if it continued on its original course or changed direction.

Winter felt an icy stillness come over her as the Proxima ship maneuvered, coming in line with the *Venture*'s course again. The Proxima had hesitated only a second before turning, and the fact that it continued to accelerate, as well as its ease in maneuvering, proved that there was nothing wrong with its power or navigational systems.

"Helm, reduce speed to point three. Ready on lasers and arm the torpedos." Winter's fingers were busy coding the weapons authorization. "Lieutenant Delieus, open hailing frequency and tell that ship to get out of our way or we'll take action."

Despite the radio officer's renewed efforts the Proxima still did not respond. The distance between the two ships was decreasing with lightning-like rapidity. The readout in front of the captain indicated 8,220 kilometers.

"They have to be crazy!" Delieus exclaimed. "They'll destroy us both!" His eyes were wide with shock as he stared at the big screen above his station.

"Mind what you're supposed to be doing!" Winter told him.

The Proxima ship seemed to be diving straight at them.

"Lasers lock on target." Winter heard the click of keys from the station where the security officer sat. In response, the viewscreen was overlaid with a red grid as the targeting computer was brought to focus on the Proxima ship.

"Fire!" the captain ordered.

The only indication of a hit was a sudden shimmering of the image on the view screen. There was no apparent damage, and Winter realized that their attacker had A-2 shielding, impervious to lasers. Damn!

"Torpedoes. Fire!" she ordered.

She immediately hit a switch on her console. "All decks, brace for turbulence!" she announced. The other ship was much too close for torpedo work, but nothing else would penetrate an A-2 shield.

The view screen flared with a blinding white light as the torpedos found their mark. There was an instant when nothing else seemed to happen, and then the Proxima ship blossomed, expanding into nothingness. The enemy was destroyed.

An instant later a shock hit the *Venture*, hurtling her backward in space. There was a shriek of mechanical protest as the ship's engines tried to compensate. Electronics overloaded, filling the air with smoke that the ventilators tried to clear. Alarms shrilled throughout the ship, and monitor lights flashed frantically. The ship's artificial gravity ceased working, and everything that was not fastened down began to drift in free-fall.

"Cut the engines!" Winter yelled, trying to be heard over the cacophony. Automatic fire-fighting apparatus shot foam at the flames flickering inside of her console. She coughed in the smoke and chemical stench. "Shut down all but essential systems! Get this ship stabilized!"

Training took over and the crew went to work. In minutes the *Venture*'s interior returned to its normal gravity-based vertical and horizontal orientation.

"Navigator," Winter said when things began to settle down. "Find our position in relation to our last course. Lieutenant Delieus, ship's status, all decks. I want the damage reports as soon as they come in."

The air slowly cleared of the last of the acrid smoke. The screen at Winter's station flickered back on, and information began to appear. She read it quickly, apprehensive of what she might see there, but it was not as bad as it might have been; damage was minor throughout the ship and injuries to the personnel were few. As the report scrolled up the screen she watched intently, interrupting the flow of data only to order repair crews to the most serious areas.

That was too close, Winter thought. In all her combat experience she had never before encountered a suicide ship. She wished she had more information and then realized that she did; the *Venture*'s sensors would have recorded the events preceding the attack. She keyed for retrieval and typed in: ?WAS THE PROXIMA SHIP MANNED?

"Affirmative," the computer replied.

?NUMBER LIFE FORMS ABOARD PROXIMA SHIP? she asked.

"Seven biological forms," computer told her. "Human."

Seven! They must have been mad, every one of them! Or drugged. Getting seven people to participate in a suicide mission seemed impossible to her. One man might be persuaded, or maybe even two, but seven? Impossible!

CHAPTER 8

Progress reports kept coming in to Winter as the crew cleaned up after the attack. She sat at her post on the bridge, busy with all of the little details that everyone considered too important for anyone but the captain to handle. It seemed as if the battle had happened only a minute ago, but in reality, hours had passed, and in all that time she had not moved except to go to check work in progress at other stations.

Winter closed her eyes during one lull and rubbed them with the backs of her hands. She was in the middle of an enormous yawn when the comlink beeped for what seemed the thousandth time.

"Captain Winter?" a voice inquired.

"Winter here," she said as she opened the link.

"Medical reporting," David said. "Everything in sick bay's stable. All injuries were minor. How's it going up there?"

"We're just about finished."

"Mind if I join you?"

"Not at all."

"Okay. I'll be right up." The communicator clicked off.

"Brought you a present," the doctor said minutes later as

he slid into the empty seat behind the captain's console. He handed her a steaming cup of coffee.

"Bless you." Winter sipped the hot liquid gratefully. It was freshly brewed and seemed to give her new energy. "What's the extent of the injuries?"

"Minor. Mostly bruises. Samuels has a magnificent hematoma on his hip. There was one burn case, but even it wasn't too bad."

"Who?"

"Walters. He was in the engine room making repairs and got too anxious to remove a metal plate. Burned his fingers."

"How's Shaw?"

"Back in the tank. He doesn't even know what happened. Did you make your report about him to Command?"

"Yes." Winter looked away, unwilling to meet his eyes.

"What did they say?" David wanted to know. "Did they give you any trouble about opening the containers?"

"Admiral Jammeson didn't come right out and say so, but I got the impression that he was pleased."

David waited for her to continue, but Winter seemed intent on her coffee.

"What did they say about Shaw?" he asked, finally.

"What do you mean?"

"Winter, you know what I mean. Why are you being obtuse? Do we let him go? Take him to Gyler? What?" The doctor's voice was laced with exasperation.

Winter sighed. "I was told to bring him back to Alpha Base after we're finished checking the lab."

"Nothing more than that?"

"That's it," she replied.

"Is he a prisoner?" David pressed.

"They left it up to me."

"And?"

Winter scowled at him. "As far as I'm concerned Shaw's behavior will determine his status on this ship. I'll take his parole—if he'll give it."

"But you're going to turn him over when we get back to Alpha Base."

"Those are my orders."

"What will happen to him after that?"

"I don't know." She drank some more of the coffee.

David was not sure why he was so worried about his patient, but after the work he had put into saving the man's life, he felt responsible for him. "Have you thought about what they're going to do to him? You may be putting him into a position that's as bad as the one we rescued him from."

"You don't have a very good opinion of the Service, do you?" Winter asked, turning her head to meet his eyes with her own. She had lowered her voice, but everyone on the bridge was too busy to pay attention to their conversation.

"I've seen things that I don't like very much," David told her quietly. "I work for the Federation. I support them and what they stand for, but I'm also a realist, Winter. What about you? Don't you care what happens to him?"

Winter's eyes narrowed. "Why should I care? I have my orders and I obey them. I'm not supposed to have feelings, one way or the other. And even if I do, I can't let them interfere." There was an angry edge to her voice, but David could not be sure if it was directed at him or at the things she had to do.

"Okay. I understand. Don't get mad at me!" he exclaimed.

She softened. "You should know better than anyone that you can't let your feelings get in the way, Doctor. We can't get emotionally involved with our work."

"Captain Winter," Lieutenant Delieus called, interrupting them.

"What is it, Lieutenant?" she inquired.

"We're being hailed by someone named McGill. He says he's the governor of Mining Station Seventy-four. That's one of the Amalgamated Minerals facilities."

"What does he want, Lieutenant?" she asked.

"He insists on speaking to the captain of the *Venture*."

"Switch the call to my console," Winter instructed.

The jowled face of a heavy-set man appeared on her comscreen. His hair was dark, slicked back from his forehead, and he was dressed in a gray, two-piece business suit. He sat at a desk in front of a wine-red drape. She could not see anything else of his surroundings.

"Captain Winter?" he asked. "Of the FSS *Venture*?"

She leaned back in her chair. "I'm Captain Winter," she said. "What can I do for you, Governor McGill?"

"For me? Why, nothing!" His face registered surprise. "Our sensors picked up a disturbance, and when I learned that your ship was in this region . . . it's very close to my jurisdiction, you understand, well, naturally I was concerned."

"Naturally." Winter was curious. Subspace communications were very expensive and usually were not made without a good reason.

"Yes," the governor continued. "I was informed that there was a battle of some kind, and while that's not unusual now-a-days, I mean with the war going on and all—not that we see too much action here, being as we're so isolated, you know—but I was wondering if there was any danger. To us, I mean."

"I can understand your concern, Governor, but there's no reason for you to worry. It's true that my ship was attacked, but we defended ourselves, and the other ship was destroyed."

"Attacked?" the governor gasped. "But who—I mean, I have to worry. There may be more of them in the area."

Winter cocked an eyebrow. "Do you know something that would lead you to suspect there are other hostile ships around?"

"H-hostile?" he stammered. "Of course not! How could I know such a thing? Besides, this station is part of Amalgamated Minerals! We're protected by the Federation and our guild treaty!"

"And yet you were frightened enough to call me," Winter pointed out.

"The treaty doesn't mean we're always safe, Captain. There are still pirates and others who aren't bound by treaties."

"I don't think you have anything to worry about, Governor. I believe this was an isolated incident aimed specifically at the *Venture*. We've taken sensor readings and it doesn't look like there is an enemy fleet, pirates, or anyone else anywhere near us."

"That's terrible! Your being attacked, I mean," he added hastily. "Do you have any idea who was responsible?"

"No," she lied. "The attack was sudden. There were no radio transmissions, and there was no beacon to give us a positive identification."

"What about your ship?" the governor asked. "Was it damaged? I want you to know we are loyal citizens of the Federation. Our station isn't much, but we do have excellent facilities for repair. We're completely at your disposal, and I hope you will pay us a visit."

Winter's eyes narrowed slightly. What was the man up to? She decided to play along. "We did suffer some damage. Perhaps it would be a good idea to take care of repairs before we go further."

"Excellent decision." He beamed. "You should come here. We're the only station within parsecs."

"How far are you from our present location?"

"I can't say," he replied. "What are your coordinates?"

"Just a second. I'll have to check with my navigator."

"Certainly. Take all the time you need. I'll wait."

The screen went blank as Winter pressed the hold button. She opened the comlink and called to Thomas in the engineering section of the ship. "How long until all systems are completely functional, Commander?"

"About three more hours at the rate we're going. Maybe a little less," he responded.

"Excellent." She switched off the communicator and turned to the navigator. "Lieutenant T'Gal, get a fix on that subspace communication. Plot a course to get us to the station and give me the ETA at most efficient speed."

"Aye, Captain. Plotting now." There was the faint clicking of keys as the navigator worked. "I've got it. Direction, seventy-two, mark oh six three. Distance two point seven NUs. ETA thirty-two point six hours at speed one point six."

"Thank you, Lieutenant."

"What in hell is this all about?" David asked.

Winter smiled wickedly at him over her shoulder. "I have no idea, but I intend to find out." She put a finger to her lips, motioning him to silence before she reopened the subspace link.

"Governor McGill?" she said. "Sorry for the delay. We'll take you up on your offer. Unfortunately with the damage my ship has suffered, we won't be able to get to you for three days."

"Three days! You must have suffered a lot of damage."

"Hopefully you'll be able to set it to rights. We'll change course for your station immediately. Thank you again for your kind invitation. Winter out."

"Yes, of course. McGill out."

The screen went blank.

"Who the blazes is McGill?" David demanded.

"I've never heard of him," Winter said.

There was a strange look on the captain's face, and David realized that she was enjoying this. "Do you think his offer is legitimate?" he asked.

"I have no way of knowing."

"But you suspect that something strange is going on."

"I am curious. His call was just a little too well-timed." Winter picked up her coffee cup and frowned at the cold contents. She sighed and set the cup down again.

"After the attack, you mean," David said. "Do you think he had anything to do with it?"

"I don't know, but as I've already said, I'm going to find out." The captain turned to speak to T'Gal again. "Lieutenant, change course for the Amalgamated station. Slow to point three and hold us there."

"Why did you lie to him?" David asked. "You led McGill to believe we'd been badly damaged."

"It will buy us some time. I want to check up on McGill and the station before we get there. It also might be to our advantage if someone is thinking of setting a trap for the *Venture*. This way they'll take our weakness into account."

"Isn't that being paranoid?"

Winter laughed. "Not after what's already happened today."

"I think the whole thing's crazy," David told her.

"Well, perhaps it is, but I can't let it go without an investigation. I'd be neglecting my responsibilities if I did." She leaned back in her chair again. "Can you imagine what that call cost? And we're two point seven NUs from the station. Consider it geometrically; in all this space, how could he have been aware of a little incident way out here? I'd say it was too much of a coincidence."

"So you think he knew what was happening from the very beginning?"

"It's possible."

"And you're going to sail right into the station?"

"Precisely." She yawned. "But not before I've had some sleep. I've been sitting here so long, I feel as if I'm growing to the chair." Winter rose to her feet and stretched hard enough that David could hear her joints crack. Then she gave him a sleepy smile and left the bridge.

CHAPTER 9

Karth, 2452 TSC

"I declare this summer Meeting open. It shall be recorded here on the sixth day of the seventh month of the year twenty-four fifty-two," the herald said, reading from the log book that lay open on the podium in front of him. "All present will hear the business of the Clans of Karth." He paused and peered out over the assembly before looking at the book again.

The space in front of the speaker's platform was filled with adults and young people. The smallest children played in sight of the huge open-sided meeting tent, sound marking their presence, their high voices and laughter drifting in and out as they moved around the perimeter.

The afternoon sun was hot, but a cool breeze blew in from the plain carrying the faint scent of grass and livestock. Somewhere a pony snorted and shook, rattling his harness. Birds sang and argued in the trees, their songs accompanied by the rustle of leaves.

"The first business," the herald continued, "is the naming of a male child born to the Winter Clan twelve years ago today. Are the child and his parents present?"

Alisia and Lorin came forward. They were alike in figure and their straight blond hair. Lorin was not as tall as his mother yet, but a lot of his growth was still ahead of him. He carried himself with an awareness and grace that was an obvious reflection of Alisia's easy carriage.

Alisia was dressed in a tunic of deep gold over trousers and boots that had been dyed the color of cloves. Lorin's embroidered tunic had been cut from the same cloth, but his pants were a more rusty brown. They made a handsome pair as they walked toward the front of the tent.

Ten paces from their goal, mother and son were joined by Knox. He was not much taller than Alisia, and his hair, also blond, had been dulled by age and too many days spent indoors. His was a handsome face with youthful features, but there was the obvious beginning of a sag about his jaw and chin, as well as shadows beneath his pale blue eyes.

Once a clansman, Knox had become a full-time trader dealing in cassia hides, fleece, and woven goods. He and Alisia had briefly shared a marriage contract until the differences in their opinions and goals had driven them apart.

When they reached the podium, Alisia left Lorin and Knox and stepped forward to give the herald a folded paper. He took it from her, and she returned to stand beside her son.

The herald cleared his throat and read: "On this day, the year twenty-four forty, a man child was born to Alisia and Knox. He was named Lorin at birth. Today he will claim his own name." The herald looked down at the blond boy. "What will we call you?"

"I will be called Maxim," the young man said, his clear, somewhat thin voice reaching everyone in the tent.

There was a sound as one or two people started to clap, but they were quickly silenced by those around them.

The herald took his time, waiting until he had everyone's attention again. "Is there anyone here who would dispute the name?"

"Nay!" The assembly's approval was expressed with cheers and applause.

"Very well, then," the herald said, not even trying to compete with the noise. "I give you Maxim Winter, child no longer, but man and clansman!"

Maxim hugged his mother and returned her congratulatory kiss, then turned to Knox and shook his hand.

Hanna watched approvingly as she stood waiting to offer

her congratulations. She knew that Knox had already spoken to Maxim, asking him to come to the city. The obvious coolness between them could only mean that the offer had been refused. Hanna was relieved. Too many of the young people were being lured not only to the cities, but even off world. The whole business with the mining consortium was not only threatening to disrupt their way of life, but was already having an adverse affect on the people of Karth. Who could know what other awful things would happen if the charter was changed and more foreigners came to their planet?

"Attention! Attention!" the herald shouted.

The crowd around Maxim thinned as people returned to their seats. Alisia and her son settled down beside Hanna, and Knox disappeared somewhere on the other side of the tent.

"Attention," the herald called again, and the babble of voices faded to silence. "The meeting today will be conducted by this year's speaker, Afton Granger."

The herald stepped back as a stocky man with dark grizzled hair took his place at the podium. Granger took a moment to look at his audience before he spoke, his voice grave. "I have here a list of those of you who have topics to introduce before the Meeting," he said. He held up a sheaf of papers that had been on the rostrum in front of him. "However there is another item of such importance to all of us that I am going to ask you to give it precedence."

The clanspeople stirred, and there was a murmur of voices.

"What's so important, Granger?" a voice called from the audience.

"A delegation from the Federation Mining Consortium has asked to address this meeting," Granger answered. "They wish to make a presentation and hopefully answer any questions we may have concerning the new charter."

"There isn't going to be a new charter," someone grumbled.

"As you all know," Granger continued, "the main issue of this meeting concerns the charter and the Federation's wish to make certain changes."

"Tell them to go back to Earth and leave us alone!" a man yelled from the back of the tent. The words were reinforced by angry shouts from his friends. The heads of the people in the front of the tent turned as they tried to identify the speaker.

"Come on, Geoff. Let them talk. What's it gonna hurt?" someone chided.

"That's fine for you to say," came the reply. "You want the Consortium on Karth."

Other voices were raised and the interchange turned into a lively quarrel. Granger raised his hands and loudly called for silence.

"I know this is not the first time that the Federation has approached us on this matter," he said. "But the government rep has asked that we consider it once again. And this time the Federation has sent someone to speak to us. Will you hear what he has to say?"

There were murmurs again.

"All right, get it over with," a woman cried.

Eric, seated beside Ilya, leaned forward as the Federation delegation climbed onto the speaker's platform. The first speaker was a balding man in a well-cut business suit with a lapel pin engraved with the Consortium's logo. But Eric was not so much interested in the mining representative as his companion. The tall man was the last one up the steps and then stayed in the background. He wore the dark blue uniform of the Federation Space Fleet, and Eric could see the gold of captain's stars on his shoulders.

"There's a Space Fleet officer here," he whispered to Ilya.

"There is?" Ilya leaned forward. "Where? I don't see him."

"There—to the side."

She rose on her knees to see over the heads in front of her. "I see him now," she said as someone behind jerked on her belt, pulling her back down. "Too bad he came with a miner," she whispered to Eric. "Both of them will get thrown out before the meeting's over."

"Good thing if they are," he replied.

"Maybe," she said. "But I'd like to meet him and find out what it's like in space."

Eric started to protest, but there was a sudden silence in the tent as the mining representative began to speak.

"My name is Bill Sconny," he said, introducing himself. "I work for the Federation Mining Consortium in an advisory capacity. I'm one of the survey team that has been working here on Karth for the past three years." The silence was ominous, and he glanced at the people in front of him. "I'm grateful for this opportunity to speak to you today." He paused, looking out over the audience again.

The scene below him was aglow with color. Everyone was wearing their festival dress, and the ground was covered with bright rugs and cushions. Despite the holiday atmosphere, Sconny knew he was in enemy territory.

"Clanspeople of Karth," he said, "we need your help. The Federation desperately needs the minerals that have been found here. For those of you who care to see them, I have brought detailed lists of the wealth of your planet. You don't have to do anything to claim these riches. The Federation will carry the entire expense of the mining operations.

"In exchange for this, we offer you one half of the profits, as well as lease payments for the land we will use. And all of it will be at no cost to you."

"But at what cost to the land?" Alisia asked, her voice easily carrying throughout the tent.

"Yes! What about our air and water?" someone else said. "You can't make us believe your operation won't affect us that way. I've seen what's happened on other planets."

"You won't even know we're mining here," Sconny replied. "The initial work will be done in the northern mountains."

"The snow there supplies more than half of the water for Astride," Alisia informed him.

Another voice interrupted. "It was a mistake to allow the survey teams in in the first place!"

"I told you that!"

A babble of sound arose.

Eric grinned at Ilya. "They won't be allowed to mine here," he told her.

"If this was supposed to be a mining world, the first colonists wouldn't have put a clause against it in the charter," she agreed. She wrapped her arms around her legs and rested her chin on her knees as she watched Granger call for quiet once again.

"If you have questions or comments, please make them one at a time so that everyone can hear you," he said.

"I've seen your maps," Alisia called out. "There are rich deposits in the northern mountains, sure, but there are even richer veins running down onto the plains. We can't allow the grasslands to be disturbed by mining. The ecology's too fragile."

"We have no plans to mine anywhere but in the mountains," Sconny rebutted. "I assure you, we're well aware of the importance of the grasslands, and I promise you they will not be disturbed."

There was laughter from the audience.

"Come on! Listen to what he has to say," a man named Haver called as he rose to his feet. "What do we have to lose?"

"Everything!" someone else yelled back. "Sit down and shut up."

"This is an open meeting," Haver replied. "I can say whatever I damn well please!"

But whatever else he had to say was lost in the babble of voices as people began to talk to each other or shout their arguments to those across the tent. A baby started to cry, frightened by all the noise and confusion, and its mother rose to take it from the tent. Granger pounded on the podium, but it was some time before he could be heard.

"Either we will proceed in an orderly manner," he said harshly, "or we will end this meeting here and now."

The silence after he spoke was complete, and he glared at the assembly for a moment more before stepping back to allow Sconny to continue.

The Consortium representative wiped the sweat from his forehead. "I know that you anticipate serious problems if you alter your charter and allow us to come to Karth. But I want to assure you that this matter has been carefully worked out. We have no intention of doing anything that will damage your planet's ecology!"

"How has it been worked out?" a voice asked from the audience.

"Well, I can't give you all of the details. That would take forever." He grinned nervously as if asking for appreciation of a small joke.

"You'll have to refine some of the minerals and gases before you ship them," the same voice said.

"Yeah. Don't ask us to believe you won't want to build refining plants and maybe even some manufactories on Karth," someone else added. "It wouldn't be profitable for you to ship unrefined ores. If you can manufacture goods at the source of the materials, the cost goes down again."

"I agree that these are problems, but I assure you they can be handled in ways that will not affect your life-style!" Sconny responded almost desperately. "Let me be honest with you. There would be some changes, some building, refining and, yes, even factories. We have to be realistic about this, and I won't lie to you. But there are two other landmasses on Karth beside Astride. We can build there."

"There'll still be changes. And how do the people who live there like your ideas?" a man called.

"They'll soon realize, as you will, that these changes will be changes for the better! Think of the jobs that will open up, think of the possibilities in careers and education. Think of what it would mean for the future, for your children!"

There were a few laughs at that last, impassioned speech, but then angry voices prevailed. Once again Granger stepped forward to call for silence.

Ilya smiled to herself. She agreed with the group of the clanspeople who wanted neither mining nor industry on Karth. She was not old enough to remember the other times when the Federation had tried to convince the people of the advantages of allowing the Federation to mine their minerals, but she understood what it would entail. The clanspeople were not so insulated from the affairs of the galaxy as their nomadic life-style would imply, and they knew the realities of welcoming industrialization to their homeworld. No one wanted Karth to deteriorate into the skeleton of a planet that so many others had become as a result of mining and factories.

Granger let the discussion continue for a brief time, but called for order before the mood could deteriorate into angry frustration. When he finally regained the meeting's attention, he carefully outlined the changes to the charter that would permit the Consortium to begin operations. When he was finished he called for a vote. The Federation proposal was voted down.

That was only one of many meetings held throughout Karth to determine the future of the planet. The Federation's campaign was long and hard, but in the end, it was decided that the original colony charter would remain in effect.

After they had collated all of the votes from the outlaying clans, the planetary government in Havensport formally presented the Federation representatives with a polite but firm refusal to the Mining Consortium's proposal. It was not accepted without argument and even veiled threats, but the government of Karth was adamant. They were, they said, not empowered to make or alter the decision without the approval of the populace. In the end, the Federation representatives had to accept their defeat.

On Earth, in the office of the Mining Consortium, other possibilities were explored. That decision also was not made without much debate and argument. And another year passed before their solution was acted upon.

CHAPTER 10

Shaw was alone in the briefing room aboard the *Venture* when Winter arrived. He was standing with his back to the door looking out at the stars. Openings such as the wide port cut into the bulkhead were for aesthetic purposes only. When the *Venture* traveled in the void of hyperspace there was nothing to see outside of the ship except a weird iridescent blue-gray light. But during the times when the ship was moving at less than light speed, the view of the stars and swirling gases was breathtakingly beautiful.

Winter paused just inside the room, her hands shoved deep in the pockets of her uniform. Shaw had been out of David's care for the past twelve hours, but she had not yet had any real opportunity to speak to her passenger.

He looked very different than she recalled, taller and a little intimidating, even though he was dressed in a plain gray jumpsuit that David had found for him. The silver-colored circlet of the wave band gleamed against his straight black hair. He held himself erect, the long slender fingers of one hand resting against the transparent barrier as if reaching for the stars that glowed in the blackness beyond. A reflection, more of a shadow than a true mirror image, duplicated his figure on the surface of the port. His long, straight nose and prominent cheekbones were highlighted, but his eyes were in dark shadow.

Winter looked past him at the stars, and for an instant she was transported beyond the ship. She remembered nights on Karth when she had slept outside of the tent, lying awake and looking up at the night sky. Then she would pretend that she was suspended, that the ground beneath her was the ceiling of some impossibly high room. As soon as she let go she would fall into that well of blackness pierced by pinpoints of intense light. With a shiver of fear and delight, she imagined that she had released herself. Closing her eyes and spreading her arms, she flew, spinning and drifting through the smoky colors of some nebula. The feeling had been wonderful, a compound of ecstasy and terror, and just for an instant she was able to recapture it. At that moment Winter felt as if she could float beyond the walls of the ship and bathe in the radiance out there. The feeling was brief, but it was intensely physical.

Reluctantly she recalled herself back to reality and her purpose in the briefing room.

Shaw had turned and was looking at her. "You enjoy looking at the stars," he said, and there was no question in his voice. "You aren't afraid of them."

"Afraid?" She cocked her head as she gazed back at him. "No. Why should I be?"

He smiled. "Many people are, even those who travel in space. The stars make them feel small and insignificant."

"I've always found the stars fascinating," Winter said, but the emotion had left her voice and she was the captain of the *Venture* once again. She turned away from the port and walked to the chairs that were arranged around a long, bare table. "Please sit down," she invited as she took her usual place at the table's head.

"You want information about the Malvern alliance with the Proxima Empire," Shaw said as he lowered his tall frame into a chair.

"That is why I asked you to meet me here." Winter leaned back and watched Shaw closely as she spoke. "I checked your background. The computer library has some interesting information about you."

"What did you learn?" Shaw asked politely.

"I learned that you're a smuggler and a spy, that you have no loyalties to anyone, and that you work for the highest bidder. You're also a fugitive in at least three systems."

"Five systems," he corrected her with something suspiciously like humor. "Two of them were, perhaps, not sufficiently important to be recorded in the Federation's files. Was there more?"

"Not much is known about you, which surprises me. The Federation intelligence agencies are usually very thorough. Still, it was enough to know you're a spy."

Shaw was still smiling. "I prefer to call myself an independent courier. The labels smuggler and spy carry such negative connotations."

"No matter what you call yourself, what you do is illegal in every inhabited system in this galaxy," Winter said with a frown. He did not seem to be taking her seriously.

"Whether an activity is illegal or not depends on your point of view," Shaw pointed out. "If an individual kills another, the act is called murder and it is considered illegal. However, if your government is at war and you kill an enemy, you will have committed a glorious act and you are called hero." He shrugged. "It is all in your point of view."

"That doesn't apply here," Winter argued.

"Does it not? Your intelligence agency engages in many acts that might be called crimes, acts such as kidnapping, arson, assassination . . . a list of activities considered highly antisocial no matter where you come from. And yet the intelligence agency is a highly respected branch of your government. Is what I do any different?"

"Sometimes the end justifies the means," Winter contended. "The intelligence agency doesn't do those things without good reason and then only when they're necessary to protect the Federation and preserve a way of life that's considered important by its members."

"Perhaps then others who perform similar acts, even though they do not work for your government, also consider themselves justified in their behavior if they have compelling reasons."

She was silent, and he continued. "I do not understand how you can call me a criminal. I assure you, I am concerned with protecting myself and my way of life in the same way that your society protects its members. This is of paramount importance to me. And do not tell me that even in your so-called democracy there is still the outmoded belief that the profit motive is suspect and immoral."

Winter was torn between amusement and irritation and had to laugh. "I don't know how this conversation became a discussion of philosophies."

"You were making a moral judgment about my way of life. That would be an excellent tactic to use if it was your intention to undermine my confidence in myself."

"Why would I want to do that?" Winter's eyes flickered to the wave shield and then back to his face again.

Shaw noticed. "No, I am not using telepathy to find out what you're thinking. You have made that impossible. It is just that I have had to be on the defensive since I woke up on your ship. I was aware of what you are trying to do because it is the logical method for you to use. In your place, I would have done the same thing."

Winter grinned ruefully. "An intelligence agent would have known how to handle this situation better than I."

"Are you admitting that you, a simple starcaptain, cannot handle a simple interrogation?"

"Obviously, since I have failed. I'm not accustomed to the methods." Winter looked down at her hands, which were clasped on the table top in front of her. "Perhaps honesty between us would be the best way to proceed."

"But you are still wondering if you will be able to trust the information I give you."

"Since you have admitted that you have no loyalties, I see no reason why you would want to be honest with me."

"What if I feel I owe you something for saving my life?" he asked.

"I wouldn't believe it," Winter replied. "Gratitude is usually a good reason for resentment."

Shaw looked at her without speaking.

"Oh, shit," Winter said, running her hand through her short curls. "My imagination is being overactive today. I should apologize for that, shouldn't I?"

"Yes."

"Then, I'm sorry. Can we begin again? Tell me what you know, and I'll let the Federation decide how much of it is true and how much is fiction."

"Agreed." He grinned. "And I will try very hard to tell the truth."

She was not sure if that was meant to be humor and decided to take his words at face value. "Then begin. What was the business that took you to Malvern?"

"I will tell you as much as I can, but I hope you understand that I cannot name my employers."

Winter nodded. "All right. I'll let that pass for now."

"The Proxima scientists have been working on some kind of a secret weapon for use against their enemies, which I understand includes the Federation. I was not informed of the details and I never knew the precise nature of this weapon, but the people who hired me were very concerned about it. There was information—notes, reports, and such—in the possession of the Proxima High Commander, Mitvale. We learned that he was on Malvern negotiating a treaty with the Matriarch. I believe the planet is of some strategic importance?"

"Yes," Winter admitted. "But others have been interested in Malvern, and the Matriarch could never be persuaded to make an alliance."

"Perhaps she has had a change of heart. All I know is that the High Commander was on Malvern. I was hired to go there and get the materials from him."

"Did you succeed?" Winter asked.

"Oh, yes, I succeeded," Shaw told her.

Despite a trace of pride in his words, she realized that he was not bragging as much as stating a fact. "Where are these materials now?"

"I put them in a hidden locker on my ship. They are still there unless someone has tried to open the locker without the proper code. In that case the tapes were destroyed."

"Where is your ship?"

"Last I knew it was in the belly of a Proxima dread-nought." Shaw shook his head. "I am certain that it has been thoroughly searched and that the information is gone."

"Then that's that," Winter said with disappointment. "I don't suppose you had a chance to examine the materials?"

"There was no time. I had to get in, steal the information, and get out again as quickly as possible. As you know, I was not completely successful in getting out." Shaw got to his feet and paced to the port while Winter watched in silence. "I have been thinking about my capture," he said after a moment. "There was a lot of confusion when my ship was boarded. Still, I was aware of the troopers—of their minds, all but one. The trooper who shot me—it was almost as if he wasn't there. His mind was a total blank. I cannot understand how that could be, unless . . ." Shaw's voice trailed off. He turned abruptly and returned to his chair. "His mind might have been shielded. That is, if he had a mind at all."

"No mind?" Winter repeated, trying to imagine how the body would function without direction. It did not seem possible to her. "How could that be?"

"He might have been artificial. An android."

"No, he couldn't have been," she stated.

"Why do you say this?"

"Robotics has produced some remarkable results, but not an artificial human—at least not one that's indistinguishable from a human being. You saw this Proxima trooper?"

"Yes."

"Was he—no, did he appear to be human?"

"He appeared the same as the others with him, except for this one difference which only I could detect. But if he was not an android, what other explanation could there be?"

"I don't know," she admitted.

Shaw sat on the edge of the chair. "David told me what I did when I was coming out of stasis, so you are aware of some of my potential as a telepath. It is possible to kill by sending a strong, controlled mental signal. I sent such a signal when my ship was boarded. But the trooper who shot me was not affected. Everyone else died." He paused. "Why?"

"I don't know. I have no experience with telepaths." Winter propped her elbow on the table and rested her chin in his hand. She frowned as she pondered the problem. "You disabled the troopers," she asked after a few seconds. "Killed them all?"

"Except for one."

"And they were all Proxima forces?"

"They wore the uniforms."

"Did you notice anything different, anything at all, about the one who survived?"

"No. But everything happened very quickly. I was in the engine room when they boarded. They went forward, directly to the control room." Shaw tried to remember. "The one who shot me came in last." He shook his head in defeat. "I cannot remember anything else."

"And you know nothing more of the Proxima and Malvern alliance except that the High Commander was there to negotiate a treaty?"

"That is correct."

Winter got to her feet and sighed. "Thank you. I'll send this information to Command. Maybe they can make something more of it. If you think of anything else, will you tell me?"

Shaw nodded.

CHAPTER 11

"Was she hard on you?" David asked some minutes later. He had come into the briefing room looking for Winter, but she had already left.

"No, she was not," Shaw replied. He had been watching the stars again, but turned away from the viewport when the doctor entered the room.

David sighed and sank into a chair while Shaw looked at him curiously.

"Did you think she would be difficult with me?" he asked. "Why?"

"I don't know. Just a feeling." David yawned. "She's been different these last few months, and sometimes it's hard to know what she'll do. She's always been distant, but lately . . ." David rubbed his eyes. He had been up working almost all of the previous night period. "I shouldn't be talking to you this way."

Shaw raised an eyebrow in surprise. "Did you imagine that you were giving up secrets to the enemy?" he inquired half in jest.

David stared at him. "No, maybe not the enemy, but—" He paused, not certain how to explain his reluctance. It was based partly on his innate good manners and partly on honor. Shaw was an unknown, but David felt that he could be worthy of trust. The man had been through a great deal, enough to bring out the worst in anyone, but Shaw had accepted everything that happened with patience and even a dry sense of humor. David thought his behavior admirable and, despite Winter's disclosure about his past, found that he liked the self-possessed stranger.

"You feel you are being disloyal to your captain," Shaw suggested. "I think I understand."

David laughed. "Sit down," he demanded kindly. "I don't know why, but I find you easy to talk to."

"I am glad you feel that way. There are many questions I would like to ask you." Shaw pulled a chair away from the table and sat where he could see both the viewport and the door.

David leaned back and stretched his legs out comfortably. "Ask. If I can, I'll answer."

"Thank you." Shaw glanced over at the stars as he tried to decide where to begin. "My position on this ship . . ." he ventured, turning back toward David.

"The captain will have to decide what that is, but she already told me you're not a prisoner."

"Am I free to go if I wish?"

"Go where?" David inquired, looking around him at the bulkheads and the void beyond the port.

"Anywhere. Off this ship when she docks."

David hesitated. "I know that Winter has made a report to Command—about finding you and everything—so the decision about what to do with you now will have to come from them. If they think what you have to say about Proxima and Malvern can be useful, they'll probably want to question you further. And who knows what other important bits of information you might have gathered during your, uh, career."

"I have already told your captain everything I can remember about Malvern. Perhaps you are unaware of it, but those in my profession are not anxious to find themselves in the custody of an authority. Not even your Command."

"But you haven't committed any crimes against the Federation," David commented. "Or if you have, there isn't anything about it in your record."

Shaw chuckled. "You read it, too?"

"Well . . . yes."

"It seems my sins preceded me," Shaw said. He made a rueful sound that was part chuckle and part sigh. "No, I have not committed crimes against the Federation, but your government is allied with New Home, for example. They might find it politically useful to hand me over to them."

David considered that idea. "They might," he agreed finally, "but not if the information you give them is important."

"Are you telling me that I might buy my freedom with useful information?"

"I wouldn't put it quite that way, but—well, maybe."

Shaw sighed. "All the Proxima wanted to do was terminate me. Had they succeeded it might have been easier for all concerned."

"Would you rather we'd left you in stasis and delivered you to Gyler?"

Shaw shook his head. "No," he said, his voice low. "No, I would not want that at all." He relaxed, leaning his elbows on the arms of the chair, his hands lightly clasped in front of him. "Tell me about this ship."

"The *Venture*? I can't tell you anything technical," David protested.

Shaw raised his eyebrow again.

"It's not my field," the doctor quickly explained. "I don't know anything about machinery. But I'll do my best about everything else. What do you want to know?"

"What kind of a ship is it? What are you doing in this part of the galaxy?"

"She's one of the new ring ships. Have you heard of them? Fast, armed, and versatile." David's mouth pulled into a crooked grin, and he shook his head. "We were supposed to be on a scientific mission. We set out for the Gallandry Yards almost a year ago. The *Venture* was going to be fitted with another ring, for labs and extra crew space. You've probably heard what happened to Gallandry."

"The yards were destroyed."

"Almost two weeks before we arrived. We helped clean up the mess. There was so much damage that it will be a long time before the yards are back in business again—if ever." David paused a minute to remember, while Shaw waited patiently.

"Anyway," the doctor went on, "after we'd transferred most of the Gallandry survivors to one of the Federation outposts, Command found other work for us. Our latest job was taking the Malvern ambassador-princess home."

"That is why you were in the Malvern system?"

"Yes. As a reward for the safe delivery of her ambassador, the Matriarch asked us to deliver a couple of containers to the Gyler Labs."

"One of them was the container in which I was confined," Shaw added.

"I've been curious about that," David said. "Why would the Matriarch ask us to deliver you to Gyler if she was an ally of the Proxima? Why didn't she ask them for transport?"

"I do not know. Unless the alliance is not everything it appears to be. She may not fully trust the Proxima."

"Well, I wouldn't blame her. Still I can't figure it out." The doctor paused. "The war's growing, isn't it? I mean, you might know more about it than I do. So far there have only been isolated incidents and a lot of politicians making noise. It seems like the Federation's been able to keep it under control, but sometimes I wonder."

Shaw looked at David for a moment, wondering how someone in the service could know so little about the workings of his own government, but the doctor seemed quite sincere. "Do you really believe that?" Shaw asked.

The doctor looked confused.

"David, if the Federation has been keeping anything under control, it has been the news about this war."

"What do you mean?"

"People have been fighting for the past ten, eleven years. Millions are dead. Entire planets have been wasted, entire populations wiped out. Have you not heard about any of these things?"

"I've heard about some of the battles, of course," David responded. "Why do you think the Federation is holding back information?"

"I do not think it; I know they are. It is not just that the news has been censored, but that no word of what is really happening is allowed to get back to your Earth."

"But, Shaw, that's serious! You must be mistaken."

Shaw shook his head. "I am not. Because of my profession," he said with a subtle emphasis, "I have been involved in this war since the beginning."

"Millions of people killed," David repeated, almost in a whisper. "Good God, millions of people. That means it's not just a case of isolated incidents."

"No, I am afraid not. There have been drastic changes in the Federation's administration of the colony worlds. The official word is that these changes are necessary because of the danger from a few rebellious planets."

"That's true," David put in.

"Perhaps," Shaw agreed. "There are some colonies that wish to remain a part of the Federation, of course, but they are very, very few. The rest have demanded autonomy. Many have already declared their independence and they are actively defending themselves." He gazed intently at his companion. "You have seen the end of the old political system, David. The colonies will win this war."

"Could you be reading more into it than there really is?" the doctor asked quietly.

Shaw laughed. "David, I have been making my living off of the war for a long time. My survival depends on knowing exactly what is happening. Most of my business has been smuggling information, so I have been in the middle of the activity. And there is a lot going on, from small skirmishes to big battles—battles with Federation forces, as well as with planetary powers that think they are big enough to carve out an empire for themselves."

"Like the Proxima?" David suggested.

"Like the Proxima," Shaw agreed. "It is hard to believe the extent of the war because the planets are so widely scattered, but the colonies are determined to be free. They have been planning this for a long time, and they are prepared to do whatever it takes. Whether they know it or not, your Federation is in a lot of trouble."

"This is hard to believe," David protested. "I know there are rebels—troublemakers—but I still believe that most of the colonies are loyal to the Federation. They have to be; they're dependent on the government to keep them supplied with—with technology, medicine, education . . . with everything. Why would they want to cut themselves off from that?"

"There have been colonies for the past three hundred years, David, time enough for them to have developed their own sources for these things. There is commerce among the stars, and the colonials no longer need Earth to survive." Shaw's silvery eyes seemed to reflect the cold gleam of the stars outside the port.

David sat stiffly, almost awkwardly in the chair. "Did you tell Winter any of this?" he asked.

"No. We spoke only of my business on Malvern," Shaw told him. "I did not think it would be appropriate to say more."

"And since Malvern has made a pact with Proxima, they'll be against us, too."

"So it would appear."

"Maybe I can't dispute your words, but it's still hard for me to believe," David said.

"My words are true," Shaw assured him. "Your news-people report nothing more than what the government wants you to know. It is like that in any war. The history of this time will also be just a small part of the truth, since it will be written by whoever wins the conflict. And so it has always been. Nothing ever changes."

David looked sadly at Shaw. "Why are you telling me this? Why didn't you tell the captain?"

"Because I wanted you to have the facts. I wanted someone of you to understand the gravity of the situation—my situation," Shaw said urgently. "I am grateful to you for saving me and, in exchange, I will share whatever information I have. But for the reasons I have given you, I really cannot allow myself to fall into your government's hands. Captain Winter is a Federation official. As such I do not know if she could hear the truth of what I say. But you, David, are different. Although you are Space Fleet, you are a doctor, not an official. Unless I am mistaken, I also believe that you are someone who cares."

But David still did not want to believe what Shaw had told him. Part of him, a very small part, was angry at being shaken out of complacency. Another part, the part that listened and remembered, knew enough to acknowledge the possibility of everything he had been told. He had seen too many things happen, things that could not be explained by the news re-leases.

"This confuses you." Shaw said, seeing the conflict in the doctor's eyes.

"Yes."

"I am sorry to have distressed you."

Was it all a trick, David wondered? Was Shaw trying to use him for something that he was planning, something that had nothing to do with his words? He looked at Shaw, wanting to know the truth, but the man's strange eyes were impossible to read; no secrets were reflected there.

He took a deep breath and let it out, dismissing the thoughts. His gut reaction was that Shaw and his words could be trusted, and David had learned to have confidence in his gut.

"No," he said. "Don't be sorry. What you've told me is different from the official version, but I believe what you say is possible. If the war is really that advanced, it's time there was truth. I just don't understand why the government thinks secrecy is necessary."

"Because they do not want you to know how desperate they are," Shaw explained. "For the first time, Earth forces are vulnerable, and they know it. They are afraid."

"The colonials are that powerful?" David asked.

"Yes, they are."

"Are you certain we don't have a chance of winning?"

Shaw shook his head. "Who ever wins a war? Battles are won or lost. When it is all over, the form of government may have been changed and different groups of people oppressed, but there is still a government, and there are still the oppressed."

David mulled that over. "What can we do?"

"Nothing. What can anyone do except what is necessary at any given moment? You have to think for yourself and make judgments based on your own morality."

"Is that why you became a spy?"

Shaw really laughed then, the sound coming out of him like something unleashed. There was joy in the sound, but there was also mockery, and David realized that the mockery was aimed at Shaw himself.

"Where do you come from?" David asked. "What happened that caused you to get involved in the war?"

The laughter vanished, and Shaw was silent for a moment. "Perhaps one day you will hear my story," he said quietly. "But not today." Shaw left his chair and walked to the door.

"But there is a story, isn't there," David called after him. "There's something even you don't want to think about."

"Thank you for listening."

The door closed and Shaw was gone.

Karth, 2452 TSC

The last night of the Turning Festival was usually the most exciting. With the Meeting concluded, the cassia trading

done, and all of the other business matters finished for another
six months, everyone could relax and concentrate on having
fun. However, that year was different. There was an added
tension as people split into two separate groups, those who
were satisfied that they had routed the Federation Mining
Consortium once again, and others who were still determined
to find a way to benefit from the mineral wealth of Karth.

On other nights people had been content to wander through
the fair, enjoying the sights and sounds, but now the clanspeople gathered together to rehash the day's events. Some of
them were not content to allow the situation to go unchal-
lenged and plotted ways to change it.

Open house was held throughout the campground as usual,
and people went from tent to tent, saying good-bye to friends
they would not see again until the Winter Festival or the next
Turning. That night there were several tents that were dark,
their owners indicating their displeasure with the outcome of
the afternoon vote. There was sadness, too, for a number of
friendships that had endured through the years had failed this
last test. The argument over the charter had caused a definite
rift among the clanspeople, and their lives would never be the
same again.

Ilya and Eric were not affected by the discord. For them
the last night of the fair was important for a very different
reason. It was the last Turning that they would have together
before Eric went to the University of Havensport. They would
be apart for over a year, and to them that was a very long
time.

They walked hand in hand through the noise and excitement of the carnival, enjoying the sights and sounds but not
wanting to be separated even for an instant. They were quiet,
more subdued than their friends, although some of them, too,
faced the same parting. When midnight came and the constel-
lations were sliding down toward the morning edge of the sky,
Ilya and Eric went off into the darkness alone.

It was high summer, but the night was a cool relief from
the heat of the day. They climbed a hill beyond the camp and
paused at the edge of a stand of towering evergreens to look
down at the lights. Voices and music drifted faintly up to
them. The smells of cooking and cassia were replaced by the
pungent resinous odor of the trees. Behind them a night bird
called, the sound low and mournful in the blackness of the
forest.

"It's so peaceful," Ilya said, sitting down with her back against a tree trunk. "Let's spend the rest of the night here."

Eric slid down to sit beside her, his arm around her shoulders. He leaned over to kiss the angle of her jaw. She turned her face to his and eagerly found his lips with her own.

"Let's make love," she whispered.

Her hair was outlined by moonlight, and the beads on her tunic reflected the soft light like muted jewels.

"Are you sure?" he asked, bemused by her intensity. "We were going to wait until our first year together at the university."

"I don't want to wait anymore. I love you." She kissed him again.

Eric's arms were tight around her as he kissed her mouth, her chin, her neck, and breathed in the clean, fresh scent of her hair.

The carpet of grass and shed leaves was soft beneath them, but still Eric hesitated. "I wanted this to be special. I want it to be right," he whispered.

"It will be special." She kissed him fiercely, her fingers tangled in his hair as her body translated its desire into action.

Eric stopped trying to argue, swept up in the strength of his own feelings for the woman he loved.

It was still dark when the morning mist touched Ilya. She burrowed closer to Eric, drowsily seeking warmth. His eyes opened at her movement, and he kissed her awake.

"I love you, you know," he whispered.

"I know," she returned as she stretched beside him, filled with a feeling of great contentment.

"When are you leaving camp?" he asked.

"This afternoon. We're letting the cassia out today. They're already grazing in the south end of the pasture."

"Our's are, too, but we won't go until tomorrow." His fingers wound in her thick hair. "I won't see you again," he said, his voice tinged with regret.

"Not for a year and three months," she replied. Then her voice changed. "I'll miss you so much."

They lay in silence and watched as the stars went out and streaks of sunlight stretched up into the sky. The land below the hill was washed in a golden light through which the colors of things were transformed, taking on a clarity and brilliance they would never have in the harsh light of day.

"You could come to the university a year early," Eric suggested. "Your grades are good enough."

But Ilya shook her head. "You know I can't. This year is very important. I have to finish my prerequisites."

"Are you still majoring in physical sciences?"

"Yes."

Eric frowned as the fear of losing Ilya returned. "What good are physics and astronomy to a herder?"

"I don't know," she laughed. "But it's what I do best."

"You're still determined to try for Space Fleet, aren't you?" Eric's feelings changed the tone of his voice.

"I always said I would," Ilya responded, trying to make him understand. "You know that."

Eric hid his face against Ilya's shoulder. "I don't want you to go," he complained, his words muffled in her hair. "You'll get off planet and you won't come back, I know it."

"Eric, why don't you come with me?" she pleaded. "Then we can go to the academy together. We don't have to join the service when our training is over, but at least we'll have some idea what life is like off Karth."

He didn't answer.

"You said you'd consider it," she pressed.

"I know . . . and I have," he replied, raising his head so that he could look into her eyes. "But somehow I always hoped you'd change your mind."

"No, I haven't," she said. She felt she had to win him over, or at least get him to accept her choice as something she had to do. "It doesn't mean I'll be gone forever. I'll be back every chance I get. And after the five years' training, I'll be back for good."

"No, you won't. You'll be so busy chasing stars that you'll forget all about Karth."

"Of course I won't." She giggled at his serious face. "Don't be silly." She gave him a quick kiss. "Come with me."

Her eyes were like stars in the golden morning light.

"You're really determined to try for the academy?"

"Yes," she said firmly.

"All right. I guess I'll have to think about going, too."

CHAPTER 12

The only part of the Amalgamated Mining Station that was visible was a scattering of pressure domes connected by tube-like walkways on the surface of the planetoid. Beyond, the asteroid field stretched into the distance. The field was not large when compared with some others, but it was such a rich source of minerals that it was worth the effort and expense of mining, even in such an inhospitable environment.

Governor McGill had been right: the station was small, Winter thought as she looked at the amplified picture that was reflected on the viewscreen on the bridge. She wondered how McGill thought he could repair something as large and complex as the *Venture*. She asked as much of the man who had answered her ship's hail and was told that a maintenance barge would link up with them. The barge was an orbital repair dock specifically designed to allow work in zero-g. In the meantime the *Venture* was directed into an orbit that would take them around the asteroid field.

"You'll pass over the station again in about seven hours," the man told Winter. "We'll make arrangements for the barge to meet you then."

"Very well," she responded.

She switched off and sat back, noting that Walters and T'Gal, who were the navigators on duty, were prepared to put the ship into the long curving orbit. The main part of her attention was on the view screen as she tried to collect as much information about the station as possible before it was out of their range. Although the scanning equipment was set for maximum penetration, the station was well shielded, and she learned very little.

David sat behind Winter, watching the results of the scanners on another monitor. Disgusted with their lack of success in penetrating the shield, he snapped the switch to "off" and sat back with a sigh.

"If I remember correctly," he said, mostly to himself, "our original mission was survey and science." Winter glanced back at him, and he caught her eye as he continued. "I didn't sign on for a war, but it looks like we're getting caught up in the damned thing, aren't we?"

"So it would seem," she said, her voice grim.

"Winter," he said very softly. "Are you still happy in the Service?"

She stared in astonishment. "Of course. This is my life. I worked hard to get where I am."

"But is being a starcaptain really everything you thought it would be?"

Winter laughed. "David, you can't begin to know how important this job is to me."

"But everything . . . our jobs, our purpose here . . . they've changed. It's different now. With the war on." He paused, remembering Shaw's words. "We've had a taste of it already, and it's going to get worse."

"Why the soul searching, David? What's this all about?"

"Sometime soon I have a feeling that you're going to be ordered to do things that go against your basic moral beliefs. What will you do then?"

"You mean fighting?" she asked.

"Yes, fighting is one of the things. But we've done that before. No, I mean other things that are even worse than combat."

"I didn't know you considered anything worse than that," she said lightly.

"But I do," he responded in all seriousness. "Things like having to deal with allies picked for political reasons, for expediency," he explained. "Remember the Malvern incident?"

Winter frowned, and David continued.

"You hated it, but you followed orders. That's the kind of thing I mean."

"You think I can't handle it?" Winter asked with an edge to her voice. "Is this what you're trying to tell me?"

"No, I'm not saying that at all," David assured her hastily. "I think you've already proved you can handle just about anything. What I am trying to say is that you have a well-defined sense of ethics, but, unfortunately, in war and politics right and wrong have nothing to do with reality."

"And you think that my moral sense will make me unfit to do my job?"

"No, I'm not saying that either. Well, not entirely. I can tell that you're already having trouble reconciling what you are told to do with your feelings. That's what's responsible for the difference I've seen in you. And we both know that things aren't going to get any better. In order to survive in the Service, you're going to have to change even more. That—or destroy yourself trying not to compromise your integrity."

There was silence, heavy and thought-filled, but through it came the sound of the captain's chuckle.

"I don't believe the future is that inflexible." She turned completely around and rested her crossed arms on the top of his terminal. "Look, David. Because of my position, I may have to make certain compromises, and they might even go against what I believe to be right and true, but it's only realistic to expect this. However, I sincerely believe I'll manage to survive with my integrity intact."

David had one more point to make. "But what about the things that have already happened? What about the changes in you that I've seen in the past year?"

Winter shrugged. "Change is a condition of life. It's inevitable. And unless I'm turning into some kind of a monster..." She cocked her eyebrow at David, waiting for his response, but he remained stubbornly silent. "You worry too much," she concluded with a smile.

Delieus's voice cut into their conversation. "Captain, there's a ship approaching. It looks like a small shuttle. They're signaling."

"Open a channel for them, Lieutenant. Find out what they want. I wonder what's happening now," she said to David before swinging her chair back around to her console.

"Captain, the shuttle has one passenger. He requests permission to link with the *Venture*. Says he has a personal message for you."

Winter's eyebrow raised. "Give him clearance, Lieutenant. Have someone meet him at the air lock and bring him here."

"Aye, Captain," Delieus said.

Minutes later the shuttle pilot was standing on the bridge. He was dressed in a tan coverall with a shoulder patch decorated with the logo of the Amalgamated Mining Consortium. There should have been a corresponding Federation patch on the opposite shoulder, but the place was bare except for a subtle shadowy outline and some threads. On his head the pilot wore a blue, billed cap with another Amalgamated patch on the front. He stared curiously around him, his lips pulled into a thin line.

"Captain Winter?" he said finally.

"I am the captain. You have a message for me?"

"Yes. I'm Bob Janes. I work with Governor McGill. He told me to tell you that he's sorry he couldn't meet you personally, but he's been pretty busy. He'll be free in about an hour though, and he'd like to discuss the repairs to your ship."

"I thought we were supposed to link up with a maintenance barge when our orbit brought us back over the station," the captain commented.

"That's right, but Governor McGill still wants to meet with you in person. He'd like to speak to you before the work begins."

"I suppose it can be arranged."

"The governor sent me to bring you to the station," Janes told her.

"What?" David interjected softly, but Winter motioned him to silence.

"You are welcome to bring another officer with you, if you wish," Janes continued. "Unfortunately the shuttle won't take more than three people."

"Thank you. I can be ready to leave in twenty minutes. Ensign," she said to the crewman who had brought Janes to the bridge. "Escort our guest to the rec room and see if he would like some refreshment. I'll meet both of you at B-airlock at . . . fourteen forty."

"You're going?" David asked when the two men had gone.

"Of course."

"You're not going alone?"

"No. I think I'll take T'Gal with me." Winter turned to the

helmsman. "Lieutenant T'Gal, call Commander Thomas. Ask him to come up to the bridge. He'll be in charge until I return. Then change out of fatigues and meet me at B-airlock at fourteen forty."

"Two of you won't be enough if there's trouble down there," David said.

"I'm not anticipating problems at the station. It's Federated territory," Winter responded. "Besides, T'Gal and I can handle anything that comes up, especially when we have the *Venture* to back us up."

"But the *Venture* will be kilometers away from the station," the doctor pointed out. "If you have to go down there, take one of our own shuttles and a security team."

"David, I don't think a show of force is necessary."

"But I do. You have no idea what you're walking into." David was becoming angry with her stubbornness.

"This is a mining station run by the Federation, not a military installation," she insisted. "Whatever's down there, it isn't dangerous. I know you think I've changed, but I'm not suicidal!"

Thomas arrived on the bridge and claimed Winter's attention.

"Thomas, you have the con. While I'm gone, put the ship on stand-by alert." She glanced at David then back again. "I don't think there is any danger, but I'd rather you were ready in case something does happen."

"Aye, Captain. You'll take a communicator, won't you?"

"Yes, but the station's shielded and I might not be able to get a signal through to you. But keep the line open anyway."

"How long will you be gone?" the engineer asked.

"I don't know. It shouldn't be more than five hours," she replied. "The *Venture* will be back in visual contact with the station by then, and I see no reason why I should be gone any longer." Winter turned her console over to Thomas and left the bridge.

David felt a combination of frustration and anger that was based on fear. Maybe Winter was right, maybe there was no danger at the station. But he had no proof of that, and the purely subjective feeling in his gut told him that she was making a mistake. At least she had taken T'Gal with her. T'Gal was a descendant of mutant stock, a woman born of a people genetically altered to survive on a heavy gravity world, and her unusual strength would deter most attackers. Still, she was not immune to a pistol or laser.

David knew there was nothing he could do to deter Winter once she was set on a course of action; he had known that when he spoke with her on the bridge. On the other hand, he could not just let her go!

Damn Winter! He left the bridge and went after her, ready to renew his arguments, but she was nowhere in sight. He turned into the dark briefing room, crossing with angry strides to the big port, hoping the immensity of space would help calm him.

"Is there trouble?" a quiet voice asked after a moment. David turned to see Shaw standing in the shadows.

"Trouble?" David repeated. "Yes, there's trouble. At least, I think there is."

"Can you tell me about it?" Shaw moved to David's side.

"It's Winter. Damned, stubborn . . ."

Shaw waited patiently for him to continue.

David sighed. "I told you about the suicide ship that the Proxima sent after the *Venture*. Winter thinks someone at the station might have been involved—specifically McGill, the governor. Now he's sent a shuttle to take her down to the station, and she's going to go!"

"Alone?"

"No. She's taking a bodyguard. One bodyguard. And with the *Venture* in a wide orbit, we'll be out of contact with her for over five hours."

"Are you convinced that there is danger for her at the station?" Shaw asked.

"I'm certain of it, but—damn it, Shaw, she won't listen to me. She never does." David ran his fingers through his hair.

Silence filled the room. Stars were bright in the port, but their multicolored glow did nothing to alleviate David's gloom.

"I may be able to help," Shaw said at last. "But only if you will permit me to do so."

David stared at him curiously. "Help? How?"

"The shuttle pilot. He might know if there is treachery planned."

"But will he tell us?" David protested. "I don't think so. You didn't see him. He didn't seem the type who would tell anyone anything."

"There are other ways of obtaining information." Shaw's

voice was low and calm as he raised his arms, his slender fingers touching the wave band.

"You can't take that off!" David exclaimed quickly.

"I know I promised I would wear it, but you should know by now that I am no danger as long as I am in control of my mind," Shaw said. "Release me from my promise just for the amount of time it will take me to find and sense the pilot's mind."

"I don't know . . ."

"Do you have any alternative?" Shaw demanded.

David looked at him, indecision naked on his face.

"You can trust me, you know." Shaw told him in a gentle voice. "If I wished to harm you or anyone on this ship, I would have broken my promise to you before this."

David couldn't argue with that. "All right," he said. "Take it off."

Shaw raised his hands to his head. When the band came off he was exposed to a sudden incredible roar of mental impressions. They displaced the silence as they poured into his mind, crashing and reverberating like the worst headache he could ever imagine. He swayed dizzily and closed his eyes.

"Are you all right?" David asked anxiously.

Shaw raised his hand to forestall the doctor's questions, and his eyes stayed closed a moment more. Then his natural ability to shield took over and damped the sensations to a bearable level.

"Shaw?" David asked again.

The telepath opened his eyes. "I had forgotten how noisy it really is," he said, shaken.

"How do you feel?"

"I am all right now."

"You went white. I thought you were going to pass out."

Shaw smiled. "So did I." He set the wave shield down on the table and rubbed his temples. His eyes stared at nothing David could see, as he carefully probed with his mind.

"There are a lot of people nearby. Help me find the shuttle pilot. Where would he be right now?"

David looked at his chronometer. "He should be at B-airlock. It's in this ring, but about a third of the way around beyond the bridge. Are you sure you can find him?"

"It is not easy to read a stranger over a distance. I will not be able to get words unless he projects them to me, but I should be able to sense his emotions." His voice stilled as he concentrated. "Is he wearing anything on his head?"

"Yes, a cap. Blue, with an emblem of some kind on the front."

Shaw was silent, then shook his head. "Nothing. I can sense the people around him, but . . . We will have to go there."

David glanced at the time again. "Then we have to hurry. It's almost fourteen hundred, and they're about to leave." He tried to keep the disappointment out of his voice. The wave band lay forgotten on the table as they raced into the corridor.

They were too late. The blast doors had already closed over airlock B when they arrived.

"David." Shaw whirled to the doctor. "Was the shuttle pilot wearing anything beside the cap on his head?"

"All I saw was the hat. Why?"

"Because I could sense everyone here—the captain and two others. But that is all. And there were four people, am I not correct?"

David felt a sudden chill of fear. "Yes."

"Then the pilot was wearing a shield. It could have been in the cap or hidden by the cap, but he was definitely shielded against a telepath."

"But why would he do that?" David asked. "Why would he expect to find a telepath aboard the *Venture*?"

"Because he knew I was here. David, they know I am on this ship and they apparently suspect that I am no longer in stasis. And I wonder . . ." Shaw stared at the closed door as if it could give him answers.

"Wonder what?" David demanded. "Tell me!"

"The Proxima went to a lot of trouble to capture me and to capture me alive. They must think I know something . . . and perhaps I do. I wonder what this secret could be."

"What does this have to do with the Proxima? Do you think they engineered all of this?"

"I was initially captured by the Proxima. Again, the suicide ship that attacked the *Venture* was Proxima, and I now believe that its purpose was to recapture or destroy me. Most likely, destroy. But by now they know that this effort has also failed. Therefore, they may be after me again," Shaw explained.

"If this is true, then why do they want Winter down on the station?"

"If I am correct, their next action will be to mount an

attack on the *Venture*. Taking the ship will be much easier with the captain gone."

David let his breath out in a loud exclamation. "So it is a trap! And she's walking right into it," he exclaimed. He shifted his weight from one foot to the other. "We have to go after her!" David whirled and headed for the bridge at a run. Shaw followed more slowly.

"Thomas," the doctor yelled as he burst through the doorway.

David had no trouble convincing Thomas of the danger to the captain. The engineer had kept silent, but he too had been suspicious of the invitation for Winter to visit the station. Within fifteen minutes the larger of the *Venture*'s two shuttles had been loaded with a security team. Shaw did not wait to be invited to go along, but strapped himself into the navigator's seat. David squeezed in, too, not willing to be left behind. Released from the grapples that held it snuggly in a depression along the lower ring, the shuttle dropped into space. The small engine flared once, and then the tiny vessel began to move away from the *Venture*.

The station's shuttle was nowhere in sight as they approached the planetoid. The *Venture*'s shuttle hovered, its pilot uncertain where to go until Shaw pointed.

"There," he said. "We can set down right next to that tanker. There's no way for us to get in without being seen, so we have to go boldly. Still, just our presence will be enough to deter them from whatever they had planned for Captain Winter."

"Unless we're already too late," David interjected, his voice full of gloom. Shaw looked at him and shook his head.

"We'll need suits to get into the station," the pilot said. "But if we ask politely, maybe they'll send one of the access tubes out and save us the trouble."

"Call them and see what kind of a mood they're in," David told him. The pilot reached for the radio.

For Winter, the ride down to the station was uneventful, which was exactly what she had expected. She had considered David's warning more carefully than he had thought, but since she could not imagine any danger in taking McGill up on his invitation, she had followed her own inclination. She also knew that mining stations were important to the Federation, and although this one was a part of the Amalgamated Consortium, it was still under Federation control.

No, Winter decided, David was wrong. And even if he was not, there could not be any danger to herself while the *Venture* was in orbit. And she was curious about McGill. His call to the *Venture* had been so well timed that he must have been aware of the Proxima suicide ship. Therefore she had her own purpose in visiting the station: she intended to learn the reason for McGill's strange call. She considered the possibility that Proxima agents were working out of the station; if that were so, Command would have to be informed. That the whole station was under Proxima control was a possibility that she did not even consider.

CHAPTER 13

Much to their surprise, the rescue party from the *Venture* had no trouble entering the mining station. After a brief conversation between the pilot and port control, they were invited to land. A flexible access tube snaked out to their shuttle and clamped tightly around the door with magnetic seals. When the connection was completed, the heavy doors hissed open, and David led the force into the station. Shaw took care to be the last man out and remained in the background, trying to be as inconspicuous as possible.

Bob Janes, the pilot who had brought Winter down, met them just inside of the station. He seemed distressed, and his eyes shifted warily from one member of the party to another.

There was a lot of noise in the immediate area, especially from a huge piece of automatic equipment that was loading ore into a tanker. Janes had to shout to make himself heard.

"It's a good thing you're here," he yelled. "I don't know what happened. One minute they were with me and the next —well, they were gone!"

David felt a renewed surge of fear. "The captain?" he shouted back. "Gone where?"

Janes started to reply, but he could not be heard over the

103

deafening rumble and clank of the machine. Gesturing, he led the team around a barrier. The noise abated as they entered a wide hallway. A group of workmen going on shift walked ponderously by, already dressed in atmospheric suits, their big, round helmets cradled in their arms. The men looked curiously at the uniformed team, but made no comment. Someone else came buzzing down the hall on a grav cart that swerved around the visitors, narrowly missing Shaw's legs. There was other foot traffic and more of the carts, but Janes halted off to one side to continue his tale.

"We were waiting for the lift," Janes explained. "I was called away for just a second, but when I turned back, your captain and her assistant were gone."

"How could you lose them in an enclosed station?" the commander of the *Venture*'s security team asked.

"It does happen."

"And you have no idea where they went?" David asked.

"I think they went down the lift," Janes replied. "We were on our way to the administrative level and maybe they went without me—but I can't be sure." He raised his hands palms up in the universal gesture that meant helplessness, confusion, and apology all in one.

David stared at him, his wide eyes and blank expression registering shock and despair.

Shaw felt all of the thoughts around him, but he could not get any useful information from the mental confusion of station personnel mingled with the *Venture*'s party. No one in the loading area or the hallway had any memory of seeing either Captain Winter or T'Gal. Once again Shaw tried to probe Janes, but the pilot's mind was very well shielded.

Shaw worked his way toward the door of the elevator that was visible just a little farther down the hall. A mine worker was standing there, idly watching the security men and the pilot as he waited for the elevator. When the doors opened and closed and the miner did not move, Shaw realized that the man was more intent on what was happening in the loading area. He listened for the man's mind and received a vague picture of Winter and T'Gal getting into the elevator. They had been alone. Shaw moved beyond the man and leaned casually against the wall.

"But you're looking?" he heard David ask.

"Of course we're looking," Janes responded. "But I'm worried. Some of those tunnels aren't safe. We've been blasting down on the sixteenth level—clearing new space for storage, mostly. But it's dangerous down there. They could get into all kinds of trouble. It was very foolish of them to go alone."

"And it was even more careless of you to let them go without you," David pointed out testily.

The security commander frowned. "Do you think Captain Winter might have gone down there?" he asked in a more consolatory tone. "To the sixteenth level?"

Keeping an eye on the miner, Shaw noticed the man's subtle but definite reaction to Janes's last words. The elevator came again, and Shaw entered it as soon as the doors opened. The miner glanced around but did nothing to stop him. Shaw punched the control button for level sixteen.

Numbers flashed one after another on the level indicator as the car began to drop. The shaft walls, visible through the grimy window on the door, changed from plasteel to rock as the car descended deeper into the planetoid. Investigating the control panel in the wall, Shaw found the switch that controlled the car's lights. He turned them off.

At level fifteen there was a slight lurch as the braking dampers came on and the car slowly completed its descent. When the car was finally motionless, Shaw pressed the button that kept the doors closed, while he looked out through the window. Outside was a huge, open space in complete darkness. There were a number of bulky objects stacked in long rows, but he could not identify them. Crates or equipment of some sort, he presumed. Still he waited, holding the door closed.

Minutes passed, measured by his heartbeats. As far as Shaw could see, nothing moved in the darkness. The level seemed to be no more than a storage area, but as his eyes adjusted to the lack of light he realized that in one of the aisles there was a shape that seemed out of place.

Finally the pupils of Shaw's eyes had dilated until there was very little of the silver-gray showing and everything was bathed with a strange, almost metallic light that was his unique form of night vision. Even then he did not see anyone or movements of any kind.

When he finally allowed the elevator doors to open, he still remained inside the car, pressed against the front wall with every muscle tensed for action. Then, in a soundless rush, he dashed out, sinking into a crouch behind a pile of crates.

As far as he could tell from a mental probe of the vast space around him, he was alone, but he knew he could not completely trust his telepathic sense anymore. At least one man on the station had been shielded against him, and there might be others.

Shaw's other senses were working, checking out his surroundings. Smelling fresh blood, he worked his way toward the dark form on the floor. It was organic and either dead or unconscious. The aisles between the towering cases still seemed to be empty. Shaw held his breath as he moved out of the shadows to where the body lay.

It was T'Gal. She was dead, shot with an exploding projectile that had taken away most of the left side of her body. There was no sign of Captain Winter.

Shaw turned to retreat into the shelter of the crates when a loud click sounded in the blackness above him. He was in motion when an electric net dropped and spread around him, holding him immobile. He struggled, but the strands held him too tightly, and he cursed himself for being so careless. The anger turned to apprehension as he saw three figures approaching. He abandoned his attempts to get free of the net and stared at the newcomers, the fine hairs on his arms rising in alarm. It was not just his helplessness that frightened him, but the realization that he could not sense the minds of his captors.

Governor McGill was so fat that he almost overflowed the chair which was placed behind the desk in his luxurious office. The floor, in contrast to the cold bare floors elsewhere in the station, was cushioned in a rich, deep pile carpet of harmony fiber. The furnishings were rich and ill cared for. The desk and chairs were constructed of savagewood from the giant trees of Blanding's World, but the sides were nicked and scarred, and the top surfaces were stained and dirty. A number of shimmering light paintings decorated the walls, along with goblin silk hangings, each worth a small fortune. The governor sat in the midst of this splendor like some maleficent presence, his air of bumbling good humor gone. In its place was an aura of quiet evil.

Shaw, still encumbered by the net, stood on the rug, and McGill stared at him through narrowed eyes.

"So this is the elusive telepath," he said. "Not quite as clever as you thought, are you?" He chuckled, making a sound like falling gravel. "You saved us a lot of trouble. We thought we were going to have to deal with the *Venture* to get you, and here you walked right into our hands." He nodded to Shaw's guards. "You can take the net off and cuff him. He won't be going anyplace for a while."

All three of Shaw's captors had accompanied him into the governor's office and they hastened to obey the orders.

Shaw did not object as they deactivated the electric net and secured his wrists in front of him. Instead he used his time to study the details of the room, looking for a weakness, waiting for a chance to escape. He still could not read the minds of anyone in the room and he was very uncomfortable at that deafness. It was understandable in the case of the governor, who wore what was obviously a wave band—a bulky black metal cap that covered his head down to the temples. But the guards were bareheaded. Shaw closed his eyes as he concentrated, probing even harder, but their minds were still blank to him. He opened his eyes again and studied the men. Was it natural shielding? He did not think so. Usually something leaked out.

"You can't use your telepathic powers on anyone in this room," the governor commented. "We took precautions, you see." He indicated the band he wore.

Shaw looked at him without speaking, and McGill laughed. "Silent? We'll change that." He nodded to the men who had moved away to stand by the door. "Bring in the other one," he said, and the guards left the office.

"So," McGill turned back to Shaw, studying him. "The Proxima want you. And they want you very badly. Perhaps you will tell me why."

"I do not know what you are talking about," Shaw said.

"Of course you do. And you'll tell me, too, before I'm finished with you."

The guards returned; one of them had Winter's unconscious form draped over his shoulder. Her once neat uniform was crumpled, and her right side was dark, covered with drying blood.

"Put her down there," McGill ordered, gesturing to a couch to the left of his desk. "Now," he said to Shaw. "I can understand why she's here—I invited her. But why did you follow her? You couldn't have learned anything from the mind of the pilot I sent, since he's one of the Proxima components. So are these guards, by the way." He watched for Shaw's reaction, but there was none. "You don't know what that means, do you?"

"No," Shaw answered wearily. "But it seems you are about to tell me."

"You should care, you know," the governor snapped. "You should care very much. What are you doing!" he yelled at one of the guards. The man was leaning toward Winter.

"She moved."

McGill swiveled his chair around so he could see the couch. "Nonsense. She's still unconscious."

"She moved." the guard insisted.

"And I said, nonsense!" the governor argued. He pointed to two of the guards. "You and you—go find Zimmerman. I want the shuttle ready to leave. And you, find out how soon they can have all of the special components loaded aboard the barge."

He turned back to the desk and shifted his bulk into a more comfortable position. One guard remained in the room, still staring suspiciously at Winter.

Shaw reached for the captain's mind. He was very careful, so that he would not startle her if she was indeed awake. As a link was established, he realized that she was conscious and alert, watching the guard from under her lowered lashes. Shaw moved forward slightly, attracting McGill's attention.

"What is so special about the guards?" he asked his captor.

"I'm afraid that I no longer have time to explain it to you," the governor told him. "But you will learn for yourself sooner than you might like." He nodded to the guard. "Put the cuffs on her. Let's get out of here before more of these Feds come looking for their captain."

The guard bent over and reached for Winter's left wrist, which hung limply over the edge of the couch. He was off balance for only an instant, but it was enough. Winter moved in a flash, twisting and coiling. Both of her heels caught the guard in the head, and there was the sickening crunch of breaking bones. Winter grabbed the guard's weapon as he fell, blood pouring between his fingers as he held his hands over his face. The captain came to her feet, backing away and holding the pistol so that it covered both the governor and the guard. There was no need for her concern, however, for the guard was dead.

"Key," she said to the governor. "For the cuffs. Hurry."

"You can't get out of here, you know," McGill told her, but

he removed an electronic key from a drawer and slid it across the top of the desk toward Shaw.

"David is at the landing area with a security team," Shaw told Winter as he unlocked the handcuffs. "We brought one of the *Venture*'s shuttles down."

"Good," Winter responded. "Get on the comlink," she told McGill, "and call the landing area. I want to talk to whoever's on my shuttle." The governor hesitated. "Now!" she yelled.

But the governor still did not move. "This is foolish. The station's full of my men. How do you think you can—"

"I said *now!*" Winter sent a bolt from the pistol into the carpet at the governor's feet. Smoke and the smell of scorched wool filled the air. McGill jerked his feet away and stared at her, his mouth gaping in shocked surprise. No one moved for a second, then McGill slowly turned his chair to the console at his side.

"No visual and no tricks," Winter warned softly. She moved to his side and pressed the muzzle of the pistol into his neck. The governor flicked a switch.

"Port control," he said hoarsely, then cleared his throat. "Port control, this is Governor McGill. Respond, please."

"Port control."

"Ah . . . let me speak to someone on board the *Venture*'s shuttle."

"Yes, Governor. Just a moment. I'll connect you." There was the muted sound of a voice calling the shuttle. McGill's breathing seemed loud in the room, and his eyes flickered between the pistol and the console. The gun in Winter's hand was unwavering.

"Patching through now," the controller's voice said.

"This is the FSS *Venture* shuttle craft A-1031," another voice announced formally.

"This is Captain Winter," she replied, leaning over McGill's shoulder as she spoke. "Ensign Samuels, is that you?"

"Yes, Captain. Are you all right?"

"I'm fine. How many in the landing party?"

"There are nine of us, including Dr. Wilson."

"Contact them. There's been some trouble. Tell them to secure the landing area—there's to be no violence unless absolutely necessary. We're outnumbered, and I want all of us to get off this station intact. Do you understand?"

"Yes, Captain. Where are you? Do you need help?"

"No. I'm in the governor's office. Shaw is here with me. We'll join you in a couple of minutes." She looked at Shaw, then back to the governor. "But if we're not at the shuttle in twenty minutes, leave without us. Get back to the *Venture* and radio our situation to Command on Alpha Base Seven."

"Captain!" Samuels protested. "We can't leave you if there's trouble!"

"You have no choice, Ensign. There's a Proxima ship on its way, and I assure you they won't be friendly. After you've tight-beamed to Command, blast this station to hell and then get the *Venture* away. That's an order. Do you understand?"

There was a pause. "Aye, aye, Captain." There was resignation in the voice.

"Twenty minutes. We'll count down from . . ." She looked at her wrist chronometer. "Now. Winter out." Winter settled her hip on the desk, the pistol still pointed meaningfully. "Okay, governor, turn it off."

"You wouldn't," he stammered, beads of sweat standing out on his forehead. "I mean, you couldn't . . ."

"I can and I will," she assured him in a deadly voice. "Don't doubt me, governor. The *Venture* has the fire power necessary to demolish this planetoid. If I'm not at the landing area in twenty minutes, we'll all be dead. So, how do we get there?"

"The elevator." He waved toward the office door.

"That's too obvious," she told him. "I'm betting that you have your own personal way of getting around. Something fast and private."

McGill glared at Winter with undisguised fury.

"Captain Winter," Shaw said. "McGill sent two of his guards on errands. They should be back here any minute."

"I heard him," she acknowledged without moving her eyes from the governor. "Time is passing, McGill. Where's your exit, or do we just sit here and wait to die?"

"You heard him," the governor said desperately. "The guards will be back any minute."

"And you're dead the second that door opens." Winter held the pistol pointed at McGill's head. "Where is your bolthole?"

McGill's lips tightened, and he seemed to deflate. He reached carefully for the console and manipulated the controls. Shaw moved closer to watch. A section of the wall behind the desk slid back, revealing an empty shaft.

"It's a grav beam. Goes straight to the landing area and my

yacht," McGill informed her. "What are you going to do with me?"

Winter and Shaw glanced at each other. Shaw could read death in her mind, mingled with the intensity of her anger.

"He has information that you need," he pointed out.

"He'll be in the way."

Shaw went to the governor and, removing the wave band, put his fingers to McGill's temples. Realizing too late what was happening, the governor began to struggle, but Winter stopped him, twisting one of his arms painfully behind his back and digging the muzzle of her pistol into his neck. McGill subsided with a moan of sheer terror.

Minutes passed in silence before Shaw stepped back, a strange look on his face. He started to speak, but Winter interrupted.

"Tell me later," she said. "Our time is almost up. We have to get out of here."

Shaw nodded and pushed the control that flooded the grav shaft with a beam of blue light. Then he twisted the switch, breaking it off. A smash of his fist on the console shattered the rest of the controls.

"It will take them awhile to figure out what's working and what is not," he told the captain. "By then we will be gone." Shaw reached for the cuffs that he had been wearing.

"Forget it," Winter said quickly. "We have to kill him."

"No!" McGill squealed. Spurred by desperation he pulled from Winter's grasp, leaped from the chair, and flung himself toward the door.

Despite his bulk, McGill could move quickly, but the captain was faster yet. She swung the pistol and fired, but the governor dropped to the floor, under the bolt. At the same time the door slammed open admitting the returning guards. Bolts of energy burned the air behind them as Shaw and Winter dove for the grav shaft. The energy was deflected by the field in a riot of bright sparks.

The prone bulk of the governor distracted the guards for an instant, and one of them remained behind to be certain that he was all right. The other bypassed the ruined controls and entered the grav beam, rising swiftly upward. Shaw and Winter were quite a way ahead of him, their foreshortened figures just visible in the blue glare of the beam.

The top of the shaft opened onto a secluded corridor off one of the landing areas. Winter stepped out, Shaw hard on her heels. After making sure they were safe, she turned back, her pistol ready for the guard.

Shaw moved in quickly and caught her arm. "No," he told her urgently. "We need him alive. You don't have to kill him; I can capture him."

Her eyebrows contracted in anger, but she gave way. Moving quickly behind a protrusion in the wall she crouched down, holding the pistol to cover the shaft.

Shaw waited out of sight, flattened against the wall just beyond the opening. When the guard reached the top of the shaft, he rushed out into an apparently empty area. Shaw slipped behind him and felled him with a blow.

Winter emerged from her shelter. "Now all we have to do is find the shuttle. Hurry."

Shaw felt for familiar thoughts and located them almost immediately. "It's not far. This way." He shouldered the unconscious guard and led the way.

As they rounded the corner, Winter was pleased to see her security team stationed around the perimeter of the landing area. The automated loading machine clanked on, heedless of the human activity around it, but all of the accesses to the area were covered and none of the station's personnel were visible. Behind the security team was the inviting opening to the tube which led to the *Venture*'s shuttle.

David stood nervously waiting in the opening. "Winter, you're hurt!" he exclaimed, starting forward at the sight of blood on her uniform.

"No," she said quickly, forestalling him. "This is T'Gal's blood."

David stopped in his tracks. "Where is she?" he asked.

"She's dead," Winter said with a great deal of anger in her voice. "Let's get the hell out of here!"

CHAPTER 14

"What did you learn from McGill?" Winter demanded of Shaw. They were on board the *Venture* and had just entered sick bay. The ship was in hyperspace, putting parsecs between herself and the AM Station.

On their return from the station, Winter had gone straight to the bridge, despite David's protests. The Proxima ship that McGill had been waiting for was located, still out of range of their weapons but approaching fast. After the fiasco at the station, Winter expected nothing but trouble. A hyperspace jump was swiftly calculated, the bridge crew in frenetic activity in response to the captain's terse orders.

Only then, when light-speed was attained and they were safe from pursuit, did Winter give in to the doctor's demands and turn the con back to Thomas. Still, as they descended to sick bay she made it clear that she wanted information from Shaw before she would answer David's questions.

"That's what you were doing in McGill's office, wasn't it?" she continued. "You took information from his mind."

"Yes. That was what I was doing," Shaw answered.

Winter looked as pleased as she could under the circumstances. "Then tell me, what's so special about those guards?"

"They are cyborgs."

"What?" the doctor exclaimed. "I've never heard of such a thing!"

"Neither have I," Winter added. "But that doesn't make it impossible. Who's doing this? And, more important, how are they doing it?"

"McGill did not know," Shaw told them. "All he knew is that their nervous systems have been altered, their brains adapted in some way so that they are able to accept programming."

"Who's responsible? Proxima?" Winter asked.

"Yes. Proxima. They are trying to refine the method so that they can have an army of these troops. The mining operation is just one of the places they have taken over as a training ground and a source of material."

"Human beings?" David asked, his voice filled with dread. "They're doing this to human beings?"

"It would appear so," Shaw assured him.

"But that's illegal!" the doctor protested. "Experimentation on human subjects has been outlawed. Where would they find the scientific personnel or even a laboratory to do such a thing?"

"On Proxima, apparently," Winter commented. "And that's why you insisted we capture the guard," she said to Shaw. She looked down at her hands and blood-stained uniform, but she kept her feelings to herself except for the dullness of her voice when she continued speaking. "Command has to know about this, but I'll have to clean up before I place the call. And then there's T'Gal . . ." She started for the door.

"Winter," David called. "Are you sure you weren't hurt?"

She paused and turned back, leaning against the doorjamb. "Yes, I'm all right. I'm bruised, dirty, and I have a splitting headache. That's all."

"The headache could mean something."

"Yes, David, it does," she retorted in a sudden show of spirit. "It means I'm tired. Just leave me alone and I promise I'll tell you when anything's wrong." She pulled herself away from the door and stuck her hands in her pockets. "Instead of worrying about me, I want you to examine our prisoner. Run him through your entire battery of tests. Take him apart if you have to. And let me know what you've found as soon as you have the results."

The doctor frowned at the departing figure. When the door closed behind her, he turned back to Shaw.

"She is angry and she wants to be by herself," Shaw told him.

David looked at Shaw's bare head. "If she finds out you've been reading her, she'll be even more angry."

Shaw shook his head. "I did not have to read her. Her feelings are so strong that she was practically sending. And after her behavior at the station, it wouldn't be difficult to guess what is going on in her mind even if I could not read."

"At the station?" David wandered over to his desk and sat down heavily in the chair. Shaw followed and perched on the corner of the desk. "What happened back there?"

"She killed a man, and I had to keep her from killing two others, including the governor."

David's eyes went wide with surprise. "Why?"

"She killed the first one to enable us to escape, but she would have killed the others in cold blood."

"That doesn't sound like her!"

"Nevertheless, it is true," Shaw assured him.

"Oh, I believe you. When she's angry she's capable of it, and she would have been furious over T'Gal's death."

"She blames herself for what happened. She did not listen when you warned her, and she allowed herself to be deceived."

David sighed wearily. "I've tried to talk to her," he said. "But it doesn't seem to make any difference." He shook his head.

Shaw watched him for a minute, a faint frown on his face. "David, are you in love with Winter?" he asked finally.

"Mind reading again?" the doctor said testily. "Sorry," he added in a different tone. "I shouldn't have said that." He ran his fingers through his hair and stared at the floor for a moment before answering. "Am I that obvious? I don't know; I'm not even sure what I feel most of the time. And a lot of good it would do me if I was in love with her. I don't think Winter believes in emotional entanglements." Abruptly he leaned forward and activated the comlink. "Security? This is Dr. Wilson. Bring the prisoner up to sick bay. I have to examine him."

When the voice at the other end assented, David switched off the unit. "Want to watch?" he asked Shaw. "This should be interesting."

The Proxima cyborg had not regained consciousness, but David took no chances and strapped him securely to the examination table. Two guards stationed themselves just inside of the door and watched as the doctor and a medtech slid the body into the diagnostics machine. Seating himself at the machine's console, David activated the unit. The tech took up her post at the computer and recorder and started them running.

"Apparently a normal healthy male," David commented as the unit made an initial scan, accessing basic body functions and muscle tone. "He's strong . . . very strong."

"Is it natural strength or has it been enhanced?" Shaw asked. He pulled over a chair and sat slightly behind David. Looking over his shoulder he tried to understand the information that paraded across the screen.

"I'd say it was natural," the doctor explained. "He's kept himself in excellent shape, and it doesn't seem that anything unusual has been done to him." David tapped keys and the unit began a deeper scan, reducing to micro to analyze tissue and chemical makeup. "I was wrong. Chemicals have been used . . . accelerated muscle development. The bone—it's a lot denser than normal." He watched the screen in silence for a couple of minutes. "I don't understand this," he said then.

"What?" Shaw inquired.

"The bones. The shape is normal—nothing's changed there. But the chemical analysis is way off. There are calcium salts . . . that's the way it should be." David shook his head in bewilderment. "I don't believe this. Platinum. What in hell is it doing there?"

Shaw was silent.

"It's in all of the compact bone tissue, but I can't imagine how it got there."

"Is it an intrinsic part or did the bones grow around it?"

"Grew around it," David supplied, his eyes fixed on the screen. He shook his head in amazement and then tapped out another command. "Let's go on. I've been saving the head for last. If the information you got from McGill is correct . . ."

Shaw sat perfectly still, watching the monitor.

An outline appeared on the screen with various parts delineated in color according to their composition and activity. But what amazed the doctor were the hundreds of brightly glowing pinpoints of light scattered throughout the head. David sat and stared in silence.

"What are those?" Shaw asked.

"I don't know," David said softly. "I've never seen anything like it. Jenna," he said to the technician. "Are you recording this?"

"I sure am," she returned, her attention on the equipment in front of her.

David tapped another command to the machine. "They're all in the right hemisphere. The left hemisphere's almost entirely depressed." He turned to look at Shaw. "Did the guard speak at all? Did you hear him? Was his voice sort of strange? Expressionless?"

"I did not hear this one but one of the others. His voice was as you have described it."

"The speech centers are affected then, probably in all of the cyborgs. Those little spots, like beads—they're organic." David checked another screen that showed chemical analysis. "Each one's slightly different. They're secreting synthetic hormones and they're all interconnected—they all react differently depending on where they are, but they feed back to each other." He zeroed in on one of the glowing spots. "This one's suppressing the left hemisphere. Amobarbital sodium— that would account for it. There's something else there as well."

Minutes passed as David alternately watched the screens and worked the keyboard. Finally he sat back in his chair and looked at Shaw. "I don't know how these implants could have been placed in the brain with such precision. It was a skillful job, but it doesn't make sense. If the Proxima intend to use these as ground troops, the cost would be prohibitive. They couldn't possibly have the resources or the time it would take to create the thousands of these cyborgs they'd need. And even if they did, the troops would be far too valuable to risk in combat."

"But McGill was certain. The Proxima are making an army of cyborgs. They are essential to the Empire's plan."

David shook his head. "I wonder what Command will make of it." He turned his attention back to the monitor. "The spots look dimmer." He punched more buttons. "They're fading."

As David made the announcement, a warning light began to blink. "The spots are dissolving, and they're releasing barbital! They're killing the brain!"

David left his chair in a rush. "Decadrin," he snapped at his aide. "Hurry. We have to get that stuff neutralized." The doctor was tugging the examination table out of the machine as the tech held out a hypo.

Shaw stood aside, watching the doctor's frantic efforts, but it was over within minutes.

"It's gone," David said finally. "It's no use. The brain's gone." His shoulders slumped in defeat.

"Doctor," the tech said. "Body functions are slowing."

"Stimulate," David said, returning to alertness. "Hook him up to life support." He turned swiftly back to the medical console, hoping to discover the reason for the sudden break-down. Only the screen showing chemical analysis was still active. The doctor and his aide worked, but as the minutes slipped by, the body functions lowered steadily out of the life ranges.

Winter was on the bridge when David called her. Once they were well out of reach of the mining station and the Proxima cruiser, Winter had ordered the *Venture* to a slower speed. The iridescence of hyperspace was gone, and the view screens showed only the stars and black of normal space.

With the ship secure, she could give David all of her attention. "Why did he die?" she asked.

"I don't know," he replied. "I can't even begin to guess until I do an autopsy. Then I have to run all of the pathology tests." He shrugged.

"Do it," Winter told him. "Prepare a comprehensive—" A blinking green light interrupted her, signaling that her call to Command was coming through. "Get back to me when you've finished," she told the doctor and switched off.

Winter took a deep breath and unconsciously straightened her shoulders as her fingers activated the receiver. "Captain Winter, FSS *Venture*," she announced.

"Captain," the figure on the screen nodded his acknowl-edgment.

She recognized Admiral Jammeson and was relieved to be dealing directly with him instead of having to go through his aide.

"I gather from your urgent call that something important has happened," the admiral said.

"Have you seen my report about the possibility of a Mal-vern-Proxima alliance?" she asked.

"Yes. I've read all of the reports you've sent since leaving the Malvern system."

"Then you know I was contacted by someone named McGill, governor of the Amalgamated Mining Station in the Ceti Three system."

"A curious situation," the admiral commented. "I hope you can explain it further."

"I can. I was down on the station less than five hours ago. Governor McGill had some information I thought you should have immediately. Proxima appears to be expanding its influence. They're using the mining station to recruit men for their ground forces."

"They're using mining personnel?" Jammeson looked displeased.

"Yes, sir. But that's not all of it. They're being fitted with some kind of implants that allow them to be controlled. Ultimately they become programmable cyborgs."

"Where did you get this information?" the admiral demanded.

"Part of it came from the governor. And we managed to capture one of the cyborgs."

"You have one of them?" he asked eagerly.

Winter shook her head. "Not anymore. Apparently there's some kind of a self-destruct incorporated with the control implants. The one we captured died before Dr. Wilson could finish his initial examination."

"Is there enough of him left for an autopsy?"

"The body is intact, but the implants are gone. I've ordered Dr. Wilson to perform the autopsy and prepare a pathology report."

"Before you send in that report, add your own assessment of the situation on the mining station. When Dr. Wilson's finished with the body, pack it in stasis. Our scientists here should probably take a look at it when the *Venture* returns to Alpha Base."

"Are you changing our orders then?" she asked.

"No," he assured her. "You're to proceed on course to Gyler. Your investigation there is even more important now that we know the Proxima are creating cyborgs." The admiral paused, looking briefly at someone who was speaking to him from beyond the pickup's range. He nodded once and then turned back to Winter. "Be sure to include your medical officer, Dr. Wilson, in the party when you tour the labs. He took part in the investigation there in '66, so he should know if something isn't as it should be. Do you have anything further to report, or any questions?"

"No, sir."

"Very well. We'll send someone to check the AM Station. And the Consortium will have to be notified, of course. Let me know if you learn anything more. Jammeson out." The screen went blank.

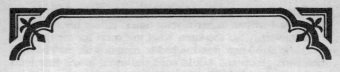

CHAPTER 15

Karth, 2452 TSC

Almost one year and three months after she said good-bye to Eric at Turning, Ilya came to the university at Havensport. She came with a group of other first-year students from the Seven Clans, and as a group, they were checked through the receiving station at the airport and loaded onto the university bus.

Ilya rode with her nose pressed to the glass, anxious for her first view of the city. At first there was not much; once they had passed though the warren of warehouses and the property used by the smaller, privately owned air services, there was a lot of open land. She could see an occasional building: some were tree-shaded dwellings, while others were factories of various sorts, with well-tended parks around them and signs set along the highway to identify the nature of the businesses.

Down the road she could see the taller structures of the city. As the bus drew nearer, the buildings were set more closely together, first a cluster of houses and an occasional apartment block, and then stores, shopping centers, and the first of the skyscrapers. There were fewer trees, although strips of green parkland were interspersed here and there. Ilya was excited by the newness and strangeness of it all.

Eric had written to her several times, telling her about life at the university, so she knew what to expect for the first two days. She also knew that she had to remain with her assigned orientation group and would not be allowed to see Eric until her free-time period. She tried to control her impatience.

The university consisted of a cluster of buildings of the pale gray stone quarried near the sea coast beyond Havensport. They were not nearly as tall as the skyscrapers, although a couple of them rose seven and eight stories high. They were scattered about five acres of beautifully landscaped grounds and the whole area was surrounded by a low wall, also constructed of gray stone. Tall galoba trees dotted the lawns, and there was a fountain in the court that opened up from the dormitory where she was assigned a room with three other freshmen.

After the first night's dinner in the school cafeteria, there was an orientation meeting in the assembly hall. Ilya and her roommates found the hall using the map in the small guidebook that they had found in their room. Everything was confusing at first, but Ilya had a naturally good sense of direction and knew that it would not be long before she was familiar with the campus. That night, she fell asleep on her bed amid a mess of papers and instructions.

The next day was taken up by the physical examination that was required of all freshmen. After that there was a tour of the university and welcoming speeches by various deans and instructors. Ilya enjoyed every minute of it, and instead of being daunted by the city, she felt exhilarated and strangely liberated. It was not that she disliked her life with the clan, but it was all she had known for seventeen years. The city was something new and different, and every minute she spent there was exciting.

The third day was Ilya's to do with as she pleased. That morning she took her map of the city and left the dorm early, before anyone else was awake. She signed out and walked from the campus into the streets, which were filled with people on their way to work. She ate breakfast at a small food stand, sitting at the counter with a group of people in worker's coveralls. The smells were new to her, and she ate ravenously. When she was finished, she resumed her walk, delighted with the opportunity for new experiences. It was as if there was energy flowing around her as she made her way to the escalator that led to a second-level pedestrian walk. But she was not completely without direction. She checked her map and sought out a certain building, where she let herself into the lobby with the key that Eric had sent her. A creaking elevator took her up seven floors.

Eric opened the apartment door, rubbing sleep out of his eyes. When he realized who was standing there, his jaw dropped with surprise.

"May I come in?" she asked, laughing at his expression.

"Ilya, is it really you?"

"Of course it is. You knew I'd be here today, didn't you?"

"Yes, but . . ." He took her into his arms. "Oh, it's so good to hold you again." He kissed her, and she clung to him, feeling silly with happiness.

"Don't ever leave me again," she whispered. "I've missed you so very much."

"And I you." He held her away from him. "Look at you. I haven't seen you for a year, and you're all grown up. What have you done to yourself?"

"Nothing! I missed you. It's been a very long year."

"It was for me, too, but you'll be proud of me."

"Why? What have you done?"

"Come in and sit down. I'll make some coffee and tell you all about it." He kissed her again before he released her.

Ilya dropped the bag filled with her belongings on the couch and looked around at the small room. The apartment, a student-housing unit, contained a small kitchen, a bathroom, and one large room that doubled as study, sitting room, and bedroom.

"Are we both going to live here?" Ilya asked.

"No. It's too small. I've already arranged for a bigger place on the next floor up," Eric called from the bathroom. "We can move in there tomorrow, after we get you registered." He emerged in clean clothes, just in time to keep the coffee from boiling.

"What is the wonderful thing you were going to tell me about?" Ilya asked, sitting beside him on the couch-bed.

"I've switched my major. I did it last year, but I didn't want to tell you about it then."

"Why not? What did you switch to?"

"I was afraid I wouldn't make it," he said. "I didn't have the prerequisites, and I had to work twice as hard to make up for it. But I succeeded. I passed the first year."

"That's wonderful, Eric."

"You'll like it even better when I tell you what my major is." He paused, then smiled. "Physical science."

"What!" She bounced in surprise, a wide grin on her face.

"I knew you'd be surprised," he said with understandable smugness. Passing with a double load in his freshman year was quite an achievement.

"But, Eric," Ilya protested. "I thought you were set on bio management. Why did you change?"

"I didn't think the Space Fleet would have too much use for a herdsman."

Ilya was not sure what to say. She leaned over and kissed Eric. "You did it for me," she whispered, awed by his devotion.

"I figured if you were set on going off into space, I'd have to go with you. I told you I'd think about it. This was my decision."

"I really didn't think you'd do it." Ilya was close to tears.

"Silly." Eric kissed her and took her cup away so that he could fold her in his arms. "I love you, Ilya. You are everything I want in life. I know that now more than ever. I will go with you wherever you go, until you're ready to come back to Karth. I'll never leave you again."

It was the night period aboard the *Venture* when Winter left the bridge. She was tired, but she went to David's cabin before her own.

The medical staff was housed on the same level as sick bay and the ship's laboratories. David, as the senior medical officer, was allocated two rooms that were spacious when compared to the living quarters on the older navy vessels. He had decorated them in warm earth tones, and the colors, along with the few personal objects he had brought with him, created a space that was a peaceful contrast to the stark efficiency of the work areas on the *Venture*.

Shaw was with the doctor when the captain was admitted, his body relaxed in a comfortable chair. Winter paused in the doorway when she saw him, but he rose politely to his feet and smiled somewhat sleepily at her.

"I didn't mean to interrupt you," she said, ready to abandon her need to see David.

"You are not interrupting," Shaw replied. "I have just been too lazy to get up. But it is late, and I should sleep."

Winter looked at the silver band he had resumed wearing.

"Thank you for wearing the wave shield again," she told him.

"David relayed your request to me."

"I wouldn't have asked, but my crew isn't used to the presence of a telepath. People with your talent are rare, and the others are uncomfortable when you're unshielded."

"If people have a difficult time living with their own thoughts, I can imagine how disquieting it would be if they imagined someone else might be aware of them. What no one will accept however, is that no esper would ever commit such a breach of privacy, and that it would be almost unbearable to be continually exposed to everyone's thoughts."

"I can accept that," Winter said. "But how do I convince my crew? I have to be careful of them, and I thought it would be best if you wore the shield."

"I do not question your right to ask it of me, and as you can see, I have obeyed." Shaw moved to the door. "Good night, Captain, David." He nodded and was gone.

"You don't like him, do you?" David commented.

Winter seated herself and stretched out her long legs before she answered. "I don't know him well enough to have formed an opinion." She smothered a yawn behind her hand. "You two seem to be on excellent terms, though."

"I like Shaw," David admitted. "Besides, I'm curious about him."

"Why?" she asked.

"I'd like to know who he really is and where he comes from."

"I'd have thought he would have told you by now," she said lazily.

"No." David got to his feet and went to a cabinet against the bulkhead. "Would you like a drink?" he asked, his hand poised in front of a row of bottles. "Or is this an official visit?"

"I'd very much like a brandy," she told him, stretching her arms back over her head until the joints cracked in protest. "What do you and Shaw find to talk about?"

David glanced up from the task of pouring the dark golden liquid into a glass. "We talk about many things. Shaw is surprisingly well educated."

"For a spy," she interjected.

"For anyone." The doctor handed Winter a glass. "Admit it. You're curious, too."

"About Shaw?" She shrugged and bent her head to sniff the

delicious fumes that rose within the crystal shell she held. "I'm curious about a lot of things. It's part of my job." She took a sip of the brandy; it lay heavy on the tongue and left a wonderful smoky aftertaste that was like a rich blend of fruit and fire.

"Is that how you see everything?" David seated himself across from her and sipped from his own glass.

"What do you mean?" she asked, sinking into a wonderful langor.

"You see things as a part of your job or not part of your job. And if they're not part of your job, you ignore them," David said, watching her closely as she relaxed. "Don't you find that limits your experiences?"

"I still don't understand what you're talking about."

He was silent for a moment. "Why did you come here tonight?" he asked finally.

"To talk," she said. "To unwind, I guess. I've been thinking about Gyler, and I'm worried. You're the ony one I could come to who has had any firsthand experience at the lab." She set her glass down beside her and shifted to a more comfortable position in the chair.

David was silent again, staring into his brandy glass, the smile gone from his face. He had been trying to shake her from her insular way of thinking, and instead she had managed to turn around and jar him.

"I know your experience there was unpleasant," Winter continued. "And if you'd rather not talk about it, I'll understand. But I think it's only fair to tell you that Admiral Jammeson has specifically requested that you accompany me down to the labs."

"I see. Thank you for warning me." David drained the brandy in his glass and got up to refill it. "It'll take me a while to get used to the idea," he commented, his back to her. "I thought I'd never set foot on Gyler again."

"I need you there, David. I have no idea what to expect. I don't really know what we're supposed to look for, and I need your help."

David closed the bottle and returned to his chair. "What can I do?"

"Tell me about the labs. Tell me anything you think will help me."

"Have you read what's in the library?"

"Yes. All of the statistics, dates." She picked up her glass again. "Why didn't they close the labs after the second time the work went bad?"

"Because the work being done there is too valuable to the Ruling Houses," David told her. "Not all of Gyler's work is controversial. Some of the things we take for granted—tissue regeneration, the benign virus that prevents organ transplants from being rejected, and a lot of less spectacular advances in medicine—have come from Gyler. If you want a testimonial, talk to any of the inhabitants of Saesar; they're indebted to the lab for the physical alterations that allow them to live on such a unique world."

"What you're saying is that despite the two slips that we're aware of, the work done at the lab is beneficial."

"In a sense, yes."

"Then why were there any slips at all? What caused these supposedly careful, caring individuals to create such monsters?"

David looked down at his drink. "I don't know. You realize that not everyone at the labs was responsible those times. There were only a few scientists involved. Maybe they just weren't able to resist all that power, the ability to create life forms in any shape that struck their fancy."

"They wanted to play God, " Winter stated, derision in her voice.

"Something like that."

She tried another tack. "What do you think the Federation suspects this time?"

"I can't imagine," David said. "My only knowledge of the recent work done at Gyler comes from the reports that they publish. And they haven't come up with anything new in the past four years or so."

"You have no idea what they might be working on now?"

David shook his head. "No. Weren't your orders more specific?"

"I was told to take a good look around and report anything suspicious. It's not much to go on, I'm afraid. But then, I don't think Command really knows what they're looking for."

"So they want me to go with you and give you the advantage of my professional eye?" David stared at the floor, seeing the pictures in his memory.

"They think you're the best person to decide if there's anything out of the ordinary." Winter yawned. "We'll be there tomorrow."

"Then I'll have just enough time to reread their last report. That way at least I'll know what they're supposed to be doing." David watched the captain, her body stretched out and limp in the chair. "Why don't you get some sleep. You look beat."

She grinned at him, but did not move.

"Is there something else bothering you?" David wanted to know.

"Yes there is. You."

"Me?" he responded, incredulous.

"Something you said to me," she explained. "About how much you think I've changed." She took a minute to sip her drink. "I've thought about it. I can't figure out what would have made you say it."

"If you can't see it, then you're in more trouble than I suspected," David said firmly.

Winter pulled herself upright. "David, how can you say these things to me? I thought we were friends."

"We are friends. That's why I say them. And believe me, I'm concerned."

"All right then, what are these changes, these differences that you see in me?"

"Maybe it would be better if I didn't tell you."

"You can't leave me wondering like this," she protested. "You have to tell me, now that you've started."

David concentrated on his drink, stalling for time. "I think you're losing some important part of yourself. Or you might be deliberately destroying it."

"What part?" she asked.

He searched his mind for the right word. "You could call it empathy."

"Empathy?"

"Empathy, sympathy . . . something like that. It's the ability to feel for other people. I don't know if this is something you're doing to yourself or if it's something that is being done to you." He stared into his glass for a moment before he met her eyes again. "I think the Service is responsible."

"The Service?"

"Yes, your beloved job."

Winter sighed. "David, do you have any idea what it takes to run a starship? I'm responsible for all of the lives on board, not to mention a lot of expensive hardware. In addition, I have to see that our missions are completed successfully. I juggle lives, responsibilities, ship, mission. And I think I'm doing a damn good job. What else can you expect from me?"

"I do know how difficult it is, but that's not what I'm talking about. It is possible to be a successful starship captain and still be able to feel for the other people around you."

Winter set her jaw. "Well, you're wrong. It isn't possible to have personal feelings in my position. They only get in the way, and that can be dangerous. And, if you haven't noticed, David, we're at war. Where would we be if I stopped to empathize every time this ship was attacked?"

"Winter—" he began, but she interrupted him.

"I have to make decisions and choices all the time. And still people are going to die, no matter what I do—or how much I care. That's what war means—fighting, killing, dying."

"And anger?" he added.

"Yes, anger, too."

"That's what you're feeling right now, isn't it?" he pointed out. "You're angry because you know what I've been telling you is the truth."

Winter laughed bitterly. "I thought you were accusing me of not having feelings. Anger is a feeling."

There was an edge to her voice, and David knew it was time to stop pushing her. He got to his feet and went to refill their glasses. "You came here tonight because it really bothered you when I accused you of being different."

"I've been dreaming of Karth," she said softly. "I've been dreaming a lot lately. I don't know if I can stand it if these dreams continue."

David gave her the refilled glass. "From what you've told me about your home world, I would have thought they would be good dreams," he said reseating himself.

"Oh, they are. They're dreams of being home, safe with my family. But they make me remember, and I don't want to remember."

"Why don't you want to remember Karth?"

"Because that part of my life is over," she said firmly. "I can't go back, and it's a waste of time to think about it."

"For someone who says she doesn't want to think about Karth, you've certainly collected quite a file on the planet."

She frowned at him, not sure how he would know that.

"You flagged the computer," he explained. "I noticed it when I was doing some research a couple of months ago."

"I have my reasons," she told him. "For your information, it has nothing to do with wanting to go home."

"All right. What are your reasons then?"

She shook her head. "I can't tell you." She got to her feet and stretched. "I think I'd better go to my cabin before I fall asleep in your chair."

"Winter, you can't go on like this," he protested.

"Can't I?" She smiled grimly and went to the door. "Once again you're wrong, David. Those dreams I've been having? I think I know what they mean; they're a way of saying goodbye to the past and to the person I was then. Right now I have a job to do, and, yes, I know you object when I talk about it like this, but my job is all that I have left anymore. I chose this life," she said with quiet emphasis. "And I want it. And if doing my job means that I have to give up the ability to empathize, well then, so be it."

David sat very still after Winter had gone, deeply troubled by the things she had said. He could not fault her performance as a Federation officer. She might be a little impetuous at times, but she was also efficient and effective. He also had to admit that her new objectivity could only enhance the performance of her duty. But unswerving obedience to the necessities of being a Federation starcaptain was killing the gentle woman she once had been. And he knew that woman still existed somewhere inside of the captain, and that her continued existence troubled Winter very much indeed.

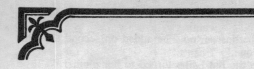

CHAPTER 16

Karth 2453 TSC

During the first summer that Ilya spent at the university, she and Eric returned to the clans for a brief visit and to attend the meeting during the Turning Festival. There they announced their engagement. The ritual was little more than a formal statement of their intent to live together and an excellent excuse for their friends to have a party, although no one ever really needed a reason to celebrate during the Festival.

Alisia was very pleased with her new son-in-law, and Hanna gave way to sentiment, crying as she hugged her foster daughter. Ilya saw her later in a corner with some of her cronies and a pitcher of ale, regaling them with secondhand tales from the city.

Ilya and Eric could only stay for one day since it was in the middle of a semester. They slept in the Winter tent and rose early. Alisia was up to wish them farewell. Maxim joined her, still rubbing sleep from his eyes and yawning.

"You won't forget about the models, will you?" he asked his sister. He had developed an interest in the Space Force and was making a collection of ships.

"I won't," she promised. "I think I know exactly where to go to find them."

"Send me a battlestar, too," he added on second thought. "If you can find one."

"I'll add it to the list." She turned to her mother. "I'll be back for the winter meeting," she said. "I love you."

Alisia hugged her. "I love you, too. Study hard."

"I will."

They started walking toward the aircar. The pilot had untied it and was stowing the cables in the luggage compartment.

"When do you get to go into space?" Maxim asked, tagging along behind them.

"Not for a couple of more months. Why don't you ask Eric about it. He's been on two training flights."

"I did. He just laughed at me and said I'd have to wait and find out all about it for myself."

"You asked me at the worst possible time," Eric told him. "You should have waited until the meeting was over."

"I did, but you went off with the other guys," Maxim complained.

"Well, next time I come, I'll give you a complete report."

"You promise?"

"Yes."

"All right!" Maxim exclaimed, delighted.

Last minute good-byes were made, and then Ilya and Eric climbed into the car. Alisia put her arm around her son as they watched the small flyer become a speck in the sky. Neither of them imagined that they would never see Ilya or Eric again.

At the end of that summer, Ilya applied to Space Fleet Academy and was accepted for the provisional year of training. If she passed that year, she would be sent to Earth to attend the academy there. In the meantime, she and Eric would continue their studies in Havensport.

On Earth, the Federation of the Ruling Houses agreed to the selection of a special task force to resolve the Mining Consortium's problems on Karth. It was decided that the minerals there were too important, especially since the colonies had launched their own space fleets, declaring independence from Earth.

The minerals on Karth represented only some of the materials that would be needed to combat the rebellion, but they were important nonetheless. One of the minerals found on the planet in large quantity was a rare silicate crystalline form noted for its unusual resonance and used in the construction of the A-type shield. In space, that shield could withstand both light and heat, making it especially effective against laser attack. The second important mineral was the foundation of the fuel for the Dillinger FTL drive. Thus the contribution of the mines on Karth was considered vital to the Federation.

One month after the Ruling Houses had appointed the task force, Captain Carlson of the Federation cruiser *Allyster* received orders to provide emergency transport for a special team of Federation marines. He did not think anything strange about the commands, for the *Allyster* was especially built for speed and such missions were not unusual.

Captain Carlson brought his ship straight into the orbital station above Earth, where it was immediately boarded by ten silent, hard-faced men. There was something unsettling about the men, something closed, secret, and potentially dangerous. There was no communication between passengers and crew during the voyage. Their destination was the Stockton Shipyards, but they made one brief stop at the Gyler Laboratories first. There three of the passengers took a shuttle down to the surface and returned with a large number of heavy, sealed canisters. The canisters were locked in a storage compartment for the rest of the journey, and there were always two of the men standing guard outside of the door.

When the *Allyster* reached the Stockton Yards, the passengers disembarked. Carlson never saw them again. He was not told what their mission was and he never asked.

Toward mid-winter Ilya was assigned to a two-month training cruise with nineteen other cadets. It would be her longest trip yet, and she was excited about it. Eric, who had missed one of his finals and had to stay behind to make it up, accompanied her to the port and kissed her good-bye before hurrying back to school.

They had only been in space five weeks when the cadets were ordered to stop whatever they were doing and assemble in the ship's lounge. Captain Maltin himself was there, standing against a bulkhead, his face set in hard lines as he waited for the cadets to enter and take their places. When the young people arrived, they stood at attention in front of the chairs that were arranged in neat rows facing the captain. Other than the footsteps of latecomers and the faint rustle of uniforms there was total silence.

Ilya realized that something unusual had happened, but she had no idea what it might be. She surreptitiously tugged at the tunic of her light blue uniform, hoping that it was not too noticeably creased. The captain and the other instructors were very strict about presenting a proper military appearance at all times. After running around the plains wearing torn pants covered in cassia and horsehair, she was finding the uniform code difficult. Still, she was getting better at it; her hair was neatly confined in one long braid down her back, and she was cleaner than she had ever been on Karth, except immediately after a bath.

Ilya was finding the captain's glare hard to endure, and judging from the nervous shifting of bodies around her, so were her classmates.

The last people were coming into the lounge, including all of the instructors and a number of other crew members, all of them looking grim. They took up positions throughout the room where they could observe the cadets.

"You may sit down," the captain said suddenly.

There was a shuffle as the cadets took their seats.

"You are no doubt wondering why I have called this meeting," Maltin said, his voice as harsh as his stare. "There has been a disaster on Karth."

The silence was total as he told of the events as he knew them. But even his awful words did not begin to describe the horror that had visited the cadets' homeworld.

First the cassia had begun to die. The disease was unlike any the herdsmen knew, and there was nothing to indicate which animal would be struck down next. One minute the cassia would be feeding and the next they were dead. Other creatures were affected, as well: drifters, the ponies, birds, fish, and insects. Even plants were not immune. Leaves withered and fell from branches; the grass shriveled and was blown away.

Then the people began to die. At first it was only the sick, the elderly, and the small children. But no one, it seemed, was immune, for not even the strongest survived. Soon there were more bodies then there were people to bury them.

The clans sent to Havensport for assistance, but the plague had reached the city, too. Scientists searched frantically for answers, but it seemed that nothing they tried was effective.

The panicked leaders contacted the Federation, asking for help, but the ships that responded could not land. Karth had been placed under quarantine, and no one was allowed on or off the planet.

In less than two weeks every living thing on Karth was dead.

No one said anything for a second after the captain's voice ceased. Then the cadets reacted. Some of them were quiet, still numb with shock. Others raged, weeping or shouting their disbelief. The instructors and the ship's medical staff moved among the cadets offering comfort and sedatives as needed.

Ilya responded to the news with silence. At first she did not believe what she was told; the words had no meaning to her. Alisia, Hanna, Maxim—all gone? It could not be. And Eric. Her mind refused to face the truth of it, that Eric, too, was dead. She had seen him only five weeks before; he had been alive and well then! It could not be true!

Ilya was sitting stiff and still in her chair, her eyes staring sightlessly at the front of the room. All around her people were expressing their grief, but she could not move. One thought repeated itself over and over in her mind. "Dead. They're all dead."

She got to her feet and walked stiffly to her cabin. She ignored an offer of help from one of the medtechs and did not even notice that he followed her back to her cabin. Without removing even her boots, she crawled into her bunk and lay down. She stayed there for three days without speaking to anyone.

Captain Maltin and the staff of the training ship did the best they could to ease the cadets' shock. After a period of mourning, those who were able were encouraged to resume their work. The rest were treated with consideration and kept out of the way. In the meantime, the ship was enroute at fastest possible speed to Alpha Base Three, which was the nearest Federation post.

When the training ship docked, Ilya disembarked with the other cadets. They were immediately admitted to the base hospital and given thorough checkups. Each cadet was assigned to a counselor, and when it was judged that the survivors of Karth were able to cope with their personal loss, they were given a choice. If they wished, they would be given transport to any other colony in the Federation, or they could go to Earth to continue their training in the Space Fleet Academy.

Ilya buried her feelings as deeply as she could, trying to insulate herself against the pain. She succeeded well enough to be one of the first cadets released from the hospital. Before she would make a decision about her future, she visited the base library. She requested access to a computer and checked all of the newscasts about Karth. She read of the plague, the quarantine, and the destruction of all life on her homeworld. It was real, she finally admitted. Everything she had ever known—her life, her family—was all gone.

Ilya sat lost in thought, in the artificial light of the space station that contained Alpha Base. She knew that her decision would dictate her future. If she went to a colony world, she might be able to re-create a life similar to the one she had lost; there would be other people to love, animals to herd, and even vast open spaces to live in, but the one thing that had made life in the clans so special could never be re-created. No, that part of her life was over, finished, and instead of looking for a substitute, she knew it would be better to go on with something new.

Ilya walked to the broad observation deck at the top of the station, were she looked out at the stars and said a mental good-bye to the young girl who had roamed the plains on a spotted pony. Tears came to her eyes and ran down her face, but no sound came from her. Silently she wept, gripping the railing in front of the port with white-knuckled hands, standing stiffly, facing the stars. Time passed and the tears ceased, but still she stood there.

She had just come to a momentous conclusion, and with it she made another decision. Ilya was the name of a young girl who belonged on Karth. The person she must become needed a new name, and she decided that it would be Winter, the name of her clan. It would be a symbol of her new life.

When she finally descended to the administration office to tell them of her decision, she was another person. It was Winter who went to the Space Service Academy on Earth.

Winter and three other cadets left the space station on board a heavy cruiser called the *Denmark*. On the ship she continued her research into the disaster on Karth. She kept to herself and spoke to no one unless it was necessary. But one of the people she did talk to was the captain of the cruiser, William Jammeson. He had been curious about her heavy computer use and called her into his office to explain. After he was satisfied, he drew her into conversation. In the course of their talk, Winter questioned him about the Service, about the ship, and about the missions he had flown, wanting anything to keep her mind busy. She did not sleep without nightmares, but all the while, inside of her the determination and will that would make her a starcaptain was beginning to emerge.

Captain Jammeson was at first only mildly curious about his young passenger, and later he was impressed with her knowledge and intensity. After they reached Earth and he had delivered his passenger to the academy, he went on leave. When he returned to D.C. Central to resume his command a month later, he stopped into the academy offices to inquire after her. While he was there, he signed his name to a form recommending her as a candidate for officer's training.

Winter completed the courses at Space Fleet Academy in five years. She graduated with honors and was assigned to her first ship, the FSS *Seeker*, an exploration and science vessel. There she served as second navigator with the rank of ensign. She worked well and was respected, but she was too reserved to be liked.

Ten years passed while Winter worked her way up in the Service and was given her first post as a captain. Two years later she was assigned to the FSS *Venture*.

Representatives from the Mining Consortium's task force returned to Karth five years after the plague and found a barren world with sparse, sickly plantlife and a greatly diminished atmosphere.

Probes were sent to the surface. Analysis of the signals that came back indicated that there were no lifeforms on the planet. A manned shuttle went to the surface. Everyone on board was dead within five hours. More probes were sent. They recorded the existence of a virulent submicroscopic organism. Unless a vaccine could be found, the minerals on Karth were inaccessible to human miners. Remotes and robots could be brought in to do the job, but additional time would be required to work out the logistics of such a complicated operation, and costs would be greater. It would be years before Karth could be made productive, and the Mining Consortium's representatives had to admit that they were defeated by the planet once again.

CHAPTER 17

The planet Gyler glittered like silver in the 61 Cygni suns, the light reflecting back from the enormous metal and window-steel construction that contained the laboratory complex. The pressure domes covered almost two-thirds of the small planet's surface. As well as the labs themselves, there was space for housing, shops, maintenance . . . everything that people in such an isolated outpost would need to keep themselves alive, healthy, and happy.

On the viewscreen above Winter's head, Gyler seemed to roll beneath the *Venture* as the ship moved into orbit. The captain made a last-minute check of the bridge before relinquishing the con. Thomas, who would be in command of the ship while she was gone, stood at the door, waiting for her to go to the briefing room. According to her chronometer, the landing party should be assembled by now. Winter straightened up and adjusted the tunic of her dress uniform, pressing the high collar closed, before stepping out into the corridor, the engineer at her heels.

"Captain Winter," Shaw's quiet voice called to her.

She stopped and turned to him as he came away from the wall where he had been waiting.

"May I speak with you for a moment?" he asked.

"Can it wait? I'm on my way to a briefing." Still, she was curious; Shaw had never before actively sought her out. "Thomas," she said to the curious engineer. "Go on ahead. I'll be there in a minute."

"I will not take much of your time," he assured her as Thomas left them alone in the corridor.

"What is it?"

"I would like to accompany your party down to the laboratory."

"Gyler is a closed facility," she pointed out. "Visitors aren't permitted."

"I know that. The only way I could hope to gain entrance would be as one of your party."

"Do you know why we're going there?" she asked.

"To deliver the Malvern containers."

"That's only part of it. We also have official business to attend to."

"Do you suspect there may be something wrong at the lab?" Shaw asked.

Winter looked suspiciously at her passenger. "There's always the possibility. Do you know anything about the current situation at Gyler?" She was not sure why he would want to go down to the labs. The possibility that he might have business there entered her mind. There would be a wealth of valuable information for a spy at the Gyler Laboratories.

"Not really, but if something is wrong, I may be able to be of assistance."

"Are you asking to come because you want to help, or do you have a reason of your own?" she asked bluntly.

"I have my own reasons," he admitted. "However, in exchange for your cooperation, I will expend my efforts on your behalf."

"Why do you want to go?" she insisted.

"I was in one of the containers consigned to this lab," he explained. "I do not know the reasons for this, and I must solve the mystery. I believe that my continued survival may depend on it."

She realized that if she were in the same position, she would feel the same way. "How do you think you could help me?" she asked, wondering how convincing his answer would be.

Shaw touched the wave shield with his finger tips. "Without this I will be able to read for you."

Winter weighed the possible problems of allowing a civilian to assist in an official mission against the advantage they would have with Shaw's unique talent. It might be a great advantage, depending on what they found down on the planet. Still she hesitated.

"What harm would it do?" Shaw persisted. He seemed relaxed as he stood, but the pupils of his eyes were dilated with excitement and there was a certain tension about his mouth.

"All right," she told him, following her instinct and making a snap decision. "But you'll have to obey my orders just like everyone else. I'm briefing the others now. Please attend." She walked past him and into the briefing room.

The assembled officers rose as she entered. She took her place at the head of the long table and motioned them to be seated also.

"Our presence at Gyler has been cleared through the lab's security," she began. "We'll take the big shuttle down to the landing pad where ground crews will offload the Malvern containers. Lt. Commander Baker, you and Ensign Creig will assist if necessary, but at least one of you is to remain with the shuttle at all times. Do you have any questions?"

"No, sir," Baker responded. He and the ensign were trained in security and would provide defensive manpower should it become necessary.

"Good." Winter looked at David. "Dr. Wilson, you will remain with me. The lab director, Dr. Swanson, has offered to conduct us on a tour of the facility. Shaw will accompany us as an observer."

She glanced around the table. Everyone was looking at Shaw.

"Are there any questions about this?" she asked.

Thomas spoke up. "How long will you be down there?"

"Four hours," Winter told him. "I'll check in with you in about two hours. By then I should have a better idea of what's involved. We're feeling our way here," she explained to the assembly. "We're looking for anything that might be out of order. I want everyone to stay alert. Baker, Creig—you especially. In the meantime, Commander Thomas will keep the ship on standby. I want constant scans, not only of the planet, but of space, as well. Command isn't sure, but they suspect that something's not right." She paused. "If there are no more questions . . ."

"I have one," David said.

"Yes?"

"What do we do when they discover that the Malvern containers are empty?"

"We don't know anything about it. We were instructed to deliver the containers, and we have done so. That's all."

"In other words, we lie."

Winter looked him right in the eye. "Yes, we lie. Are there any other questions?" She looked at each of the people around the table. "That's it then. Assemble at the landing bay in fifteen minutes. David, find something for Shaw to wear, but make sure it's not a uniform."

David was dismayed by the welcoming committee that met the landing party in the reception area of the lab. Dr. Swanson, the director, was there with all of his staff and, it seemed, all of the other scientists presently working at the lab. David quickly lost count of the names. He felt as if he had been introduced to everyone at least twice.

He looked around for Winter and saw her standing, a cup of coffee in her hand, her head inclined in polite attention as she listened to something that the director was telling her. The director looked vaguely annoyed by the invasion of the *Venture*'s personnel, but at least he had seen that an effort was made to be hospitable to the Federation's representatives.

"Or is all of this a decoy? An elaborate ruse designed to lure us into false complacency?" a soft voice whispered. David recognized Shaw.

"Did you learn anything?"

"I have. We are—"

"Dr. Wilson?" a voice interrupted loudly. "David, is that you?" A tall fair-haired man took the doctor by the arm. "I thought I recognized you! Do you remember me?"

"Of course I do. Jon Avery," David said, surprise in his voice. "But I can't believe it. You came here with me when we were assigned to inspect the labs . . . when was it? Seven years ago?" He shook the outstretched hand and was treated to a friendly clap on the shoulder.

Shaw turned unobtrusively away, pretending to be interested in the conversation of a group of scientists standing next to him, but he remained close enough to listen to what was said between David and Avery.

"Yes, I'm still here. Amazing, isn't it? But there was some work that attracted my attention and I was lucky enough to get hired on. What about you? Still in the Service, I see."

"It's my career."

"Why have you come to Gyler?" Avery asked casually. "This isn't another Federation bust, is it?"

Shaw glanced back at David. Avery's thoughts were not clear, but the telepath read treachery behind the smiling face. Did David suspect anything? Shaw moved closer.

"No," David replied. "We're here to drop off some containers at the request of the Matriarch of Malvern. Since we were here, the captain decided to see the lab." He changed the subject, anxious to get off the subject of the Malvern containers. "What have you been doing?"

"Same old stuff—biochemical synthesis. Let's get out of this zoo and I'll show you my lab. I've come up with some interesting ideas lately, and you're probably one of the few people who would appreciate them."

"I'd like that," David said. "I should clear it with the captain first."

"Oh, don't bother, " Avery told David, taking him by the arm. "Unless I'm mistaken, Swanson's off on one of his lectures about the glorious work we're doing for mankind. Your captain won't be able to get away from him for at least an hour. By then we'll be back, and she'll never know you've been gone."

"Well . . ." David was torn between leaving Winter and his curiosity to see the work. Still, the whole purpose of coming to the labs was to look around for anything unusual. Avery's offer might be the only chance that he would have to take a look behind the scenes.

"It's not far," Avery urged. "We've got a priority project for a private client going on. It's pretty special. Just about everyone in the lab's involved. I really think you'll be interested."

"Priority?" David abandoned his coffee cup on a convenient table as they started walking.

"Dr. Wilson?" Shaw said, coming up behind them.

"Oh! I'd wondered where you'd gone," David said, startled. "Jon, I'd like you to meet a friend, well, a colleague of mine from the *Venture*. Dr. Jon Avery, this is, ah, Dr. Shaw."

"Dr. Shaw." Avery beamed and shook his hand. "What's your specialty?"

"Actually, he's——" David began.

"Psychology," Shaw said quickly. "I am studying the abnormalities induced by space stress. I am especially interested in motivation."

"Is that your work aboard the *Venture*?" Avery asked, curiously.

"I'm little more than an observer this trip," Shaw supplied. "I'm just collecting information now. The collation and conclusions will come later."

All three of them were moving out of the reception area and into the corridor as they spoke.

"Interesting," Avery commented. "Perhaps I'll read the results of your work someday. I often find useful information in areas other than my own." He waved a hand at the closed doors they were passing as they moved through the hall. "These are just offices, nothing to see. The labs are down here."

He operated a handlock and opened a door, standing aside for David and Shaw to enter another hallway before him. There were very few people in that part of the lab, and those who were there all seemed intent on their own errands. No one displayed any interest in the visitors.

"Can you give me some kind of an idea about the work you're doing?" David asked.

"There's no way to put it simply. In essence we've developed a microminiature bioelectric generator. It's sequence coded and injected into the body. We've made it hemosympathetic, so it travels through the bloodstream to a specific area and then grows to its full size in a specified area of the nervous system."

"A generator?" David asked.

"That's what we call it," Avery explained with a depreciating smile. "It's more like a computer, really. It can be programmed, but like a generator, it gives off electrical impulses."

David suddenly realized that what Avery was describing sounded like the beads that controlled the cyborgs. The implications of Jon's words frightened him, and he wondered why he was being told so much. He looked at Shaw, but his friend was silent, his face expressionless as he gazed around him.

"What is this generator supposed to do?" David asked gingerly, half afraid of what he might hear next. "What is the purpose of the programming?"

"It's a way of compensating for any problem area in a natural system," Avery told him. "Take the case of a paraplegic, for example. One or more of these generators would be programmed to replace damaged nerve parts. They grow a metallo-organic pseudodendrite and function exactly as the damaged part would have." Avery stopped walking. They were standing in front of two doors, one on either side of the corridor.

"It would have to be an incredibly small generator," David commented.

"That's why they are grown in place. It saves the physician from having to perform a difficult and potentially risky operation. And the best part is that the generator has a genetic code to preselect the area where it will grow and eventually function."

"What's behind this door?" Shaw asked, cutting off David's next question.

"Here?" Dr. Avery turned to him, distracted for a moment. "Why, nothing. Storage, mostly. The work that you'll be interested in is done in the lab up ahead." He pointed. "If you'll excuse me a moment, I'll call security and warn them we're coming. There's no problem with visitors in the lab, but the guards like to know."

"Of course," David responded. "We'll wait."

But Avery did not have a chance to go anywhere. Shaw looked quickly up and down the corridor; no one was in sight. He seemed to flow as he stepped swiftly behind Avery and hit him with a short, chopping blow where the neck joined his shoulder. Shaw caught the doctor's body as it fell.

"Shaw! What in—" David exclaimed.

"Quiet," Shaw grated. "Get that door open." He nodded across the hall. "Hurry up before someone comes."

David did as he was told and followed Shaw as the telepath dragged Avery's body into the empty office. "What's going on? What are you doing?" he asked, confused and more than a little apprehensive.

"This is a trap," Shaw explained in a whisper.

"A what? What are you talking about?" David asked, more bewildered than ever.

"This is what I was about to tell you back at the reception area when Avery appeared."

"Do you mean Jon Avery is part of a plot against us?"

"Avery and most of the others here are involved. He was about to tell his accomplices that we were on our way and to order your capture."

David knelt and felt for his old friend's pulse. The heart was beating steadily. "That's why he told us all about the work he was doing, about the generators," he said softly. "I'll bet anything that what he described are the cybernetics' devices. Were you able to learn anything more about what's going on here?"

"Just impressions of treachery aimed at you and the captain," Shaw said. "Getting you here alone was part of it."

"Damn," David breathed. "Avery was such a good researcher."

"He may still be," Shaw suggested. "It is the focus, not the work itself, that has been perverted."

"How could this have happened? He was as furious as I was when he found out what was going on here back in '66. How could he have sold out, corrupted his own work?"

"It can happen to anyone if there is sufficient incentive." Shaw cracked the door open and peered into the hallway. "You will have to go back to the reception area and warn Captain Winter."

"Me? What are you going to do?" David asked quickly.

"There's something of great importance behind the closed door across the hall. I have to find out what it is before I rejoin you and the captain. Stay close to her, and be very careful," he warned.

"I think I should stay with you."

"No, you should not," Shaw began, but the doctor met his eyes calmly, his mouth set in a stubborn line. Rather than waste time arguing, Shaw gave in. "All right. Perhaps the captain will be safe for a little while longer. Come, but be very quiet."

The door that Avery had said led to storage was locked, but Shaw was adept at getting into secured places. He worked swiftly at the mechanism, and in seconds the door swung inward. The two men slipped inside and found themselves in a room lit only by the glow of the stasis units that filled the space, row upon row. David moved wonderingly forward, peering through the transparent fields at the figures preserved there. According to the instruments on each unit, some were dead and some were alive.

"What is this?" he whispered. "Shaw?" David looked up when there was no answer. He saw his friend standing by one of the units by the far wall. "Shaw?" he repeated. "What's wrong?"

Shaw's face was a ghastly white and devoid of all expression. He stood still and held himself so rigidly that he seemed not even to breathe. David lightly touched his arm, and Shaw flinched.

"Shaw?" the doctor said again. And then he looked into the container to see what had shocked his friend.

It was the body of a young woman. At first David thought he was seeing another one of the lab's attempts to redesign the humans into more exotic forms, but closer examination made him realize that this figure was something much more than that. She was of an alien species not yet encountered by man.

The alien looked as if she were made of silver. Her skin, stretched over long, fine bones, was covered with a fine, downy hair that had a luster that reflected back the blue light of stasis. Her hands and feet were long and fragile looking, but David knew that such a look could sometimes be an effective disguise for more than adequate strength.

She was definitely humanoid; the skeleton sketched beneath the skin upheld that, and the swell of small breasts with a darker nipple proclaimed a mammalian type. But the wings were difficult to understand.

As David looked at the web-thin skin relaxed around the figure, he tried to imagine what it would look like when she was awake. She would stand about two meters tall. Her head was topped with long, straight, black hair that was arranged around her shoulders. Whoever had put her into the stasis unit had been very careful to place her precisely, as if she was a prized specimen. And she probably was. The body lay in the blue light of the field like a priceless sculpture of precious metal. David could not help but glance up at the monitor to assure himself that she was really alive.

"This is amazing," David said, his voice hushed. "I wonder what she is."

Shaw stirred at his side, and David saw his friend's eyes shining strangely in a rock hard face as the man fought to control his emotions.

"I can not tell you what she is doing here," Shaw said, his

voice hoarse. "But the implications of her presence are more important than anything else in this lab."

"Why do you say that?" David asked. "Do you know what she is?"

Shaw nodded. "Yes, I know," he whispered. "She is an Al'laan."

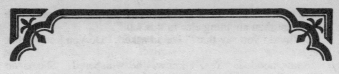

CHAPTER 18

In the year 2348 TSC a lone scout ship, the FSS *Ranger*, was exploring a nonmagnetic anomaly in a distant part of the galaxy. Such phenomena were rare, and Federation scientists would be glad of any information the *Ranger* could bring them, but in their eagerness to obtain the data, a safety factor was overlooked and the small ship was caught in an ion surge.

The result was disaster. The damage included the inversion and complete shutdown of the propulsion system, a breached hull, loss of precious oxygen, and the death of seven crew members. Even if the engines could be reactivated, there was little hope that anyone on the ship would live to see their home again. The *Ranger* was crippled, drifting far from charted space and beyond the reach of subspace radio.

That was when a miracle occurred . . . or so it seemed to the remainder of the *Ranger*'s crew. Just when they had abandoned hope, they were rescued. Their saviors arrived in a large disk-shaped ship and identified themselves as the Al'laan.

Since humans first left Earth to explore the stars, they had encountered only one other spacefaring race. The discovery of a second alien nation was a historic event. The crew of the

Ranger was overjoyed at their rescue and excited by the meeting. The Al'laan, however, were not pleased.

Despite the efforts of the *Ranger*'s captain, the Al'laan commander refused visual contact, even though, after the computer had managed to translate the language, there was almost continuous communication between the two ships. The *Ranger*'s crew were never certain if it was the actual Al'laan or robots who performed the various tasks as the repairs were made. The workers were concealed within unusual, almost globular environment suits whose faceplates or viewports, if there were any, were opaque.

When the *Ranger*'s hull was finally patched and her engines reactivated, the Al'laan prepared to depart. Their commander did consent to take word of the Federation and humankind back to his government. If the leaders were agreeable, then a communication could be opened between the two nations.

The *Ranger* limped back to Federation space with her news, but almost a full Terran year passed before word came from their new neighbors in space. The Al'laan government had been divided over the question of initiating relations with the Federation. The more conservative voices had prevailed, and when contact was reestablished, it was to be continued only as long as certain strict rules were met. Chief among them was that the location of the Al'laan homeworld would remain unknown, and that there would be no contact between the two nations except by subspace radio, which was to be relayed through an unmanned satellite provided by the Al'laan.

The Al'laan proposed that after a better understanding of each other had been reached, it might be possible to ease the restrictions. Until that time, any violation of the requirements would result in immediate termination of positive relations between humankind and the Al'laan.

There was curiosity on Earth, of course, and curiosity bred speculation. Arguments went back and forth for months before the members of the Ruling Houses finally agreed that it would be to Earth's advantage to accept the Al'laan's terms. It was hoped that the advantages would outweigh any problems caused by the limited terms.

There was also apprehension among the Houses, as well as among the populace. That apprehension was not so much voiced as felt. It grew from a kind of xenophobia and bred a faction in the government that advocated forcing the Al'laan to agree to their demands. It was only with difficulty that the few warlike voices were silenced. No one wanted to find out how the Al'laan would enforce their conditions. Their strength and weapon capabilities were unknown and, because unknown, feared.

No one knew anything about the Al'laan except that they were somewhere out there and that they possessed the capability of space flight. No one knew what they looked like, what kinds of weapons they had, or whether or not they would go to war against the Federation. With so many unknowns, no one wanted to be the one to create the incident that would allow those questions to be answered.

A short time after the Al'laan's requirements had been accepted, an unmanned station began broadcasting, and communications between Al'laan and humankind were begun. At first every word was followed with excitement. They were reproduced in the news and expounded upon in tri-vee specials. But as the years passed and the patient dialogue continued, public interest, at least, turned to other, more spectacular events, and for most people the Al'laan became just another one of the curiosities of space.

Winter was aware that David and Shaw were absent from the reception area. She wondered about their desertion, but thought it best not to call attention to the truants. They must have a good reason, she thought. They had better have a good reason.

She listened to the director's lecture on the lab, emphasizing her attention with questions whenever she could fit them into the flow of words. At the same time, the continued absence of the two members of the landing party began to worry and even anger her.

A short time later Winter was relieved to finally see Shaw coming toward her. He stood silently at her shoulder as the director drew other members of his staff into his audience. In that brief interlude Winter felt a light touch on her arm and Shaw's voice . . . in her mind.

Have information. Speak in private.

"Dr. Swanson," she said, breaking smoothly into the director's talk. "I am interested in what you have been telling me, but my time is short and I'd like to see the labs now, if I may?"

"Of course," the director agreed. "That is why you're here, after all."

"Before we begin, however, I'd like to speak to your security chief. Is he available?"

"Yes, I believe he is in his office—just beyond this room. Will you follow me?" He moved off toward the exit, giving Winter a chance to turn to Shaw.

"Where have you been and where's David?" She spoke softly, but there was a definite sound of anger in her tone.

"Dr. Wilson is in one of the labs. He is all right," he added at her look of concern. "He is waiting for us there. I had to come back to warn you to expect treachery here."

"Can you be more specific? Who's involved?"

"Many of the lab personnel and most of the administration."

"The director?"

"He is a part of it, but he is not, as you might suspect, the leader."

"Captain Winter, are you coming?" Swanson called.

"In a moment, Doctor," Winter answered. "Stay with me," she said quietly to Shaw.

Winter was on edge as they followed the director into the corridor. What had Shaw meant by treachery? What form would it take? And what in hell was David up to? She forced the questions into the back of her mind, concentrating on her immediate surroundings.

Lab security was handled by the Bosh Agency, which was a private organization able to provide everything from a bodyguard to a small army. They were a group of elite mercenaries whose loyalty belonged first to the agency, and second to their employers. No matter who might be trying to take control of Gyler, the security men could not be bought. Winter hoped she would be able to get information from the Bosh Agents stationed on Gyler.

She had watched the director for signs of nervousness when she asked to meet with security, but the man had appeared unperturbed. If he had anything to hide from her, it probably did not involve the Bosh agents.

The security office was large, its walls crowded with surveillance screens and computer banks. A crew was on duty, but their chief stood out from everyone else in the room. He was big, even by the standards of the agency, and his chief's bars gleamed gold on the shoulders of his crisp tan uniform.

"What can I do for you, Dr. Swanson?" he asked as the director and his guests arrived.

"Chief Echard, this is Captain Winter from the FSS *Venture*. She is, as you know, touring the lab and has asked to see security."

Winter shook the tall man's hand. She wondered if he was the best one to help her and glanced at Shaw, hoping he would understand her question.

Echard followed her look and turned to Shaw, his eyebrow raised in inquiry.

"This is . . ." Winter began, wondering how she could explain the presence of a civilian in her landing party.

"Dr. Shaw," Shaw filled in for her, extending his hand to the agent. "I'm an observer temporarily attached to *Venture*'s medical staff."

"Chief Echard," Winter said, averting attention from Shaw. "I was wondering if you would be able to accompany us on the tour. I have some questions, and you may be the only one qualified to answer them."

"I don't see why he shouldn't come along," Swanson said. "But I don't know if he will be able to give you any answers."

"Oh? Why is that?" the captain asked.

Echard grinned at her. "What Dr. Swanson means is that I'm new here. I was only assigned to the lab two weeks ago. I'm still learning my way around."

Winter's hope vanished. She looked at the rest of the agents in the room. "Your men can't all be as new to Gyler as you are."

"No, most of them have been here for a longer time. I brought six new agents with me, but the rest are old hands."

"What information did you want from the security chief?" Swanson asked curiously. "Perhaps I will be able to tell you what you want to know."

"I wanted to know the details of your defense system," Winter said. "As a member of the military, I'm interested first in the area of my own specialty. With the spread of the rebel influences, the lab is in a sensitive position."

"Yes, I understand," Swanson replied, a thin smile on his lips.

"Captain," Shaw interjected. "Perhaps I could continue the tour with Dr. Swanson while you discuss security with Chief Echard. You can rejoin us when you are satisfied."

Winter realized that Shaw had seen her dilemma and was

thus drawing the director away. "That's a good idea," she answered. "You can report your observations to me later. Is this agreeable with you, Dr. Swanson?"

The director did not look pleased, but he agreed to continue the tour with Shaw as Winter's representative. "You should join us as soon as possible," he said. "You'll want to see at least part of the lab with your own eyes. Bring her to module six in ten minutes, Echard. That should give you ample time to discuss security," he added, smiling again.

Echard was grinning at her when the door closed on Shaw and the director. "Come into my office," he said. "It's quiet, as well as private, and I'll supply you with whatever information you want." He led the way through the main security room.

"Well, Captain," he asked when the door was closed. "What do you really need from me? By the way, this is the one room in the whole complex that I know isn't bugged, so you can say anything you want. You might also tell me why the Federation is so curious about Gyler Laboratory."

Winter took the chair that he offered, and he sat down behind a rather cluttered desk. "Have you seen anything here that would make you suspicious?" she asked.

"I am still learning how not to get lost in the corridors," Echard told her. "I haven't discovered anything in the time I've been here, but I'm pretty sure that my predecessor did."

"Did you question him?" she asked eagerly. "What did he say?"

"He didn't say anything. He's dead."

"Dead?" Winter repeated. "How did he die?"

"The official report listed Fitkin's syndrome," the security chief said. "According to procedure with all contagious diseases, the body was cremated without an autopsy." He looked down at the surface of his desk, turning a pen end over end, his lips pursed. Then suddenly he raised his head, his eyes like dark flints. "I've been trying to get more information. Very quietly, of course."

"So you don't believe the report?" Winter asked.

"No, I don't. Especially now, taking the other circumstances into consideration." He drew a deep breath, and pushed himself back in his chair. It seemed to Winter as if he had just that moment decided to reveal everything to her. "As I suggested to you, I think he found something here. I was sent out to investigate his death, as well as another problem that's come up." Echard left his desk and went to look out into the main office through the transparent door. "I was told to expect you, by the way. My orders are to make an evaluation and then cooperate fully with you, if I decided you could be trusted."

Winter was nonplussed by that disclosure, but she ignored the feeling and concentrated on obtaining information.

"Who gave you those orders?" she asked. "I thought the agency worked for only one employer at a time."

"That's true," Echard replied, with a small smile at the captain's confusion.

"If you help me now," she continued, "won't you be going against agency policy?"

"Not in this case," he explained. "You see, despite appearances, I don't work for the Gyler Laboratory. I was hired by a special committee representing the Ruling Houses of Earth."

"The Federation? That implies the problem here is even more serious than I was led to believe."

"What were you told?"

"Very little. I was ordered to observe and report anything suspicious. That by itself could mean anything, but I had the impression that Command—or someone even higher than Command—suspects there are irregularities."

"Have your observations substantiated this?"

She gave a mocking snort of laughter. "So far I've been treated to a VIP reception and a lecture on the lab—all of the typical press-release material. I haven't seen anything, and quite frankly, I don't know where to begin looking. But you've been here longer. What can you tell me?"

"I reviewed the last transmissions that McTeigue, my predecessor, sent back to agency headquarters. From what I've been able to put together, if something was going on, they were able to keep it from him for an awfully long time. It was only toward the end that he began to be suspicious and started looking for evidence. He mentioned a report that he was preparing. I've searched for it, but . . ."

"It was erased?"

"It doesn't seem possible. Those files would have been in agency code," Echard said, his frustration visible for the first time. "All I found under his lock were routine matters—personnel files, status reports, and so forth. There was nothing to indicate a special investigation of any kind."

"So you're as much in the dark as I am," Winter commented.

"Not quite. There was enough in McTeigue's last transmission to give me a starting point."

"And?"

"The lab is no longer under Federation control, although for some reason it suits them to maintain this appearance."

Winter let her breath out in a hiss. "Who is responsible? Who has taken over?"

"I don't know for certain, but Proxima seems the most likely. A large part of the lab is devoted to secret work—work so secret that even I can't go into those sections. There's a picked squad of security men who rotate shifts for the areas involved. No one else is allowed access."

"Are these men Bosh agents?"

"Yes." Echard let his breath out in a derisive snort. "I'm supposed to be their superior, and yet it would seem that they have a higher security rating. You explain that to me!"

"I can't," Winter admitted. The memory of the Proxima cyborgs intruded into her thoughts. But how could they have been substituted for Bosh agents? The idea seemed farfetched, and she turned her attention back to Echard.

"I thought agency conditioning couldn't be circumvented," she said.

"It can't. Or it couldn't until now. You can imagine that Bosh headquarters is as anxious as the Federation to know what's going on here."

"But when McTeigue got too close to the truth, he conveniently died," Winter said.

"That's the only explanation that makes any sense," Echard replied. "He was getting too close to something."

"Then you'd better be careful. You might be the next one to contract a mysterious, fatal illness."

"Oh, I'm careful," Echard replied with a cheerful grin. "You'd better look out, yourself. McTeigue took sick and died very quickly."

"Do you have access to the lab's data banks?" she asked.

"Only the nonrestricted portions. Of course," he added with a hint of humor in his voice, "I did manage to get into one or two of the locked files."

"One or two? How many exactly?"

"Four of them."

"That might be what we need," Winter exclaimed. "What did you learn?"

"Not much I'm afraid. The files contained a lot of lab notes—diagrams and stuff like that. My secondary science classes didn't prepare me for anything advanced, so most of it was incomprehensible."

"Then as far as you know, they could have any kind of information coded in those files."

"I'm afraid so. Maybe your tech staff could figure it out. I know it would take time . . ."

She shrugged. "Then it takes time. Will you get me copies?"

"I've already made them. I was hoping you'd be able to smuggle a data button out of here. I want headquarters to see this."

"I'll be glad to take it with me when I return to my ship," Winter said. "My tech crew can go to work on it immediately."

"And send a copy to Bosh headquarters," he reminded her.

"Certainly."

"Good. The agency will be grateful." He glanced at his chronometer and got to his feet. "We have to rejoin Dr. Swanson. He wasn't very happy to let you out of his sight, although I'm not sure what he imagined I could tell you. They've been very careful to keep me from nosing around."

"Are you aware that Swanson is involved in whatever's going on?" she asked.

Echard paused in the act of reaching for the door handle. "I wouldn't have thought Swanson was capable of duplicity. What makes you suspect him?"

"One of my landing party is an esper," the captain admitted.

Echard stiffened and the smile left his face.

"He picked up impressions of treachery." Winter explained. "He's certain there's something more than just a tour planned for us."

"Did he give details? Did he tell you who's involved—besides Swanson?"

"I'm afraid not. I didn't have much of a chance to talk to him. Still it all fits together. And I agree with you; I also think that Proxima is involved. I suspect they're using the lab to develop cybernetic techniques and applying them to human subjects."

"Programming people? For what purpose?" Echard walked back and perched on the edge of the desk, his arms crossed over his chest.

"Control," Winter said. "From what we've been able to learn, they intend to develop an army of cyborgs."

"How did you learn of this?" Echard demanded.

"Several sources. We captured one of the cyborgs. My ship's medical officer was able to do a preliminary examination before the cyborg destroyed himself. He had a number of implants in his brain. Dr. Wilson thinks they act as a transceiver of some sort."

"Why do you think Proxima is behind it?"

"I have no evidence," she admitted. "So far it's just a suspicion, but I think it's well founded."

Echard looked at his boots and frowned as he considered. "All right. I think I may be able to get evidence for you. If Proxima is creating cyborgs, it could explain the defection of Bosh agents. It would also explain McTeigue's death."

Winter looked at him, not understanding.

"Level-one agents," Echard explained, "are mentally conditioned against mind control. If an attempt was made using either chemical or telepathic means, it wouldn't work. If they tried to force the conditioning, the agent would die."

"And McTeigue was a level-one agent."

"All squad leaders and security chiefs are at least level-one."

Winter nodded. "That has to be it then." She took a deep breath. "David—Dr. Wilson—is somewhere in the lab. I don't know what he's up to, and I'd like to find him before we return to the tour. Can you help me?"

"Of course. Almost the whole lab is covered by spyeyes. Unless he's in one of the secret areas, he'll show up on the monitors outside."

Echard led the way from his office. Displacing one of the agents who was seated in front of the bank of security monitors, he flipped switches and scanned the interior of the lab, section by section. Winter watched over his shoulder, but David was not revealed by any of the surveillance cameras.

"Let's get back to Swanson," she suggested. "Shaw knows where David is."

Echard relinquished the monitors, and he and the captain left the security office. They found Shaw and the lab's director almost immediately, and it was obvious that Swanson had been stalling, waiting for Winter and Echard to rejoin him.

"So, Captain Winter. Did you get your questions answered?" the director asked as they appeared.

"Thank you," the captain responded politely. "I find your security measures very interesting."

"They're not particularly unusual," Swanson commented as he turned to lead her farther down the hallway. "Shall we continue our tour now?"

"Dr. Swanson," Winter said, stopping him. "Rather than tour the entire lab, there are a few specific areas I'd like to see."

The director shot her a look of annoyance.

"Shaw, where's David?" Winter asked, ignoring Swanson for the moment. She looked up at the telepath, wondering why he was so silent. He had not said anything to her, mentally or audibly, although she knew he still had something that he considered important to tell her. His stony expression gave away nothing of what he might be thinking or feeling.

"But—" the director began.

"Not far from here," Shaw said quietly. "Come this way." He turned to go back down the hallway.

"But that's a restricted area," Swanson protested, walking fast to keep up.

"As a Federation starcaptain, I have clearance." Winter told him bluntly as she followed Shaw.

CHAPTER 19

David stood looking down at the silver figure in the stasis tank for a long time after Shaw had left. An Al'laan, Shaw had said, but how did he know? He had spoken with such conviction, though, that David could not doubt him.

He transferred his attention to the stasis machine. It was a field generator, and unlike the container built by the Malvern, it was not portable. Once the field was deactivated, the body could be revived much more easily and quickly than from chemical stasis.

One end of the room contained a number of computer terminals. David checked Jon, who was still unconscious, before he went to one of the terminals and pulled out the chair. He knew there would be security blocks on most, if not all, of the information in the lab's computer, but he might be able to gain access to one or two files.

He played the keys, and the screen flashed the expected response: a request for a password. He tried a couple of likely words, but the key could be anything. He wished he had paid more attention in his computer classes at the academy. He also wished Shaw was there; the telepath would know how to break through computer security—it was part of his job, after

159

all. David tried to get in a fourth time, but the screen showed nothing but the Gyler logo with a flashing request for the password superimposed over it. He was staring at it, wondering what to try next, when a hand reached over his shoulder and the fingers keyed the correct word.

"There's no reason why you shouldn't see all of it," Jon said. He sat on the arm of the chair beside David and massaged his sore head.

David turned in startled haste. "Jon—" he began, embarrassed at being party to the assault, as well as being caught snooping. Avery looked shaken, but he was in control of himself and, David realized, of the situation once again.

"I woke a couple of minutes ago. I've been watching you," Avery said, behaving as if nothing unusual had happened. "I'm glad your friend is gone. I wanted to talk to you alone, to invite you to join us in our work here."

"At Gyler?" David asked, his mind spinning as if he, not Jon, had been struck.

"You would be a welcome addition to our staff."

"What work?" David was horrified at the changes in his old friend, but determined not to let it show.

"I serve the Empire," Avery declared.

And he's proud of it, David realized, appalled and disgusted at the defection of someone who had once been a respected doctor.

"All of the work at the lab has been dedicated to their cause," Avery said.

"What work?" David asked, careful to keep his voice neutral.

"We're creating the greatest fighting force in the history of mankind."

Avery's eyes gleamed. In what? David wondered. Anticipation? Delight? Pride? He felt sick.

"Fighting force?" he asked. "Are you speaking of the Proxima cyborgs?"

"I suspected that you might know something of our work here. Yes, you are correct, although I'm certain you've put the wrong interpretation on what we're trying to do. But if you join us everything will become clear. What do you say? Do you want to enlist on the winning side?"

"You know that isn't possible," David said quietly, wondering what his refusal would bring. He had already been told too much to be allowed to live. "What you're doing is not only wrong—it's immoral. It goes against all laws—against everything we've been taught. I could never work with you under such circumstances."

"Pity," Jon mocked. There was a strange expression on his face and a twisted smile on his lips.

David could feel the nervous sweat running down his sides, but he tried to prepare himself for whatever would happen next. He was not good at combat, but he would attempt to defend himself if it came to that.

"I knew that was what you'd say, and I tried to warn them," Avery said. "But Swanson insisted that I try to recruit you. He's a fool. I was right." There was a metallic gleam in his hand as he came to his feet and took a step toward David. "I'm sorry, my old friend. Remember that I did give you a chance. Now we'll do things my way."

"What are you going to do?" David stood abruptly, putting the chair between the scientist and himself.

Jon held up a silvery tube. "This is a narcotic. You won't feel anything, and when you wake up, like it or not, you'll be one of us." He started forward.

David grabbed for the hand that held the tube, but the chair was in his way. He stumbled as Avery lunged at him, and the two men wrestled for an advantage. Neither one of them heard the door behind them open.

"What's going on here?" Echard shouted, authority ringing in his voice.

Winter rushed to David's assistance, but she was an instant too late. The tube hissed its contents into David's chest, and he froze for a moment, his eyes wide with astonishment, before he crumpled. Winter caught him and gently lowered his head to the floor. Shaw pulled Jon away from them, taking the empty tube from his hand.

"Arrest these two!" Avery demanded of Echard. He tried to pull himself from Shaw's grasp, but the slender hands held unusual strength and his efforts were futile.

Avery stopped struggling and jerked his head toward Shaw. "He attacked me! And I caught Dr. Wilson trying to get access to confidential files! They're spies!"

Winter ignored the words and felt for David's pulse. It was there, slow but steady, she noted with relief. She sat back on her heels and looked at Avery.

"You may think fast," she told him. "But no one here is

going to believe anything you have to say." She got to her feet. "What did you give David?"

"I? Nothing! I had to defend myself," he blustered, looking toward Swanson for support.

"What was in the tube?" Winter demanded.

"A harmless narcotic," Avery growled. "He's asleep, that's all."

Winter looked at Shaw, who nodded; Avery was telling the truth. "What was David doing in this part of the lab?" she asked.

"Dr. Avery brought him," Shaw told her. "He said he wanted to show us the work he has been doing."

"That's not true," Avery protested. "I never brought them to this room. The work here is very sensitive. There's nothing for outsiders to see."

"I can imagine," Echard said as he looked at the stasis containers, disgust clear on his face.

Avery, released by Shaw, sank down in the nearest chair, rubbing his sore arm.

Shaw felt it was necessary to explain to the captain. "When Dr. Avery led us through the hallway, I felt his concern for this room as we passed the door," he said. "I suspected there might be something important inside."

"Obviously you were right," Echard agreed. "What's this all about?' he asked Avery. "Why are all these bodies in stasis?"

"It's part of some highly sensitive work," Swanson said, breaking into the conversation. He seemed very nervous but determined to bluster his way out of trouble. "However, everything we're doing is within the approved parameters. It's all perfectly legal. I'll explain—"

"You don't have to justify anything to these people!" Avery snapped. "We're no longer under their jurisdiction."

"And just who do you answer to?" Winter asked him.

"To the Empire," Avery told her proudly, sitting tall in the chair.

"Proxima?"

"Of course," he said, his tone implying that there could be no other empire.

Winter and Echard exchanged glances. "We'll have to se- cure the lab. How many of the security men can you count on?" she asked him quietly.

"Only the six I brought with me when I came here," he said.

"It won't be enough," she told him. "I'll bring more people down from the *Venture*."

"Even with your crew, we still won't have enough to take the lab by force," Echard pointed out.

"No, but we might be able to neutralize the leaders before anyone realizes what's happening. Once they're out of the way it'll just be mopping up," she explained.

"It might work. It'll be risky, but I don't see an alternative."

Winter's mind was busy planning and anticipating problems. "We'll have to be very fast and quiet about it," she said. "I'll send Dr. Wilson back to the *Venture* on the shuttle, and have every available crew member armed and sent down."

Swanson had been edging toward the door as Winter spoke, but Shaw had been moving unobtrusively toward him. As the director reached for the door handle, Shaw caught his wrist, pulling him back into the middle of the room. The director tried to struggle, but he, too, was no match for Shaw's strength.

"You can't do this!" Swanson complained, looking fearfully up at the tall stranger. "You have no rights here! You won't get away with this!"

"I suggest you come quietly," Echard said, dropping his hand to the holster of his handgun. "I will not hesitate to use this the next time you make a move."

"You're bluffing," Swanson said, his eyes riveted to the security man's right hand just inches from the gun. His words came fast and fearfully. "You're an agency man. Your loyalty is to me—to the lab. We're your employers."

"You're mistaken. The Federation of Ruling Houses hired me. And since you've admitted that you're working for the Proxima Empire, you're the enemy."

"That's not true! I admit nothing. It's Avery you want. Not me. I'm loyal to the Federation!" Swanson babbled.

"You are lying," Shaw said. "Your mind is trying to devise ways of putting all of the blame on Dr. Avery, but you were involved with Proxima from the beginning."

"How—how can you say that? You can't know any such thing," Swanson stammered.

"He knows," Winter told him. "He's a telepath." She looked speculatively at Shaw. "Which gives me an idea. You would know which of the lab personnel can be trusted. Will you help us?"

"Yes," he replied.

"Good," she said. "Work with Chief Echard. You'd better check the security staff first. As you find people we can trust, enlist them. Explain what's going on if you have to, but work as quickly as possible. I don't know how long it will take, but we don't have much time. Remember, we need all the help we can get, so everyone you find is important." She looked down at the doctor. "In the meantime, I'll get David to the shuttle and start sending the *Venture*'s crew down here."

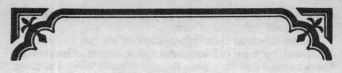

CHAPTER 20

It took two days for the Bosh agents and the *Venture*'s crew to take control of the Gyler Laboratories. Despite their allegiance to the Proxima Empire, most of the lab personnel were not fighters. They gave up readily when faced with armed opponents, and eventually more than a hundred Proxima supporters were rounded up and confined under guard in the residence wing to await the arrival of Federation forces.

One group of technicians, however, resisted capture. They fought fiercely despite the superior numbers against them. The battle raged through the corridors, but the resisters were slowly pushed back. They finally barricaded themselves in a lab and held out there until Echard thought to have the room flooded with a narco gas.

Echard and Winter waited the required fifteen minutes before they donned respirators and entered the lab. The bodies were scattered where they had collapsed when the gas took affect, and all of the thirty-seven were dead.

A medic was called in, but only after he had performed an autopsy and conferred with David on board the *Venture* did he make his report. Apparently all of the men and women in the room had implants, which had been programmed to kill when under extreme stress. Evidently the narco gas had provided just the right kind of stress.

Winter received their information as she sat in Echard's office waiting for a call to go through to Admiral Jammeson. She was tired and dirty from the fighting and wanted nothing more than to shower and sleep, but the call had to be made first. David found her there, sprawled in a chair with her legs over the arm.

"What are you doing here?" Winter said to him by way of greeting. "You're supposed to be resting." She turned in the chair and dropped her feet to the floor.

"I've rested enough to last me a week," he told her bluntly. "Heard you were short on doctors, so I came down in the shuttle."

Winter smothered a yawn. "How long have you been here?"

"Almost twenty hours. Good thing I came, too."

"Were there more casualties than first reported?" she asked, fearing the news.

"No. Two lab techs were killed. One of the *Venture*'s crew was wounded, but not badly."

"Ensign Peters," Winter supplied. "How is she doing?"

"She'll be up in about a week. She had a pretty bad burn on her leg, but the first graft has already started to take."

"It could have been worse." Winter shifted restlessly. "Why is this call taking so long?" she complained suddenly.

"Someone said the Brandywine relay satellite's down. We have to rely on the Fed comlink, and traffic's backed up," he told her.

"This is supposed to be priority," she muttered, and then yawned again.

"Have you ever known that to make a difference?" he asked wryly. "Relax."

Winter scowled at him.

David reached into the medkit slung over his shoulder and pulled out a hypo.

"What's that for?" she demanded.

"Something to cheer you up—vitamins and stimulants. My prescription." He pressed the hypospray against her arm. "This will keep you going for a couple more hours." David glanced up as the door opened. "Well, hello, Shaw. I was beginning to wonder where you'd disappeared to."

David smiled at his friend, but there was no answering smile on Shaw's face.

"Have you told Captain Winter about the Al'laan?" he asked David.

Winter straightened up in the chair and looked from one man to the other.

"There hasn't been time," David explained.

"Well suppose you tell me now," Winter said, irritation in her voice.

The doctor replaced the hypo in his kit as he spoke. "In the stasis room, there's a humanoid—a female. Shaw thinks she's an Al'laan."

"She *is* an Al'laan," Shaw affirmed.

"How do you know?" Winter asked, suddenly aware of the unusual tension in Shaw. "No one has ever seen an Al'laan," she added.

"I have. You have to get her out of stasis," Shaw told her almost desperately. "And if you do, there may still be great trouble because she is here."

"Why?" David asked.

"Can you imagine how she got here?" Shaw replied.

David shook his head, bewildered at the changes in his friend.

"I think it is safe to assume she is here against her will," Shaw continued.

"Oh, great." Winter rubbed her eyes. "This could just be the incident that plunges us into war with the Al'laan and we're right in the middle of it. Why didn't you tell me any of this before, David?"

"I couldn't tell you. I was unconscious," David said. "Then when I came to, I was too busy. What difference does a few hours make anyway? She isn't going anywhere."

Winter started to get to her feet to go to the stasis room, when she remembered her call and sank back down. "You'll have to take care of this for me, David. I want you to get her out of stasis immediately and handle things until I get there. Can you do it?"

"Certainly. When have I ever failed you?"

"Never." She met his gaze, and the corners of her mouth twitched. "Get the Al'laan—if that's what she is—out of stasis." She glanced at Shaw as she spoke. "While you're there, determine the condition of the rest of the bodies. We can leave them until the Federation team gets here, but Jammeson will want a report." She rubbed her eyes. "How many of your medics are down here?"

"Just one. Jenna."

"Get her to help you. And there's some of the lab's techs. Put them to work, too."

"Right away." David went out the door, and Shaw started to follow.

"Shaw, wait a minute," Winter said. "I want to talk to you. Please sit down."

Shaw's face went stony and his movements were reluctant, but he obeyed. Silence built between them as Winter took time to consider her words before she spoke.

"You said you've seen the Al'laan before. When was this?" she asked.

"Can you not guess?" he asked, his voice bleak.

"No. How could I?"

Shaw turned his head away from her. "You forget, I can read you. You accepted some time ago that I am a mutant, but occasionally you have thought that I might be alien."

He deliberately looked at her, his silvery eyes hypnotic. Winter imagined that she could see herself reflected in those eyes, caught and helpless to break away. Her breath caught in her throat as she felt him reaching into her mind. She felt her heart pounding and the blood coursing all through her body, taking with it her will, her resistance. She knew that she should not continue to meet his gaze, and yet she could not look away.

His hand slowly reached out to touch hers as it gripped the arm of the chair.

"Deep within your mind is the sound of oceans and hooves drumming on the sand," he said softly, almost whispering, his eyes never wavering from hers. "It feels of wind and night skies . . . and of terrible sorrow."

The interior of Echard's office faded as Winter saw Karth, the pictures conjured up by Shaw's words more vivid than any dream. The visions of her past came, flowing unchecked and completely out of her control. She felt powerless in the face of the assault, and in her shock at the intensity of the memory, it took her a minute to realize what Shaw was doing.

"No! Stop that!" she shouted, jerking her hand from under his. "Get out of my mind!"

Shaw blinked and turned away from her, his face cold. "And you get out of mine," he said. His level, almost toneless voice was a sharp contrast to the threat of hysteria in hers. He flicked a glance back in her direction and saw the degree of her distress. "I am out," he said more gently.

Winter was breathing hard, trying desperately to control her trembling. How could he have done that? How could he have known to do it, her mind cried out in panic. In those few seconds Shaw had dug into her memory and released things that she had hoped were buried forever.

It was the habit of command that finally came to her rescue. "Go find David," she said abruptly. "You should be with him in case he needs your help." She kept her eyes on the desk as she spoke—anywhere but on Shaw.

"I will go. And you are right, David will need my help. It is never wise to underestimate a frightened Al'laan." He rose to leave but paused, looking down at Winter.

She sat very still, her eyes deliberately turned away from him.

"Captain Winter—" he began.

"Please don't say anything else. Just go and find David. Now."

Shaw bowed his head and did as she ordered.

After he had left, Winter continued to fight the flood of emotion and memories released by his invasion of her mind. He had brought back a part of Karth that was so close to her, so much a part of what she was despite her efforts to deny it.

Karth was gone, she told herself fiercely. Gone forever.

But one day she would know why, another part of her mind added. One day she would learn who was responsible for the destruction of her home, and on that day her life would have a new direction. Until then, however, she needed to block out the pain. She forced herself to breathe deeply, to recapture calm.

"Be still as a mountain," she repeated to herself in a whisper, quoting the ancient tai chi master Wu Yu-hsiang. "Still as a mountain."

In response to the litany, Karth retreated to the secret places in her mind, and she locked the door behind it. Once again, it would only escape as the echoes that disturbed her dreams.

Over the years she had found a peace of sorts, and although it was not perfect, it allowed her to function, to live without the burden of memory. How dare Shaw threaten that peace!

* * *

Winter's call finally came through, and Admiral Jammeson appeared on the screen in Echard's office. When she reported that the lab was secure, Jammeson seemed pleased.

"There is one other thing . . ." she said. She hesitated, then plunged on. "In the stasis room. One of the bodies there is alien. She's been identified as an Al'laan."

"A what?" Jammeson leaned forward in his chair. "Explain."

"Yes, sir." Winter's voice was without emotion as she recited the information. "She was discovered and identified by Shaw. I've ordered Dr. Wilson to revive her. I thought this would be best in light of our tenuous relations with the Al'laan. We have no way of knowing how she got here, and I thought it was important to deal with the matter immediately."

"Shaw made the identification?" Jammeson repeated. "How certain was he?"

"Very certain."

"And you believe him?"

"Yes, sir. I believe he knows what he's talking about."

"Damn," the admiral said softly.

He leaned over to talk to someone out of the transceiver's range. "It would have been better," she could hear him saying, "but it's out of our hands. We'll have to work with it as it stands."

He turned back to Winter. "How long before she's out of stasis?" he asked.

"Dr. Wilson estimated about two hours, maximum. He reported just before your transmission to say that she appears to be in excellent health. As far as he can tell, they haven't done anything to her except put her to sleep."

"Thank the heavens for that! I'll wait here, Captain. I want to speak with you again in two hours no matter what has happened. And if it is at all possible, at that time I would also like to speak to the Al'laan."

"I understand."

"In two hours then. Jammeson out."

Winter shut off the receiver and sat immobile, her fingers still on the switch. Something about the transmission had been wrong. She was not sure exactly what it could have been, except that Jammeson had not seemed very surprised to learn about the Al'laan. She wondered briefly if he might have suspected it before she told him. But how could he have known?

It puzzled and troubled her, but she was too weary to pursue it just then.

Two hours, Winter thought as she hauled herself to her feet. She tugged her uniform straight and headed for the stasis room.

The field stasis unit had automatic controls which cued the operator by sounding a buzzer at the conclusion of each step of the cycle. When Winter arrived, the process of reviving the Al'laan was almost complete. The blue glow was gone from around the alien, and where her skin had appeared to have a metallic sheen, it was obviously covered by a fine, short fur that refracted the light. She lay between the field generators, but her chest rose and fell as she breathed independently again. The EEG monitor beside David showed that she was still unconscious.

"How much longer?" the captain asked.

David glanced up. "Soon."

Winter stood watching him work, then went to the computer terminal where Echard sat.

"Avery did us a big favor," the security chief commented as he made a note on the pad beside him.

"What is it?"

"He was so sure of himself. Too sure. He unlocked all of the master files. Now we have access to everything that was going on here. There's a lot of information on other projects, as well."

"Data on the cyborg project?" Winter sank into a chair and watched the words scroll up the screen.

"Look at this."

Echard interrupted the flow of words on the screen. With a couple of key strokes he called up another file, and a diagram appeared, a gridlike representation of a human head marked off by spots of light. The spots were very similar to those in David's autopsy report on the cyborg captured on the mining station.

Winter nodded with satisfaction.

"As much as I understand, it's all here," Echard told her. "And what might interest you is the file on the Al'laan. I'll prepare copies for you to transfer. While we're in here, can you think of anything else that you might want?"

"Why don't you tape a directory? I'll go through it when I have more time, and then you can copy any of the files that I or my tech staff think are important." She sat back, stretching her legs out. "I assume you've made a report to your agency?"

"Yes."

"Is there any chance I can get a copy of that, too? I'd like to include it with the information I send to Admiral Jammeson."

"I can have it ready before you leave. What's your schedule?"

"I have to return Admiral Jammeson's call in a little over an hour. After that our orders are to return to Alpha Base." Winter glanced back at David, who was still intent on the stasis machinery. "The admiral wants to talk to the Al'laan."

"Are you certain that's what she is?" Echard asked.

"Aren't you?"

"You can settle that question once and for all," David announced. "Ask her yourselves. She's awake."

CHAPTER 21

Shaw leaned against the back wall as far away from the Al'laan as he could get, his arms crossed over his chest, a meager protection against what was happening in the room. After so many years he had thought he would never see an Al'laan again—yet right there in the room was not just any Al'laan, but Shamask!

He closed his eyes, blocking his sight of the people around the control consoles, but he was still aware of them, and of the technicians who were making an inventory of the bodies in stasis. He shielded his mind and retreated deeply into himself, trying to get away from the distraction and the confusion that he felt.

When he finally opened his eyes and focused on the group around the stasis unit, he did not move from where he was standing. It was almost as if he was afraid to call attention to himself, afraid to be there in the same room with Shamask, but at the same time unable to leave.

David had moved to the side of the container, Winter and Echard beside him while the technicians hovered just beyond. All of them radiated one emotion: curiosity.

The Al'laan opened her eyes. The pupils, surrounded by

huge silver irises, contracted as they adjusted to the light.

Winter stared at the eyes and then glanced quickly at Shaw. It can't be! she told herself in amazement.

The Al'laan lay without moving as she blinked and gathered information to tell her where she was. Shaw remained against the wall, rigid and still as if he had turned to stone, but his mind was alert, waiting, listening.

The Al'laan moved. She shifted her weight to her elbows, trying to raise herself to a sitting position. David went to help her, but at his movement she dropped back, her hand coming up to ward him off. A thin web of skin stretched from her wrist behind her, the pale silvery color shimmering in the artificial light of the lab.

"Hu-mans," the Al'laan said, her voice deep and rich. Anger was there. Her lips came back from her sharp, bright teeth in a snarl.

David froze in apprehension, not knowing what to do or what to expect.

The Al'laan sat up unaided, an expression of undisguised rage contorting her features. The wings billowed at her movement and then subsided, draped against her back.

"No!" Shaw called, walking swiftly forward. "These are friends."

The Al'laan's head turned in his direction. Then Shaw said something in a strange language. The spoken words trailed off, replaced by a telepath's communication. A long time seemed to pass as they stared at each other. The people around them waited, too confused and apprehensive to interfere.

The Al'laan broke away first and slowly looked at the others around her. Shaw turned without a word and walked heavily to the door and out into the hallway.

"Who is the leader here?" the Al'laan asked. She spoke Standard, and although the tone was still angry, the words were without inflection.

"I am," Winter told her. "I am Captain Winter of the FSS *Venture*."

"You have a ship? That is good. You will take me to my people immediately."

"If that's what you want, and if my superiors will give me permission, I will certainly do so." Winter indicated Echard and David, who were standing beside her. "This is Security Chief Echard, who is now in charge of the Gyler Laboratories, and this is the *Venture*'s medical officer, Dr. Wilson. Will you let Dr. Wilson help you? You've been in stasis and we'd like to make sure that you haven't been harmed."

"Better if I had not been brought here!"

"You're right, but we had nothing to say about it." Winter hoped to soothe the angry alien, but it seemed that nothing she said was working.

"Your lack of responsibility does not negate the facts. I am here. I do not wish to be here," the Al'laan said sulkily.

"David, I have a transmission to beam to Admiral Jammeson. He'd like to speak to our guest," Winter said, looking down at the Al'laan. "When you're ready, would you bring her to Chief Echard's office?"

Winter was becoming annoyed at the position she had been forced into. She was feeling more tired then ever and was not sure she would be able to make the decisions that such a sensitive diplomatic situation required.

David looked at the Al'laan. "Well . . ." he began, taking a minute to assess her condition.

"I am the one to be consulted," the Al'laan interrupted. "Who is Admiral Jammeson? Why must I speak to him?"

"He's my superior officer," Winter told her. "And he's the one who'll decide whether or not I'll be allowed to take you back to your people."

The Al'laan raised her chin stubbornly. "I will speak to him now."

"First I have to make the initial connection. The communication board is in the security office. You'll have to come there," Winter said.

"Proceed with preparations. I will come."

Winter looked at David.

"Don't look at me," he told her, his irritation tinged with humor. "Everything seems to have been taken out of my hands."

"Bring her to security when you're ready," the captain said. "You might also find her something to wear."

Winter went into the hallway, glad to leave the unhappy alien to David. She wanted to get to security as quickly as possible so she could speak to Jammeson alone. Hopefully she could warn him of the alien's imperious manner and demands. She also realized that she needed to see Shaw and find out what he knew about the Al'laan. She felt reluctant to face him after their last painful episode, but she reminded herself that duty came before any personal consideration.

Shaw was in Echard's office. He was sitting in a chair, his body rigid. His face was very pale, the skin drawn tightly over the high planes of his cheekbones, his silver eyes ringed with shadow and as unreadable as ever.

Winter felt a sudden compassion for him. If what she suspected was true, then she did not envy his position. Hiding the truth and hiding from the truth must have been very difficult for him.

"I knew you would want to talk to me, so I waited," he told her when she arrived. His voice was very quiet. "I would also like your permission to return to the *Venture* as soon as possible."

Winter looked at him curiously. "That can be arranged," she said. "And you're right—I do want to talk to you. I can't figure how you knew about the Al'laan unless you are one of them. But . . . although there are some similarities, you don't really look like the woman we took from stasis."

"Nevertheless, I am an Al'laan."

So she was right! Winter pulled another chair over and sat down facing Shaw. "I don't understand," she said gently. "Why are your people so secretive? Are there other Al'laan living among mankind?"

"There may be, but I have never met any. I also do not want to talk about my origins, if you please."

His pain was obvious despite the control he kept over his voice, and Winter felt a flicker of sympathy. Still, she reminded herself, she had a job to do and what passed in the next few hours would have a profound affect on all of humanity. Personal considerations could not be allowed to interfere.

"I'm sorry if this is difficult for you," she said. "But you must understand how delicate this matter is. I need to know anything you can tell me about the Al'laan. I'll be talking to Admiral Jammeson in a few minutes and I'd like to give him as much background as possible. He's going to have to make some difficult decisions."

Shaw nodded and looked away. "All right. I will do what I can." He drew a deep breath. "She is frightened, and that is why she seems so angry. She blames mankind for the predicament in which she finds herself. She knows the fact that she has been exposed to mankind as an Al'laan will have serious repercussions in the relationship between our two races, but she wants to return to her people with as little trouble as possible. She wanted nothing to do with this situation."

"What would you recommend that we do?"

"Let her go," Shaw said, sudden intensity in his words. "Do everything that you possibly can to return her unharmed. Make certain that Admiral Jammeson understands the importance of this. There will be some very unpleasant repercussions if she is detained further . . . if it is not already too late."

Winter frowned as she tried to make sure she understood correctly. "Do you mean that the Al'laan may place the blame for her capture on all of us, not just the ones responsible?"

"Yes."

"But that's illogical," Winter protested. Yet she had to accept the possibility. "All right. What can we do about it?"

"Do everything in your power so that your admiral will allow her to have her way. He may want to see her, to talk with her in person, but this cannot be permitted. For your people to do anything more than to help her to get home could mean serious trouble."

"Then you'll have to help me convince Admiral Jammeson, and help me explain to the Al'laan . . . make her understand that we weren't the ones responsible for her capture."

But Shaw shook his head. "I cannot do that. Please do not ask it of me."

Winter's brow furrowed in confusion. "Shaw, what's wrong?"

"If I did as you ask, there would be questions. Right now I do not think I can face them."

Winter took time to consider his words. She could see the strain that he was under and she was wise enough to realize that he had helped her all that he could. "All right, go to the shuttle. We're moving personnel back up to the ship, and you can ride up with them."

Shaw stood, then hesitated before going to the door. "She will seem unreasonable and even demanding," he told the captain. "And you must remember that she is terribly frightened and too proud to endure this experience without trying to assert herself. This is the reason for her manner with you and the rest of the humans she will be in contact with."

"What did you say to her back in the stasis room?"

"That I think you will do whatever is possible to help her. You may not realize it, but you were all in danger. She might have harmed you."

"I think we understood that. Thank you for your intervention."

Shaw nodded. "I will go to the shuttle."

Winter stayed in her chair after he had gone, trying to think of ways to approach Jammeson, but her tired mind was not up to the task. She would just have to improvise and hope it was good enough to avert disaster. Jammeson would have to be responsible for his own decisions.

Winter turned her chair to the communications panel and began punching in the sequence that would connect her with Alpha Base across parsecs of space. The PLEASE WAIT signal was flashing on and off, and as she stared at it, her eyes began to close despite everything she did to try to prevent it. It took her several seconds to realize that the signal had been replaced with the face of the Base communications officer, Major Morrace.

"You look terrible, Captain Winter. Has it been that rough?" the major inquired sympathetically.

"Probably," Winter said. "You can't imagine what it's been like."

Morrace grinned. "Well, prepare yourself. There's more to come. You managed to stir up everyone here. The admiral and most of his staff have been in and out and on the beam to Earth almost continuously since your last transmission. They're waiting for you now."

Morrace's face was replaced by Jammeson's. Winter forced her protesting body to sit straighter in her chair.

"Admiral," she said, "the Al'laan is awake and wishes to speak to you."

"Good work, Captain. We are very anxious to have this opportunity to talk to her on behalf of the Federation of Ruling Houses of Earth. Where is she?"

"She's still with Dr. Wilson. They'll be here any minute, but I wanted to talk to you first."

"What is it, Captain?" the admiral said politely.

"I'm afraid she may prove troublesome, sir. She's already demanded that I take her back to her people immediately. She's understandably angry because she was brought here, and I'm afraid she may blame us for it. I have spoken to Shaw about her, and he strongly recommends that we return her as soon as it can be arranged."

"Well, of course we will!" Jammeson said jovially. "But we must also show her the courtesy that she is entitled to in her unique position as the first ambassador for her race."

Winter was afraid of what that meant. "Sir, I don't think

she considers herself an ambassador. I think she considers herself a prisoner."

"Nonsense," Jammeson insisted. "She couldn't think anything like that at all. She will be grateful to you for her rescue —that is, unless you've bungled it in some way. You haven't let your famous temper get out of hand, have you?" The admiral glared at Winter.

"No, sir," the starcaptain responded wearily. "I didn't have time."

"Well, I'll speak to her and get this straightened out. I suppose we can't expect you to be a diplomat as well as everything else."

Winter realized that Jammeson was annoyed that she was there instead of him. He could have the honor, she thought bitterly. All she wanted right then was sleep.

At that moment the Al'laan swept into the room. She was dressed in a lab coat and a pair of overalls that had been modified for her anatomy; she held herself regally, her head up and her long black hair swirling down to her knees. David hurried after her, looking harassed, and Echard trailed behind.

Winter switched the comscreen onto wide angle so Jammeson would have a clear view of everything that happened in the room.

"Is the transmission prepared? I wish to leave quickly," the Al'laan demanded.

"I am Admiral Samuel T. Jammeson, Federation Space Service, representing the Federation of Ruling Houses of Earth," Jammeson said formally.

"Order Captain Winter to transport me immediately," the Al'laan told him.

Jammeson looked surprised. "Well, certainly! We will see that you are returned to your home. However, I'm certain you will agree that it would be better if you wait until we have a more suitable transport for you. The *Venture* is just a working ship, not really as comfortable as you might like."

"A ship is a ship. I will travel on Captain Winter's ship. It is here. I wish to leave now."

Jammeson leaned over to speak with someone in his office, out of the pickup's range, then addressed the Al'laan again. "We will, of course, defer to your wishes. Captain Winter will take you anywhere you want to go. Before you leave, however, I would like to express my most sincere apologies for any inconveniences you may have suffered as a result of your visit with us. If there is anything we can do to make amends, I wish you would tell me."

"You may terminate this conversation." The Al'laan turned to Winter. "You have permission to take me home. Where is your ship? We will leave immediately."

Winter looked at David. "Would you please conduct our guest to the shuttle? I'll finish here and join you as soon as I can."

The Al'laan strode out of the office even as Winter was speaking. David nodded to the captain and rushed after her.

"Captain Winter," Jammeson called from the monitor. His face was very stern, and Winter knew she would have to endure his frustration. "Here are your orders. Convey the Al'laan to whatever destination she selects. I want a report, of course—of the entire trip. Make tapes. You're in a unique position, and I hope you'll be able to handle this. I don't want another incident like the one with the Malvern Ambassador-Princess."

"Yes, Admiral."

"I want to know where you take the Al'laan and who meets her there. I want a report of any conversations she may have with you or any of your crew. If it is at all possible, I want Dr. Wilson to do a complete med scan."

"Yes, Admiral."

Jammeson continued to glare at her from the screen. "None of this went as I anticipated."

"I realize that, sir. I'm sorry."

"You did try to warn me, I'll admit that." He sighed and sat back in his chair. "Okay, Winter, it's in your hands. Don't bungle it. Jammeson out."

CHAPTER 22

David was lying on his stomach when he opened his eyes. After the confusion of the past couple of days he was glad to be back in the peace of his cabin on the *Venture*. His jaw dropped in a huge yawn and he stretched, savoring the comfortable pull of his muscles. He let his breath out and turned over, knocking his pillow to the floor. When he rolled over to retrieve it he remembered the Al'laan.

David groaned. He was a doctor, not a diplomat. He had tried to be patient and understanding, for he could imagine the difficulties she had endured. Yet on several occasions he had still come within millimeters of losing his temper.

He retrieved the pillow and stuffed it behind his head as he lay back, his hands clasped behind his neck.

At least he knew her name now. Shamask, or at least that was what she had told him to call her when he had asked. But she still treated him as if he was a member of some inferior species, not worthy of her attention. Her attitude would have amused him if she had not been so damned impatient! Shamask's biggest show of anger had come upon learning that Winter would not accompany them back to the ship and that the *Venture* could not leave orbit for at least twelve more

181

hours. But David had made her understand the necessity for the delay—at least, he hoped he had made her understand.

When they finally boarded, Shamask had insisted on contacting the communications satellite that her people maintained, but Commander Thomas refused to allow her to use the ship's tight-beam equipment without Winter's authorization. She had raged until David suggested that they contact Winter. Thomas complied and the captain gave permission, adding that he should record the call. Winter also informed them that she would be back on board by 0900 the next day, and that they would break orbit shortly after that.

David looked at the chronometer strapped to his wrist; it was 0917 hours. He swung his legs out of the bed and hurried into the shower. While he was dressing, the message light on his comunit came on.

"Wilson, here," he said, belting his shipsuit as he spoke.

"This is Winter, David. Have you slept enough?"

"I just woke up. Did you get any sleep?"

"Yes. I finished up on Gyler about five hours ago and rested there before I came up. Meet me on the bridge. We're breaking orbit as soon as Shamask tells me where we're going." Her voice implied that she did not relish having to deal with another difficult passenger on the *Venture*. She had all of David's sympathy, although he suspected that he would be the one who would have to deal with the Al'laan most of the time.

"I'll be up as soon as I get my boots on," he replied and switched the unit off.

"Where did you put Shamask?" Winter asked as David joined her several minutes later.

The bridge was busy as the crew readied the *Venture* for the voyage. Lights blinked as systems were activated, checked, and put on standby. The techs' faces reflected the eerie glow from the many screens that banked their stations. There was a faint hum of machinery and the clicking of keys, as well as quiet voices reporting the status of the systems.

"She's in the empty cabin beyond the infirmary," David said, taking his usual seat behind the captain. "Since you seem to have delegated me as babysitter, I thought it would be best to keep her nearby."

"Thank you for that. I decided that you were the best person for the job." Winter smiled as she turned around to face him. "You're famous for your patience, and I'm not." She handed him a steaming cup of coffee.

"She is a bit of a problem, isn't she?" David commented, taking a careful sip.

Winter retrieved her own cup. "That's an understatement. But Shaw says she's just scared, so we have to be patient with her." Winter indicated a box of computer buttons on the console beside the doctor. "Here's another job for you. These are a main directory and copies of files from the Gyler computer. You'll need them for your report on the lab. You might also scan the medical data on the cyborg process, and whatever else you find that's relevant. And see if you can find something on the Al'laan. Have the reports, or at least a preliminary, ready to beam to Alpha Base as soon as you can."

David grimaced at the size of the job. "That's a lot of material to cover."

"Put some of the medtechs to work on it," she suggested. "I'm sure it's not as bad as it looks. Most of the buttons are the directory. Echard promised to buzz us any other files we want. I didn't have enough time to go through any of it while we were at the lab." Winter drank from her cup again before setting it aside. "I still won't have time to give it any serious attention until the Al'laan is off our hands, but I thought you should get a start on it, in case there's something you think we'll need right away."

"Captain Winter," Lieutenant Delieus interrupted. "Message coming in on tight beam. Audio only, priority indication."

"Origin?"

"The Al'laan satellite."

"Relay it to my terminal and tape it," the captain ordered. She swiveled her chair around. The distance was great and static almost obscured the words. Winter reached forward and adjusted the audio pickup on her panel.

"... calling FSS *Venture*." The words came through the hiss and crackle.

"FSS *Venture* here. This is Captain Winter speaking. Proceed with your message."

"Captain Winter. Message is being relayed through communication satellite. Can you hear me? What is quality of reception?"

"Your signal is fluctuating, but I can understand you. Please proceed."

"We have received transmission from FSS *Venture*. We are aware of presence of Al'laan on board the FSS *Venture*. Please confirm."

"The message was correct. The Al'laan, Shamask, is on my ship. We are preparing to bring her to whatever destination she specifies."

There was an increase of static.

"Lieutenant Delieus, compensate," Winter said. "We're losing the signal."

"It's not us, sir. The signal has been interrupted."

David sat silently behind the captain, coffee growing cold in his cup. Winter turned to look at him and began to say something when the transmission resumed. She snapped back to her board.

"Captain Winter, are you present?"

"Winter, here."

"We have examined charts. We will provide directions according to Federation navigational codes. Please proceed to point space identified as A dash three, oh six four, point B, seven, point eight, two eight. Is this clear?"

Winter repeated the coordinates. "You wish us to travel to these coordinates?"

"Affirmative. Estimate duration of transit."

Winter turned to ask Delieus, but he had anticipated her, and the information began to form on her monitor. There were a couple of alternatives based on fuel consumption, but that would be critical only at sublight speeds. The most efficient way to cover the distance would be to make a superlight jump.

"We'll reach the coordinates in one hundred and sixty-nine hours," she said.

"This is excellent," the voice said through the static. "At such a time we, Al'laan, shall cohabit those space coordinates. Do you anticipate necessity for further clarification of information?"

"The coordinates you've given me are for an area of empty space," Winter said as she looked at the tri-dee map that was projected on her screen. "There are no planetary systems nearby. Will you be able to find us when we arrive?"

"We do not foresee difficulties locating FSS *Venture*," the voice told her.

"Then I have no further questions."

"Termination."

The hiss of static increased until Winter switched off the audio.

"Brief and to the point." David commented.

"Why was I not informed of transmission with Al'laan?" Shamask demanded as she came through the doorway to the bridge.

Winter swiveled her chair around. "Because there was no time, and because the call was specifically for me."

"I should have been summoned," the Al'laan argued.

Winter got to her feet, and David could see the muscles of her jaw tense. He started to speak but realized that the captain would resent his interference. Why, he wondered, do we always get such difficult passengers? Then he remembered Shamask's unique and probably frightening position as an alien in the power of an unknown race—a race that had captured and imprisoned her. And she was a telepath, sensitive to the emotions of everyone around her. In her position he would be scared stiff. Shamask glanced at David, and he realized that she was aware of his thoughts.

"There was no time," Winter repeated firmly. "However you can listen to a tape of the transmission, if you wish. Its purpose was to arrange a rendezvous with your people. If you have no further business on the bridge, we are preparing to leave orbit."

Shamask looked at the crew whose activities she had interrupted. She sensed curiosity and apprehension, as well as the captain's irritation and David's sympathy.

"I will wait in cabin," she said and left.

David picked up the box of computer buttons. "I'll get started on these," he told Winter, who stood looking after the departed Al'laan.

She turned and nodded to him. "Okay. See if she needs anything, will you? I don't have the time to play host right now." Winter slid back into her seat. "I'll talk to her again as soon as we've made the jump. Will you have some background material for me by then?"

"What do you want?"

"Details of her capture . . . where they found her, all that. It should all be in one of the files that Echard included. Signal me when you have the information transferred to our computer."

"I'll do that." David wanted to say more, but Winter's attention was taken up with maneuvering the *Venture* out of orbit and preparing for the jump. As the countdown began, David left the bridge.

It was not until the big screen on the bridge showed the iridescence of warped space that Winter turned her attention to the message signal light. She keyed retrieval and read David's note saying that the information about Shamask's capture was in the computer. Winter called it up and glanced around the bridge while she waited.

The *Venture* was on automatic, and most of the crew had left their posts. The lights on the main navigation control panel rippled a signal as the ship made some minute maneuver. Winter noted that the watch officer seemed attentive, although he really had very little to do until it was time to return to real space. She understood that his zeal was for her benefit and smiled to herself before turning back to the words that were appearing on the screen.

There was no information about where the Al'laan had been captured. Shamask had been brought to the Gyler Labs in a Proxima ship only a week before the *Venture* had arrived. Winter read further and saw that they had known she was an Al'laan! Proxima's purpose in sending her to the lab was to have a secure place to keep her until they could arrange safe passage to the Empire. They hoped to use her to set up their own exclusive communication with the Al'laan and eventually form an alliance with them against the Federation.

Winter culled that information from between sections of medical data. The Proxima, it seemed, had been almost desperate to discover a way to protect themselves against an Al'laan's anger. Shamask had defended herself well. Like Shaw, she had been stunned and captured by the special troops, but not before she had killed a number of people. The report called them "unamplified humans."

"Amplified humans" were the cyborgs, also called the "special troops." Winter read some more and then decided she had had enough for a while. The cyborgs at the lab had fought as if they had no fear of pain or death. She also remembered the suicide ship. It was logical to assume that it had been manned by a cyborg crew.

She cleared her screen and went to find Shamask.

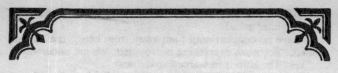

CHAPTER 23

Shamask opened the door before Winter could knock, and the two women stared at each other for a silent moment. Shamask was the more slender of the two. Her bones were attenuated, covered with a soft down that glistened in the ship's light. Winter stood in her uniform, the severity of the styling accenting her military carriage. Her thick, brown hair was neatly cut in a short spacer's crop that would not be a nuisance in either an atmosphere suit or free-fall.

Shamask wore a garment made from multicolored strips of cloth intricately draped across her torso to allow the freedom of her wings. The wings themselves were arranged down her sides like an additional item of clothing, the silver skin looking like some rare, metallic silk. Beneath them a long skirt flowed from her hips to brush the deck. Her black hair was confined at her forehead by another strip of cloth, allowing the ends to fall to her knees.

"I see Dr. Wilson has programmed the quartermaster for you," Winter remarked, indicating the gown.

"He is sympathetic to my needs, yes," Shamask replied politely. She stood aside to permit the captain to enter her cabin. The door hissed shut behind them.

"Is there anything else we can do to make you comfortable?" Winter asked.

"I have no comfort until I am away from here," the Al'laan replied. "For now, everything is provided. We are underway?"

"Yes. The ship is in warped space now."

Shamask nodded. "What is destination? I have heard tape of transmission with Al'laan. Numbers meaningless."

"They indicate an area in the Amergau sector, an area that hasn't been extensively explored. There are no planetary systems. It's just open space."

"Al'laan are there?"

"That's what they said. Where did you learn to speak Federation Standard?" Winter asked.

Shamask cocked her head, reminding the captain of a bright bird. "All who work with problem of mankind have learned language. Linguistic materials provided scientists were adequate."

"You were involved in this work?" Winter asked. "What did you do?"

"I was one who listened to transmissions and relayed selected material for specialists. I served as translator for others who would not learn your language."

"Do you know how you got to the Gyler Labs?" Winter shifted the subject. "Can you tell me anything about it?"

Shamask's face hardened, her eyes narrowing to angry slits. "I do not forget," she said. "Captors simulated distress. I took my ship to help. This is contrary to Al'laan law. I will be punished." Her hands clenched at her sides for a moment, and then she continued with her story. "We landed. We searched, and no one was there. I was apart from others. Men came." She fell silent.

"According to the report I read, you fought well before you were captured."

"It did not good," Shamask said bitterly.

"What happened to the others who were on your ship?"

"I do not know. I do not know what happened until I awakened. This story is in report?"

"The report contains mainly medical data. There were some notes and commentaries, but other than that very little about your capture."

Shamask looked at Winter as if she was listening to something. "What are cyborgs?" she asked after the time of uncomfortable silence had passed.

Winter realized that Shamask had been reading her, and although she resented the intrusion, she decided to be frank. "Cybernetic organisms—humans, in this case. They are humans adapted so that they can be programmed and controlled. The words 'programmed' and 'controlled' are the ones used by the Proxima, but they do not describe what's actually done."

"Proxima." Shamask tested the word. "These are ones who captured me?"

"Yes."

"This is outrage. What was purpose?"

"Because they hoped to make your people their allies," Winter told her.

Shamask considered that contradiction for a moment, then frowned. "These are your enemies?"

"They are opposed to the policies of the Federation," Winter said. "But there has been no formal declaration of war between us—as yet. Alliances are always uncertain when a war is building."

"These disagreements of your species are meaningless to Al'laan," Shamask said rather pointedly. "Why do they want Al'laan?"

"They hoped to gain a powerful ally," Winter repeated.

"These are not wise. These are foolish to think this is possible. To force an alliance is not right. We will never assist in war."

"I agree that they were foolish, but if they could have succeeded—"

"Impossible," Shamask interrupted. "Al'laan would never have considered this thing."

Winter was silent as Shamask, wings rippling, paced off her agitation.

"You are foolish," the Al'laan said, "to make this plan." She flung herself into the only chair in the cabin. "Why is Shaw on board this ship?" she demanded.

Winter was startled by the abrupt change of subject. "Shaw?"

"He is Al'laan. Why is he here?"

"How do you know he's an Al'laan?" Winter hedged, playing for time. "He doesn't look at all like you."

"He is. You do not know this?"

"I've considered the possibility, but his appearance . . ."

"Appearance altered so he can look as one of mankind."

"He refuses to tell anyone about his past," Winter said. "Do you know him personally?"

"I know him," Shamask said. "How does he come to be here?"

"He was also a captive of the Proxima Empire. Through one of their allies, the Malvern, he was being sent to the Gyler Labs in a stasis container. My ship was chosen for transport, but when Dr. Wilson learned the cargo was a live human, I ordered him removed from stasis."

"What do you do with him now?" Shamask asked.

"My superiors wish to talk with him. He may have some information they need," Winter admitted.

"He is prisoner?"

"No," the captain assured her. "He will be free to go after questioning."

"This is truth? How can you say for others?"

Winter stiffened. "I only follow orders. I cannot say what will happen, but the Federation has no reason to detain Shaw. He has not broken our laws."

Shamask looked intently at her. "Your mind does not know this."

"I have no way of knowing exactly what will happen to Shaw," Winter said tersely, nettled by the Al'laan's use of her esper ability. "I cannot predict events, speak for my superiors, or take responsibility for their actions. I just follow orders."

"You repeat."

"What is Shaw to you?" Winter asked, trying to get the conversation to safer ground. "Why are you so concerned about what will happen to him? I'd also like to know why he has been altered to pass for human and sent to live among us. Is he a fugitive from your people?"

"This is not for you to know." Shamask came to her feet and paced across the cabin again. "I did not know he is here. I am curious," she continued. "This matter is not important. I am important."

"We are doing everything possible to take you back to the Al'laan, quickly and safely," Winter promised. "And now that I know Shaw is an Al'laan, perhaps he will want to go back with you."

"This is not permitted," Shamask said quickly. "He is not wanted in Al'laan."

Winter's brow furrowed in confusion. "Why not? What did he do?"

"This is for Al'laan to know."

"But it isn't right," the captain protested. "He's an Al'laan —you're his people."

"In Al'laan, he will die."

Shamask was adamant, and Winter knew she would not get anywhere if she continued to press. Shaw would obviously have to provide the answers to her questions himself.

Winter turned and went to the door that hissed open in front of her. She paused just outside of the cabin, her hand on the control. "Thank you for speaking with me. I'm sorry that my duties do not permit me to spend more time with you, but if there is anything you need, please ask Dr. Wilson." She removed her hand, and the door slid closed.

Winter walked thoughtfully down the corridor. She wanted to see Shaw and started to go to his cabin, but then she realized that she was more likely to find him with David. When she arrived at sick bay, the doctor was alone, sitting at his computer terminal and making notes on a thick pad.

"David, do you know where Shaw is?" the captain asked.

"Not here," David replied, his attention on his work. "I'm amazed at this directory. We must have gained access to the main system. There are files on almost every subject, not just the medical records."

"I want to talk to him," Winter said, going back to her original topic. "Do you know if he's in his cabin?"

"Shaw?" David turned then, all of his attention on the captain. "I think so. Why? Has something happened?"

"I just spoke to Shamask. She implied some things about Shaw, but she refused to elaborate."

"What kinds of things?"

"She admitted he's an Al'laan, for one. When I suggested he might return with her, she told me he wouldn't be welcome."

David turned the chair and stretched out his legs, crossing them at the ankle. "I suspected he was an Al'laan when I saw Shamask's eyes," he said quietly. "There's something going on, though. Did she say why he can't go back?"

"No. She refused." Winter leaned against the side of med console.

"I'm not sure if that makes sense." David was silent a moment, gazing down at the keys in front of him. "I don't think Shaw will tell you anything. He's refused to talk about his past every time I bring the subject up. And now he won't even talk to me. He's in his cabin and he's asked to be left alone."

"Is he all right?"

"Physically, yes. But he's obviously pretty upset about something—probably Shamask. I suggest you leave him alone for awhile. I imagine finding Shamask the way he did was a shock. Give him time to get over it."

"Is this your medical opinion?" Winter asked.

"It is."

"All right. I'll leave him alone, but keep an eye on him for me and let me know when he comes out of it." She turned to leave.

"Before you go," David said, "would you look at some of the titles I found in the directory?"

"I will, but not now. Later, when I have more time. Beam your list to Echard and have him send whatever files you think are important."

"But, Winter—" he protested.

"Later, David. With the Al'laan to deal with I can't even begin to think about Gyler now."

She was gone before David could tell her about the files on Karth.

CHAPTER 24

While the *Venture* made the jump across warped space, Winter sat on the bridge composing her report for Admiral Jammeson. The watch commander sat at the navigator's console, monitoring the ship's systems as the computer took the vessel through the superlight maze.

In sick bay David worked on his notes, read, and waited for the ship to return to normal space so that he could contact Echard. He never had another chance to tell Winter about the files on Karth, but he thought he should send for them just the same.

Shamask occasionally was seen walking in the corridors, but she spoke to no one, and the crew was too apprehensive of her to initiate conversation. Shaw stayed in his cabin and refused to see anyone.

One hundred sixty-nine hours passed until the computer on the bridge signaled that it was time to return to real space. Winter watched as the sublight systems came humming to life.

"Mark, one minute," Thomas announced.

David appeared and slid into his seat at the science station.

"Weapons, check," Lieutenant Nelson said. "All banks fully charged and operational. On standby."

"Weapons?" David commented.

"Under the circumstances they are required by regulations and also, I think, advisable," Winter told him without turning around.

"Five seconds," Thomas called. "Four, three, two, cutting in sublight engines."

The deceleration was automatic and had been going on for the past four hours, but still the transition from warped space was abrupt and, as usual, upset David's stomach. The iridescent blue-gray in the port flashed and darkened to normal space with its decoration of brightly colored stars.

"Coming up on the coordinates," Thomas said. "Speed point five and holding."

The bridge crew watched on the navigational grid as the light that represented the *Venture* slowed and seemed to come to a stop, reflecting the contrast between their current speed and superlight.

"Right on target." The engineer's voice was filled with satisfaction.

"David, what does your scan show?"

He checked the bioscanner. "Sensors show a blip off to starboard—point oh three two degrees."

"Lieutenant Delieus, invite Shamask to come to the bridge," the captain ordered. "Tell her we have arrived at the rendezvous point."

"Aye, Captain." He spoke softly into the communicator, then switched it off. "She's on her way." He paused, looking at something on his panel. "Captain, there's a transmission coming in."

"Main speakers. Let's hear it, Lieutenant."

". . . ission. FSS *Venture*, are you receiving? I repeat, initiating transmission. Federation Survey Ship *Venture*, please respond."

Winter pressed a button and spoke. "This is the FSS *Venture*, Captain Winter speaking. We have your signal. Please proceed with your transmission."

Just then Shamask entered the bridge. She called out in her own language and was answered by a voice from the speaker.

Winter smothered a curse. "Delieus, tape this! Tie it into the computer and translate," she snapped. "Shamask, what are you saying to him?"

Shaw had come up to the bridge after Shamask and was standing unnoticed in the doorway. He answered Winter. "She is identifying herself and demanding to be taken off of the *Venture* immediately."

The voice from the Al'laan ship cut in, speaking in Standard again. "Captain Winter, activate visual circuits."

Delieus looked at the captain, his eyes opened wide in amazement. Never before had the Al'laan permitted a visual communication. Winter signaled him to comply.

The main viewing screen flickered and changed to show the interior of the Al'laan ship. Two of the Al'laan were in sight, one seated before a control panel, the other standing facing the view screen. Both were pale and dark haired. They were dressed in what Winter assumed was a uniform of some kind: breast pieces of a leatherlike material, heavily embossed and subtly colored, and from the waist down, short kilts. Their dark wings were draped down their sides, flowing out and then subsiding with every movement.

"Dorticia Shamask, transport is arranged," one of the Al'laan said. "Captain Winter, indicate suitable hull interception point."

"The air locks are marked by concentric rings and numerals. On the flat side of the ring nearest to you there is an air lock marked with this symbol." Winter keyed her console and the number "three" flashed on the screen. "Can you see it?" she asked.

"We see this symbol," the Al'laan responded.

"We will be waiting for you at the air lock with this symbol," Winter said.

"Comprehend," the Al'laan captain told her. "Arrival momentary. Dorticia Shamask, go to air lock. Captain Winter, further communication necessary. Remain."

"Certainly, if you wish. One moment, please." Winter turned to speak to David. "Would you take Shamask to the air lock?"

"Right."

Winter watched until they had left the bridge. Her eyes strayed to Shaw, who was standing just inside the doorway. His posture was stiff and his face blank. His eyes shifted to meet hers for a second before turning back to the viewscreen. Winter returned to her panel.

"Shamask is on her way," she said.

Thomas was monitoring the arrival of the Al'laan shuttle using one of the hullside cameras. "Docking completed. Cycling air lock," he told Winter.

"Captain Winter," the Al'laan said. "Intersect with transport complete." He stopped speaking and looked off screen for a second. Another Al'laan appeared at his side. Clearly older, the newcomer had white streaks in his long black hair and wore, as well as the uniform worn by the others, a large glittering jeweled disk suspended from a chain around his neck.

"Captain Winter? I am Dortem Vidor. I was to have been in charge of communications with you, but when your ship was sighted I was unavailable. I hope there have been no difficulties?"

"No, there have been no problems."

"That is good. Our captain will be gratified, as he was not pleased at the necessity of learning your tongue and not certain he could make himself understood." He paused. "I have an unpleasant task facing me. You are aware of Al'laan preference for maintaining complete physical isolation from mankind?"

"That has been one of the main stipulations of our continuing communication with your race," the captain said.

Dortem Vidor nodded. "Yes. It is unfortunate our wishes have been ignored in matter of kidnapping Dorticia Shamask. Our government is angered by this breach of trust."

"I hope they understand the circumstances surrounding the capture and that the Federation is not responsible. The Proxima Empire is our enemy. They kidnapped Dorticia Shamask."

"We know those responsible are not Federation, but they are yet of your race. Therefore it has been decided an example must be made so none of you will ever attempt to repeat this offense."

"What do you mean an example?" Winter asked, experiencing a sudden chill of apprehension.

"We are not a violent people," Vidor assured her. "Believe this and know I am deeply pained by necessity; nevertheless, I have orders. Your ship is to be destroyed."

Winter unobtrusively tapped a message that would show only on Commander Thomas's board: ACTIVATE WEAPONS BANKS. PREPARE TO FIRE ON MY ORDER.

"Don't you think we might have something to say about that plan?" she said out loud.

"We were certain you would attempt to defend yourselves, but I think you will find your weapons have all been deactivated. Test them."

"Commander Thomas, pick a target away from both ships and test all weapons banks," Winter ordered.

"Aye, Captain." Thomas busied himself at the board.

David returned to the bridge and quietly slipped into his seat. He had heard the last of the conversation between Winter and the Al'laan. He looked over at Shaw, who was standing unobtrusively in the back of the bridge.

There was a series of metallic clicks as Thomas pressed the firing controls. "Captain, nothing's happening. All banks are nonfunctional."

"Thank you, Commander," Winter said quietly. She stood and looked into the screen, her growing rage evident in her posture, her voice icy. "I don't know how you're doing this, but you have managed to deactivate our weapons. I protest this action. If you are as fair and peaceful as you say, you wouldn't destroy an unarmed opponent."

"As I have said," Dortem Vidor responded, "the necessity grieves me, but I have orders and I must obey."

"Who gave you these orders?" Shaw's voice cut into the dialogue. He stepped forward, stopping beside Winter and for the first time in range of the viewer.

Winter glanced at Shaw when she saw the look of amazement on Dortem Vidor's features. Shaw stared up at the screen, his face expressionless.

"You! Why are you here?" Vidor snapped.

"My movements are no longer any of your concern. However my presence on this ship should be a factor in your decision to carry out your orders."

The Al'laan's face was twisted with rage. "Wait," he growled. The screen went black.

"What's this all about?" Winter demanded of Shaw.

He looked down at her. "Vidor obviously did not know I was aboard the *Venture*. I thought it was time I corrected that misinformation."

"And Dortem Vidor knows you?"

"Yes, he knows me very well."

"Do you think you can dissuade him from destroying my ship?"

"I don't think he will be allowed to do so while I am on board."

"Shaw, there are obviously too many things that I don't know about you and the Al'laan," Winter told him, her voice tight with anger. "Our safety depends on my having as much information as possible. What can you tell me that will help us here?"

"I was not sure if they would go to this extreme or I would have told you sooner. Right now there is no time to correct that, but let me talk to Vidor. If there is a way to get the *Venture* out of this, I will have to find it."

Winter could see no other way to handle the situation. She turned away from him. "Thomas, get the *Venture* ready to leave here at a moment's notice. Delieus, put in the coordinates for a hyperspace jump. I don't care what destination you pick just as long as it's back in Federation space." The crew moved into action. "I'm not going to sit here and wait to be destroyed," she told Shaw.

She sank back into her chair and turned to David. "Can you scan their ship? How many are on board?"

"They're moving around, so it's hard to count. I'd say twenty, maybe twenty-two. They're receiving a transmission now."

"They've probably called to find out what to do about Shaw," Winter said. "Delieus, can you pick it up?"

"Sorry, Captain. It's a shielded transmission," the lieutenant told her.

Winter looked up at Shaw. "We are forced to depend on you," she told him. "Still, while we may be weaponless, we can still run, and I'll be damned if I intend to just sit here. Talk to Dortem Vidor. See if you can convince him to let us go."

"They're hailing us again, Captain," Delieus called to her.

"Thank you, Lieutenant. Switch them on." Winter watched the screen as the interior of the Al'laan ship reappeared. "Dortem Vidor—" she began, but was interrupted.

"I wish to speak to Denylan Khaire, Prince—the one you call Shaw," the Al'laan demanded. He looked beyond her to Shaw.

Vidor said something in Al'laan, and Winter noted Delieus keying the computer to translate.

"Stop!" Shaw interrupted before she could protest. "My friends do not understand our language. For the sake of clarity we will speak only Standard."

"Very well, Your Highness," Vidor conceded, but there was a sneer in his voice. "Once again you have managed to cause trouble. Much against my will, I have been instructed to treat you with courtesy to which birth entitles you, instead of blowing you into Asortez's seventeen hells as you deserve."

Shaw smiled and gave Vidor a nod. "You have not changed, cousin. You still are charming."

"Nor have you changed. From all the reports I have seen I am surprised you have not managed to get yourself killed. It would save all of us much shame."

"I'm sorry I have not met your expectations. What are your instructions concerning the *Venture*?"

"I am to discuss those with you privately. We are sending transport for you. You will join me on this ship."

"I will not leave the *Venture*."

Vidor leaned forward, glaring out of the screen. "I order you to come aboard this ship."

"I do not recognize your authority, Vidor. I am staying. Anything that concerns this ship can be said to me here."

Vidor leaned back and muttered something in Al'laan.

"You forget, Vidor," Shaw said. "We grew up together. I know you. You were always too obvious. Since you have orders not to harm me, you want me off the *Venture*. Then you will be able to execute your original plan. But if I do not leave, you will have to let this ship go."

"One day you will go too far, Your Highness," Vidor said, the title more of a taunt than a form of courtesy. "One day you will not be able to talk yourself out of trouble. That day will make me very happy," Vidor said. He looked at Winter. "Go quickly, then. The prince has saved you this time, but I may yet decide ridding the universe of my royal cousin is worth the anger of the council. After all," he concluded, looking back at Shaw, "not many of them still agree that your breeding should keep you from the fate you deserve."

"Fly well, cousin," Shaw said with a little bow. "Hurry. Get us out of here," he whispered to Winter.

She nodded to Thomas. "Sublight now. Jump to hyperspace just as soon as we've achieved maximum acceleration."

Thomas did not bother to answer. His fingers flew, and his anxious eyes watched the gauges as he pushed the *Venture* to the limit and then some.

David realized that he had been holding his breath and let the air out of his lungs in a sigh.

"We are not out of trouble yet," Shaw warned.

"But he said that the Al'laan wouldn't do anything to the *Venture* while you're on board," David protested.

"He had to say that," Shaw explained. "His communication was being monitored by his superiors as carefully as yours was being recorded by the Federation. His words do not mean that Vidor would not try to destroy us if he finds an undetectable way to do it."

"Such as?" David prompted.

Winter was wondering the same thing. She looked thoughtfully at Shaw. "What did they use to keep our weapons from firing?" she asked.

"A scrambler signal," he replied. "They would have programmed it to intercept your signals from the bridge to the weapons banks."

"They can do that from their ship?" she asked. "How could such a device work across space?"

"It is not possible," Shaw said. "They would have to use an amplifier somewhere on the *Venture*." Then he nodded as he, too, realized how Vidor could yet manage to achieve their destruction.

Where? Winter asked herself as her mind ran a rapid inventory of the possibilities. They could be only one place. "At the air lock," she said out loud. "Thomas, do we have a camera on lock three?"

"Aye. I'll scan." His head bent over the console as his fingers rapidly punched the keys.

"Put the picture on the main viewer and send someone to check the inside of the lock. We've got to find that scrambler," the captain told them.

"Captain," the engineer warned. "We've got a jump calculated to begin in seven minutes."

"We'll make it. We'd better," she finished in an undertone.

The camera panned over the outside of the *Venture*'s foremost ring. The painted number three just outside the lock was plain on the screen. Equally clear was a small oval device attached to one side of the hatch.

"Damn!" Winter exploded from her chair and was racing to the corridor before anyone else could react.

"Winter!" David yelled starting after her. "What are you doing? There's no time! We're going to jump."

She had a locker open by the time he reached her. The tech was helping her load an environment suit into the air lock.

"Winter, there's no time," David repeated, frantic at the thought of what she was attempting to do.

"There's time. Just shut up and don't waste it," she said

shortly. She nodded to the technicians who closed the door after her. Through the port David could see her struggling into the suit. She started evacuating the air even as she worked the helmet over her head.

David clenched his fists as if his tension could help her. He knew she was going to try to retrieve the Al'laan device before the *Venture* made the jump to superlight. But if she was caught outside the ship when that happened, she would be lost. There was no way they could find her in the vast other dimensions of warped space.

Winter fastened the safety line from her suit to a ring inside the lock, and without waiting for all of the air to be evacuated, she opened the hatch. The remaining air streamed out into the vacuum of space, the change of pressure hurling Winter from the ship. David watched horrified, but the safety line held.

Thomas's voice came from through the wall speaker. "Four minutes and counting."

Three minutes have passed, David thought. Already it felt like an hour. Winter gave a tug on the safety line, and the momentum set her drifting back toward the *Venture*'s hull. She reeled in the line, pulling herself along even faster than the drift.

"Come on, come on," David muttered through clenched teeth, his hands gripping the edges of the port. Winter was hidden from his sight by the hull.

"Three minutes."

Winter's hand, then her leg appeared in the opening. She floated into the lock, an oval shape cradled in her arm.

"Two minutes."

The outer lock was closing, but it seemed to move very slowly.

"One minute. Counting . . . nine, eight . . ."

The outer hatch inched shut as Thomas counted out the last of the seconds. Then there was a lurch as the *Venture* hurled herself into warped space.

CHAPTER 25

Winter was still in the suit, sitting on the deck where she had landed when the ship jumped. David and the tech helped her get the helmet off.

"Of all the people on board, you're the one we can't afford to lose!" David yelled. He was shaking with anger and relief.

"I had to do it," she defended herself. "Here." She handed the Al'laan device to the tech. "Take this down to the engineering lab. Tell Commander Thomas that it's there and I want it taken apart. Find out what makes it work." The tech nodded and hurried off, holding the device very carefully, as if it might blow up at any moment.

"You could have sent someone else after it!" David continued.

"There wasn't enough time to explain what had to be done," Winter insisted. "I knew, so I had to be the one to go. Can't you understand that? If I had tried to send anyone else it would have been too late."

"You could have been lost when we jumped."

"And we all might have been killed if that thing had been left out there. Help me up." Winter staggered to her feet, holding on to the wall. David caught her arm, alarmed at how pale she looked.

"Are you all right?" he asked, his concern softening his voice.

"I'm fine. Just feeling the aftereffects." She gave a shaky laugh. "You don't have to scold me, David. I know what I did—how risky it was. If I'd had time to think about it, I don't know if I would have gone out there. But then I've always had good reflexes." She laughed again. "Help me get this suit off. It's hot."

David helped her with the fastenings. She was shaking by the time he got her out of the suit.

"You'd better go to your cabin and lie down," he recommended.

"I will as soon as I've checked the bridge. I still have a ship to run, you know."

She took a deep breath and steadied herself, and David watched her walk down the corridor as if nothing at all had happened. He looked down at the deck where the crumpled atmosphere suit still lay and swore softly to himself. Then he hurried after the captain.

Delieus and Nelson, the communications and engineering officers, were the only ones left on the bridge when Winter arrived.

"Status report," she said as she came through the doorway, David a few steps behind her.

"All systems functioning," Nelson told her.

"Our destination is the Cassiopeia system, sector two three B seven," Delieus reported. "ETA eighty-two point oh seven hours."

"Thank you. Lieutenant, do you know where Shaw is?"

"No, sir. He left the bridge just after we jumped."

"Thank you. I'll be in my cabin until the morning shift. Call me if anything happens." She turned to David and gave his shoulder an affectionate squeeze. "And thank you for worrying about me," she said softly as she went past him.

"It's my job," he replied. "Sleep well."

When she left the bridge, Winter did not go directly to her cabin. She walked in the opposite direction and stopped at Shaw's door. He had been expecting her and opened it before she could decide whether to knock or leave.

"I thought you might be asleep," she said.

"No. I knew you would be impatient for answers to your

questions about the Al'laan. And you were right. Not telling you what I know put your ship in danger. Please come in." He stood aside for her to enter the cabin.

"You had a lot of time to think about the consequences before we made the contact. Why didn't you tell me then?"

"I have not had to think about the Al'laan for a very long time. I thought I would never have to deal with them again." He paused. "You saw that my relationship with my people is not the best."

"What happened? Dortem Vidor called you 'prince.' What did he mean by that?"

"Please sit down. It is a long story and perhaps you should hear it all." Shaw waited until Winter was settled before he began to speak.

"The Al'laan are an ancient people, perhaps a little older even than mankind. We evolved on a light gravity planet, one that is so rich in minerals that organic life carries large concentrations of it in their cells. This is what accounts for our coloration and dense bone structure.

"The atmosphere of our planet is turbulent. There are constant high winds, and most of the life forms, including the Al'laan, have evolved to use the winds instead of resisting them. Only in the last ten thousand years or so have we begun to build permanent structures—cities—and those are built underground or in the caverns that lace the mountain ranges. Because we are such a mobile society, our evolution was slower than yours, but despite that, we are similar in many ways to mankind."

Shaw was silent for a moment, remembering. Then he spoke again in a softer voice. "My homeworld is very beautiful, although perhaps you would not find it so. You might think it wild and even frightening. Everything moves, changes constantly, but we move and change with it. We fly on the winds . . ." He was silent again.

"Why did you have to leave?" Winter asked.

Shaw looked at her. "Our people are ruled by a dynastic house—by an emperor. He is the head of a government composed of a noble court. I was the leader of a group who tried to change that. At first we attempted to work through the court, but the Al'laan are tradition-bound. So my friends and I tried to overthrow the government."

"You *what*?" Winter had not tried to imagine what Shaw had done to alienate himself from his people, but somehow she would never have imagined him as the leader of a rebel band. But then, why not? The profession of spy was not all that dissimilar.

"I headed a revolution," Shaw said. "Why are you so surprised? It has happened many times in your history. In my world, however, it is not that common."

"All right. Your revolution failed."

"And I was exiled as my punishment." Shaw dropped down on the edge of the bunk, his hands limp between his knees.

"In Earth's history the traditional punishment for treason is death," Winter told him.

"The Al'laan have the same penalty," Shaw said. "They rounded up almost all of those who worked with me. When we were together in the prisons beneath the emperor's city, my friends were killed, one by one. It was not pleasant to watch." He stood and began to pace. His voice remained calm, almost expressionless as he spoke, but the words came faster. "And I had to watch. They were my friends. We believed in the same things, had the same ideals. And I watched them die. I hoped they would kill me, too. I expected it. But they had something else planned for me." He paused to catch his breath.

"They changed me into what you see. They turned me over to the scientists, the gentle doctors who worked on me for almost a year, altering my chemistry, my skin, my coloring. It was to make me more like one of mankind they said, so I would be able to survive among you. But I knew it was really to make sure I would never be able to return to the world of the Al'laan." Shaw laughed. "They did leave me with a reminder of what I had been." He touched the scar that was visible where his arm came out of his sleeve. "They left me with a reminder of what I can never be again," he whispered.

Winter watched Shaw, his movements graceful despite the confines of the small cabin, his pain evident in his inability to remain still. The words were pouring out of him as if he could no longer endure keeping them inside.

"The emperor's family is almost sacred to the Al'laan. They have—we have—ruled in an unbroken line for centuries of our time. What I had done was unheard of and I should have been killed, but I was a member of the royal family—I was one of the heirs and untouchable. They could not bring themselves to kill me outright, and their only alternative was to send me into your worlds as an exile. Exile," he whispered bitterly. "The slow killing."

"They gave you a chance to begin a new life," Winter suggested carefully. "They changed you so that you could survive."

"But they left me with my memories . . . memories of the killing of my friends. And they left me with the knowledge that I was responsible for the deaths. I was also allowed the realization that I will never again be one of the Al'laan." He paused and looked down at the captain. "To you they are alien, but I am alien to both races now. I am neither Man, nor am I Al'laan. They have made certain of it. I belong nowhere. Alien and alienated forever and from all people. How can you imagine what that would be like? To be denied your home, your family, your world. To know you can never go back, never again be part of anything in just that way."

Winter felt the words he spoke. How could she know, he asked. But she, of all people, *did* know what it was like never to be able to go back.

"Others have had these feelings of alienation." The words came out of her mouth, but she felt as if someone else were speaking. The sound was harsh.

Shaw was silent, looking at her as if he had had a sudden realization.

Winter took a deep breath. "The only thing that concerns us here is your information about the Al'laan. Please continue," she said firmly.

"This means something more to you," Shaw said slowly. "I think it has something to do with the images I saw in your mind when we were on Gyler—the horses on the beach."

Winter got quickly to her feet. Her head was beginning to ache with the day's accumulation of stress. Shaw was standing before her, sympathy in his face as he confronted a suddenly very vulnerable starcaptain.

"You carry a burden, too, don't you?" he said softly. He put his hands on her shoulders, holding her gently and making a complete link of their minds. And the memories of Karth came, conjured up by Shaw.

Winter jerked herself from Shaw's grasp and leaned against the wall, shaken and shaking. "Don't ever do that again," she gasped.

Shaw just looked at her, his eyes still filled with the vision she had remembered.

"Winter?" It was the first time he had ever called her by her name without the prefix of her rank. He wanted to reach for her again, to understand the resistance she felt to her memories. He knew what she was feeling, and although his own hurt was still fresh and strong, he wanted to ease the anguish he saw in her. The feeling was strange for him, but he did not take the time to try to understand.

"I think this has been a difficult day for both of us," Winter said quickly. Her appearance of composure had returned. "But it's over now. Finished." She left the cabin.

Back in her quarters, it was Winter's turn to pace. Admiral Jammeson would want a complete and detailed report of everything that had happened that day, including her conversation with Shaw. She should set it down while the events were fresh in her mind, but for some reason she felt reluctant to expose Shaw's story to the cold and unfeeling analysis of her superiors.

Why? a voice in her mind demanded. Because parts of his story were so very like her own? Winter did not want to think about it, and turmoil set her feet moving back and forth across the deck. This was, she realized, one of the few times she had ever questioned what she had to do in the service of the Federation. She was deeply troubled by all that had happened and by the intrusion of doubt into her orderly, well-regulated life.

Winter walked back and forth, pushing herself farther into exhaustion. The adrenaline rush that had sustained her outside the ship had gone, leaving her depressed; weariness made it an effort just to support the weight of her body and force her legs to move. In contrast, her mind was alive with thoughts that came rushing, out of her control.

Back and forth Winter moved, not knowing what she wanted or needed; back and forth until she fell onto her bed, sleep stilling her body but not her mind.

CHAPTER 26

Early in the afternoon Admiral Jammeson received a priority message on the privacy shielded screen in his office. When the call was finished, he summoned his aides and the head of Information Services, Oliver Gerny. He sat with his elbows on the desk, his chin resting thoughtfully on his clasped hands while he waited for them to arrive. There was both anger and apprehension in his mind as he mulled over his orders from Command Headquarters. It was just like them to dump such a difficult problem in his lap! The fact that he had done precisely the same thing to them not a week before was something that he did not choose to remember. Now he had to deal with the Al'laan again, and the new problem promised to be even worse than the first.

Jammeson's thoughts were not pleasant. Fortunately the wait for his subordinates was not long. There was a knock at the door and then it opened to admit four men in spotless uniforms, their ribbons and bars of rank bright and gleaming.

"Gentlemen," he greeted them, coming from behind his desk. "Please be seated. I have some rather startling news for you."

The aides exchanged silent glances as they found seats around the small oval table.

Jammeson remained standing as he looked down at the expectant faces. He clasped his hands behind him, rocking back and forth on his feet as the silence grew.

"I have just had an unusual message from Earth," he said finally. "We are facing a difficult task, but one which I am certain can be brought to a satisfactory conclusion. I have just had word from Command headquarters that they have received an ultimatum from the Al'laan."

"What is this?" Gerny spoke his surprise. "When did this happen? I thought the situation with the Al'laan had been taken care of." He wondered briefly if Captain Winter had bungled her assignment. If she had, it would mean trouble.

"Yes, I, too, was amazed at this unprecedented occurrence," Jammeson said ponderously. "But I was shocked even more so by the content of their ultimatum. It seems that the smuggler, Shaw, who was rescued by the *Venture*, is a member of the Al'laan race." He paused a moment to let that sink in.

Gerny's eyes narrowed. His brain was quickly searching for the various ramifications of the disclosure. The aides were silent, understanding that the new information was going to make their jobs even more difficult.

Jammeson continued. "The essence of the ultimatum is this: the Al'laan are angry that Shaw has been . . . well, let us say, detained by the Federation, and they demand his immediate release. Since the *Venture* is under my command, the matter has been given into my hands.

"Gerny, I want you to set your computers to work on this problem. At the moment it would appear that there is nothing for me to do but order Captain Winter to take Shaw to the nearest inhabited world and release him, *but*," he said, "I want confirmation and/or alternatives to this plan."

"You want me to plot probable end results of all possible actions?" the information officer asked.

"Yes." Jammeson leaned over the table, his weight resting on his braced hands. "I can't help but think that Shaw might also prove to be a valuable asset to the Federation. In this case, I want you to add this possibility when you question the computer; I want to know if there is any way for us to keep Shaw without the Al'laan becoming aware that we have done so."

Gerny slowly shook his head from side to side, the expression on his face forbidding. "Since we have no way of knowing the extent of the Al'laan information net, or even if such a net exists, your proposed action could prove to be very risky."

"That's why I want a computation. I believe we have to try to find a way to keep Shaw for the Federation. If he's running around loose, there's always the chance that the Proxima might get to him. They did so once before, if you will remember." Jammeson frowned at his subordinates. "Therefore, if it is at all possible, Command wants him detained."

"Why is Command leaving such an important matter up to us?" one of the aides ventured. "I mean, their data retrieval complex is so much larger than ours."

Gerny already knew the answer: Command wanted Alpha Base to take the responsibility if anything went wrong.

"As I have already said, Lieutenant," Jammeson responded, "the *Venture* is under my command. And the computers here are certainly adequate for the task." The admiral looked intently at the three men around the table. "Are there further questions?"

"When is Captain Winter due to check in again?" Gerny asked.

"Not for another twenty hours or so," the admiral told him after glancing at his chronometer. "I see no reason why her new orders shouldn't be ready at that time."

And thus he passed the problem on.

Winter and the chief engineer were in the workshop in the second ring of the *Venture*. The shop was cluttered with spare parts, meters, and the racks of tools that Thomas and the other techs used in their work. The Al'laan device that Winter had removed from outside of the air lock was partially disassembled in a small isolated chamber beyond a thick protective panel. The engineer used a pair of waldos to reach it as he spoke.

"These circuits are controls for the scrambler," Thomas told Winter. "It's all very neatly planned and very specific."

"How could the Al'laan know enough about the *Venture* to design such a device?"

"I don't know." The engineer was grim. "They'd have to know exactly what they were doing in order to deactivate a specific system without affecting the others. They're getting their information somewhere, that's for certain. This thing wasn't built by guess work."

The captain's face was equally grim as she looked at the device.

"And here's what really scares me," Thomas continued, his big hands deftly manipulating the waldos to unclip a section of the Al'laan device. He set it carefully aside. "Now watch." He fastened an external energy source to the unit. There was a sudden loud clicking sound from the machine.

"What did you do? I didn't see anything," Winter said.

"I disconnected the unit's internal power leads, but I need some juice to show you this." The waldo picked up a heavy wrench and held it in the air over the device. "Watch," he repeated.

Thomas opened his remote fingers and moved the waldo away from the wrench, but the tool remained suspended a foot above the alien machine.

"What—" Winter began in amazement as she watched the bulky wrench twist and float gently in the air.

"Antigravity," the engineer told her. "The device can be focused and has a considerable range. Quite powerful for such a small generator. When I first tried it, it was set for a hundred meters or so. We can be thankful I had the damn thing pointed at a bulkhead and space when I turned it on the first time. Look at this." He touched two wires together, and a sharp beam of light hit the wrench. It dissolved into nothing. "If that beam had hit the engines . . ."

"We wouldn't be standing here talking about it," Winter finished for him.

"Aye," Thomas said respectfully. "We would have been blown to eternity in a second—and probably even further than that." He disconnected the energy source. "I cannot tell you the purpose of the beam, but I do know it had a remote trigger, as well as a sensory trigger attached. We also know that it was trained on the weapons controls and, by extending its range, it could reach the engines, as well. If the beam had been activated it would have vaporized all ship's controls and the engine failsafes."

"And the engines would have been critical within seconds," the captain concluded. She released her breath in a hiss. "For a peaceful people, the Al'laan are certainly thorough in their destruction." She made a decision and turned away from the window to look up at the big engineer. "Make certain that device is completely dead and then pack it up so there won't be a chance of anything triggering it accidentally. I think it would be best if we turned it over to the techs at Alpha Base."

"That I'll do." The engineer's fingers traced the edge of the window, and he was silent for a moment, obviously concerned and trying to find words to express himself. "Captain Winter," he said, his voice unusually gentle. "You scared us something terrible when you went outside the ship after this thing. We didn't know what was happening, and I thought you were being rash—but if you hadn't gotten it when you did . . ." His words trailed off.

"But I did get it." Winter smiled at him, recognizing the unspoken gratitude behind the words he spoke so hesitantly. "Just be sure the device stays safe."

David pushed himself back from the computer terminal in his office. He was tired of the never ending reports his position required. Keeping records of his work was one thing, but having to rewrite everything in the jargon so beloved of the bureaucratic mind was another. He also had to reword all of the technical data so that the navy brass could read it. David did not see any sense in it, especially when he always sent duplicates of his own records to his superiors on the science staff. Why could they not just send the information on to the brass?

He had a sudden vision of Command deluged by a veritable sea of data. The higher one got in rank, the more of it one had to deal with. Maybe being a lowly tech was not such a bad thing after all. At least he had time to sit around with his feet up now and then. At the moment, that did not seem like such a bad idea.

David poured a fresh cup of coffee from the insulated pot and sat back, lifting his feet to the desk top. Winter found him that way when she entered sick bay.

"Are you finished with your work already?" She seated herself across from him.

"When are these blasted reports ever finished?" He reached over and poured a second cup of coffee. "I've decided that the military runs on red tape—or did someone else say that?" He leaned forward to give her the cup. "It doesn't matter; I agree with them. Command will have to do without us for a while anyway, since we can't send anything 'til we're back in real space. Having come to this conclusion, I decided to take a break."

"I'm having trouble writing my report, too," Winter said.

"You?" David told her, his eyes wide in mock surprise. "I thought writing reports would be a snap in a life devoted to military procedure. Just like breathing for you—you know, inhale, exhale, write reports. Simple." He drank from his cup. "So what's wrong?"

"Nothing a lack of conscience wouldn't cure," she told him, but she would not meet his eyes.

"Well, well," David intoned slowly. "Someone's finally gotten through those tough defenses of yours." She frowned at him, but he ignored her look and continued. "I bet you talked to Shaw. What'd he say that made you question your sacred duty?"

"I thought you'd know all about it by now. Have you talked to him since yesterday?"

"No, I know better than to butt in to sensitive areas." Despite his flippant tone, David watched her carefully.

"I hadn't noticed," she commented.

"Oh, not where you're concerned," he explained. "It's my job to ride watch on you."

"Thank you very much, but I don't need it."

"Oh, yes, you do. Starcaptains may be the toughest people in the galaxy, but even they have a breaking point. That's why every starcaptain has a special nursemaid," David said lightly.

"You mean a personal spy, don't you? Who do you report to anyway? Jammeson?" There was a distinct edge to Winter's words.

David's hurt was patent. "That's not fair, Winter. You know I've always been on your side."

"I hoped so." But she did not seem convinced.

"I am. You have to believe it."

His face displayed his very sincere distress, and Winter stopped baiting him. "I really have no choice, do I?" Winter said much more gently. She sighed.

"What's wrong?" David asked. "What did Shaw say to make you so uneasy?"

"It isn't so much what he said as how I feel about it." She made a sound of disgust. "I hope you believe that I don't want to do anything to make life harder for Shaw . . . but I keep remembering what Shamask said about him. And, now that the Federation has their own Al'laan, I have the feeling that they're going to use him to find out everything they can."

"You can bet they will," David said emphatically. "They'll take him apart. They were only interested in his information about the Proxima-Malvern alliance before, but now that they know what he is— I'll be surprised if they ever release him. He'll be passed from division to division until everyone from state security to pathology gets a piece of him."

"You don't really believe that, do you?" Winter protested. "There are laws—"

"Shaw's an alien," David interrupted. "You know damn well that he has no more rights than some experimental animal. Besides, no one ever bothers with the law in wartime. Expediency and the good of the state are all that matters."

"David—"

"No." He quickly forestalled her. "Shaw's an unknown, possibly hostile element, and that makes him a threat. And, since he's a member of such a mysterious race, the Federation will have to keep him in custody just so he won't fall into enemy hands."

"It's called protective custody," she suggested. "That's not the same thing as criminal incarceration."

"Very nice differentiation," David said sarcastically. "That's what's wrong with the military mind; it's so naive. Winter, remember, this is wartime. Shaw might be better off if he was stuck on a prison planet somewhere. But they're going to take him back to Command, and he'll disappear in that underground warren of theirs. He'll never see the light of day again. It will be as if he never existed."

"I may be naive, but I think your viewpoint's equally simplistic," she countered.

"Winter, how can you think that way? Do you really believe that anyone in Command will care one way or the other for Shaw's rights—or even his life? Be realistic! He's an Al'laan, and now that they've learned he's a highly placed Al'laan they'll decide that he has information vital to Federation security. They'll want to use it against the Proxima or—or the Malvern, or whoever our enemy is at the moment. They'll probably even want to use his knowledge against his own people before they're through."

"What are you saying, David?" Winter was aghast at the bitterness of his words even as she tried to ignore the shiver of apprehension they evoked.

"The Al'laan are a race that are not under Federation control. You can't imagine how nervous that makes the political mind. And if I know the brass, they've already classed the Al'laan as our enemies."

Winter was silent, staring at her half-finished coffee. David watched her, noting the changes the past months had made. She was still every inch the starcaptain, but she was thinner and she had a fine-drawn quality that made him think she was running on nervous energy more than was good for her. Winter was approaching her breaking point.

"Winter, how can I help you?" he asked softly.

"You can't. These are decisions I have to make for myself, but it does help to have someone to talk to." Her voice faltered. "Sometimes I think you're right, but it's hard . . . What you're saying goes against everything I believed in."

"It's never too late to correct that kind of mistake."

"But to know you've been living a lie . . ."

"Don't be so hard on yourself," David said.

"No, I don't think I'm being too hard, but things have been happening—things that I can't explain. I'm worried."

"You'll work it out," he insisted. "I have faith in you."

"Thanks." She chuckled sadly. "It's good to hear, even if I can't find it in myself anymore."

David wondered again what Shaw had said to her, but he knew he could not ask; if Winter wanted him to know, she would tell him. He also wondered if he should mention the tapes of Karth, but decided to wait until they arrived and he had a chance to review them. When he knew for certain what they contained he would tell her, but not until then. She was having too much trouble with the responsibility for Shaw's fate.

"Where is Shaw?" Winter asked suddenly. "Have you seen him at all?"

"No, I've been too busy working on these damn reports. As far as I know he's either in his cabin or in the gym."

"The gym? When did he start going there?"

"I took him over a couple of days ago. He's not that different from the rest of us. Even an Al'laan can't go forever without exercise, and I think captivity is beginning to get to him." David could not resist that one last try. He cared very much for Winter and was loyal to her, but he also intended to do everything he could to see that Shaw regained his freedom.

The captain drained her coffee and stood up. "Thank you," she said quietly.

Winter was not sure what she wanted to say to Shaw, but she knew she had to see him again before she wrote her report. The problem of how to represent him and his situation was worrying her even more after her talk with David, and she had to settle it.

Responsibility for Shaw's life was not the only thing troubling Winter. She was constantly making decisions, having to consider the crew's well-being and the safety of the *Venture*. While those decisions involved putting them all into danger at times, she had never faced the necessity of condemning a living being. According to David, that was precisely the decision that faced her now.

Winter respected David's judgment even though she was impatient and sometimes angry with his concern for her. But despite their conversation, she was not completely convinced that the Federation would disregard Shaw's rights. She could not allow herself to believe it.

It was not her place to question orders, even though she might not approve of what she was told to do. An efficient military depended on each part working together under the direction of Command, and only Command knew how each of the actions fit into an overall plan. And yet Winter could not help but be torn between her training and her feelings. Such a dilemma was new to her and it was not welcome in her orderly life.

Shaw was playing. He somersaulted and dove through a huge padded ring suspended in the middle of the free-fall gym, his eyes half-closed as he focused on the movements of his body. He did not seem to notice Winter in the doorway.

She watched him rebound from the wall with a light touch of his foot, twisting his outflung body to curve backward and head first through the ring. He changed direction and swung slowly and gracefully around the ring, controlling himself in free-fall with an ease that reflected practice—or was it his experience flying?

Shaw was beautiful to watch, and Winter felt an impulse to join him, in flowing around the ring in a celebration of the body's ability to move and express freedom. She felt the strange compulsion grow in her, but she forced herself to ignore it.

Rather than deal with another conflict, Winter decided not to disturb Shaw just then and turned away, back to her responsibilities. She did not see the look of regret that he sent after her.

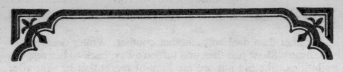

CHAPTER 27

Lately Jammeson was beginning to feel that there were things happening behind his back, that command decisions were being made without his knowledge or approval. He knew he was not being paranoid because he saw evidence of that at every staff meeting. His presence seemed to serve no purpose other than to give official sanction to some action that his staff had agreed upon before they even met with him.

Jammeson had that feeling again as the operations team discussed the problem of the Al'laan, Shaw. The admiral suddenly felt old and useless as he looked at the hard young faces around him. Everyone there was new, he realized, with the exception of Gerny. They had been sent out from Earth to fill positions created by the war, and despite their deference to his rank, they were the ones who really ran the base. The thought sent a pang of guilt through him. He was peacetime military and lacked killer instincts. That no doubt was what made the presence of such men necessary.

Jammeson knew he might as well be invisible at the meeting as the words flew past him. He knew what the others were trying to do. They wanted him to agree to some action, but more and more he seemed to be working from inside a fog.

Why could they not just tell him what they wanted without all of those words?

Then something penetrated, recalling his wandering attention. ". . . fisher," he heard. "It can be in position within eight hours."

"I thought that idea had been scrapped," he heard himself say and desperately hoped that he had not missed some vital piece of information. "Didn't design and development decide that they would never work out?"

"They did, Admiral," Williams told him. Williams was a snotty-nosed specialist who looked as if he should still be in school. "The design was one of the best the Stockton Yards had ever come up with, but the drive couldn't be made safe. Then when the Dillinger drive came along, someone in research had the idea of incorporating the principle of the warp regulator into the fisher prototype. This work is classified, of course, but all of the tests were successful. We now have a flex-warp drive."

"The ships are small," Gerny added. "They carry a crew of four, but their speed is at least ten times that of the conventional warp drive ships."

"And you're proposing to send one of these fishers after the *Venture* to bring Shaw back here—back to Alpha Base Seven," Jammeson said.

There was no response except the nervous shuffling of papers somewhere and a furtive exchange of glances around the table. Jammeson wondered again what he had missed.

Gerny cleared his throat. "Admiral," he began. "On your orders I ran all of the information through the computers. My staff has been over all of it thoroughly. There's really only one viable solution to the problem of Shaw."

Jammeson fastened his eyes on his old friend, the only one he thought he could trust. "And?" he prompted.

Gerny sought silent support from the others before he continued. All eyes were on him.

"Shaw is a great danger to the Federation. As long as he's safe in our hands we have no reason to fear him. But his past record of involvement is, to say the least, antisocial. If he is permitted to go free, who can predict what he will do? And what if he were to fall into enemy hands? What if the Proxima were to get him again? Think of it, Admiral!"

Jammeson did think of it. "I see your point. What do you propose we do?"

There was a silent sigh of relief around the table. Half the battle was won.

Gerny continued. "The demands of the Al'laan must be met. There is no question of the Federation attempting to keep Shaw." The information officer looked at the men seated around the table again. "What we propose to do must never go farther than this room. There won't even be an official report of the action."

"Get it out, man!" Donaldson almost shouted, drawing Jammeson's attention to him. He was a short, bullet-shaped man who had been silent throughout the meeting. Donaldson wore the uniform of the Federation Security Service and was the newest addition to the command staff at Alpha Base Seven, but Jammeson did not really understand the reason for his assignment.

"Please, Colonel," Gerny said. "I think it's necessary to explain all of the background first."

"What is the solution?" Jammeson prompted.

"We must destroy the *Venture*, and Shaw with her," Gerny said in a rush. "If it is done correctly, no one will know it wasn't an accident. It will be tragic, and we will be suitably dismayed, especially in our report to the Al'laan."

"That's a solution?" Jammeson asked angrily. A chill seemed to invade his mind, but for the first time that day, his thoughts were clear. He knew then why Donaldson was there. Donaldson, the Federation butcher . . . but that was only whispered. No one really wanted to admit that the Federation kept a corps of assassins.

"We've researched this thoroughly," Gerny told him.

"I won't allow it." Jammeson's voice carried all of the force he could manage. "We're civilized! The Federation of Ruling Houses would never condone such an action." Jammeson stood. "I want an alternative solution," he said. "This meeting is adjourned until such a solution is found." He swept his staff with an angry glare and then strode swiftly out of the room.

"Damn," Gerny intoned softly when the admiral was gone. He slumped in his chair. "I was afraid of this."

"Nonsense," Donaldson growled. "You have your orders. We will proceed with the plan."

"Yes, of course. But it would've been better if Jammeson approved it."

"He's finished," Williams said nastily. "He'll be recalled to

Earth anytime now. In the meantime we've got to get this action underway."

"Do we know where the *Venture* will come out of warp?" Donaldson asked.

"Not really. The computer's given us three possibilities," Gerny said. "All based on the entry point. Your best bet is to go to a point equidistant from all three. From there, with your drive you can reach the *Venture* in less than twelve hours."

"What about armament? I mean, the fishers are small," Williams said.

"There's more than enough. The new ship design incorporates the latest in both laser and torpedos—maximum firepower. You've seen the specs. The drive is at one end, and the crew works in a capsule at the other. There isn't a lot of room, but then the fisher is a warship, not a luxury liner," Donaldson told him.

"Captain Winter trained as a fisher pilot," a quiet voice announced. "I hope you took that into consideration."

"She worked with the old fishers, and it was years ago," Donaldson retorted. "Besides, our whole plan depends on speed. She won't have a chance to identify the attacker. She'll never know what happened, and that's the beauty of the plan."

"When it's over," Gerny added, "we'll report it as a regrettable accident, an act of war attributed to one of the colonies."

"We'll blame it on Proxima," Donaldson growled as he collected the papers on the table in front of him. He turned to Gerny. "Let's get moving. I need the coordinates so I can get going."

The *Venture* made the transition to real space at fourteen hundred hours ship time, three and a half days after leaving the Al'laan rendezvous point. Winter joined the watch officer well before the change and sat on the bridge as the crew came to report to their stations.

As systems were switched on and the humans on board prepared to take back control from the computer, the ship seemed to be slowly coming alive again. There was the sound of voices making status checks, mingled with the clicks and beeps as manual controls were put on line. The captain experienced a feeling of satisfaction at the smoothness of the transition. The big screen that could be seen from all stations went black and then cleared to show a star field. The *Venture* was back in real space and time.

"Sector thirty-two B seven, Cassiopeia system dead ahead, mark zero, three point four, six," Ensign Nelson reported.

"Thank you, Ensign. Maintain position," Winter said. "Lieutenant Delieus, shoot all transmissions to Alpha Base Seven. Report our position and tell them we are preparing a jump to their sector. Commander Thomas, program the jump and let me know when you're completed."

"Captain," Delieus called for her attention. "Our position report has been received by Alpha Base. Command was waiting and sent an order for us to hold position. Priority class transmission coming in for you. Code and scrambled."

"Send it to my station." The words TRANSMISSION ON STANDBY flashed on the screen in front of Winter. She typed ACCEPT, and the face of Admiral Jammeson appeared.

"Captain Winter," he said. "We have been waiting for you to report on your successful return of the Al'laan."

Jammeson's face was unusually grim, and Winter wondered what was happening.

"Yes, Admiral. There were some problems, but we were successful. I had the ship's reports beamed to Base as soon as we'd left warped space. You should have them by now."

"We do, but it seems that the Al'laan are disturbed because of the presence of another one of their people on your ship. The one called Shaw," Jammeson said.

"Sir?" Here it comes, Winter thought. Shaw will now be delivered to the authorities.

"The Al'laan have issued an ultimatum." The admiral glanced down, then back at the screen. "It seems that the one you call Shaw is a prince of some kind. The Al'laan have demanded that we release him immediately. In order to comply, you are to take him to the nearest inhabited planet. Do you have any questions?"

Winter was stunned. She had been agonizing over Shaw's fate, and suddenly Jammeson had settled the question for her—and in a way that would be more than satisfactory to Shaw, David, and, she had to admit, herself. Winter felt as if an enormous weight had been lifted from her shoulders.

"No," she replied, hiding her relief. "I have no questions."

"Good. Your navigator has reported your position as the Cassiopeia system. There are two inhabited worlds there, but I think Evendore would be the logical choice. They have excellent spaceport facilities and it's neutral—for the time being, at least. Propose this to Shaw. Then after you have left him, return to Alpha Base Seven."

"Understood."

"Jammeson clear."

The screen blanked.

Jammeson sat back and turned his chair to face Gerny, who had been sitting just out of the pickup's range during the transmission.

"Not having second thoughts, are you?" Gerny asked.

"I guess not—not really. But it does seem a waste. Are you certain there's no way we could keep the Al'laan from knowing we have Shaw?"

"My boys have been all over the possibility. Hell, we pushed the question so hard the computer was beginning to get mad at us. There's no way, Bill. No way at all unless we want to risk bringing those winged buggers down on us."

"You still recommend destroying him?" Jammeson insisted.

"Better that than have him in Proxima hands. The Al'laan won't say anything if he's dead. If they think he's alive and being held somewhere in the Federation, they'll be in here kicking ass before we can turn around." Gerny shifted uneasily in his chair. When he resumed speaking he did not look Jammeson in the eye. "Why don't you take me up on my offer. Let me take over while you ship back to Earth. You know, it would really help us if you speak for Command before the Houses."

"I have been thinking about it," Jammeson replied. He did not look directly at Gerny, either. "But the idea of letting Donaldson loose with this . . ." Distaste molded the admiral's face despite his efforts to remain noncommittal. "The man's completely without feelings or honor. He's little more than a butcher the way he handles his assignments."

"You have to remember this is war, Bill, and he's the best there is. All of us find ourselves in positions where we have to make compromises. Despite his reputation, right now I think

Donaldson is exactly what we need. He'll see the job through."

"I'm sorry it has to be this way."

"I know. You've worked with Winter for a long time, haven't you?"

"I put her name up for officer training."

"Too bad it had to be her ship, but then, those are the breaks," Gerny said, and Jammeson almost hated him for his lack of sympathy. But he also knew that Gerny was right.

"Maybe I should take the trip back to Earth. If I start having personal feelings for this project, I might do something to endanger its success," he said in a moment of weakness and self-pity.

"I'm glad to hear you say that," Gerny said soothingly. "It will be best; I think you'll see that in time."

"Where's Donaldson now?"

"He and the fisher left."

"They're gone already? Who gave the order?" Jammeson's eyebrows raised in surprise.

"Earth Command. The order came through a couple of hours ago. The fishers are Donaldson's pet project. He commanded a squad of them on their first mission."

Jammeson snorted in derision. "He wants to make the kill. I should have guessed. He pushed this thing through over my head."

"It's out of your hands now."

"I guess it is, if he's already gone." Jammeson sighed. "I wonder how soon I can make connections with an Earthbound ship."

"Well, if you leave within the next five hours you can link up with the *Morgenstern* by tomorrow afternoon."

"The *Morgenstern*? That's a resort orbital."

"On Earth trajectory. If you catch that ship you'll have a month and more of R and R in some of the most luxurious surroundings you can imagine. I'd hop to it, if I were you. The next vessel heading your way might be a freighter. It would take you twice as long, and from what I hear the food is awful—not to mention the accommodations."

"It would be best . . ." Jammeson almost whispered.

"You know it would be. Call your aide. Get packed and catch that shuttle."

Jammeson looked up at his old friend. "You're right. What would you like me to bring you from Earth?"

"Surprise me. Find something I don't have."

"I will. In the meantime, look after things here for me."

"Don't worry. Nothing will have changed when you get back," Gerny lied. He was almost sorry to lose the admiral. Almost, but not entirely.

CHAPTER 28

At sublight speeds Evendore lay four days away from the *Venture*'s position, and Winter set Thomas to work at plotting a course. After she assured herself that everything else was running smoothly on the bridge, she left him in charge and went to find David. She wanted to tell him about their new orders personally. There was proof that Command was not nearly as unconcerned as he had imagined. Her faith in the Service rekindled, she made her way to sick bay.

David was staring at a computer screen. Winter walked up behind him and could see nothing but the words IN PROGRESS flashing on and off.

"David?" she said.

He turned, startled. "Sorry. I didn't hear you come in."

"I made as much noise as usual. You must have been thinking about something," she said. "We have new orders. I wanted to tell you about them."

"I was wondering when a new complication would show up," he said, his voice anticipating doom. "What's happening now?"

"I think this will please you. Shaw is free. We're to take him to the nearest inhabited world and release him there."

"What?" David expressed his amazement, something Winter could not do in front of Admiral Jammeson. It was her turn to laugh, sharing David's obvious relief. "I can't believe it! What happened?" he demanded.

"It seems that the Al'laan raised a fuss and applied pressure."

"Irresistible pressure it would seem, if they're going to let Shaw go just like that." David snorted. "I'm finding this hard to believe. What's the catch?"

"No catch," Winter told him. "I thought it would make you feel better to know that you don't have to worry about Shaw's future anymore."

"For his sake, I'm glad. But the decision doesn't make me feel any better about Command. Did you think it would?"

"I hoped it would make a difference." Winter's voice was calm but did not hide her disappointment.

"Winter, they aren't releasing him out of the goodness of their hearts! They're under pressure, otherwise they wouldn't have considered it for a moment. Expediency is their motive. Always. The word 'compassion' is not in their vocabulary."

Winter was silent. They were at an impasse. Nothing she could say would change the way David thought.

"Have you told Shaw yet?" he asked her.

"No. I wanted to tell you first. Why don't you ask him to come up here? We'll tell him now."

David dialed the com, acting quickly as if in fear that somehow Command might change its mind and snatch away his friend's only chance for freedom.

When Shaw arrived he accepted the news of his imminent release without any sign of emotion. He watched Winter carefully as she perched on one of the lab tables, telling him of her orders. David watched the two of them, sensing something different but unidentifiable in their attitude toward each other.

"The Adevi alliance is supposed to be based somewhere in this system," Shaw commented when Winter had finished speaking. "Evendore is supposed to be under their protection."

"I thought it was neutral," Winter said.

"It is, as a free port, but it is the alliance that keeps it open and free."

"Would you prefer another planet?" the captain asked. "I might be able to arrange it."

"That will not be necessary," Shaw replied. "Evendore is perfect for my purposes. I should be able to get a ship for any number of systems there."

"You might even join the alliance," Winter said sarcastically.

"I might do that, if I was inclined to join anything," Shaw agreed calmly.

Winter was nettled by David's continued skepticism and by Shaw's calm acceptance of her news. She slid off the table and started for the door.

"Captain Winter," Shaw called after her. "Thank you."

"Gratitude is not necessary," she snapped. "I'm only following orders."

"I wonder what's wrong with her now," David commented when she was gone.

"She is confused," Shaw told him.

"Confused? Not her. She's stubborn. She decided this was a gesture of kindness on the part of Command and she's mad at me because I don't agree." He got to his feet and went to a chemical digitizer set up against one wall. "Well, let's celebrate your release from the clutches of Spacefleet Command. This thing can synthesize a number of edibles and potables including a fair assortment of ethanol-based beverages." He paused and looked quizzically at Shaw. "You do drink alcohol, don't you?"

Shaw laughed. "I've been known to do so, yes. My altered system reacts exactly as yours to recreational chemicals."

"Well, what will you have then?" David asked, his hand poised over the controls.

"I enjoy beer and various wines. Perhaps brandy would be suitable on this occasion."

"Okay, but that's in a special place." David opened a cabinet and removed a wide bottle. He poured the contents into two glasses and gave one to Shaw. "Here's to your freedom," he said, raising his glass.

"And to yours, someday, I hope."

"Thank you." David took a sip of the mellow liquid. It lay smoldering on his tongue, threatening to burst into flame, while the fumes rose through his sinuses into the back of his head. He swallowed hastily. "What will you do when you reach Evendore?"

"I am not sure. I need a ship, credits . . ." He shrugged. "I will do whatever is necessary to secure these things."

The doctor's brow furrowed in concern. "You're not planning to return to your old profession, are you?"

"I doubt it would be possible. Very soon there will be too many people who know what I am. They would be looking for me for the wrong reasons. Such interest can prove a fatal liability for a smuggler."

"Then what will you do?" David asked.

Shaw sniffed the brandy before tasting it. "I do not know. My main concern for the moment will be to keep out of the hands of the political powers."

"They want to influence the Al'laan through you."

"For what purpose?"

David shrugged. "To form an alliance with them—for the added strength, advantage."

"The Al'laan would never allow themselves to be drawn into a conflict between factions of mankind," Shaw said, echoing Shamask's words to Winter.

"Satisfy my curiosity, Shaw," David said. "Why do the Al'laan insist on secrecy?"

"We have been aware of your people for a much longer time than you have been aware of us and have had ample time to study you and your ways. We know, for instance, of the human tendency to absorb other nations into your economic social structure. The Al'laan do not want this to happen to them. There are also physical differences between us that might generate ill will or even disgust toward the Al'laan from certain factions of mankind. Although you may deny it, there is a very strong prejudice among your people. They believe anything that is different is wrong—or at least inferior."

"What differences? I haven't seen any in you, and I've watched you very closely."

Shaw laughed. "I know you have. But did you realize that I have been changed—physically altered to blend in with your people?"

"Changed in what way? I mean, I can see the wings are gone and your skin color is different from Shamask's, but aside from your esper ability and your eyes, I don't see any difference—and especially not a dangerous one."

"My blood elements have been changed," Shaw told him. "Its mineral content has been altered. That accounts for the difference in my skin tone. And my metabolism has been altered so my diet is more in keeping with yours."

"But Shamask ate our foods with no ill effects," David pointed out.

"She also requested large amounts of protein supplements from you, did she not? The Al'laan requirement for protein is at least twice that of a human."

"Yes, she did," David agreed slowly as he remembered. "I was surprised by that."

"She would have been seriously malnourished otherwise. I can live on your diet, but even my protein requirement is slightly higher than yours. It is not enough to cause problems or to arouse comment, though."

"How could a high protein requirement be enough to cause bad feelings for the Al'laan race?"

"Among certain vegetarian or even protein-starved groups such a difference would be enough. Considerations such as this are what caused the conservative members of the Al'laan council to insist on isolation. We have no desire to be assimilated or conquered, and those would have been the only alternatives."

"Your people believe it would have come to that?"

"If mankind continues to repeat its history, it most certainly would have come to that."

"But we exist peacefully with other alien races," David protested.

"Only those who fit into your society and who contribute to your goals. And they're still aliens—second-class citizens in your worlds, at best. Is this not true?"

David was silent.

Shaw drained his brandy. "So, as Captain Winter tells me, I have four days until my freedom."

"I'm glad this has happened. I was worried about you."

"You have been a good friend, David. I am grateful for everything you have done on my behalf. I know it has been considerable, and I wish there was something I could do for you in return."

David hesitated for a moment before he spoke. "You might tell me what's wrong with Winter," he said. "I've watched her changing over the past year and I'm worried about what I think is happening."

Shaw looked at him gravely. "Why do you think I might know? It would mean invading the privacy of her mind. If I did anything so intimate, I could never tell another."

"No. I didn't think you would. And that's not what I

meant. I sensed something earlier today between the two of you. I might be wrong, but I thought you might have something to do with her mood today."

"Your captain is trying to protect herself with blind faith and obedience to Command. I unwittingly removed a barrier to her real feelings and she is struggling to rebuild her wall."

"I'm not sure I know what you mean."

Shaw laughed softly. "I'm certain your captain will be all right. Her conflict will disappear as soon as she has answered her questions about Karth."

"Karth! I'd almost forgotten!" David exclaimed. "There's a file on Karth among the tapes Echart beamed to me." David turned his chair to face the terminal.

"Does she know about this?" Shaw asked.

"No." David's fingers were on the keys. "I didn't have time to tell her."

Shaw watched as the doctor called up the information on Winter's homeworld. The people in the Gyler Labs had access to a wide variety of classified materials. From what David read, not all of the material was scientific, but he did not question why they would also have military documents.

The words rolled up the screen, telling a tragic story. They held the answers to the questions that Winter had been searching for all these years. Silence filled the sick bay as David and Shaw read the report describing the murder of a planet, the death of Karth.

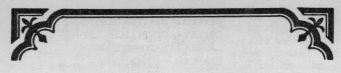

CHAPTER 29

"There they are again, Captain," Delieus told Winter.

She stood behind him, watching a read-out of the long-range sensor over his shoulder.

"Put the section on main screen and increase magnification," Winter said, sliding into the seat at her station. Her face bore no expression as she watched the section of space represented on the big screen. Once again they were about to have an encounter with an unknown—what? Was it another Proxima ship? Or the Al'laan? She did not know and tried to reserve her emotional response until she was more certain, but she could not prevent a ripple of apprehension.

The bridge crew was tense and silent as they stared at the screen.

The captain keyed for a tactical definition of the area in view, and green letters arranged themselves at the upper left corner of the screen:

MASS = FOURTEEN UNITS
DISTANCE FROM *VENTURE* = 102.01 KM
TOTAL DISTRIBUTION = 32.01 SQ KM
ENERGY = POSITIVE/ION DRIVE/GRAVITY

DRIVE/ANTIMATTER DISPERSAL/
DRIVE/REACTION CHAIN DRIVE/
LASER/ULTRASONIC WAVE.
BIO SCAN = POSITIVE/400+

Ships, Winter translated in her mind, not one but fourteen, and they were all manned. From the activity it would appear that the *Venture* had come upon a battle.

"Thomas, activate our shields and take us closer, speed point five," she instructed. "I want a better look at this."

"Aye, Captain. Shields on. Changing direction to three twenty-nine mark twelve."

"Lieutenant Delieus, check their beacons and then scan for transmissions," she ordered. "Let's see if we can find out who they are and what they're up to."

He bent over his board, working hard for a moment before he spoke. "Beacons identify two as Proxima. The others don't have a signal. Transmissions are in battle code."

"Let the computer have them. Set to translate." She leaned back, her elbows on the chair arms, eyes narrowed, watching the display enlarge as the *Venture* moved closer.

"Aye, Captain." His fingers worked for a moment and then he gave a start of surprise, adjusting the clip in his ear. "Captain, we're being hailed."

"Federation intruder, identify yourself. What do you want here?" a voice called into the bridge.

"This is the FSS *Venture*. Captain Winter speaking. Our intentions are peaceful. Who are you?"

"Captain Adenue of the alliance ship, *Portern*. What is the precise nature of your business in the Cassiopeia system?"

"We have a passenger for Evendore. May we proceed?"

"At your own risk. We are under attack by the Proxima."

"Proxima, here?"

"Yes, here!" Adenue said. "They've been raiding Dunnor. The whole planet is in ruins. By the time we found out about it, most of their fleet had gone back to the Empire, but we managed to destroy the end of their convoy. Now we have to capture that freighter."

"Do you wish assistance?" Winter asked.

"It's not necessary. We are sending boarding parties to the freighter now. It's full of refugees from Dunnor, and fortunately we were able to capture it intact."

"The *Venture* will stand by and monitor. Please signal if you wish assistance. Winter out."

The fisher sent a tight-beam subspace radio transmission to Alpha Base Seven. They had sighted the *Venture* one day out from Evendore. Since their sole objective was locating and destroying the vessel, they had spent valuable time avoiding a fleet of Proxima ships that were also in the area for some reason. Donaldson was irate at the delay. He was beginning to be worried lest Shaw get to the planet before their plan could be put into action.

Gerny received the transmission in the Base Information Office.

"We could change Winter's orders," he suggested. "We could have her bring Shaw back to Base."

"What good would that do?" Donaldson snapped impatiently, without thinking about the possibilities opened up by such a change.

"I didn't say they would arrive," Gerny replied pointedly. "There's a lot of space to cover between the Cassiopeia system and Alpha Base. A lot could happen—if you know what I mean."

"Yeah," the fisher captain agreed slowly as the realization hit him. "I do see." He thought quickly. "All right, but do it only as a last resort. The sensors have picked up something going on here. A big force of Proxima ships just jumped into hyper, but it looks like a couple of them have been left behind."

"For what reason?"

"How would I know?" Donaldson said peevishly. "Maybe they're trying to recruit allies."

"They'd be foolish to try it there. That territory's under the control of the Adevi alliance."

"It still doesn't mean they wouldn't try," Donaldson said, his impatience showing. "They're having a fight with someone—could be the alliance. And . . ." His voice slowed as he had an idea. "The battle would be a perfect cover for what I want to do to the *Venture*."

"As you say," Gerny agreed dryly.

"Let me see what happens. I'll keep you informed."

"I certainly hope so," the information officer replied.

He switched off the radio and sat back. Sometimes Donaldson was a hot head, and he hoped the man would be able to resist attacking the *Venture* in front of witnesses. Then he sighed; Donaldson was also notorious for his successes. He would have to trust that the trend continue.

Far away from Alpha Base, in the Cassiopeia system, Donaldson began to maneuver the fisher, getting into a position where he could remain undetected and still watch the battle. Then he waited—and fumed, for Winter was apparently keeping the *Venture* well clear of the battle. The execution of his orders was going to be more complicated than he had expected. The difficulty made him even more determined to succeed. That bitch was not going to ruin his perfect record!

The battle was almost over when the *Venture* arrived. The bridge crew watched as the Adevi destroyed the last of the Proxima escort fighters and boarded the freighter. In less than fifteen minutes of hand-to-hand fighting, it, too, succumbed.

"FSS *Venture*, this is Admiral Adenue. Are you there?" the voice called into the bridge.

"Captain Winter here."

"Captain, do you have a medical staff? I'm aboard the freighter, and there are over three hundred people crammed in here, many of them ill or wounded."

"Call Dr. Wilson to the bridge. Hurry." Winter told her communications officer. "I have a doctor, Admiral, as well as nurses and medical aides. We'll send them over in the shuttle. Do you need anything else?"

"Thank you, no. We'll tow the freighter to Evendore as soon as we have the passengers stable, but we need medical help now. We'll await your med staff. Adenue out."

"What's this?" David asked as he walked into the room.

Winter explained. "They're expecting you," she said when she had finished.

"We'll take full field packs." The doctor headed for the door.

"David, be careful," Winter called after him. He turned back.

"I will, Captain. I suppose we should stay with the freighter until they reach Evendore."

"I'll have a shuttle pick you up there."

"Okay. See you then." And David was gone.

* * *

The *Venture* proceeded to Evendore surrounded by Adevi ships. Donaldson watched, knowing she was safe from him as long as there were so many witnesses. He paced them, careful to keep the fisher out of scanning range until the *Venture* went into orbit around the planet. Then he called Gerny again.

"Captain Winter, message from Alpha Base." Delieus called to her.

"Thank you, Lieutenant." Winter keyed accept. The screen showed Gerny. His face radiated cheerfulness, but Winter had never been able to trust him completely even though she knew he was Admiral Jammeson's close friend and assistant.

"This is Captain Winter. Go ahead."

"Captain, this is Oliver Gerny speaking. I'm in command in the absence of Admiral Jammeson. There has been a change in your orders."

"What change is this, sir?"

"You are to return to Alpha Base immediately and bring Shaw with you."

"Excuse me? Isn't this contrary to my last orders?" Winter was curious and strangely, she thought, suspicious. According to Jammeson the Al'laan had been adamant about releasing Shaw. From what she knew of the aliens, it would be dangerous to the treaty to disobey. What could have happened to make such a risk necessary?

"I know," Gerny told her. "This has been sudden, but we have only just learned that Evendore is not secure. You must realize that we have to be certain of Shaw's safety before we can permit him to leave our custody."

"But Evendore is held by the alliance. It's a freeport," the captain protested.

"There are rumors of Proxima infiltrations," Gerny said. "And Shaw must not be allowed to fall into their hands again." Then his tone changed. "Are you arguing with me, Captain Winter?"

"No, sir, I'm not," she assured him. "I was just surprised."

"Keep your surprise to yourself, Captain! And carry out your orders," Gerny snapped.

"Yes, sir."

"We will expect you then, in about ten days. Gerny out." The screen went blank.

CHAPTER 30

It was late in the night period on board the *Venture*, and Winter was alone in her cabin. The room was as dark as her mind, shadows filling the spaces and carving the furnishings into gargoyles, but Winter was immune to the visual fantasies. She was trying to unravel the tangle of thoughts that had been twisting in her mind ever since the transmission from Alpha Base. The only light in the cabin was a dim glow above the bunk. The soft radiance brought out the inviting contour of pillow and cover, but the captain felt disinclined to sleep. She sprawled behind her desk, the chair angled so she could stretch her legs, concentration making a frowning mask of her face.

The ship was in a tight orbit around Evendore, and David was still down on the planet helping with the refugees from Dunnor. Winter planned to join him in the morning, to meet face-to-face with the survivors of the Proxima raid. She suspected that she should also make a detour to Dunnor and personally check the damage there before beginning the trip back to Alpha Base. As far as she could see, the Adevi alliance seemed to have the situation well in hand, but after the Proxima attack, Command still might think the Federation should

237

extend their patrols to include the Cassiopeia system. Any information she could bring would help them in their assessment of the situation.

The destruction of Dunnor was not all that occupied Winter's thoughts. Once again there was the matter of Shaw. She had been instructed to bring him to Alpha Base, but uncharacteristically she resisted the necessity of following the order. Perhaps she was only reacting to David's suspicions, but Winter felt that Shaw should be allowed to make the decision for himself.

Something had not felt right about Gerny's transmission. She could not imagine what it was; the man's words and manner had not been in any way out of the ordinary, but she felt a prickle of apprehension whenever she remembered it. Perhaps it was the expression in his eyes. Accessing, shifty—that was the only way she could describe them. Or was she being overly fanciful?

Winter hated feeling such conflict. Orders were orders and she was duty bound to obey, and yet . . .

The soft sound of a chime interrupted her uncomfortable thoughts as someone requested permission to enter her cabin. She called out, and Shaw stepped inside, the door hissing closed behind him. For a moment neither of them spoke. Shaw could sense her depression and confusion as he stood beside the door, his tall body sketched by the dim light.

"I hoped I would find you awake. I am not intruding, am I?" he finally asked.

"No."

"I wanted to know when we will be going down to Evendore."

"In the morning." Winter avoided the necessity of telling Shaw about the change in her orders. She straightened herself in the chair and switched on the cabin lights, keying down to a soft gleam that banished the gargoyles and returned reality.

"Winter, what is wrong?" Shaw asked. He could sense her confusion; there were visions of himself mixed with a fear of disaster.

"Nothing. I just have a lot to think about. Command will want a report of the Proxima raid, the refugee situation—" A light on her desktop console began to blink. "Excuse me a moment. The bridge wants me." She turned her chair and activated the com link. "Winter, here."

"Captain," Nelson's voice said over the familiar clicks and

beeping of the bridge. "Admiral Adenue wishes to speak to you. He says it's urgent."

"Patch him through, Lieutenant."

The sounds of the bridge were replaced by Adenue's voice. "Captain Winter?"

"Winter, here."

"Captain, I am down at Adevi headquarters. One of our perimeter patrols has just returned. They report that the *Venture* was followed into our system by another ship. It's out there now, behind Evendore's moons, trying to stay out of scanner range."

All of the lethargy left Winter in a rush. "Did your patrol identify the ship?"

"It didn't have a beacon, and all of its transmissions were coded, but it's small—some kind of a fighter. We have a visual."

"And they think that this ship has been following the *Venture*?" she asked.

"They were positive of it. When we became aware of them, we thought it might be another of the Proxima fighters, but it hasn't displayed interest in anything but your ship."

"I'm sorry, Admiral, but I have no idea who it might be," Winter said.

"We're positive that it's a Federation ship."

Winter stopped breathing. "How do you know that?" she asked, frightened but not sure why.

"Our scouts taped two of its transmissions, and we have set our computer to decode, but so far all we've learned is that it's from your Space Service."

"Damn, that's odd," Winter said softly to herself. She shook off her fear and faced the situation, trying to find ways to understand it. "If the transmissions were in a Federation code, the Venture's computer can make a translation," she said to Adenue. "Would you send me copies?"

"We were hoping you would offer. We're prepared to send it now."

"Hold on. Let me alert my communications officer. He'll process them." Winter flicked a switch and spoke to Nelson. "Lieutenant, prepare to receive copies of coded transmissions. Feed them to the computer for decoding and call me when it's finished."

"Aye, Captain."

She could hear keys clicking in the background.

"Transmission in progress," Nelson reported.

"Captain Winter?" Adenue's voice called.

"Yes, Winter here."

"You will share the decoded messages with us, won't you? This is our system, and we're naturally concerned with what happens here. We have a right to know."

"Of course, Admiral. Unless the transmission concerns sensitive information, I'll inform you as soon as I have a translation. Winter, clear."

"Thank you. Adenue, out."

"Were you expecting another Federation ship?" Shaw asked.

She had forgotten that he was there. "No, and I have no idea what it's doing here. What really worries me is that they haven't tried to contact the *Venture*. Why weren't we contacted?" Even she could hear the anxiety in her voice.

"It may not be a Federation ship."

"Adenue is sure that it is." The light on her desk was blinking again. She switched on the audio at her terminal and typed in a request for the translation. There was a lot of static despite the computer's attempts to compensate, but the words came through clearly.

"Gerny, here."

"The *Venture* is already in orbit around Evendore," a strange man's voice said. "They didn't get into the battle at all."

"You want me to recall Winter?"

"Affirmative. Get her out in the open, and then I can deal with her. Just make sure the Al'laan is aboard—and make it fast."

"I'll put the orders through immediately. You're sure you can still do this?" Gerny asked.

"They'll never know what hit'em. Donaldson out."

The hiss and crackle continued although the transmission had ended. Winter sat, stunned, until Shaw reached over her shoulder and switched the audio off.

"What do you think now?" he asked.

"I don't understand," she said softly, her eyes staring blindly at the bulkhead.

"It is very clear to me. Once your Command found out that I was an Al'laan, they never intended to let me go," Shaw said wearily.

"What did Donaldson mean when he said 'deal with her'? Deal with me? The *Venture*? What?"

"You are going to have to accept the obvious. The Federation has sent a ship after us—after me."

"They wouldn't . . ."

"No? The evidence proves otherwise. Perhaps we should see what this ship looks like. Is there a visual? Did Adenue send it as well?"

Winter switched on the CRT and keyed a request for the visual and identification. The machine complied.

SHIP = FSS 107/FISHER CLASS/LONG RANGE INTERCEPTOR
MANUFACTURED = STOCKTON ASTRONAUTICS/STOCKTON
          YARDS/SIRIUS SECTOR
DRIVE = HYBRID/DILLINGER-WALDROSE FLEX-WARP
          GENERATOR
ARMAMENT = VARIES
DEFENSE = CLASS A-2 SHIELDING/HIGH DENSITY
          PLASTEEL ARMOR
PERSONNEL = FOUR CREW

"Fisher!" Winter exclaimed, coming to life again. "I trained in a fisher, but then the design was scrapped. They couldn't make the drive safe."

"They seem to have overcome that difficulty. Flex-warp drive," Shaw mused. "If that works, it would be a ship worth having."

Winter got to her feet and began to pace. "Why have they sent a fisher after the *Venture*? All right, you were right—it has to be after you. But it isn't logical. They've already decided to let you go, and if anything happens to you, they'll have to answer to the Al'laan."

"Unless I am dead," Shaw said. "That would be one way they could eliminate the whole problem."

"You mean problems such as the possibility of the Proxima getting to you. But could they consider blowing up an entire ship?" She stood still, the truth dawning on her. David had been right, she thought. She looked at Shaw, who was watching her steadily.

"What are you going to do?" he asked.

"I received new orders earlier today. I have been instructed to bring you to Alpha Base. I was trying to figure out what

Command's motives were when you came in. Now it's clear. The *Venture* was being maneuvered into a trap. All of this— it's been nothing but lies . . ." She turned away, despair washing over her.

"Winter," Shaw said softly. He stepped forward and carefully touched her shoulder. When she did not respond one way or the other, he gently took her into his arms.

At the touch of her he felt deeply into her mind. There was pain there, pain and grief that went back almost twenty years. He stroked her hair, sending thoughts of peace until she relaxed and raised her face from his shoulder, her eyes wet with tears.

"I feel as if everything I have ever believed in," she whispered, "everything I've worked for all this time has been a lie."

"No," he began.

"Yes," she said firmly. "I've been betrayed, but I have also been the betrayer."

"It isn't too late to change."

She looked up at his face so close to hers and was about to retort when all of the sorrow seemed to wash away, replaced by the reality of his silver eyes looking intently into hers. She wondered at the comfort she felt with his arms around her and, despite her earlier grief, nothing else seemed important. His mouth touched hers in a light kiss, and she became aware of his body along the length of hers.

"Do the Al'laan make love?" she murmured, her mouth against his.

"This one does," he replied, his lips barely moving. "And I have wanted to know you since the day I touched you in my cabin."

"I was afraid of you," she admitted.

"And now?"

"No. I'm not afraid of you anymore. I had too much to hide from you then, but not now—not anymore." Her hands came up to the back of his head, caressing his thick hair as her lips met his. Slowly she became aware of his mind, but the thoughts and feeling were so wrapped in her own that she could not be sure where one ended and the other began.

The thoughts at first were faint, as if Shaw was consciously shielding her from them, but slowly his mind opened and she accepted what came. There was the constant pain of alienation and a longing of such intensity that she almost cried aloud.

She felt the feeling of loneliness and the grief of knowing the aloneness, blending with the desire for some kind of union, for the touch of another living being.

His face was bent over hers, the silver eyes as watchful as ever. She did not draw back from him, but allowed his mind to continue in its learning of hers. He slowly kissed her face, her eyelids, her cheek, tasting the salt of her tears. His lips found hers, gently at first, then possessively as her mouth responded. Her arms held him tightly, her body molding itself to his.

A link had been established. Everything he felt was known to her, and all of her feelings were his, but the emotional sharing was rapidly being drowned out by their rising passion. They clung together, and Winter reflected to him what her body felt in response to the mental and physical sensations in his mind. Slowly their passion built, and in the union of their bodies, they found the delight and the comfort that they both so badly needed.

Winter was blind and deaf, beyond all feeling and at the same time able to see and hear and feel more clearly than she ever had before . . . and Shaw was there with her, in the same places at the same time, as much a part of her as she was a part of him.

Winter opened her eyes. She was alone in her bunk, the cabin around her faintly visible in the not quite total darkness. For a second her mind fought against accepting the reality of the familiar surroundings. Those hours with Shaw had been a dream, her mind insisted, but she knew that was not so. Or was it?

Startled, she sat up, her eyes searching the room for some evidence that Shaw had been there. There was no sign of him.

Winter took a fast shower and pulled on a clean uniform. A quick check of her chronometer showed that six hours had passed since Shaw had come into her cabin. Only six hours? It must have been longer!

She breathed deeply and forced her frantic thoughts to stillness. As calmness returned to her mind, the familiar hum of the ship around her brought comfort and strength, but she was curious at the persistent feeling that she had lost something precious. Her mind sorted feelings and memories as she looked around her cabin. Only then did she notice the message light flashing on her desk. Winter sat in the chair and, after a moment's hesitation, activated the unit. Shaw's face appeared on the screen.

"Ilya," he said, calling her by her childhood name.

She felt a moment of panic, flashing back to the last time anyone had called her that. He would have gotten the name from her mind, she realized.

"Since I have come to live among mankind, I have always been alone. I learned to prefer this self-imposed solitude . . . until the brief time I spent with you. This experience has made me realize that there are some among your people with whom I can share my thoughts and feelings, and at the same time ease the unhappiness that can come from too much loneliness. I would very much like to be with you again, but I know this is not possible just now. You have decisions to make, and I do not wish to influence your thinking during this time. This is why I have gone.

"I have also done this so that you will not have to compromise your sense of duty, if you should still feel loyalty to the Federation and to the Space Service after the things we learned yesterday. Officially, I have escaped. I have gone down to Evendore on the shuttle, and from here I will be able to make my way into the galaxy. If you look for me now, you will not find me.

"Among the files from the Gyler Laboratory is one that David showed to me, but he did not have a chance to tell you of its existence. I think it is time for you to know of this file, for it contains the answers to questions that you still have about Karth. You came from a lovely world, Ilya, and I understood the reasons for your anger and sorrow when I learned of your planet's fate. .

"Perhaps after you have seen the tape and made your decisions, you will be able to find the peace you deserve. I sincerely wish it for you. Good-bye, Ilya."

The screen blanked, and Winter sat there staring at nothing. Shaw was gone, and in going he had solved one problem for her: the need to worry about his future. But she would still worry about him alone in a society where many people would be against him.

Shaw.

Where was he now? What would he do?

It was not for her to worry or wonder anymore.

She focused on the screen in front of her and remembered how David had tried to interest her in the files from the Gyler Lab. She took a deep breath and activated the computer, calling up the data. When the menu appeared, she selected the report on Karth.

CHAPTER 31

When Winter entered the bridge Delieus was still on duty. Thomas was there as well, checking a connection behind a panel of the navigator's terminal. He glanced up as the captain came in, then stood when he saw the expression on her face.

"Captain Winter, are you all right? Is something wrong?" he asked.

"Nothing's wrong, Thomas," she replied, her voice carefully controlled and completely expressionless. "If anything I'm much better than I have been in a long time." She seated herself. "Lieutenant Delieus, open the comlink shipwide. Tell the crew I want to speak to them."

"Captain," Thomas said. He abandoned his job and straightened up, his face reflecting amazement. "What's happened?"

"You'll know in a minute, Commander," was the captain's reply. But a little more than a minute passed before Delieus told her that the crew was ready. Winter nodded her thanks and opened the channel that would allow her voice to reach every part of the ship.

"This is Captain Winter," she said quietly. "I'm going to tell you about the events of the past days because I want you to be able to make a decision based on this knowledge. I want to emphasize the gravity of our situation and hope you'll realize that I'm not making a rash judgement. I gave sincere consideration to what I intend to do, and as far as I'm concerned, this is my only alternative. I'll be asking some of you to join me, but I want you to do it with full knowledge of the consequences and of your own free will."

Thomas and Delieus exchanged startled glances.

"I've served the Federation Space Service for seventeen years," she continued. "During that time I've been a faithful and loyal officer. I have never contemplated an action that was not in the best interests of the Federation—until now.

"Yesterday I received orders to take the *Venture* into a situation that would mean her certain destruction and the death of everyone on board."

"What?" Thomas exclaimed. Winter could hear the murmur of voices from the crew members who had been standing in the doorway to the bridge. She glanced at the engineer while she waited for silence so that she could continue.

"I'll explain," she said. "Because of pressures from the Al'laan nation, the Federation was forced to agree to release Shaw. This is the reason we were sent to Evendore. But Command also wants to keep Shaw from falling into an enemy's hands. To be sure that this doesn't happen, they've decided to kill him and have sent a ship, a fisher, to destroy the *Venture*. In their desperation, and they've got to be desperate to contemplate such a mad act, they're willing to sacrifice all of us.

"The fisher is waiting for us now, out beyond Evendore's moons. It's captained by Colonel Donaldson of the Federation Special Security Force. He's also the officer who headed another task force seventeen years ago—the task force that destroyed my homeworld, Karth. So you can see that I have a double and very personal interest in going after Donaldson.

"This is what I propose to do; I intend to take the *Venture* and try to destroy the fisher, but I cannot go alone. I'll need at least ten of you to run the ship. The rest of you are free to take the shuttles down to Evendore.

"Whatever you decide, may peace go with you all. Winter out."

There was silence throughout the ship as the crew realized the implications of the captain's announcement. Looks were exchanged and then words, hesitantly at first and then in emotional torrents. Sympathy was with the captain. Most of them had served with her long enough to give her their allegiance.

On the bridge, Thomas spoke for them all. He made an adjustment, reattached an optic fiber, and replaced the navigator's panel with tender care. Then he slid into the seat. "Helm on standby, Captain. Ready to break orbit at your command."

"Here are two more critical burn cases," David said.

His audience was Dr. Granor Pena, a stout, grizzled man who headed the medical facilities at Adevi headquarters. Behind him two other doctors and four nurses moved through the improvised triage that had been set up in the dock of Evendore's capital city, Brice.

"I've got them stabilized and sedated," the *Venture*'s doctor continued, "but there wasn't enough dermafoam to start regrowth."

"We'll get them straight to Brighton General. They have an excellent burn unit there." Pena gestured to one of the other doctors, who in turn summoned orderlies. Stretchers were brought and the wounded taken away.

David and Pena moved on through the chaotic scene as the injured continued to be unloaded from the captured Proxima freighter. More often than not they were accompanied by the remains of their families, and cries and lamentations added to the din in the huge covered space.

The space port at Brice was an open field surrounded by hangars and warehouses. The freighter had been towed in close enough that its entry bay opened directly into an empty warehouse that had been commandeered as a place to sort the survivors from Dunnor. Several of the hospitals had sent members of their staff to assist. Since David and the rest of the *Venture*'s med team were familiar with the wounded and had already begun treatment, the task went relatively smoothly. The most critical cases were sped to the nearest hospital, while the rest were divided among the others that had room to take them.

Fortunately there were many more uninjured survivors, who were assigned to temporary housing facilities in the city. The inhabitants of Evendore were horrified at a Proxima attack so close to their own world and rallied nobly in the cause of the victims. A number of hotels, schools, and even a convent opened their doors to the refugees.

David felt as if he were on automatic pilot as he moved through the crowds. He wore an armband that identified him as a temporary member of the Adevi medical staff, and although he received more than one curious look because of his Federation uniform, the armband allowed him freedom of movement while the caduceus on his collar earned him respect.

He had been working among the refugees for over twenty-four hours, and although he did not feel fatigued, he knew he would not be able to keep going much longer. When Dr. Pena and the group from the other hospitals arrived he was relieved, especially when Pena proved both knowledgeable and sincerely concerned for the plight of the survivors.

"What will happen to them?" David wondered aloud.

"What?" Pena asked, rising from his examination of a woman who had a crushed arm and shoulder. "Get her to OR," he told an orderly. "Tell McPherson she'll need a partial graft." He turned back to David. "You and your medics did a good job here. Fortunately the colony on Dunnor was small. Terraforming was only just completed last year."

David nodded. He was watching two uniformed officials working their way toward him through the crowd.

Pena looked for what had attracted David's attention and saw the officials. "Ah, Admiral Adenue. You're back."

"We landed a half hour ago. I see the refugees are being cared for," the leader said.

Pena introduced David. "This is Dr. Wilson of the *Venture*. His team had the work well underway before the freighter was even landed. In most of the cases, thanks to him, we only have to continue treatment."

Adenue extended his hand to David. "I am very grateful to you, Doctor, and to your captain for being generous enough to spare you to us."

"We could hardly do otherwise and still call ourselves civilized," David responded, shaking the man's hand. "You are welcome to any assistance my medics or I can give. This has been a terrible tragedy."

"More than you can know," Adenue replied gravely. "Allow me to introduce Captain Duncan Clark, my second in command.

Greetings were exchanged all around before the admiral continued. "I have been informed that another member of your crew is in detention at headquarters. He refuses to state his business and has been asking for you. Perhaps you will accompany us there?"

"I'm not sure . . ." David looked at Pena, torn between what he felt was his duty and curiosity about whoever was at headquarters.

"I am certain you can be spared. And when the work here is finished, Dr. Pena will see that your medical team is taken care of," Adenue said.

"We are almost finished," Pena assured the *Venture*'s doctor. "Your men will be fed and given a place to sleep before they return to your ship."

"All right then." David turned to Adenue. "Who is it—the one from the *Venture*, I mean?"

"A man named Shaw. I am told he came down in a shuttle early this morning. He could not give a convincing reason for his presence, and security wanted my permission before they released him. Do you know this man?"

"Yes," David admitted, his mind suddenly filled with questions. Did the Adevi know who and, more important, what Shaw was? "I know him very well. He isn't dangerous."

"The security men couldn't be sure. He hasn't been harmed," Adenue assured him. "Merely detained. Come, I'll take you to him."

Shaw was sitting cross-legged on a cot in the day room that was set up behind the security officer's office. There were no windows, and the only exit was through the locked door. His gaze was fixed on the far wall as if he was engrossed in a duty chart hung there, but he did not turn away from it when the door opened.

"Shaw?" David inquired.

His friend slowly turned to face him. As usual there was nothing to read in his face or silver eyes.

Get me out of here. The words formed clearly in David's mind.

"Of course," the doctor said out loud. "I mean," he continued quickly, trying to cover the lapse. "Shaw, I'm glad to see you, of course, but why are you down here? Where's Captain Winter?"

"I left her with the files of Karth," Shaw said. "She had decisions to make, and I thought it would be best if she was left to do so without interference."

"Will you vouch for his man?" Adenue asked.

"Certainly," David said. "Shaw was, uh, rescued from the

Proxima, and we were in the process of conveying him to a safe place when we came here."

"Is that the reason the *Venture* came to Evendore?" Adenue wanted to know.

"That's it," the doctor said.

"Hmm," Adenue intoned. "Why wouldn't you answer my men's questions?" he asked Shaw.

"I am sorry if I seemed discourteous," the Al'laan replied. "I was not sure what my reception would be."

"Where are you from? Were you a citizen of the Proxima Empire?" Adenue asked.

"No. I was their prisoner. They intercepted my ship and killed my copilot."

Adenue frowned, obviously wanting to ask more questions, but they were interrupted by the arrival of a breathless courier.

"Admiral," the man panted. "We have been looking all over for you. The *Venture* is leaving orbit. The watch officer thought you should be informed."

"What!" David and Adenue exclaimed at the same time.

How could the *Venture* be going without me? the doctor thought.

Adenue went through the door, David hard on his heels, Shaw and Clark behind him.

"What about the prisoner?" the security guard shouted when he became aware that Shaw was following them.

"He may as well come," the admiral replied. "I want to talk to him anyway."

They arrived at the headquarter's control room within seconds.

"The *Venture* broke orbit about five minutes ago," reported a man who was seated before a console. "They haven't communicated with us, and they don't answer our radio hail."

"Damnation," Adenue said. He keyed open a channel on the transciever and spoke. "Calling FSS *Venture*! This is Admiral Adenue. Respond please."

One of the artificial satellites around Evendore was transmitting a picture of the Federation ship as it moved slowly away from the planet.

She's really leaving, David thought, wondering what would have made Winter do such a thing. She knows I'm down here, and she's leaving!

"She's going after the fisher," Shaw said quietly as he watched the screen.

Everyone in the control room turned to look at him.

"That's madness!" Adenue exclaimed.

"Not if you know her reasons," Shaw explained. "The captain of the fisher is the man who led the force that destroyed her homeworld. She wants revenge."

David stared at him, wide-eyed in shock.

"Not here, she doesn't!" Adenue said with barely concealed rage. "This territory is under my jurisdiction, and I won't have her endangering it by bringing the wrath of the Federation down on us! Crispian! Clark! Alert the navy and get our ships out there. I want her stopped."

"Yes, sir," the officers replied, and ran to obey.

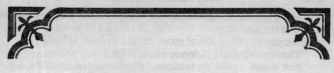

CHAPTER 32

The *Venture* headed away from Evendore, her wide-range sensors scanning space for the fisher. Winter watched the planet dwindle behind them and spared a second of thought for the people she had abandoned. She felt guilty, but she attempted to console herself with the knowledge that they would be safer back on the planet. The coming confrontation had nothing to do with them, and she would have left more of the crew behind if it had been up to her. But it was not . . . and the absence of David and his team left the ship with no medical staff except a single medtech. It would do. It would have to do, she decided.

And Shaw? a nagging little voice in her mind asked. What about him?

It was not her place to make decisions for Shaw, she told herself firmly. Just the responsibility for him while he was on her ship had been enough to disrupt her mental equilibrium, and she wanted nothing more to do with such a disquieting individual. For all concerned, Shaw was best left on Evendore, she said to herself, and knew that she lied. She dragged her mind away from the subject of Shaw.

"Torpedos, armed and ready," the second engineer reported

softly to Thomas. "Shields set on maximum." They were in a huddle over the weapons console checking and rechecking the armament.

"Any sign of them?" Winter asked Delieus, who was bent over the small screen that displayed information from the external scanners.

"Nothing," he replied. "We're still being hailed by Adenue, though."

"Ignore him," she instructed.

"Yes, sir," Delieus said, his eyes still on the scanner's screen.

Winter flipped switches and watched as a readout of ship's functions appeared. Everything was going well so far. All they had to do was find the fisher. The advantage of surprise was all they would have, and she was determined to make good use of it.

Delieus sat up in his seat. "There's a trace of residue behind the moon—ionic interference. They were there all right." He bent forward again.

"Can you tell which way they went?" Winter asked.

"Looks like they were heading out toward the near edge of the system. Traces are more dense in that direction."

"Increase distance of scans," she instructed. "We have to find them before they find us."

"Aye, Captain."

Winter shifted in her seat and wished David was there. She suddenly missed having him behind her at the science station. He would probably have something suitably caustic to say, something that would put all of this into perspective. She knew he would not approve of what she was doing, but then she had always suspected that David was a pacifist at heart.

Winter fiddled with one of the knobs on her console, wrapped in thought. David would never sit in the seat behind her, and even if the *Venture* survived the encounter with the fisher, she would probably never see him again. She raised her head and stared around the bridge. After the coming battle, not only the Federation but the Adevi alliance would be after her and the *Venture*'s crew. They were about to become outlaws.

It could not be helped, she told herself. Since the fisher was under orders to destroy the *Venture*, she had to see to it that the fisher was destroyed instead. And her own peace of mind required that she confront Donaldson, the man responsible for the destruction of Karth.

Winter hoped that David would fare well with the Adevi. She knew that doctors were always in demand in the colonies, so she did not fear too much for him. What did trouble her was that David had been a good friend, and she had not had a chance to say good-bye.

Shaw was another matter. He could have been a friend, too . . .

And there she was, thinking about him again, she realized. Winter sighed. "Status," she asked Delieus.

"Definite ion trail," he replied.

That was what they were waiting for. The bridge crew paused in their work, listening as he continued.

"Heading two seventy-two point oh three. I think we've got them!"

"All right!" Nelson exclaimed under his breath.

"Change course," Winter told him. "Heading two seventy-two point oh three. Delieus, keep on the scanner. I want to know the minute you locate them. Thomas, armament status."

"All systems green, Captain," the engineer reported. "We're ready for them."

"Load torpedos in both launchers," she instructed. "We have to hit them with everything at once. We'll only have one chance."

"Aye, Captain," the engineer responded gravely. He keyed the communicator and relayed the order to the crew at the torpedo bay.

Delieus suddenly spoke. "Visual, Captain. They're dead ahead."

"Display on the big screen. Have they seen us?"

"They're continuing along their original heading. They don't seem to realize we're after them."

"Good," she said with savage satisfaction. "We'll announce ourselves."

"Sir," Shaw said as Adenue was about to leave the control room.

The general had already briefed the landbased controllers and was preparing to board his flagship. Adenue turned back.

"I want to come with you," Shaw said. "I believe I can be of assistance. I am experienced in combat."

"I'd like to come along, too," David quickly added. "I

think we both have a vested interest in what becomes of the
Venture."

Adenue frowned from one to the other. "I want to make
one thing clear if you go. Federation or no Federation, I give
the orders here—and I expect them to be obeyed instantly. Is
that clear?"

"Very much so," David said. Shaw nodded.

"Very well then. Shaw, find Captain Crispian Adenue. He
lost three crew on the last mission and can use you. Jenkens,
radio my son's ship and tell them to expect Shaw."

"Yes, sir," the woman at the radio answered.

"Dr. Wilson, come with me." Adenue strode from the control room.

A crewmember of Crispian's ship, the *Swift*, had just
enough time to show Shaw where to strap in before the
fighter's engines caught and hurled them into space. The ride
was a bumpy one, since the craft was stripped for battle. It
would not have had the amenities of a yacht anyway, and for
the first time Shaw thought sadly of the lost *Nighthunter*.

When they achieved orbit, the *Swift* rendezvoused with the
rest of the fleet, awaiting the general's battle orders. They
were not long in coming, and the *Swift* was delegated with
two other fighters to go after the fisher while the rest of the
fleet went to intercept the *Venture*.

The *Swift* carried a crew of forty—forty-one with Shaw—
not because they needed so many to man the ship, but because
their battle tactics usually included boarding and hand-to-hand
combat. The small ship was crowded, and Shaw waited in the
crew's quarters with the others while the ship was underway.
When an ensign found him there, he was trying to fend off the
questions of a curious marine sergeant named Wilber. Shaw
was summoned to the bridge.

When he reached the bridge, he occupied himself identifying the controls while he waited for Crispian to finish a radio
transmission. The captain was talking to one of the other
fighters.

The *Swift*'s engines were apparently the older reaction–
chain drive systems, but Shaw had heard that some of the
colonies had made modifications that gave them subspace capability. It would be interesting to know what the Adevi ship
could do. There was the same type of captain-navigator console that he had installed in the *Nighthunter*, as well as sepa-

rate weapons and copilot station. Each of those was manned, and the captain stood leaning over the gunner's shoulder to place his call. He straightened up when he was finished and turned, extending his hand to Shaw.

"Welcome aboard. I'm Crispian Adenue. Let's go out here where we can talk."

Shaw read him as they made their way into a very small combination office-stateroom that was tucked just behind the bridge. There was nothing in the captain's mind except curiosity, a very natural apprehension for the coming battle, and determination that his ship would make a good showing. Crispian appeared to be basically an uncomplicated and good-humored individual.

"I don't get to use my cabin very often, except to sleep," Crispian said as he waved his guest to a seat. "I'm usually stuck on the bridge." He slid behind the desk and sat down. "I wasn't told anything but that you would be a replacement fighter. I have a feeling that you're a little more than a simple trooper."

"Although I have no doubt that I can perform adequately as a fighter, your assumption is correct," Shaw replied.

"You're from the *Venture*," Crispian continued. "Dr. Wilson told the admiral that you were rescued from the Proxima."

"That is true."

"Where are you from?" Crispian asked. "What did you do before you became a guest of the Proxima Empire? I need to know how best to use you in my crew."

"I have piloted a ship somewhat like this one," Shaw told him. "Mine was a Blessard racing sloop."

"Nice ship," Crispian said admiringly. "Thirty-five ton?"

"Smaller. Fifteen metric tons. I chose that model so I could handle it solo."

"It's still a lot of ship. Think you could handle the *Swift*?" Crispian asked, watching Shaw carefully.

"If it was necessary. However my experience has been evasion rather than direct confrontation of the enemy. And you do not seem to need another pilot."

"One never knows," Crispian commented as he made a decision. "I want to take the fisher intact, if possible. The plan is for the other two ships to run interference while we try to get into position and board. Are you any good at hand-to-hand?"

"When I have to be," Shaw admitted.

"Then you can be one of the boarding party. Stay with me. You might learn something about direct confrontation of the enemy."

"Thank you," Shaw said gravely.

Crispian got to his feet but remained behind the desk. "Standard isn't your native language, is it?"

"You are perceptive. What made you suspect?"

"You speak it fluently, but you don't use contractions. That's a dead giveaway."

"I will—I'll try to remedy that," Shaw said carefully, and Crispian laughed.

"The Adevi alliance has room for all kinds," the captain said. "Don't worry about it. Let's go forward."

When Donaldson realized that the navigator was neglecting the scanners, a vital part of his duties, he cursed the man roundly and ordered an immediate spherical scan. The *Venture* was there and closing fast.

The fisher maneuvered just as torpedos from the *Venture* sped through space. Even though they did not impact, Winter ordered them remotely detonated; the shock was enough to toss the fisher out of control.

"Again!" Winter ordered, sitting forward in her chair, her hands clamped on the arms.

In the lower bay, the crew had the next round waiting and dropped them into the tubes. Two and then two more of the deadly silver shapes streaked from the *Venture*'s central shaft. All of them missed as the fisher flashed into flex-warp just in time to avoid detonation and the turbulence.

Winter pounded her fist on the arm of her chair. "Where did they go?" she wondered out loud, her voice carefully controlled to show none of the frustration she was feeling.

"They flexed," Thomas supplied, although he knew that the captain was as aware as he was of the fisher's unique capability to wink in and out of spatial dimensions. "They'll be back any second—but they could show up anywhere."

"Keep a sharp watch," Winter warned. "They'll be shooting at us this time. Double-check the shields and—"

"There they are!" Nelson shouted, pointing at the big screen.

The fisher was coming directly at them. Winter ordered two more torpedos launched, but the fisher was firing, too.

"Evasive!" she ordered.

The *Venture* maneuvered, but not soon enough. The laser struck the foremost ring just aft of the bridge, and although the shields deflected some of it, there was still enough to cut into the hull. The scream of tortured metal was quickly joined by an alarm klaxon. From outside of the bridge there came the sound of shouted instructions as a repair team went to attend to the damage.

"They're coming at us again," Thomas warned, but Winter was ready and ordered a maximum spread of the *Venture*'s lasers. Again the fisher had to dodge to avoid them.

"Ships coming in," Delieus announced. "It's the Adevi fleet. We're being hailed."

"I have no time for them now," the captain snapped. Still, she cast one quick look at the big screen in time to see three of the alliance vessels break formation and go after the fisher. The rest were preparing to circle the *Venture*.

"Evasive," she called to the navigator, whose fingers were flying over his console.

The *Venture* responded, but moving away from the Adevi brought her back into the fisher's range. Donaldson fired a torpedo that hit the second ring dead on. A mighty shock raced through the *Venture* as two of the spokes holding the ring to the hub came free. The ring swayed gently for a moment and then more violently. Its movement took it back and then forward, the arc getting wider each time until it finally collided with the first ring, the point of impact directly behind the bridge. The first ring shuddered and also snapped a spoke.

The bridge crew were thrown from their places as consoles and seats were jarred loose. The artificial gravity ceased to function, and somewhere there was the ominous roar of escaping air. Alarms were screaming even louder than the injured, and beneath it all was the boom and screech of metal cracking and bending. Fires broke out as wiring shorted, and the air was quickly filled with choking smoke. Flame licked its way into the bridge, greedily feeding on anything it could find. There were miniature explosions as floating objects collided with the small individual screens, spraying knifelike shards of plastic and adding to the danger and confusion. Above, the big screen hissed with static, displaying a mottled surface of madly dancing colors like some angry pointalistic painting.

The sounds were deafening and the sights those of complete chaos. Overwhelmed by the total confusion, the senses were incapable of comprehending what was happening. Winter was stunned as she looked around the bridge, barely able to understand what was happening, much less accept the pain that laced through her shoulder. Thomas, the closest one to her station, appeared to be unconscious. As a finger of flame made its way toward him she released herself from her seat restraints. Another shock went through the bridge as the loose ring impacted again, and Winter was thrown against the science console, landing heavily on her injured left arm before she started to drift across the bridge. She gave an involuntary cry and, enraged by everything that was happening, pushed herself back around. She grabbed onto anything that was handy to pull herself along, angrily deflecting floating debris as she went to try to help the engineer.

Then suddenly a third shock went through the forward ring. Something in the big screen exploded in a bright white light that spread outward, engulfing the bridge and everyone in it.

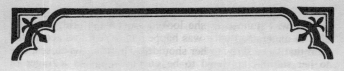

CHAPTER 33

"What I wouldn't give for a ship like that!" Crispian said. His eyes were gleaming with appreciation that came very close to being lust at the promise of controlling the awesome power inherent in the slender fisher.

"That will take some doing," commented Maurier, who had slipped from the pilot's station to the copilot/navigator seat when the captain returned to the bridge.

"Nonetheless, we'll manage." Crispian grinned at him. "We always have before."

The older man grunted. He had served with the young captain on a number of missions and no matter how much he might deplore Crispian's rashness, he had to admit that they had never failed to achieve their objective—yet.

"Daws and Jacques will engage as planned. We'll use their cover to maneuver," Crispian commented, his attention on the keyboard in front of him. "All right, that's set." He punched RUN and looked back to where Shaw had been standing beside the inner hatch. "Get aft with the rest of the boarding party. Sergeant Wilber will see that you're properly outfitted. Tell him I'll be down as soon as I've finished here."

"I thought you were staying with the *Swift*," Maurier com-

261

mented with an apprehensive glance at the captain.

"I think I'll go with the boarding party this time," Crispian told him offhandedly.

"You know your father won't like it. He gave you strict orders after the last time," the second in command argued.

"But he won't know anything about it until this is all over," Crispian responded without the least bit of conscience.

Shaw left the bridge. He had seen the *Venture* hit and was wondering about the extent of the damage. From what he could see, it looked bad. Despite its size, the fisher was a formidable adversary, and he wished he could be sure that the *Swift* would have success where the more powerful *Venture* had not. It was also frustrating not to be in control—the result of having been the captain of his own ship. Crispian was overeager, a characteristic of his youth, but he and the rest of the crew were apparently seasoned veterans who had triumphed in a number of such encounters, an admitted advantage. Still their current target was a completely new type of warship.

Shaw made his way back to the crew's quarters. The men and women there were enthusiastic and eager for the coming confrontation. They had no doubts like the ones that troubled their alien companion. A selection of them was preparing to board while the rest helped or got in the way, offering unnecessary suggestions and good-natured ribbing. Spirits were high and those who were going were envied by the others who would remain behind to fight the *Swift*.

Shaw donned the atmosphere suit that Sergeant Wilber provided, pleased to note that it was of a modern, lightweight design. He checked the weapons: a handgun that shot explosive charges and a wicked-looking laserdag that could slice through anything from flesh to thin metal. The latter was worn in a sheath attached to his right calf within easy reach of his hand. It would be of more use than the gun; bullets could breech the ship's hull and thus end the encounter for everyone, friend and foe alike.

A helmet with a retractable visor completed Shaw's uniform. It contained a transceiver that would allow him to be in visual and audio contact with the main ship and the rest of the boarding party. He was unfamiliar with the controls, but some brief instructions were enough to remedy that situation.

"All right," Wilber called. "Everyone pay attention!"

Activity ceased and everyone focused on the sergeant.

"We'll go in as soon as the captain gets the ship into position. Simson, you and Krakow go first with the grapples. When we're attached, get the hell out of the way while Mark and Goodman cut the hatch open. The rest of you will provide cover, but as soon as there's a way in, you move!"

"Which of us're going in, Sergeant?" someone asked.

"Simpson, Mark, Blake, Howards, and Goodman will stay with the shuttle," the sergeant informed them. "Patten, Broodmore, Krakow, and you, Shaw, will board the fisher with the captain." Wilber paused to let that sink in.

"That's only five of us," the sandy-haired man called Patten complained.

"What's the matter? Scared?" Simpson jeered good-naturedly.

There was laughter at Patten's expense and a loud hubbub as the other crewmembers joined the taunting.

"Get it under control!" Wilber yelled, quelling the noise. "The fisher only holds four, so five will be plenty. The main problem'll be to disable the crew while Captain Crispian takes control of the ship. Then the shuttle will return to the *Swift*, and we'll escort the fisher while the five of you pilot her back to Evendore. Any questions?"

"Yeah. What do the rest of us do?"

"You provide backup," Wilber retorted. "We don't know anything about this ship, and there could be some nasty surprises. That's why the second team has to be ready." He paused again, fixing his charges with a steely glare before he concluded the briefing. "So let's get on it."

"We could have stayed at home," someone complained. It was one of the crew that was to remain on the *Swift*.

"Get out and walk back if you don't like it here," Wilber snapped in response.

"Hey, sarge! Just kidding!"

Isolated in their quarters, the crew were not aware of the battle that raged in space outside the *Swift*. The fisher was a new and unique design, but in the end the machinery was only as good as the operators. Despite their less advanced equipment, Crispian and the other captains had been fighting in space for many years, and that experience enabled them to pull off a number of maneuvers that the fisher's crew could neither anticipate nor copy. The balance of advantage was increased when they were joined by seven additional Adevi ships that had been released after the *Venture* was disabled.

Still the battle was a bitter one. The *Swift* rocked sharply several times, and Shaw wished he were on the bridge where he could see what was happening. What he missed was one of the Adevi fighters being blown to vapor. That attack seemed to spur the Adevi on to greater effort, and they fought with renewed ferocity and, in one case, recklessness, for another ship fell victim to the fisher's guns. In the end it was a lucky shot from the *Swift*'s sister ship, the *Sweep*, that knocked out the fisher's drive. Unable to maneuver, the smaller ship began to drift, and the fighters carefully closed in for the kill. Laser bursts came from the crippled Federation ship, but the nimble Adevi fighters dodged easily. Finally, realizing the futility of wasting his ammunition and power, Donaldson ordered a cease fire.

The *Swift*'s communicator gave a loud ring, and Crispian's voice announced to the crew that they would be in boarding position within minutes.

Shaw followed the picked members of the crew as they made their way to the air lock where the boarding shuttle waited. They donned their helmets and made last minute adjustments to equipment as they walked. At the lock they were joined by Crispian, who was still securing the top of his suit. Wilber went to help him.

"Everything set?" the captain asked the sergeant.

"Yes, sir. Teams picked and instructed as you ordered," Wilber replied. "You're really going, sir?"

"Looks like it. Shaw here?"

"Right over there, sir, though I don't know why you wanted him instead of one of the others," the sergeant complained.

"The admiral sent him along, and I thought it might be a good idea to see how he handles himself."

"You think there'll be trouble, sir?" Wilber cast an apprehensive glance at the tall stranger in the midst of the *Swift*'s crew.

"I wouldn't have let him come along if I did. But maybe he'll make a good recruit."

"As you say," was the noncommittal reply.

His captain grinned and clapped Wilber on the shoulder before putting on his helmet and following the team into the lock. "Look after everything for me. See you back on Evendore."

"Luck, Captain," Wilber said.

The boarding shuttle was easily large enough to fit all of

them, but once the door had cycled shut there was an unpleasant feeling of claustrophobia as they sat shoulder to shoulder on the benches that ran the length of the craft. The overhead lights were on, and additional illumination was provided by beams from individual helmets as their owners made another last check.

"We're ready," Crispian reported to the bridge through his throat mike.

"Preparing to launch shuttle," Maurier replied.

There was a burst of acceleration as the *Swift* ejected the shuttle, and then a complete silence as the small craft slid into space. Through the row of large square ports that had moments before given them a view of the interior of the air lock, there was a spectacular view of stars. Shaw knew that one of the brighter lights was Evendore, although they were already too far out for him to be certain exactly which one it was. Behind, between them and the sun, was the dark bulk of the *Swift*, and ahead was the sliver shape of the fisher.

With a burst of maneuvering rockets the shuttle shifted position heading for its target while the *Swift* drifted rapidly away behind them to join the other fighters circling the enemy ship.

"There!" Crispian exclaimed suddenly, pointing.

An opening had appeared in the side of the silver vessel and two suited figures emerged, dragging something bulky at the end of a tether line.

"They are either trying to make repairs or jury rig a maneuvering engine," Shaw said. "They must be desperate if they will take such a risk just now."

"Saves us the trouble of cutting our way in," Goodman commented.

The figures outside the fisher apparently became aware of the *Swift*'s shuttle and, abandoning their project, headed for the hatch. Their movements were awkward in the vacuum of space, and despite the help of the tether line, they did not move quickly.

"Not spacemen," one of the team commented with sour satisfaction.

"Which probably means they're Federal Special Security forces," Crispian warned. "Don't underestimate them." He turned to the shuttle pilot. "Get us over there fast as you can."

"Aye, Captain." the woman replied. She requested acceleration, and the shuttle's small rockets gave another burst. "Impact in two seconds. Tractor's on. Be ready with the grapples."

Simson and Krakow were getting into position even as the pilot spoke. The rest of the team were snapping their visors shut and loosening weapons in their sheaths. Shaw copied them and then waited.

The shuttle made contact, and the team entered the air lock, Shaw following closely behind the captain.

The pair of figures that had been outside of the fisher in atmosphere suits met them, handguns drawn. Before anyone could stop them, one managed to get off a blast that ruptured the shuttle's hull. The small vessel lurched away from the fisher, escaping air frosting the space around the gash in the hull.

Before anyone even had time to worry about the fate of the crew members still inside, a blast marked the end of the shuttle. The projectile had apparently hit something in the engine, causing a reaction.

The blast also rocked the fisher, knocking the boarding team from their precarious hold in the air lock. With one hand Shaw managed to grab on to a ring just inside the hatch, while his other caught the sleeve of the captain's suit. Two other members of the team were also lucky enough to find something to hold on to, while the fifth went spiraling into space, still struggling with one of the fisher's crewman.

When they finally got themselves sorted out, the remaining crewman was aiming his gun. Without thinking Shaw sent a mental blast. The figure crumpled instantly. Crispian bent over him as the two remaining members of the team squeezed past, going to work on the air lock's inner door. Simson cycled the outer door closed, sealing them inside the ship. Air began to hiss into the lock and pressure gradually increased.

"He's dead," Crispian said, his words coming to Shaw through the helmet speaker. "What did you do?"

"I will explain to you later," the alien informed him as he nodded toward the inner door. "There is another just beyond, armed and ready, and one alone in the cockpit. They know we are here, and they are determined to fight to the last possible moment."

"How do you—" Telepath, Crispian suddenly realized, staring wonderingly at Shaw. But there was no time to think about that. He was furious over the destruction of the shuttle and even more determined to capture the fisher.

When the door finally opened, Krakow unsheathed his laserdag and engaged the Special Services man waiting there. Shaw worked his way past them, heading for the cockpit with Crispian following. They were greeted with the sound of Donaldson's laughter.

"That's another one," the assassin reported, swiveling his seat to face them. "My ship may be without maneuvering power, but I can still outfight you colonial bastards."

The viewscreen above the control panel was filled with the bright light of an explosion that slowly cleared. Seconds later the fisher was hit by turbulence and began to drift sideways.

"So," he continued. "You really think you've won this little encounter, do you?" His voice was very nasty.

"He's rigged the fisher to self-destruct," Shaw told Crispian quickly. He moved forward as Donaldson reached for the control panel and caught the man's hand, twisting it up and back. There was a loud crack as the bone gave way.

Donaldson dropped to his knees on the deck, cradling his broken arm and laughing even as tears of pain rolled down his face. "That ship," he gasped. "The one I just blew? It was yours," he told Crispian. "And I radioed before I fired—told them I'd destroyed the boarding party. With the shuttle blown, they'll believe it, too."

Crispian pushed past him and examined the control panel, looking for the communicator.

"Don't bother," Donaldson said. "I busted the radio just before you got here. I'm gonna die, but you're gonna die with me."

Crispian looked at Shaw, who nodded an affirmative. "The radio is destroyed. This ship is completely disabled except for the weapons firing mechanism and the self-destruct device."

"Well I don't want that," the captain said with some asperity. "There has to be some way we can communicate with the fleet and let them know we've succeeded in capturing the fisher."

"There isn't," Donaldson told him. He struggled to his feet and gasped with pain as the movement jarred his arm. "They'll blow up this ship and you with it."

His mad laughter crescendoed as the viewscreen filled with a bright light and then flashed to black.

CHAPTER 34

When Winter woke she was stretched out on a bunk. Her left arm felt numb, and when she lifted her other arm to examine it, someone caught her hand.

"Take it easy," a familiar voice said.

She opened her eyes, squinting in the bright light, and slowly focused on David.

"Where am I?" she asked.

"In the brig," he said.

"What?" She struggled to rise.

"Be still," David told her. "You've busted your collarbone."

"Damn." She looked around the bare walls and then returned her gaze to the doctor. "This isn't the *Venture*," she stated.

"No. You're on the *Portern*. We took the wounded off the *Venture*, and the ship's being towed to Evendore."

"What was the damage?"

"Not as bad as we first thought," David said. "She's pretty unstable with both rings loose, but Adenue says they can have her spaceworthy in a matter of months."

"How many—how many casualties?" Winter asked.

David scowled. "Enough. What made you do such a stupid thing?"

"What do you mean, stupid?"

"I mean stupid," he returned. "What in hell made you think you could take on the fisher? Why did you do it?"

Winter turned her face away and stared at the bulkhead. "Donaldson was on that ship."

"Donaldson?"

She faced him again and saw his look of confusion. "Donaldson. You should know who he his; you gave me the files."

David frowned. "Not the files on Karth," he ventured.

"Yes!" she shouted. "Karth. Donaldson. He was the leader of the team that destroyed the planet."

David was silent for a moment. "You mean you went after the fisher for revenge? You took the *Venture* and her crew into an impossible situation just so you could destroy that man?"

"What else did you expect me to do?" But he was silent. "David, you were the one who gave me the files. You were the one who wanted me to know the truth."

"Yeah, but I didn't expect you to risk your life, your ship, and your crew on an impossible stunt!" He was breathing hard when he finished.

She sulkily averted her eyes, and he maintained the silence.

"Winter, what made you think you could succeed?" he asked, his voice gentler. She did not answer, and after a moment more, he got to his feet. "Have it your own way. I have other wounded to see to."

That was not exactly true, for the *Portern*'s doctors were on the job, but he did not see that anything would be gained by arguing with Winter when she was in one of her moods.

"How many?" she asked in a very small voice.

"Twenty-three wounded. Five dead," he said bluntly.

"Who?"

"You want a list? I'll have one sent down to you." He stalked out the door.

Winter struggled into a sitting position. "David," she called toward the door, but it was too late.

Five dead, she thought. Who were they? Thomas? Nelson? Delieus? Who?

"Damn!" Winter muttered. Then she sighed and looked down at herself. She was still wearing her uniform, but it was torn and smelled of smoke and chemicals. Not that the uniform mattered anymore, she thought. When she returned to Alpha Base she knew she would be facing a court-martial. The best that could happen was reduction in rank, the worst a term in one of the military penal institutes. If that happened, she would never again wear the uniform of a Space Service officer. Strangely Winter found that the idea did not bother her as much as she thought it would. After what had happened to Karth and the planned attack on the *Venture*, she was not sure if she wanted to remain in the Service. She did not know what she could do instead; the service had been everything to her for so many years.

Winter's left arm was tightly strapped to her chest. The shoulder ached slightly, but it was nothing she could not live with. She gently touched the bulky bandage and realized from the warmth that David had used an amplified regrowth hormone. She would be using the arm again in a week.

Use it for what? she wondered. Her future was not very clear. She was a prisoner of the Adevi, and when they finished with her, the Federation would have its turn. Maybe she should escape, find Shaw, and they could go smuggling together.

Winter moved restlessly, trying to find a comfortable position in the bunk. She did not bother trying the door; it would be locked. Then she heard a clicking sound, and the door opened for David. The doctor's face was still furrowed with lines of worry, but he was not angry anymore.

"I'm sorry," he said, closing the door behind him and coming to the bedside. "That last shot was unnecessary."

"I don't blame you," she admitted.

"You should. You were in no position to defend yourself."

"What's going to happen now?" she asked.

"To you?"

"To all of us."

"I don't know. It depends on Adenue. The crew were following orders, so they probably won't be facing charges. But you went against Adenue's orders when you engaged the fisher. I should warn you, he was furious. As for what the Federation is going to do to you...I can't say. You'll be lucky if you get a court-martial. They'll probably shoot you on sight."

"Gee, thanks." She let her head drop back on the mattress.

David looked at her, pity in his eyes. He really did not know what would become of her, but one thing was certain:

her career in the Space Service was finished. That would be a blow even though she might not want it to continue after learning what the Federation had done to her homeworld. The knowledge must have come as quite a shock, especially on top of finding out that her own Service had sent a fisher to destroy her and the ship she commanded. He knew her too well; the decision to fight could not have been an easy one for her to make. He sat facing her on the edge of the bunk.

"What do you want to do?" he asked.

"What options do I have?" she responded.

"I could name you a few."

"Such as?"

"Join the Adevi," he suggested. "They can always use a good officer."

She considered that. "I thought you said I was under arrest."

"You are, but I get the feeling that Adenue would be lenient if he understood your motives."

"Karth and the fisher?" she said. "Won't he have to ship me back to the Federation?"

"He has no love for them. The Adevi alliance came into being as a way to protect the outlying colonies from the Proxima when the Feds decided the area wasn't important enough for them to do it. Although the Adevi haven't been active against the Federation, the feeling here is not good, and I suspect there will be an official break sometime in the near future."

"The Feds wouldn't like the idea of a group of colonists developing this much strength in space," she said. "They'd see it as a threat."

"There have already been warnings," David told her. "Adenue has even been ordered to disband the Adevi alliance."

"That sounds like something the Houses would say," she commented wearily. "They wouldn't even consider that the colonies might find it necessary to defend themselves."

"And the Proxima have been very active in this area. The Empire is becoming a force to reckon with."

"We saw that on the mining station and at Glyer," she said.

Winter stared at the overhead bunk, and there was another time of silence until David spoke again.

"I'm joining them," he said.

She turned her head toward him. "The Adevi?"

He nodded.

"What about your oath to the Federation?"

"I won't be bound to an organization responsible for the things I've seen. I don't know if the Adevi are any better." He shrugged. "If they aren't, then I'll go someplace else. Maybe I'll become a colonist. Maybe there's a world somewhere that can use a worn-out old sawbones."

"They'd be lucky to get you," Winter murmured, feeling a pang of sadness. She was losing another good friend.

"Winter—" he began, but stopped as the door opened and Adenue entered the cabin.

David got to his feet as the admiral came to gaze down at the captain. Adenue's face was lined with fatigue, and his anger was apparent in his stiff posture as well as the tight control that made his voice almost neutral.

"You were fortunate," he said. "You and your crew."

"I wouldn't call the five dead fortunate," she retorted. "They were the ones who had to suffer for my mistakes."

"I'm glad to see you have the decency to take responsibility for what you did," he said. When she did not repond, he continued. "I'm here to tell you that the fisher has been captured. It's being towed to the space dock."

"You defeated the fisher?" Winter asked, her eyes suddenly glowing with life again.

"We did," the admiral replied. "Although not without considerable cost."

"So you're adding that to my list of offenses?" she asked resentfully.

"Winter," David softly warned. Adenue held her future in his hands, and it would be worth her while to placate the man—if that was possible. David looked at the stiff back and wondered.

"No, she's right," Adenue said. "I did consider her responsible. But I realize the Federation is to blame. They sent both the *Venture* and the fisher into the Cassiopeia system." He sighed and ran a hand through his thinning gray hair.

"You said cost. Exactly what do you mean?" David prompted, apprehensive of the answer.

"Three Adevi fighters were destroyed," Adenue said. "One of them was captained by my son."

There was a moment of silence until Winter spoke. "I'm sorry," she said softly. She realized that David was staring at the general, his eyes wide with shock. "David?"

"The fisher destroyed your son's ship?" the doctor asked Adenue.

"Yes," was the low-pitched reply.

David hesitated as he slowly turned his head and fixed his eyes on Winter. "Shaw was on that ship," he told her, and watched as the words sunk in and she went white. "The Federation had its way after all," he added softly. "He's dead."

Winter bit her lip and then slowly closed her eyes, hiding an expression of intense anguish.

Adenue looked from one to the other, realizing that his words had had an even greater affect than he had suspected. David was so surprised by the captain's response that he set his own sorrow aside and went to kneel beside the bunk.

"I'll get you something," he suggested.

"No, don't bother," she replied. "Just . . . please leave me alone."

"There's more," Adenue said.

"How could there be any more than that?" Winter asked him, opening her eyes. She blinked rapidly, trying to control the wetness there. The muscles along her jaw were tight with the effort it cost her to maintain control.

"You must realize that you're in a very difficult position," the admiral began.

Winter spoke bitterly. "It would appear that way." She took a deep shuddering breath and then was still.

Shaw is dead, dead, dead, a little voice in her mind said again and again. Somewhere a wailing started up, but she forced her emotions into the background and tried to deal with the present. Later she would mourn, but not now.

"You have a choice," Adenue continued. "We could send you back to the Federation—but in light of our confrontation with the fisher, I'm not sure if they would be appeased."

"No," she agreed sarcastically, her pain showing despite herself. "I don't think they will appreciate the destruction of millions of credits worth of military hardware."

"Winter," David warned her again, but he could see that she was beyond caring what happened to her.

"We could also try you ourselves," Adenue continued, ignoring both of them. "You have committed offenses against the Alliance."

"What about extenuating circumstances?" David suggested. "I explained to you what happened."

"And I'm sympathetic," the admiral conceded. "But in this

situation you shouldn't have allowed personal feelings to interfere with duty."

"My duty?" Winter said bitterly. "I was ordered to take my ship to certain death—you might consider that I did exactly what I was supposed to do. I took the *Venture* out where the fisher could get her."

"You went against my express orders, and I am the authority in this system. The ultimate result of what you have done could bring the Federation down on us."

"I thought you said that they were the ones responsible," Winter argued. "You can claim interference and that your ships were only defending themselves."

"Since that is what happened it is precisely what I will do." He was silent, examining the woman before him. "What do you plan to do?" he asked finally.

"Right now everything seems to depend on you," she said.

"True, but you do have choices."

"And what are they?"

"As I said before, we could ship you back to the Federation and hope they see this as a gesture of good will."

"For some reason that doesn't appeal to me," Winter interrupted bitterly.

"You could also renounce your allegiance to the Federation and join the Alliance," Adenue told her. "We just captured a ship that could use a good captain."

David's jaw dropped open, and Winter stared in amazement.

"You would give the *Venture* back to me?" she asked.

"I've been talking to your crew. They speak highly of you. They also told me that before you went after the fisher, you gave them a choice of either staying with the ship or going down to Evendore. That in itself tells me a great deal about your character. We need good people in the Alliance."

"You would trust me?" she demanded.

"Are you telling me that you aren't trustworthy? That your word is no good?"

She laughed bitterly, the sound as brittle as breaking glass. "If I renounce my oath of allegiance to the Federation . . . I wouldn't consider that a particularly good recommendation."

"If we betrayed you the way they did, no one could blame you for defecting," Adenue pointed out.

She looked from the admiral to David. "I want to get up," she said, easing her legs over the edge of the bunk. David started to help her to stand, but she shook off his hands and did it herself.

"Very well," she conceded. "I'll join the Alliance."

Adenue smiled, although his eyes were still filled with sadness. "I was hoping you would say that." He held out his hand. "The Alliance welcomes you to the ranks of the Adevi Raiders, Captain."

David grinned as he watched Winter take the proffered hand.

"I have to get back to the bridge," Adenue said. "We're about to dock. The fisher will be coming in right behind us. You might want to be there when we open her up. If you feel up to it," he added.

"I heal faster on my feet," Winter said, following him to the door. Heart, mind, and body, she told herself, they would all heal faster with something to do besides dwell on the deaths of her friends. But it was going to be very hard.

The space station above Evendore was alternating bright and black shadow as it reflected the light of the sun. It rose in a series of cantilevered decks, pierced by ports and hatches. The uppermost level, which contained the control station, was bristling with antenna. A series of broad arms extended from the decks, and ships were hitched to their surfaces like remora. Beyond the pale structure Evendore hung in the sky, huge and impossibly close. The strata of clouds were visible above the planet, and through openings here and there the surface could be seen, the distant blue of oceans surrounding the brown and green of land.

The station was not as large as some Winter had visited, but she was impressed with the efficient way they handled the ships. A pair of tugs nudged the *Portern* to her mooring, while others fixed grapples to the disabled fisher and brought her directly into a good-sized bay.

Winter disembarked through the tube that connected to the *Portern*'s main hatch, and she and David hitched a ride on a grav sled with Adenue and a couple of engineers.

"We won't start cutting through until the repair bay is secure," one of the engineers said. She was a big woman with short salt-and-pepper hair. "But already Wally said he thought he heard someone pounding inside. He thinks there might be survivors."

"Have you taken sonic readings?" Adenue asked.

"I called security to bring their equipment over. They'll check the ship as soon as they're allowed into the bay."

As Winter listened, she realized that David was watching her closely. How was she supposed to be taking the information that Donaldson might still be alive, she wondered? Then she saw that Adenue had turned to face her as well.

"He's mine," the admiral said grimly, his eyes locked on hers. "He killed my son, and I want him to stand trial."

"Just as long as you let me help you convict him," Winter told him. "That's all I want."

Adenue smiled like a shark in sight of its prey. "I promise you'll have a hand in it."

After the round sides of the fisher had been propped up on stabilizers, the door of the repair bay was closed and air pumped back in. There was a loud creaking as the weight of the Federation fighter settled to the deck, but the grapples held and it did not roll.

As the grav sled reached the bay, a group of people in green uniforms converged on the ship with various pieces of equipment. Winter assumed they were the security team. She climbed off and accompanied Adenue and the engineers to the fisher, which did not look nearly as formidable now that it was their captive. There were black blast marks streaking the silver sides, and the area around the hatch and the nose were fused metal. Still, it was an impressive sight. Hatred for the thing and the men who flew her twisted in Winter's gut. Her lips narrowed, and she controlled the emotion with an effort.

"There is someone inside," one of the security men shouted. "They're pounding on the hull."

"Cut the hatch open," Adenue ordered. "And stand by with your weapons. We don't know if they're friendly or hostile."

"Yes, Admiral!" one of the green uniforms replied.

There was a hissing and a lot of sparks as the laser cutter did its work. The security men stood as close as they dared, squinting in the smoke, their pistols held ready.

With a bang that reverberated throughout the bay, the hatch swung free. Smoke obscured the opening as the ventilating system labored to suck it clear. Two figures appeared, coughing on the fumes. The first was a rather disheveled Crispian, pushing a sulky Donaldson before him. The captain spotted his father and, relinquishing his captive to security, came running.

"Mission accomplished, sir," he said with a grin. "What in hell took you so long getting us out of there?"

His father caught him in a fierce embrace, stopping the flow of words.

Winter watched them, warmed by the old warrior's happiness at having his son again. Then she looked back to the fisher just in time to see Shaw emerge, helping an injured Krakow down an improvised ramp. Technicians and security ran to relieve him of his burden. Shaw straightened up and turned to face Winter.

David spotted his friend at the same time and went quickly toward him.

"Are you all right?" the doctor demanded.

"I am uninjured," Shaw assured him. He looked over David's head at Winter as she slowly approached. David followed the direction of Shaw's gaze and then looked from him to Winter before he stepped aside.

"Hello, Ilya," Shaw said quietly, holding out his hand. She smiled as she took it.

It was a more brilliant smile than David had ever seen, and he realized that he would not have to worry about the captain anymore. She had slain her demons and could begin to live again. We'll all have a second chance at making something for ourselves, he thought. A fresh start even in the middle of a war was more than most people ever got.

David laughed for the sheer joy of it and carefully hugged them both.

ABOUT THE AUTHOR

Johanna M. Bolton was born an Army brat in New York City and moved for the first time at six months of age. She has lived in Japan and Germany, as well as a number of the states, a childhood she would recommend to anyone. She has studied fine art, biology, and mathematics, taught pre-school, high school, and college, ridden dressage horses, written for newspapers, trained show dogs, bred tropical fish, ridden her BMW motorcyle, and tried being married.

She now lives in Santa Fe, which the ancient Indians called "the dancing place of the sun." Her household includes a giant dog named Max, two cats, and a lot of fancy carp. She plays the flute, piano, and guitar, practices karate and Tai Chi, collects dragons, and one day she will learn to fly.